The Cockney Angel

Dilly Court grew up in North-east London and began her career in television, writing scripts for commercials. She is married with two grown-up children and four grandchildren, and now lives in Dorset on the beautiful Jurassic Coast with her husband and a large, yellow Labrador called Archie. She is also the author of *Mermaids Singing, The Dollmaker's Daughters, Tilly True, The Best of Sisters, The Cockney Sparrow, A Mother's Courage, The Constant Heart* and *A Mother's Promise*.

Also by Dilly Court

Mermaids Singing
The Dollmaker's Daughters
Tilly True
The Best of Sisters
The Cockney Sparrow
A Mother's Courage
The Constant Heart
A Mother's Promise

Dilly Court

The Cockney Angel

arrow books

Published by Arrow Books 2009

2 4 6 8 10 9 7 5 3 1

This novel is a work of fiction. Names and characters are the product of the author's imagination and any resemblance to actual persons, living or dead, is entirely coincidental

First published in Great Britain in 2009 by
Arrow Books
Random House, 20 Vauxhall Bridge Road,
London SW1V 2SA

www.rbooks.co.uk

Addresses for companies within The Random House Group Limited can be found at: www.randomhouse.co.uk/offices.htm

The Random House Group Limited Reg. No. 954009

A CIP catalogue record for this book
is available from the British Library

ISBN 9780099519355

The Random House Group Limited supports The Forest Stewardship Council (FSC), the leading international forest certification organisation. All our titles that are printed on Greenpeace approved FSC certified paper carry the FSC logo. Our paper procurement policy can be found at www.rbooks.co.uk/environment

Typeset in Palatino by Palimpsest Book Production Ltd,
Grangemouth, Stirlingshire
Printed and bound in Great Britain by CPI Bookmarque Ltd,
Croydon CR0 4TD

For Irene, Tony, Adrian and Christine, with love.

Chapter One

Wood Street, Cheapside 1865

She was alone on a bleak street corner; daylight was fading and the grey stone buildings towered above her like eyeless monoliths. Tiny, terrified and just five years old, Irene bit her lower lip in an attempt to prevent herself from crying. She shivered as pellets of sleety rain slapped her cheeks and pooled around her bare feet. The pavement was ice cold and her thread-bare garments were no protection against the elements. Soon it would be completely dark and she had lost sight of her father, who was so busy taking illegal bets that he seemed to have forgotten her existence. She wanted to go home to Ma, but she did not dare move. She was on the lookout for coppers. It was her job and she must not let Pa down. Cops were the enemy – Pa said so. In desperation she sought shelter in the doorway of a big building but a man in uniform appeared from the interior, scowling at her and telling her to clear off. His bewhiskered face loomed above her and she stared transfixed by fear at the purple thread-like veins that spread like a spider's web across his cheeks. His breath smelt like sour milk and a dewdrop hung from the tip of his bulbous nose. The brass buttons on his jacket were as big as pennies and she was certain he was one of them. 'Pa,' she screamed. 'It's the cops.' But there was no reassuring reply to her agitated cries. Blind panic overtook her and she began to run . . .

Gripped by a cold sweat, Irene opened her eyes and snapped into a sitting position. She breathed a sigh of relief as she realised that it was the noisy, quarrelsome inhabitants of the ancient plane tree on the corner of Wood Street who had awakened her from the recurring nightmare which had haunted her since childhood. For once she welcomed the dawn chorus of rooks cawing to each other like a raucous band of fishwives. She yawned and stretched her stiff limbs. It was just a dream after all, and she was safe at home in the family's cramped living quarters above the pickle shop. Heaven knows, she was used to lying on the floor with only a straw-filled palliasse between her body and the rough-hewn bare boards, but the nights were growing colder now that autumn was here. Soon winter would claim the city. Pea-souper fogs would smother the streets in an evil-smelling blanket, and then the frosts would set in followed by rain and snow. She raised herself to a kneeling position, moving slowly so that she did not disturb her sleeping parents, but a quick glance at the old iron bedstead revealed just one small shape huddled beneath the coverlet.

She shook her head. So Pa was up to his old tricks and had not come home last night after all. He must have had a good hand of cards to keep him from his bed, although it was not uncommon for him to return in the early hours of the morning reeking of cheap grog and tobacco smoke, more than a little tipsy, but never violent. She sat on her haunches, deliberating whether or not to go looking for him. It wouldn't be the first time she had gone on such a mission and found him sleeping off the excesses of celebrating a good win, or having imbibed too freely in order to drown his sorrows after making a heavy loss. Pa would gamble on anything from a toss of the die, a dog fight, or even two flies crawling up a windowpane. When his luck was in he would bring home his winnings, which would sometimes be enough to keep them in relative comfort for a whole year, but of course the money never lasted that long. Billy Angel could never allow a sure thing to pass him by. Money slipped through his fingers as fast as the waters of the River Thames flowed through London.

A muffled moan from the bed and the groaning of rusty springs indicated that her mother was also awake, and probably in pain from the chronic arthritis that gnawed at her joints, twisting her fingers and toes into gnarled lumps like the knotted branches of the plane tree. A sliver of anxiety shafted through Irene's stomach. She hated to see her much-loved mother suffering from the debilitating illness. Ma had always been a tower of strength before she was laid so low. She had borne the trials that had beset the family with such courage and good humour that it seemed unfair she should be the one to suffer now. Irene wished with all her heart that there was something she could do that would relieve Ma of her pain. 'Are you all right?' she whispered.

Clara Angel raised herself with difficulty but she managed a smile. 'Just a bit stiff, ducks. Nothing to worry about.' She glanced at the empty space in the bed and her lips trembled. 'I stayed awake half the night waiting for the sound of his key in the lock, but now I'm really worried. I hope he's all right.'

Irene scrambled to her feet. 'Of course he is, Ma,' she said, forcing herself to sound cheerful. 'It ain't as if it's the first time Pa's stayed out all night. He'll probably turn up any minute with a bad head and a pocket full of money.'

'Then he'll be gasping for a cup of tea. I'll get

the fire started if you'll fetch water from the pump, Renie.' Clara swung her legs over the side of the bed and her face contorted with pain. 'Silly old legs are playing up a bit this morning. There must be rain in the air.'

'Take it slow, Ma. There's no need to rush.' Irene reached for her stays and fastened them over her shift. She yanked at the laces, reducing her waist to a mere hand's span before slipping on her much-darned cotton blouse and linsey-woolsey skirt, which had also seen better days. Lastly, she thrust her bare feet into her ill-fitting second-hand boots and she bent down to tie the laces. 'I'm off then. I'll call in at the dairy and get some fresh milk.'

'Get a loaf too, love. There should be just enough money left in the tin. Your pa will be starving when he gets home.' Clara slid off the bed and pushed her feet into an old pair of men's dancing slippers; the only form of footwear that would accommodate her deformed feet without causing her excruciating pain.

Irene took the battered cocoa tin from the mantelshelf and tipped its contents into the palm of her hand. Twopence was not going to go far, but it was all they had. 'Is there anything I can do for you before I go, Ma?'

'I'm fine, ducks,' Clara said, with a ghost of a smile. 'Just give me a minute to get me old bones moving. I'll be down in the shop before you get back from the bakery.'

Irene knew better than to argue or to appear over-sympathetic. Ma might be as fragile as a jenny wren, but she was a proud woman, and not one to give in easily to infirmity. She snatched her shawl from its hook behind the door, wrapping it around her shoulders as she descended the steep wooden staircase to the tiny shop below. With its crudely plastered whitewashed walls and low ceiling it was little larger than a cupboard, but the small income it provided had kept them from the workhouse when times were bad. The pungent smell of pickled onions and vinegar caught at the back of her throat, causing her to cough as she crossed the flagstone floor in two steps to take the milk jug from beneath the counter. She picked up a wooden pail and looped the handle over her arm before unlocking the shop door and stepping outside.

The air was pleasantly cool and the sun was just breaking through a bank of grey clouds. The sound of the rooks squabbling in the plane tree was louder than a school yard filled with noisy children. The flapping of their wings sent showers of dead leaves floating down to carpet the pavement in bronze and gold like a hoard of pirates' treasure. In stark contrast the cobbled street was strewn with mouldy straw, horse dung and the occasional carcass of a dead rat, left half eaten by the feral cats that roamed the city after dark. The night soil collector was doing his rounds and the stench from his cart preceded him. An aged crossing sweeper leaned against his broom, still apparently half asleep, until a brewer's dray pulled by two sturdy carthorses almost knocked him down. He leapt out of the way, shaking his fist at the driver who shouted a stream of obscenities with a cheerful grin and a rude gesture as he drove on.

Irene picked up her skirts and started off towards the pump, but there was a long queue of people waiting to take their turn and she decided to go to the dairy first. Having filled her jug with creamy milk, she went on to the bakery where she bought a loaf of bread hot from the oven. When she returned to the pump she found just a handful of people standing patiently in line, and with a resigned sigh she took her place behind young Sal Hawker, a maid who worked for the silk merchant whose house was situated a few doors away from the shop. Sal was always ready to impart a tasty bit of gossip, and not seeming to have any luck with the dour-faced matron standing in front of her she turned her head and spotted Irene with a delighted smile. Once started, Sal was only too pleased to pass on the news that Janet, the daughter of Rattray the fan maker and his snooty wife who thought herself a cut above the rest of the neighbourhood, was in the family way by a married man.

Irene could not share Sal's obvious pleasure in this piece of news. She was extremely sorry for Janet. The poor girl was unlucky enough to have a toffee-nosed mother and a father who would not say boo to a goose, let alone his domineering wife. Mrs Rattray had always made it clear that she looked down on the daughter of a notorious gambler and a woman who sold pickles for a living, and Irene wondered how she would react to the news that her one and only daughter was about to have an illegitimate child. She made appropriate noises in response to Sal's tittle-tattling, although it was almost impossible to get a word in edgeways. Irene was quite relieved when it was Sal's turn at the pump as the strenuous exercise of drawing water kept her quiet for a few minutes. A shout from an upstairs window of the silk merchant's house sent the maid scurrying off in response to an angry summons from a red-faced woman wearing a white mobcap. Taking Sal's place, Irene filled her bucket and was about to heft it off the ground when a man's hand covered hers. 'Allow me, young lady.'

She straightened up and smiled with genuine

pleasure at the sight of her oldest and best friend. 'Hello, Artie. You're up and about early.'

Arthur Greenwood doffed his top hat and grinned. 'Haven't been to bed yet, girl.' He lifted the heavy bucket with ease and fell in step beside her.

'You're as bad as my pa,' Irene said, with a heartfelt sigh. 'I don't suppose you've seen him recently, have you?'

'Didn't the old devil come home last night?'

She shook her head.

'As a matter of fact I did see Billy,' Arthur said, dodging a large turnip that had fallen from a costermonger's barrow. 'He was at the Sykes brothers' place in Blue Boar Court.'

'What time was that?'

'Past midnight. I wasn't exactly keeping an eye on the clock.' He winked at her and patted his jacket pocket. 'Won a packet, I did. D'you fancy a night out?'

'Not at the sort of places you'd be likely to take me.'

'That's not fair. I know how to treat a lady.'

Irene pulled a face. 'That's ripe, coming from a fellah who once took me ratting. I was sick for a week afterwards.'

'Well, I admit that wasn't one of my better ideas, but it was a long time ago.'

'It was three years ago and I was just fifteen.'

'I was just a boy then.'

'You were two years older than me and you should have known better.'

'I won't make the same mistake again,' Arthur said, tweaking a lock of Irene's hair that had worked its way loose from the knot at the nape of her neck. 'C'mon, Renie, I'm flush for a change thanks to my winning streak.'

Irene frowned. 'What am I going to do with you? You've got to stop gambling now, before it takes you like it did my pa.'

'I said I would, didn't I?' Arthur said with a mischievous grin. 'Last night was the last time. Honest.'

'I've heard Pa say that more times than I can count. You've got to mean it, Artie. Stop now, or it will be too late.' Despite her stern words, Irene couldn't help smiling. It was impossible to be cross with Arthur for long, even if he did sometimes drive her to distraction. When he smiled his green eyes crinkled at the corners and his cheeks dimpled, giving him the look of a mischievous satyr. He was always joking and teasing her, but just being with him made the day seem brighter.

They had arrived outside the shop and Arthur stopped, setting the bucket down on the step. 'I won't get like Billy, that I can promise you.'

'I hope not, Artie, I really do.' Irene unlocked

the door and opened it. 'Are you coming in to see Ma?'

He shook his head. 'Not now. In fact, I'd better get a move on or I'll find myself looking for another apprenticeship. My old man might be the best silversmith in London but I'm sure he's the worst-tempered man in the city.'

'When do you take your journeyman's exam?' Irene asked, changing the subject. She had seen Cuthbert Greenwood in one of his tempers and she knew that what Arthur said was no exaggeration, but it wouldn't do to dwell on it just now.

'In less than a month's time. If I happen to pass, which I rather doubt at this moment, I'll be able to work for myself and I won't have to listen to the old devil ranting at me and saying I'm a disappointment to him.'

'Fathers!' Irene said with feeling. 'I love mine even though he drives me mad at times. I wish I knew where he was at this minute.'

'Stop worrying about Billy and say you'll come out with me tonight. We'll sample some of their steak pudding at the Old Cheshire Cheese and maybe go to a penny gaff afterwards. What d'you say to that?'

'It sounds fine, but if my pa doesn't turn up soon I'll have to spend the rest of the day looking for him. It could take a while to go round all his old haunts.'

'I think you're wasting your time. Anyway, they won't let you in. Women aren't allowed in the gaming rooms.'

'I know that, and I don't hold with gaming hells or any kind of gambling, but sometimes I'm just a little curious to see inside one. I can't think what the attraction is and I'd like to find out first hand. Then just maybe I could understand Pa a bit better and try to persuade him to mend his ways.'

Arthur shrugged his shoulders. 'I think it's more complicated than that, Renie. Gambling is like a fever that gets into a fellow's blood. It's not easy to stop. Anyway, I'd best get to work.'

'Good boy,' Irene said, giving him a gentle shove. 'Go and make something splendid in silver for the toffs to eat off or drink out of, while I go and sell pickles and sauces. You may think you're hard done by, but sometimes I think I'll never get the smell of onions and vinegar out of my hair.'

He leaned towards her and dropped a kiss on the top of her head. 'My favourite perfume, ducks. See you tonight.' He doffed his hat with a flourish and swaggered off in the direction of Silver Street.

Somewhat reluctantly, Irene stepped over the threshold into the gloomy interior of the shop. Having deposited the milk and bread on the counter, she went back to retrieve the heavy bucket of water, taking care not to spill any of the precious liquid, as it would have to do for all their needs until she made a return visit to the pump. She looked up hopefully as she heard a footstep on the stairs, but it was just her mother making her painful descent.

'Oh, it's you, Irene,' Clara said, pausing to catch her breath. 'I thought it might be your dad come home.'

'No, it's only me. I'll make us some tea and then I'll go looking for him.'

'I don't think that's such a good idea, love. You know it makes him angry when we fuss. Anyway, I need you in the shop this morning. Mr Yapp will be making a delivery and me hands is too painful to stack the bottles and jars on the shelves. But a cup of tea would be lovely, and a piece of toast would go down well. I got the fire going upstairs so it shouldn't take long.'

After a hasty breakfast of tea and toast, Irene insisted that her mother went back to bed in order to catch up on some of the sleep she had lost worrying about her errant husband. Sometimes Irene despaired of Pa and this was one of those moments. With all the love in the world she had to admit that he had many faults. It was true that he could charm the rooks from the plane tree if he put his mind to it, but at the best of times he was irresponsible, and at his worst he was outrageously feckless. At forty-five he was still a handsome devil, with flashing brown eyes and hair that gleamed black like the best coal. He loved life but never took anything seriously, especially when it came to earning an honest living and providing for his family. And yet, for all his many failings, to Irene he was a dashing corsair and she could never hold his misdemeanours against him – at least, not for long. She struggled to cope with his addiction to gambling and she grew impatient with him when he showed little concern for her mother's ill-health. Then, by something close to a miracle, he would redeem himself by coming home with some frippery that he had picked up in a street market, or a bunch of flowers that were more than likely to have been stolen from a graveyard, which he would present to his wife with the aplomb of a great stage actor. Irene smiled to herself at the very thought of it. Occasionally, she felt that she was his senior and he was little more than a wayward child, and that made her feel even more protective towards him.

She spun round at the sound of the door opening, but it was only Yapp's boy, Danny Priest. 'Delivery for you, miss.'

Through the grimy windowpanes Irene could see Yapp's cart laden with wooden crates and wicker baskets lined with straw and filled with bottles and jars of pickles and sauce. 'Ta, Danny. Bring it in, if you please.'

He backed out of the door gazing at her with moonstruck eyes. Irene gave him an encouraging smile. Danny could not be more than twelve or thirteen, and he was a skinny little monkey of a boy, all gangly arms and legs that did not seem to be properly coordinated. He blushed beneath his freckles whenever she spoke to him and he was so eager to please her that he almost fell over himself in his efforts. She watched him rush to the cart and lift off a box which was so heavy that he had to bend almost in two in order to prevent it from dropping onto the cobblestones. With an obvious effort, he straightened up and staggered into the shop, turning red in the face, with his pale blue eyes bulging. He managed to heft it onto the counter, setting it down so hard that the glass jars jangled together. A look of consternation puckered his face. 'Old Yapp will beat the daylights out of me if I've broke anything.'

'I'm sure there's no harm done,' Irene said, keeping her eye on Yapp, who was perched on the driver's seat of his cart with a clay pipe clenched between his teeth. He peered through the window, scowling at Danny, and his hand went automatically to clutch the large horsewhip at his side. Irene smiled and waved to him. 'Morning, Mr Yapp,' she mouthed.

He nodded curtly and she saw his fingers relax on the whip handle.

'Ta, miss,' Danny said, gazing at her as if she had sprouted wings and a halo. 'You're a blooming angel, that's what you are.'

'If only that were true,' she said, patting him on the shoulder. 'Best get on with your work, or you'll be in real trouble with old Yapp and I wouldn't want that to happen.'

Danny made a grab for a basket of bottles and shot out of the door, dodging a cuff round the ear from Yapp as he deposited the basket of empties in the cart and picked up one that was ready for delivery. He staggered back into the shop and dumped his burden on the counter.

'Cash on delivery, the boss says,' he said breathlessly.

Irene reached beneath the counter for the cash box. She opened it and frowned. Yesterday's takings had been reasonably good, but all that remained now was a threepenny bit and a handful of coppers. There was only one person who would rob the till and he still had not made an appearance. She looked up and met Danny's anxious gaze. 'I'm afraid I can't settle the account in full, but I will have the right amount later in the day.'

Danny shook his head and his bottom lip trembled. 'He'll beat me if I don't get the cash, miss. You know he don't allow credit.'

She emptied the coins onto the counter and pushed them towards him. 'Take this to Mr Yapp and tell him that I need an hour or two, but he will be paid by close of business today. I promise.'

'I'll tell him but he won't like it.'

A shout from Yapp made Danny glance nervously out of the window. He scooped up the coins and hurried from the shop. Irene watched as the boy handed the money to his master, receiving yet another clout round the head for his pains. Yapp stood up in the well of the cart and for a moment Irene thought that he was going to climb down and come blustering into the shop, but he shook his fist at her mouthing words that she was glad she could not hear. Having apparently vented his feelings he slumped down on the seat and cracked the whip over the horse's rump, causing the poor animal to lurch forward. Danny was left to run along behind until he gathered enough speed to take a flying leap onto the footplate at the back of the cart.

Praying silently that Pa would return home soon with at least some of his winnings intact, Irene set about the task of stacking the shelves with jars of Yapp's Best Pickled

Onions, beetroot and mustard pickle. She lined them up like soldiers on the parade ground, and having satisfied herself that all the labels were clearly visible and any stickiness had been wiped clean, she started on the bottles of sauce. Taking each glass container from its nest of straw, she wiped and polished them until they sparkled in the shredded shafts of sunlight that filtered through the small windowpanes.

Tomato, anchovy and hot chilli sauce with tamarind were all specialities created by Obadiah Yapp, as he was proud to tell anyone who was prepared to listen. As a young man he had joined the army and when his regiment was sent to India he had developed a taste for hot and exotic foods. On his return home he had missed the spicy condiments with which they flavoured their food, and had experimented until he discovered the exact recipe that would titillate the taste buds of Londoners. Irene had heard the story so many times that she knew it by heart.

She set the last bottle on the shelf and stacked the boxes and baskets beneath the counter to await collection. It was still early and trade was slow, but as the morning wore on a gradual trickle of customers came through the door to make their purchases. Irene kept glancing anxiously at the clock on the wall, and every time the door opened her hopes were raised, only to be dashed when it was not her father who walked into the shop.

Clara came downstairs at midday, looking pale but slightly less drawn than she had first thing. She leaned against the newel post at the foot of the stairs. 'He hasn't come home then?'

Irene was quick to hear the note of despair in her mother's voice and she forced herself to smile cheerfully. 'Not yet, but I'm sure he'll arrive any minute now with a sore head and feeling very sorry for hisself.'

'I don't know, Irene. I got a bad feeling about this. He's usually home afore noon. I heard the church clock strike twelve and that's what woke me.'

'Do you want me to go looking for him, Ma?' Irene glanced out through the window at the sunny street. Suddenly she longed to be free from the dark little shop with its low ceiling supported by beams that resembled the spreading roots of the great plane tree. Sometimes it felt as though the tree itself was reaching into the room to strangle and overpower her. Spending twelve hours a day behind the counter was not her idea of fun, nor was it her chosen path in life, but Ma needed her. Unless Pa mended his ways, which was very unlikely, she knew that there was little chance of leading her own life. Sometimes she almost envied her older sister Emmie who had married the first man who came along as a means of escape.

She had married Josiah Tippet, a middle-aged draper with a taste for mustard pickles and a house in Love Lane. He had buried two wives and had apparently been on the lookout for a third when he came into the shop and had laid eyes on Emily, who was quick to spot the main chance. Emmie was a sweet girl and a loving sister, but Irene had to admit that she had always had ideas above her station, and now she fancied herself as quite a lady, wed to a man who was a well-respected member of the Drapers' Company and cherished hopes of becoming an alderman before too long.

'Would you, ducks?'

Her mother's voice broke into Irene's thoughts, dragging her back to the present. 'Of course, Ma. I'll find him and bring him home safe and sound.'

'Don't go too far then. Just take a walk around the courts and alleys where he goes at night, and if you see any of his mates you might ask them if they know where he might be found.' Clara's voice broke on a sob and she clutched her hand to her throat. 'I'm afraid he might have been set upon by thieves and left for dead in the gutter somewhere. My poor Billy.' Tears welled in her eyes and she raised her apron to cover her face.

Irene hurried round the counter to hook her arm around her mother's shoulders and she led her to a bentwood chair that was normally reserved for privileged customers. She pressed her gently down onto its hard seat. 'Don't upset yourself, Ma. It's just your imagination taking over. Pa can look after hisself. I expect he's just lost track of time. You know how he is when his luck is in.'

'I know I'm probably worrying over nothing, but I just can't get these thoughts out of me head.'

Irene snatched up her shawl. 'I'll be as quick as I can, and you mustn't worry or you'll make yourself ill. Trade's slow today, so you shouldn't be too busy while I'm gone.'

'You're such a thoughtful girl,' Clara said, wiping her eyes. 'I dunno what I'd do without you.'

'I'll be back in two shakes of a cat's tail, and I'll bring Pa home with me.'

Irene stepped outside into the warm sunshine of a late September afternoon. Wood Street was now thronged with horse-drawn vehicles both private and commercial. Hansom cabs, brewers' drays and wagons laden with sacks of hay or crates filled with everything from tea to cow horns clattered over the cobbles, jostling each other for space. Barefooted street urchins stood on street corners selling matches or bootlaces, and others, too young or too poor even to afford small amounts of goods to trade, begged for money to buy food. Office clerks, merchants, law writers, housewives going to market and servants running errands crowded the pavements, making Irene's progress slow and difficult.

She headed for Goldsmith Street and the rabbit warren of dark alleys and courts that led off Gutter Lane. Opium dens and gambling hells were tucked away behind respectable city offices, banks, small shops and businesses. She knew them all by heart. As her recurring nightmares reminded her, she had stood on street corners from the age of five, acting as lookout while her father worked as a bookie's runner, risking arrest by taking illegal bets. She had been too young to know what she was doing, but she had been instructed to watch out for the copper on his beat, and to warn her father if she saw one so that he had time to pocket the cash and run. They would slip into the shadows and disappear down the very alleyways that she was searching now. It had been terrifying at times but there had also been an element of fun, like playing a game of hide and seek. Pa could make the dullest day turn into an adventure, especially when they were escaping the clutches of the law, which Pa said was designed for the benefit of the rich toffs and not for the likes of them. Irene had been indoctrinated at an early age to be wary of anyone wearing a uniform and above all to distrust the police. On the other hand, Ma had taught her the difference between right and wrong, and insisted that the cops were only doing their duty and should be respected. It had been very confusing.

As her search progressed with no sign of her father, Irene was beginning to fear the worst. By late afternoon she was tired and hungry. Her feet were sore, her legs ached and she was just about to give up and go home when she heard a man's voice raised in song. There was no mistaking the melodious notes of Pa's pure baritone, and she had heard that particular ditty often enough to know that it was one of his favourites, only sung when he was well oiled. The sound was coming from the depths of a narrow alley in the shadow of Newgate prison. Without thinking of her own safety, Irene entered the twilight world between the grim buildings with soot-blackened windows peering blindly into the gloom. Men lounged in doorways smoking strange-smelling substances. She could tell by the other-worldly look on their faces that they were drugged with opium, but they paid her scant attention as she hurried towards a patch of light where the tenements and warehouses formed a square open to the sky. Sprawled on a pile of old sacks, she saw the familiar figure of her father who lay flat on his back singing loudly and interspersing the risqué words with loud guffaws of laughter. But he was not alone, and she skidded to a halt at the sight of a man dressed in black bending over her father. Her heart gave an uncomfortable thud against her ribcage. Was he robbing Pa? Or was he attempting to help him to his feet? She ran at the stranger and grabbed him by the arm. 'Leave him be, mister. Don't hurt my pa.'

He straightened up, flicking free of her grasp as if she were a small and irritating insect. 'Don't be ridiculous. I mean him no harm.'

He was much taller than she had at first supposed, and this man was no common thief. His dark suit was well cut and his shirt collar and cuffs were starched and dazzling in their whiteness. From the crown of his black bowler hat to the tips of his shiny black leather shoes he had the appearance of a City gentleman, but the piercing gaze of his startlingly blue eyes set beneath straight dark eyebrows seemed to bore into her soul. She was unused to such scrutiny and she backed away, feeling distinctly uncomfortable. Unless she was very much mistaken, this bloke was a copper. She had been trained to spot one a mile off. 'I'm sorry, mister. My mistake.'

He inclined his head in a brief acknowledgement of her apology. 'If this man is your father, I suggest you take him home before he gets into real trouble.'

She bent down to tug at her father's hand in a vain attempt to drag him to his feet. 'Get up, Pa.'

Billy opened his eyes, grinning foolishly. 'Hello, Irene my duck.'

'Please get up, Pa. I've come to take you home.'

'I'm nice and comfy here, girl,' Billy said, closing his eyes again and snuggling into the pile of dirty sacks as though it were a feather mattress. 'I'll just have forty winks . . .' His voice trailed off into a loud snore.

Irene knelt down on the filthy cobblestones. 'Wake up or you'll get done for being drunk and disorderly.' She shook him by the shoulders, but Billy did not respond. She glanced over her shoulder and saw that the stranger was about to walk away. 'Excuse me, mister,' she called. 'Could you give me a hand, please?'

He turned his head and regarded her with raised brows. 'I have more important things to do right now.'

'I don't think I can lift him on me own,' Irene said, attempting to heave Billy to a sitting position. The alleyway had suddenly cleared of the men who were previously hanging about, but she knew they would reappear the moment that the officer of the law departed, and she was afraid that if her father had any of his winnings left in his pockets they would fall on them and take his money by force. She met the police officer's cynical gaze with a straight look. 'I'd be obliged, mister. Since it's you who wants him moved on.'

He was at her side in two long strides and he hoisted Billy to his feet. 'Can you stand on your own, man?'

'Shall we dance, cully?' Billy asked with a tipsy grin, throwing an arm around the police officer's neck.

'Behave yourself, Pa,' Irene said, blushing with embarrassment. She took her father's free arm and hooked it around her shoulders. 'I think I can manage him now, mister,' she murmured.

'Are you sure of that?' He allowed her to take Billy's full weight for a second or two but her knees buckled beneath her and she almost fell to the ground.

'It's obvious that you cannot,' the officer said, relieving her of her burden and signalling to two uniformed constables who came hurrying towards them.

'I'm afraid we lost them, Inspector Kent,' the

elder of the two said, eyeing Billy suspiciously. 'Is this one of the gang, guv?'

'That's my pa,' Irene said hastily. 'He's a bit swipey but he's no criminal.'

'Take him, Burton.' Kent thrust Billy's swaying frame into the arms of the fresh-faced younger officer. 'He might have been involved but he's too drunk to give us any useful information.'

Irene plucked at Kent's sleeve. 'My pa don't have nothing to do with the street gangs, mister – I'm sorry, I didn't catch your name.'

His lips twitched and a glimmer of humour lit his eyes. He inclined his head in a formal bow. 'Inspector Edward Kent of the City of London Police – and you are?'

'I'm Irene Angel, and this here is my pa, Billy Angel. We're respectable folk. My mother has a pickle shop on the corner of Wood Street and Cheapside. Pa likes a drink occasionally but he's not a bad man.'

'We all know Billy Angel, sir,' Constable Burton said in a low voice. 'He's a professional gambler, and he's known to frequent illegal gaming houses. He's also suspected of having dealings with the Sykes gang.'

'Now that's a big black lie,' Billy said, shaking his fist. 'I've never been near Blue Boar Court in me whole life. It's a case of mistaken identity.'

'I never mentioned Blue Boar Court,' Constable Burton said with a triumphant grin. 'See, guv, he's convicted hisself out of his own stupid mouth.'

Irene rounded on him. 'Here, you watch your tongue, young man. You can see that my pa ain't quite hisself. He don't know what he's saying.' She turned to Inspector Kent. 'You wouldn't hold what a drunken man says against him, would you?'

'I'm afraid I haven't got time for this. Take him home, Miss Angel, or I will arrest your father for being drunk and disorderly.' Kent dismissed her with a wave of his hand and he turned to the more senior officer. 'I've business to attend to in Newgate, Davies. You'd best get back to the station and write up a report.'

The constable saluted smartly and marched off towards the main road.

Billy watched him go with a mocking laugh. 'That's right, Officer. Go away and leave a fellow in peace.'

'Come along, Pa,' Irene said, tugging urgently at his arm. 'Let's get you home.'

He pulled free from her, and grinning stupidly he tapped the side of his nose. 'I'm on to a certainty, ducks. You go home and I'll follow later.'

Constable Burton seized Billy by the scruff

of the neck. 'You heard the guvner, Billy. Do as he says or I'll clap the cuffs on you and you can sober up in the cells until the magistrate's court tomorrow morning.'

'Come quietly, Pa,' Irene pleaded. 'Ma's out of her mind with worry and you know that always makes her rheumatics worse.' She turned to Kent. 'I promise I'll keep an eye on him in future.'

'All right,' he said coldly, 'but if I come across Billy Angel in similar circumstances I won't be so lenient. Burton, you'd best help Miss Angel get her father home.'

'Yes, guv.'

A floodtide of relief surged through Irene and she reached out impulsively and shook Kent's hand. 'Thank you, Inspector. You're a toff. I won't forget this in a hurry.'

He drew his hand away and his expression remained impassive. 'Take my advice and keep away from your father's cronies, Miss Angel, or we might meet again in even less fortunate circumstances.' He turned on his heel and strode off into the dark alleyway.

'Let's get your pa home, miss,' Burton said, struggling to keep Billy on his feet.

Irene took her father's free arm once again, and wrapped it around her shoulders. 'Come on, Pa. Please be a good boy and do as the constable says.'

'Damn coppers!' Billy muttered, changing in a moment from tipsily happy to belligerent. 'Never trust a cop, Renie. Don't have nothing to do with 'em, that's my advice.'

Irene cast an apologetic glance at Burton, who was looking distinctly wary at Billy's sudden change in temper. 'He don't mean it, Constable. It's just his way.'

'Don't you talk to him, my girl,' Billy said, slurring his words. 'Remember what I've always taught you. Coppers are bad news. If I ever catch you stepping out with one of 'em, I'll have to disown you, even though I loves you.'

Chapter Two

Clara was not alone in the shop when Constable Burton manhandled Billy through the open door. Irene's heart sank at the sight of her sister Emily sitting on the chair in front of the counter with her gloved hands folded primly in her lap. Clara uttered a cry of relief as she hobbled from behind the counter to fling her arms around her husband's neck. 'Billy. Oh, Billy, you bad boy. You had me so worried.'

'Hold on there, Clara my sweet. You're strangling me.'

She drew back, eyeing the constable with some alarm. 'My Billy's not under arrest is he, Constable?'

'No, ma'am. Not this time.' Burton released his grip on Billy, who lurched towards the staircase and sat down heavily on the bottom step.

'Ta for the help, mate,' Billy said in a slurred voice. 'You're a good 'un, and I can't say that for most coppers.'

'Pa!' Irene cried, feeling the ready blush rise to her cheeks at her father's tactless words. She glanced nervously at the young policeman.

'He don't mean what he says, and I thank you for helping me to get him home.'

'Happy to oblige, miss.' Burton headed for the doorway and then hesitated, beckoning to Irene.

She followed him outside onto the pavement, closing the door behind her so that Emily could not hear whatever it was that he had to say. 'Yes, Constable, what is it?'

'A friendly word of warning, miss. You'll keep Billy away from Blue Boar Court and the Sykes gang if you've got any sense. The Sykes brothers are a bad lot and we're keeping a close watch on them and their doings.'

'I will,' Irene promised. 'But I'm sure that Pa doesn't have dealings with the likes of them.'

'I hope not, for his sake and yours, but bear my words in mind, miss.' With a cheerful salute, Burton strode in the direction of Cheapside. Irene watched him go with mixed feelings. She knew that he had meant well in warning her about Vic and Wally Sykes, but it rankled that he thought her pa had anything to do with a well-known gang of blackguards and bullies. The sun had gone down and a chilly breeze rustled the dying leaves on the plane tree. She shivered and went back inside the shop, bracing herself to face Emily and the inevitable interrogation which she knew was hanging over her like an imminent thunderstorm.

As she came through the door, she saw her father crawling upstairs on his hands and knees with Clara urging him on like a harassed mother hen. Emily had remained seated on the chair by the counter, and her expression was anything but encouraging. Irene faced her sister, knowing full well what was coming. She had heard it all before, and she was not disappointed.

Emily rose to her feet, arranging her blue poplin skirt over the swaying hoops of a wide crinoline. She smoothed the matching bodice, trimmed with blond lace, and her hands fluttered to adjust the straw bonnet cunningly dyed to the exact shade of her gown. Irene watched the procedure with a sigh of resignation; even in a state of extreme agitation she had never known Emily to be anything other than particular about her appearance. To say she was vain might be a bit unkind, but it was true nevertheless. Emily had always been the pretty one, and she knew it.

Apparently satisfied that her appearance was no less than perfect, Emily shot a reproachful look at her sister. 'How could you, Irene? How could you allow Pa to get into such a state that he had to be brought home by a policeman? The whole of Wood Street must have witnessed the spectacle.'

'Don't talk rubbish, Emmie. How could I stop Pa doing anything that he wanted to do? I'm not his keeper.' Avoiding Emily's accusing stare, Irene dodged behind the counter and began tidying the jars and bottles that her mother's rheumaticky hands had not been able to replace on the shelves.

'No, but you promised me that you would keep an eye on him. You obviously haven't done so or he wouldn't have got himself into that disgraceful condition. I don't know what my Josiah will say when he hears of this.' Emily began to pace the floor, although there was barely room for her and her crinoline. It swung from side to side as she moved, giving her the appearance of an agitated bluebell.

Keeping calm with an effort, Irene concentrated on re-stacking the shelves. 'I can't help what Josiah thinks. I did my best to find Pa, and it was bad luck that some bigwig police inspector happened to come across him flat on his back in an alley behind Newgate and more than a little swipey.'

Emily stopped pacing for a moment and clasped her hands to her breast, eyes wide with horror. 'How embarrassing. You say a police inspector found him?'

'That's what I said.'

'That's even worse. You know that Josiah has hopes of becoming an alderman this year.

What if it got about that his father-in-law was known to the police?'

'I don't suppose the cops go in for gossip,' Irene said, smiling at the thought of the aloof Inspector Kent doing anything so mundane as to exchange chit-chat with his colleagues over a cup of tea and a plate of cucumber sandwiches.

'But you said it was an inspector who found Pa. Who was he? Maybe Josiah is acquainted with him.' Emily sat down heavily on the chair, fanning herself with her gloved hand. 'Do you know his name?'

'Inspector Edward Kent. He was a stuck-up toff and he looked more like a blooming clergyman or a lawyer than a copper. I didn't like him one bit.'

'Edward Kent! But that's terrible. We met him at a function at the Guildhall. I was struck by his perfect manners and his air of good breeding. Josiah said that he's the youngest police inspector ever, and that he could be made up to superintendent before he's thirty, which is virtually unheard of, so Josiah says.'

'Josiah says this and that. I'm sick of hearing what Josiah says, Emmie. And I don't care about Inspector Kent. At least he let Pa off and we're never likely to meet him again, so I shall just put him out of me mind.'

Emily opened her velvet reticule and pulled

out a lace-trimmed handkerchief. She waved it at Irene. 'Brussels lace,' she announced, delicately mopping her brow. 'Josiah imports it direct from Belgium. It's one of his best selling lines, so he—'

'Says – yes, I know,' Irene interrupted. 'Why are you here, Emmie? Did you come just to lecture me, or is there another reason for your visit?'

Emily's cheeks flushed a delicate shade of pink and she twitched her shoulders. 'You make it sound as though I only ever come to complain when it's just the opposite today.'

'Go on then. Tell me what's so special about today?'

'Well.' Emily hesitated and her blush deepened. 'I've come to take Ma back to Love Lane for an extended visit.'

'What? But that's impossible. We have the shop to run, and you know that Ma wouldn't go anywhere without Pa, unless, of course, you're thinking of inviting him too?'

'Heavens, no! Josiah would have a fit if I suggested it. No, this is for Ma's health and well-being. We have more than enough room in our house.'

Irene chuckled. 'I know. You have eight bedchambers, a cook general and a maid of all work, plus a poor skivvy who comes in daily to do the cleaning.'

Emily smiled proudly, seemingly oblivious to her sister's teasing. 'Don't forget the horse that Josiah keeps at livery and the dog cart he puts at my disposal should I want to venture further than I can comfortably walk.'

'Oh, for goodness sake, drop the airs and graces, Emmie. This is me you're talking to. It weren't so long ago that you lived up above the shop with the rest of us with only one pair of shoes to your name and they was second hand.'

'I'm doing my best to forget it. I've risen in the world since I married Josiah and I'm learning to speak proper – I mean properly. I want our children to be proud of their ma and not ashamed of a poor girl who came from the pickle shop in Wood Street.'

Irene stared hard at her sister. 'What do you mean, children? Are you . . .' She broke off and ran round the counter to hug Emmie. 'You are, aren't you? Oh, Emmie, that's wonderful. You never could keep a secret.'

Emily smiled, but she held Irene at arm's length. 'Be careful, you'll crush my best poplin, and this lace cost more than you'll earn in a month. But, yes, I am in the family way and that's another reason for Ma coming to stay with me. I need a woman's company what with my Josiah being so busy with business and his two stupid sons refusing to leave home even though they are full-grown men. Big babies, that's what I call them. If they didn't both work in Josiah's emporium, I would suggest that they moved out, but unfortunately he relies on them.'

'Never mind the vile brothers. You mustn't allow them to upset you, especially in your condition,' Irene said, giving her another hug for good measure. 'I'm really pleased for you, Emmie. I can't wait to be an aunt.'

'You could come and live with us too, you know. I'm sure that Josiah wouldn't mind, and it would get you away from this horrid little shop.'

'Ta, but you know I can't do that. Even if you manage to persuade Ma to come for a visit, I couldn't leave Pa on his own. Heaven knows what sort of bother he'd get himself into.'

'Perhaps you're right, but you'll soon be nineteen and you ought to be looking for a husband. You need to find a man who would take you away from all this.' Emily sighed heavily, shaking her head. 'I'm afraid you'll never meet anyone suitable stuck behind that counter.'

'Well you did,' Irene said amicably. 'Your Josiah walked right through that door and bought a dozen jars of assorted pickles and sauces just to make an impression on you.'

'That's as maybe, but I made an effort to be charming, whereas you say exactly what you think, and men don't like that.'

'I can't help it if I'm honest.'

'You need to be careful, or you'll end up as an old maid. Anyway, it's late and I must get home. I didn't mean to stay so long.' Emily rose to her feet and glided to the foot of the stairs. 'Ma, I'm going now, but I'll be back tomorrow with the dog cart to take you home with me, and I won't take no for an answer.' She cocked her ear, and when there was no reply she shrugged her shoulders. 'Until tomorrow then.'

Irene frowned. 'I very much doubt she will come with you.'

'Leave it to me,' Emily said confidently. 'Tomorrow morning, when Pa's sobered up, I'll tell him he must make her come, for her own health if nothing else. Another winter in this dreadful shack and she'll be crippled for life. You just leave it to your big sister. I'll show you how to handle a man, even a stubborn and selfish one like our pa.' She made her way to the door and opened it, peering out into the gathering dusk. 'Oh, dear. I should have left an hour ago. Now it will be quite dark by the time I get home and Josiah will be so cross with me for walking out alone.'

'I'll see you home.'

'But then you'll have to walk home in the dark.'

'I'm not scared. I can look after meself, ta very much, sister. Right now I'm more worried about you and your babe.' Irene snatched up her shawl as they left the premises. She had been lying when she said she was unafraid of walking the streets after dark. Only a fool would ignore the dangers of the night, but she was more concerned for her sister than she was for herself. She linked her hand through Emily's arm. 'Come on, girl. Let's get you home before your Josiah sends out a search party.'

They had not gone more than a couple of paces before Danny caught up with them, red in the face and panting as if he had been running. He held out his hand. 'Mr Yapp wants his money, miss.'

'What's this?' Emily demanded. 'Don't tell me you're in debt to that dreadful man, Renie?'

Irene hung her head. 'I didn't have quite enough to pay the full amount.'

Emily thrust her hand into her reticule. 'How much, boy?'

'A shilling, missis.'

'Here, take it and tell your master he's a money-grubbing old reprobate.' Emily dismissed him with a wave of her hand.

Danny pocketed the coin with a grin. 'Ta, missis.' He walked off with a jaunty swagger, leaving Emily facing Irene with eyebrows raised.

'I don't have to ask why you hadn't the funds to pay old Yapp.'

Irene shook her head. 'No, it was Pa, of course. And thanks, Emmie. I'll pay you back as soon as I can.'

'No matter,' Emily said grandly. 'Josiah is very generous with my pin money, but we'd best hurry. He hates unpunctuality.'

They set off, heading north towards Love Lane. Above them the sky was rapidly turning from velvet blue to inky black, and twinkling pinpoints of stars pierced the haze of chimney smoke that hovered above the rooftops. The street lamps sent out warm pools of yellow gaslight and the pavements were still crowded with late evening shoppers. Dark-suited businessmen and bank clerks with shiny elbows and frayed cuffs hurried homeward from their offices in the City, and costermongers shouted their wares, offering last minute bargains to clear their day's stock of fruit and vegetables.

Emily clung nervously to Irene's arm and was soon out of breath. She said that her new shoes pinched and she had to keep stopping to rest, holding her side and complaining that she had a stitch. But even allowing for their slow progress, it did not take very long to walk the half-mile or so to Love Lane. Josiah Tippet's five-storey townhouse with its elegant eighteenth-century façade and imposing portico made a definite statement. It was only a well-to-do merchant who could afford to dwell in such a residence and everything about it, from the sparkling clean windows to the highly polished brass door furniture and fresh paint-work, spoke of money and success.

Emily rattled the doorknocker, stamping her feet as she waited for the maid to answer her summons. 'Where is that wretched girl?'

'Don't be so impatient, Emmie. Give the poor creature a chance. As I recall you've more steps for her to climb than in the Monument.'

This brought a smile to Emily's lips. 'Yes, it is a grand house. I'm very lucky.'

Irene stifled a sigh. No matter how large the house or how many servants and fine clothes Emily might have, Irene couldn't help feeling that she paid a high price for her rise in society. Josiah was not a bad person, nor was he ever anything but pleasant in his dealings with his wife's family, but he was fat and well past middle age. The thought of being intimate with a man who was even older than her father appalled Irene, but then she did not have to suffer his attentions, and to be fair to Emily, she seemed to be genuinely fond of her ageing husband.

The door opened and Emily stepped over the threshold, scolding the young servant for keeping her waiting. The girl, who was little more than a child, hung her head and muttered an apology. Emily turned to Irene, who had remained outside on the pavement. 'Well, are you coming in or not?'

Irene shook her head. 'No, ta. I'd best get back to the shop.'

'Suit yourself,' Emily said, shrugging. 'But you will take care on the way home, won't you? There's all sorts hanging about who might do you harm.'

'Don't worry about me. I'll run all the way and I won't speak to strangers.' Irene walked off with an exaggerated spring in her step, but as soon as she heard the door close she picked up her skirts and broke into a run. She had just reached the end of Love Lane and was about to turn into Wood Street when she heard a familiar voice calling her name. Glancing over her shoulder, she saw Arthur striding towards her from the direction of Silver Street. Gasping for breath she was only too pleased to stop and wait for him to catch up with her.

Holding his top hat on with one hand, and with his muffler flying out behind him like a pennant, Arthur ran across the street, dodging in and out between hansom cabs and private carriages. He arrived at her side, smiling but breathless. 'What are you doing out after dark, Renie? You know it ain't safe.'

'I just saw Emmie home.'

'You should have taken a cab.'

This made Irene chuckle. 'Yes, I shouldn't have given me coachman the evening off.'

'It's not a joking matter,' Arthur said, falling into step beside her. 'Lucky I came along when I did.'

'Did you get into trouble for being late this morning?'

'No. The old man was out visiting a rich client so he didn't realise I wasn't there.'

Irene shot him a sideways glance. 'Shouldn't you be going home for your supper?'

'Steak pudding at the Old Cheshire Cheese. Had you forgotten?'

She had forgotten but she did not want to hurt his feelings by admitting it. 'Oh, I don't know, Artie. Pa was in a bit of bother with the police earlier today. Maybe I ought to stay home this evening to back Ma up if he says he wants to go out again.'

'I'm sure Mrs Angel can cope with Billy for one evening. Anyway, you promised.'

'No, I never. I told you I had to find Pa, and I did.'

'So what happened?'

'The cops think he's mixed up with the Sykes gang.'

'That's bad.'

'He ain't one of them, you know that very well.'

'No, no, of course not,' Arthur said hastily. 'I didn't mean to say he was. It's bad that the police think he might be.'

Irene quickened her pace. 'I really must get home.'

'All right, but I'm coming with you.'

It was unnaturally quiet when they entered the shop. 'Wait here, Artie.' Irene ran upstairs and opened the door to the living room, but it was a peaceful enough scene that met her anxious gaze. Ma was sitting in a chair by the fire, and Pa was lying on the bed still fully dressed and snoring loudly.

'Are you all right, Renie?' Clara asked anxiously. 'You look flushed, ducks. Have you been running?'

'I was worried that Pa might have gone out again, but I see now that it weren't necessary.'

'Yes, he's sleeping like a baby,' Clara said, smiling serenely. 'I daresay he'll have a sore head when he wakes up.'

'Serve him right,' Irene said with feeling, but seeing her mother's face fall, she repented. 'What about you, Ma? Can I get you something? I don't suppose you've had anything to eat since breakfast.'

'I'm not hungry, love. I had some bread and

jam for me dinner and I don't think that your dad will feel much like eating when he wakes up. He can't take the drink like he used to.'

Irene went over to the bed to take a look at her father. His face was flushed and his jaw slack, but he was in a deep sleep and unlikely to awaken for hours. The thought of a good supper was too tempting to brush aside and Arthur was waiting for her downstairs. 'Do you mind if I go out with Artie, Ma? Just for a bite to eat.'

'You go, ducks. You deserve a nice night out with your young man.'

'He's not my young man. He's just a friend.'

'You go out with your friend and have a good time. Change your clothes and brush your hair, Renie. You look like you've been dragged through a hedge backwards.'

'Yes, Ma.' Irene smiled to herself. That was more like the old Ma. Irene could still remember a time when her mother had been a handsome woman of spirit, but that was before ill-health and worry had taken their toll.

Irene stepped out of her soiled garments and slipped on her one good frock; a hand-me-down from Emmie. She peered into the shard of fly-spotted mirror over the mantelshelf and tidied her hair into the snood at the nape of her neck. Even so, curly tendrils managed to escape around her forehead and no amount of brushing could persuade them to behave.

'There,' Irene said, straightening the white collar on her plain grey bodice. She held out her skirts, mimicking the fullness of a crinoline. 'How do I look?'

'Beautiful,' Clara said, misty-eyed and smiling. 'I'm a lucky woman to have two such pretty daughters.'

'Not forgetting your handsome son, Ma.'

Clara looked away, biting her lip. 'We don't speak about him. You know that, Irene.'

'I can't forget Jim. He's me brother.'

'Well, he's forgotten us.' Clara's voice hitched on a sob. 'Running away to sea when he was little more than a boy. Ten years he's been gone and no word from him. He might be dead for all I know, and I can't forgive him for the misery he caused your pa and me.'

'You don't mean that, Ma.'

Clara tossed her head. 'I do. That boy broke me heart when he run off. I won't never mention his name again.'

'But you keep his clothes in that old wooden chest,' Irene said gently. 'Just in case he does come home.'

'I should have taken them to the pop shop years ago.'

Irene stifled a sigh. She had tried in vain to make Ma talk about Jim, but her negative response was always the same. One day, Irene was certain that her big brother would come home. He would walk through the door, tall and handsome, having made his fortune in some foreign country. Why couldn't Ma see it that way?

Down below in the shop, Irene could hear Arthur shuffling about and calling her name in a hoarse stage whisper. She patted her mother's hand. 'I've got to go, Ma. But you're wrong about Jim. I know he's alive and he would have contacted us if he was able. He'll come home one day, you'll see.'

Clara made no response to this, but sat rigidly staring into the glowing embers of the fire. Irene left the room and made her way slowly downstairs with a deep feeling of sadness. She had been eight years old when Jim had left home after a fierce row with their father, who had threatened to beat him black and blue for stealing food from old Noddy, the pie man. Jim wasn't a bad boy, he had simply been hungry. If Pa had not lost everything on a certainty at the race track, they might have had vittles in the house and Jim wouldn't have been tempted to steal to fill his belly. It made Irene shudder even now when she recalled the scene. Jim had been her idol and she had cried for a week after he had gone. One of Billy's mates on the docks told them that Jim had sailed as cabin boy on a ship bound for Australia, and that was the last they had heard of him. Irene liked to imagine that he had survived the rigours of life at sea, and had prospered on the other side of the world, but sometimes when she awakened in the middle of the night during a bad dream, she feared that he was dead from drowning or disease. The uncertainty was the worst thing.

'What's up?' Arthur demanded. 'You look like you lost a tanner and found a farthing.'

'It's nothing. I'm hungry, that's all.'

'Well then, lady. We can soon put that right.' Arthur reached for her bonnet and shawl which she had discarded carelessly on the chair. 'Haven't you got anything warmer, Renie? It's cold outside.'

She snatched the shawl from him, wrapping the flimsy, much-darned material around her shoulders. 'I save me ermine-trimmed cloak for best, silly,' she retorted, jamming her bonnet on her head. Her cold fingers fumbled with the ribbons, but Arthur took them from her and tied a bow beneath her chin with such expertise that it made her chuckle. 'You're turning into quite a lady's man, Artie.'

'Not at all. I just like to see things done proper. It's the artist in me.' His eyes twinkled mischievously as he looked her up and down. 'Very pretty. You'll do.'

'Ta very much. I'm glad that you ain't ashamed to be seen out with a girl in her one and only decent set of clothes.'

He fingered a wisp of hair which had escaped her attention. 'You'd look lovely even if you was wearing an old flour sack.'

This made Irene laugh outright. 'Now I know you're teasing me.'

'No indeed. Cross me heart and hope to die, you're the prettiest girl in Cheapside, although that grey dress don't do you justice. You should wear green or blue to bring out the colour of your eyes.'

'Oh, come now, Artie. You're having me on. Do I look as though I come down in the last shower of rain? Me eyes are neither green nor blue but some strange colour in between and me hair is plain brown like a sparrow's wing. As me old granny used to say afore she died and went to heaven or the other place, "Irene, you was behind the door when good looks was handed out. God give 'em all to that flighty sister of yours." She was right too; the only trouble is that Emmie knows it.' Irene opened the door and shivered as the cold night air hit her. 'You weren't lying, Artie. It's blooming chilly. Let's get to the pub as quick as we can. I'm starving.'

Arm in arm they set off for Fleet Street and found it buzzing with activity as the gentlemen of the press set about their work of producing the next day's newspapers. Light blazed in the office windows and there was a continuous flow of hansom cabs dropping off reporters with notebooks clutched in their hands as they raced into the brightly lit buildings. The scent of burning charcoal in a brazier and the tempting aroma of hot chestnuts made Irene even hungrier, and her mouth was watering at the thought of the famous steak pudding served at the Old Cheshire Cheese.

By the time they reached Wine Office Court she had worked up quite an appetite. She did justice to a plateful of steak and kidney pudding, washed down with a glass of red wine and followed by apple pie swimming in a pool of thick yellow custard. Arthur ate well too and kept her entertained with anecdotes about the people he met in his work, and grumbles about the strictness of his father who, in his opinion, expected impossibly high standards from his own son and was far more lenient with the other apprentices.

'He says I spend too much time carousing and gambling,' Arthur said, wiping custard from his chin with a table napkin. 'But I say a fellow has to let off steam somehow. What d'you think, Renie?'

'Hmm,' Irene murmured, leaning back against the wooden settle. She was so full that her stomach hurt, but it was a good feeling and not one that happened very often. Their diet at home was frugal at the best of times, and quite often the family were reduced to eating bread and scrape for weeks on end. The taproom was filled with tobacco smoke and the smell of sap oozing from the burning logs, which made pleasant snapping and crackling sounds, adding to the general hubbub of conversation and occasional guffaws of laughter from men drinking at the bar. She was pleasantly sleepy and filled with a sense of well-being, and had not really paid much attention to Arthur's question.

'Don't you agree?'

'Agree to what, Artie?'

'That a fellow should be allowed to have a bit of fun at the end of a hard day.'

'I'd have to say yes to that, but it all depends on what type of fun you're talking about,' Irene said, suddenly alert and cautious.

'Let's have a laugh or two. I know a place where we can go to round the evening off. You'll love it.' Arthur rose to his feet, holding out his hand. 'Come on, Renie. I'll take you somewhere exciting.'

Unaccustomed to wine, Irene allowed her better judgement to be overruled, but she was still questioning Arthur's intentions as they crossed Fleet Street and made their way towards the river. She was excited but also a little nervous, and she clutched Arthur's arm more tightly as they walked the cobbled streets between tall buildings that seemed to bend and bow to each other above their heads in Hanging Sword Alley. The night-time sounds of the waterside were softened into an eerie background music of muffled hoots from steam whistles, the rhythmic flapping of sails and the splash of water as it lapped the stone steps. There was a pervading smell of cess and rotting vegetable matter and she covered her mouth and nose with her hand. They had come to the end of the alley and the small court was momentarily illuminated by the moon as it struggled out from behind a thick bank of clouds. Irene was aware of shuttered windows and an almost deathly hush, which was shattered when a door opened and a man staggered outside much the worse for drink. The sound of loud music and laughter flooded out in his wake, accompanied by a gust of stale air smelling strongly of tobacco smoke, ale and raw spirits.

'This is it,' Arthur said, taking her by the elbow and thrusting her into the narrow, dimly lit passageway.

'Artie, if this is a gambling club I won't stay,' Irene said anxiously.

'Don't worry, I'm not taking you into the gaming room.' Closing the door behind them,

Arthur led her down the corridor and knocked three times on a door at the far end.

'I don't like this,' Irene protested. 'I want to go home now.'

Even as she spoke, the door opened and she found herself in a large room lit by dozens of candles in wall sconces and candlesticks placed on long trestle tables. Women sat on benches chatting, drinking tumblers of what smelt like gin, and smoking clay pipes and cigarillos.

'Good evening, ladies.' Arthur doffed his hat with a flourish.

A few heads turned, although most of the women were seemingly too immersed in conversation to bother about the newcomers. Irene gasped as the heat and tobacco smoke hit the back of her throat, but as she looked round the room she recognised a couple of familiar faces. That flaming mop of curls and the gaudily painted visage could only belong to Fiery Nan, a prostitute who had a liking for pickled cucumbers and frequented the shop in Wood Street. Sitting next to her was her friend Gentle Annie, who had been known to break a punter's arm if he reneged on his promise to pay for her services.

Arthur gave her hand a squeeze. 'So, are you happy to stay with the ladies while I play a game or two at the tables?'

'You shouldn't have brought me here,' Irene

said in a low voice. 'You know what I think about this sort of place and you promised you'd stop gambling.'

'This will be my last time – my final fling before I take my exams and become a respectable citizen.' He backed towards the doorway and Irene could tell by the glint in his eyes that the gaming fever was already upon him, and nothing would prevent him from climbing that staircase.

She went to follow him, intending to leave the den of iniquity, but she was stopped by a hand clamping on her shoulder. She turned her head and found herself looking into the raddled face of Fiery Nan.

'Hello, Irene. What are you doing here, girl? Your dad would have something to say if he knew you was keeping such company.'

'I should go,' Irene murmured. 'It was a mistake.'

Fiery Nan glanced at Arthur's retreating back and she pursed her lips. 'Brought you here, did he? I'll have a few words to say to that young man.'

'I must get home,' Irene insisted.

Nan shook her head. 'No, ducks. It ain't safe this late at night. You stay here with Gentle Annie and me. We'll look after you until your fellah's taken a drubbing at the tables, which won't be long if I'm any judge of character.'

She took Irene by the shoulders and guided her through the packed room to a table where Annie sat with a clay pipe clenched between her teeth.

'Make room for a little 'un,' Nan said, nudging Annie in the ribs.

Gentle Annie turned her head and grinned, causing her thick makeup to crack at the corners of her blue eyes and making tiny lines radiate from her carmine lips. She gave the girl who was seated next to her a shove that sent her tumbling off the end of the form onto the floor. 'Well, if it ain't young Renie from the pickle shop. Come and sit here, ducks. Get her a glass of Hollands, Nan.'

Irene managed a weak smile as she perched nervously on the edge of the wooden bench. 'No, ta, Annie. I've just had supper across the road and I couldn't eat or drink another thing.'

Fiery Nan slapped her on the back with a hearty chuckle. 'A drop of good gin will go down a treat. You don't want to offend Annie, now do you, ducks?'

'Well, no,' Irene said reluctantly. She could see that both of them had been drinking, and although they were good-humoured now she knew only too well that this could change in a flash. They were attracting some attention from the rest of the women, who could smell a fight a mile off, and Irene did not relish a scratching, hair-pulling contest with Annie who was built like a Thames sailing barge. She accepted a glass of blue ruin from Nan and took a tentative sip, trying not to pull a face at the strong taste of the raw spirit.

'Drink up, girl,' Fiery Nan said with an approving smile. 'We need to make the most of our free time afore the men get bored with losing and come looking for sympathy.'

'And not just that, dearie.' A small woman sitting at the table closest to them turned to them with a wide grin, exposing a row of blackened stumps where she once might have had a set of good teeth.

'Shut your trap, Ivy,' Nan said, scowling. 'She ain't one of us, so hold your tongue.'

'Oh, pardon me,' Ivy retorted, curling her lip. 'I didn't know that the Princess Royal had come amongst us.'

Irene sensed an argument brewing. She rose swiftly to her feet, holding out her skirts and curtseying to Ivy with a wink and a smile. 'If I'm the Princess Royal, then you must be Queen Victoria. Pleased to meet you, ma'am.'

There was a moment's silence and then Ivy threw back her head and roared with laughter. A wave of merriment rippled round the room and soon everyone was laughing uncontrollably, holding their sides and clapping their hands as if they had just heard the best joke in the world. Irene glanced anxiously at Fiery Nan, who shrugged her shoulders and was about to make her way back to her place when the door burst open and suddenly there was chaos. The women's laughter turned to screams and shouts as a dozen or more uniformed police officers surged into the room, making arrests in what appeared to be a random fashion. Irene made for the door and found herself locked in a steel embrace.

'Good God. Miss Angel, what are you doing in a place like this?'

Chapter Three

Fighting against a rising tide of panic, Irene managed to control her instinct to struggle as she realised that her captor was none other than the young constable who had helped her take Pa home only that morning.

'It was a mistake,' she murmured, biting her lip.

Burton's youthful features were creased with concern and he raised his arm protectively as a bottle flew over their heads and smashed into the wall. A shower of broken glass clattered to the floor with red wine trickling down the wall like a bleeding wound.

'It certainly was,' Burton said, swinging her off her feet and depositing her in the narrow hallway. 'Let's get you out of here, miss.'

'No, thank you, Constable, but I'll be all right,' Irene insisted. 'I can't go without my friend.'

'Some friend if he brought you to a place like this,' Burton said, frowning. 'I don't think you quite understand, miss, but you could end up spending the night in the clink with the rest of the females, if you get my meaning.'

Irene glanced over her shoulder in time to see Gentle Annie butting a constable in the stomach while Fiery Nan struggled with a burly sergeant. For a moment it seemed that Nan was winning, but another officer grabbed her from behind and cuffed her wrists. It was so unfair, Irene thought angrily. She was torn between the desire to break free and rush upstairs to warn Arthur, and anger at the treatment of women who had been simply enjoying a social evening. They might not be angels and it was true that most of them had at one time or another had a brush with the law, but on this occasion it appeared that they were being victimised by an over-zealous police force.

'This is all so unfair,' Irene cried, angrily. 'They weren't doing anything wrong.'

Burton's cheeks were suffused with a rosy blush. 'A young lady like you shouldn't mix with their sort. Let me escort you outside, miss. Please.'

'But my friend won't know what's happened to me. He'll be worried.'

'Your friend will be up before the magistrate in the morning unless I'm very much mistaken. A night in the cells will hopefully make him think twice before he visits such a place again.'

Irene opened her mouth to protest but,

without a by your leave, Burton tightened his grip on her shoulders and he propelled her along the passageway, past the foot of the stairs where the punters were being arrested one by one as they came down to discover the source of the uproar. 'This is becoming a habit, miss,' he said cheerfully.

As they reached the street door, Irene shook off his restraining grasp. 'I can find me own way, ta.'

'The inspector gave me my orders this morning. I was to see you safely home then and I know he would say the same now.'

She hesitated, torn between the desire to find out what had happened to Arthur and the longing to be as far away from this place as was possible.

Burton opened the door. 'Shall we go, miss?'

With a final glance at the fracas ensuing in the hallway Irene had no option other than to follow him through the dark passage that led into Hanging Sword Alley and then into Fleet Street. It was raining and the gutters overflowed with filthy water polluted with horse dung. In the flickering lamplight, the cobblestones glistened with an oily sheen, and the thin soles of her boots slipped and slid as she tried to keep pace with the young constable.

'What was all that about?' Irene demanded breathlessly. 'What right have the cops to arrest women who were just enjoying a peaceful evening out?'

'It's not for me to say, miss. We were just following orders.'

'Well, I call it downright bullying.' Irene shivered as the rainwater seeped through her thin clothes, and she sneezed.

Burton glanced down at her and his stern expression softened. 'You're soaked to the skin.' He took off his uniform cape and wrapped it around her shoulders. The heavy garment was still warm from his body and it smelt strongly of wet wool and cheap pomade.

'Why did you do that?' Irene demanded, eyeing him suspiciously.

'Just following orders, miss.'

'Well, I wouldn't want to get you into trouble with your boss, Constable.'

'Don't get the wrong idea, miss. The inspector is tough, but he's fair. I won't have a word said against him.'

Irene could see that it was useless to argue, and they walked on briskly and in silence until they reached the corner of Wood Street. She stopped and took off the cape, handing it back to him with a grateful smile. 'I hope you ain't too wet.'

'I'll soon dry out. Goodnight, miss.'

'Goodnight, Constable, and thank you.'

'I hope we meet again in more pleasant circumstances,' he said shyly.

Irene angled her head, eyeing him with mixed feelings. He was a nice-looking young chap and kind too. Had the circumstances been different she might have warmed to him, but she could hear Pa's voice in her head warning her not to trust a copper. It was a hard lesson, learned young, and memories of tonight's fiasco were still fresh in her mind. She knew very well that Constable Burton was waiting for a word of encouragement, but she said nothing, merely nodding her head.

If he was disappointed, his well-schooled features did not betray his feelings; he saluted her smartly and hurried off with long strides in the direction of Fleet Street.

Irene let herself into the shop, locked the door behind her and tiptoed upstairs. The only sound in the darkened room was that of her father's stertorous breathing and the occasional soft sigh as her mother moved in her sleep. It was cold, and despite the constable's chivalrous act, her clothes remained damp. She undressed to her shift and climbed into her bed, but it was a long while before she succumbed to sleep. She couldn't help worrying about Arthur and wondering what had befallen him after the police raid on the gaming club. Old man Greenwood would be furious if Arthur was up before the beak in the morning, and it might even jeopardise his journeyman examination. She felt her eyelids growing heavy and, with a deep sigh, she turned on her side and curled up in a ball.

Next morning, she awakened to find that her father was up and dressed, seemingly none the worse for wear. He chucked her under the chin with a disarming smile and announced his intention of going to Faulkner's bath house in Newgate Street.

'But, Pa. That costs money and we need food.'

Billy smiled benevolently. 'Of course we do, my pet. And I will bring something back with me when I am bathed, shaved and fit to mix with society.' He dabbed ineffectually at the patch of mud on his frock coat and sighed. 'Goodness knows what happened to me on the way home last night, but I seem to have taken a tumble.'

'It was the night before last, Pa. Don't you remember nothing?'

'Not a thing, my little cabbage. It's all a merciful blank and I daresay is not worth bringing to mind.' Billy took his battered top hat from the mantelshelf and rubbed it on the cuff of his coat before placing it at a rakish angle on his head. 'At least I look like a gent, even if I smell like a goat.' He reached for his silver-headed cane and tucked it under his arm. 'There, now Billy Angel is ready to face the world. Give your mother a kiss from me, petal, and tell her I won't be long.'

Irene was speechless as she watched him saunter out of the room, but at the sound of his footsteps on the stair treads she realised that once again Pa had neatly sidestepped all his responsibilities, and disregarding the fact that she was wearing nothing but her shift, she ran after him. 'Pa, wait!'

He stopped at the bottom of the stairs, turning his head to flash a questioning smile in her direction. 'Yes, poppet?'

'If you've got money, please let me have some so that I can buy food and coal.'

'You know that I would give you my soul, my dear girl, but sadly I have only enough coin for a hot bath and a shave.'

'But you said . . .'

He raised his forefinger to his lips. 'Hush now, my dove. We don't want to spoil a beautiful morning by a sordid argument about money. When I am fit to rejoin the human race, I will go to my club and collect a debt or two. We will dine like kings tonight. That's a promise.' He unlocked the door and opened it with a flourish. 'Au reservoir, my cherry, as they say on the Continent.'

Irene opened her mouth to protest, but Billy had already departed, leaving the door swinging on its hinges. She shook her head, sighing with frustration. Pa was a trial and no mistake. Whatever money he had left in his pocket after his visit to the public baths would be earmarked for the gaming tables, and if his luck was in they would not see him again that day. She retreated upstairs to dress, moving about the room on tiptoe so as not to disturb her mother. Having knotted her hair in a chignon at the nape of her neck, she went downstairs to open up.

Outside the window she could see people scurrying along the pavements on their way to work. It was unlikely that any of them would stop to buy sauce or pickles, but she had to be ready to catch any passing trade, and she busied herself about the shop. Her thoughts returned to Arthur, and as she polished the wooden counter she wondered if he had been allowed to go free with just a caution, or whether he had spent the night in a police cell. She hoped and prayed for his sake that he had not, but she knew that there was nothing she could do except wait and hope to see him breeze through the door with a big smile on his face.

She dusted the glass bottles and jars on the shelves, and as there were still no customers she picked up a besom and began to sweep the floor. She was sweeping the dust out onto the pavement when Josiah's smart green and yellow dog cart drew to a halt at the kerb. His storeman, Tompkins, who also acted as coachman when required, tipped his cap to her and tossed the reins to a small ragged boy, promising him a halfpenny if he held the horse. The child nodded his head and grabbed the reins whilst keeping a safe distance from the animal's mouth, eyeing the horse as if he feared it might gobble him up. Tompkins climbed stiffly from the driver's seat and let down the hinged tailboard.

Emily was attracting some curious glances from passers-by as she alighted from the vehicle. She laid one kid-gloved hand on Tompkins' arm, keeping the other tucked inside a rabbit-fur muff. She smiled, inclining her head to acknowledge an old acquaintance as regally as if she were Queen Victoria herself. She sailed past Irene and entered the shop, but as soon as she was out of public view her smile froze on her lips. 'Well? What have you to say for yourself, Irene Angel?'

Irene stared at her in genuine surprise. 'What are you on about?'

'Don't act the innocent with me, Renie. You were seen last night, being dragged along Fleet Street by a police constable. As if Pa's gambling habit wasn't bad enough, now you've got yourself into trouble with the law. How could you do this to me?'

Irene closed the door so that a curious Tompkins could not hear. 'I was not dragged along Fleet Street as you say. Who told you that?'

'It was Ephraim who saw you, so don't deny it. He had been doing business for his father in one of the newspaper offices and he saw you.'

'Your nasty-minded stepson got it wrong then. I was being escorted home if you must know, for my own safety.'

'For pity's sake, why? Where had you been?'

Irene bit her lip; this part was not going to sound so good. She shrugged her shoulders in an attempt to appear casual. 'It was all a misunderstanding. Artie took me to supper at the Old Cheshire Cheese and we went to a place he knows afterwards.'

Emily's eyes narrowed to slits and her delicate eyebrows winged together over the bridge of her pert little nose. 'What sort of place?'

'It was a kind of gaming club.'

'Women aren't allowed in those sort of places. Even I know that,' Emily said suspiciously. 'No decent woman would be seen dead in a gaming hell.'

Irene hung her head. It was impossible to argue against the truth, and she could not meet her sister's fierce gaze. 'It was a mistake,' she murmured.

'This is worse than I thought,' Emily snapped. 'You were caught socialising with a gaggle of common prostitutes and dollymops. How could you be so stupid, Renie? If this gets back to Josiah he will be absolutely furious.'

'Does he have to find out?'

'I won't tell him, but I'm afraid that Ephraim will take great pleasure in passing on bad news and then Josiah will be so angry. I just don't know what I'm going to say to him.'

Irene could see that Emily was working herself up into one of her states, and she was stricken with guilt. 'I'm sorry if I've upset you, Emmie, but you've got to stop worrying about us and think of yourself and the baby.' Irene gave her sister a hug, and she pressed her gently down onto the one and only chair. 'Now sit down and stop fretting. I doubt if your friend, Inspector high-and-mighty Kent, will even remember my name today. He's got better things to worry about than a girl who works in a pickle shop.'

Emily smiled reluctantly. 'I suppose you're right, but I wish you would try to keep out of trouble, Renie. It makes things very difficult for me, and I just know that Ephraim and

Erasmus spend their time looking for bad things to say about our family. They can't forgive their pa for marrying me and now that there's a baby on the way they are even worse. That's another reason why I want Ma to come and live with me. You won't try to stop her, will you?'

Irene saw her sister's lips tremble and the tears sparkling on the tips of her long eyelashes, and she had not the heart to argue. She patted Emily on the shoulder. 'No, I won't, but you've got to stand up to those two bullies. Tell Josiah what they're like and let him deal with them.'

Emily opened her reticule and took out a handkerchief. She wiped her eyes and sighed. 'Josiah thinks that the sun shines out of their arses.' She clamped her hand to her mouth and her eyes widened in horror. 'Oh, dear heaven, it just slipped out.'

'Spoken like a true Angel,' Irene said, chuckling.

This drew a reluctant smile from Emily and she shook her head. 'I only have to be back here for five minutes and I forget everything I've learnt. Anyway, I'm going upstairs to talk to Ma. Promise you won't say anything to put her off coming home with me.'

'I promise.'

Emily rose to her feet and she laid her hand

briefly on Irene's shoulder. 'You ought to come too, you know. Leave this horrid little shop and let Pa look after himself. I love him as much as you do, but he's a selfish man and he'll never change.'

'I know what he's like, but he needs me, Emmie. I couldn't just walk out on him.'

'Suit yourself, but the offer still stands.'

Irene watched her sister ascend the narrow staircase with mixed feelings. She knew that Ma would be much better off in the Tippets' house with servants to wait on her and good food in her belly, but it seemed as though her family was gradually disintegrating. Jim had been the first to leave home, and then it had been Emmie's turn. If Ma agreed to go, it would leave just her and Pa, Irene thought sadly. The offer of a comfortable and easy life was tempting but she could not bring herself to abandon him. Pa was a child when it came to looking after himself; a charming irresponsible child.

She picked up the duster and began to polish the counter, straining her ears in an effort to eavesdrop on the conversation upstairs, but she could only hear the low murmur of voices. She couldn't help wondering how Pa would react if she was forced to tell him that Ma had gone to stay with Emmie in Love Lane. It would be a temporary measure, until the baby was born.

At least, that was what she would tell him. She hoped he would understand.

'What?' Billy cried, smiting his forehead with the flat of his hand. 'My Clara has left me? Why would she do such a thing?'

Irene poured a generous measure of gin into a glass and added a splash of water. She handed it to him. 'Drink that, Pa. I know it's been a shock, but Emmie did it for Ma's own good as well as her own.'

Billy tossed back the drink in one go and held out the glass for a refill. 'I thought you had no money,' he said suspiciously. 'How could we afford the booze?'

'I took money from the till, and I bought us a pie for supper. We have to eat, and as to the gin – I thought you might need it.' She handed him the stone bottle.

'Hollands,' Billy said appreciatively. 'None of that jigger gin. You're a good girl, Irene. But your sister is an ungrateful serpent. What right has she to spirit your mother off like that? You tell me.'

'I did tell you, Pa. She's in the family way and she needs Ma to keep her company and give her good advice. Emmie thought that a stay in Love Lane might help Ma's rheumatics.'

Billy poured himself another drink, omitting the water. He drained the glass, frowning.

'But what about my needs? How am I to manage without my little Clara?'

'I'm here, Pa.'

'Yes, you're here, but it's not the same. My luck will run out if your mother is not here by my side. We'll be ruined.'

'Don't talk that way,' Irene said, controlling her temper with an effort. 'That's just superstitious nonsense, Pa. Your luck is a fickle thing and it has nothing to do with Ma or anyone else.'

Billy eyed her speculatively. 'Is there any cash left in the till, Renie? I could do with a stake for the game tonight.'

She was tempted to lie. There was a shilling left from the day's takings. She had done well in the shop after Ma's tearful departure, mainly due to a visitation from Fiery Nan, who had bought three jars of pickled walnuts, two jars of piccalilli and a jar of pickled lemons. These, she said, were for her nerves, which were all jangled up after being locked up in a cell all night when she'd done nothing to deserve such treatment. Gentle Annie was nursing a black eye, but the copper who arrested her would have sore ribs this morning, if not one or two of them broken, and Ivy had a handful of torn fingernails. They were all out of sorts and it was all because of an ambitious police inspector: Nan knew where to lay the blame for last night's raid. There was, she grumbled, no justice in the world. Then Fiery Nan, having vented her anger, stacked her purchases in a wicker basket and had stomped out of the shop, leaving Irene breathless and even more worried about Arthur, from whom she had heard nothing. If she had not been stuck in the shop all day, she would have marched down to the police station in Old Jewry and demanded to know what had happened to him. As it was she had to be patient, and that was not in her nature.

She had spent the day fuming and fretting, and had not been in the best of humours when her father had breezed into the shop just before closing time. She was now finding it extremely hard to be patient with him.

'Come along, poppet,' Billy urged in his most cajoling tone. 'Surely you could trust your old pa with a stake for the game tonight.'

'Pa, you said yourself that your luck is out. You've already lost a whole shilling so why not give it a rest this evening? Stay home with me, or let's go out to a music hall. We haven't done that for ages.'

'Ha!' Billy cried triumphantly. 'So you have got some money.'

'A little, Pa, but I need to keep that to pay Mr Yapp what I owe him and to buy more stock. I can't trade if I have nothing to sell.'

'But I'll recoup all my losses and you'll have money to spare. You can buy all the pickles on Yapp's cart and still have the price of a fish supper. You trust me, don't you, darling?'

Irene met his appealing gaze with a sinking heart. No matter how much of a fight she put up, she knew that Pa would win in the end. 'All right, but promise me you won't lose the lot.' She put her hand in her pocket and took out a florin.

Billy took it, chortling with delight. 'There's a good girl. I knew you wouldn't let me down.' He seized his top hat and cane and made for the door.

'Pa, you haven't had any supper.'

'Don't worry, my dove. I'll eat later. Don't wait up.' He left the room, taking the bottle of Hollands with him.

She stared at the pie and suddenly her appetite left her. Without her mother to back her up, Irene knew that she was going to have an uphill struggle to keep Pa in line. She listened for the sound of his key in the lock, but all she heard was a dull thud as the door slammed and then there was silence. Sighing, she went downstairs to check and was barely surprised to find that in his hurry to be off Pa had forgotten to lock the door. She was about to do so when Arthur's father Cuthbert Greenwood barged into the shop, almost knocking her down. 'Where is he? Where is that scurrilous ne'er-do-well?'

Irene staggered backwards, saving herself from falling by clutching at the newel post. 'If you mean Arthur, he's not here.'

'Then where is he? I'll warrant you know where I can find him. He didn't come home last night, and he wasn't at his workbench this morning.'

'I don't know where he is,' Irene said defiantly. It was not exactly a lie. She only suspected that Arthur had been detained by the police, and even if she had known it for a fact, she would not have admitted it to Mr Greenwood. He was a bad-tempered bully and she had never liked him; moreover, she was certain that the feeling was mutual.

He glowered at her, baring his teeth like an angry bull terrier. 'I'll warrant you do know something, young lady. Whenever my boy got himself into trouble in the past, you were always lurking somewhere in the background, so don't put on that innocent face. Tell me where he is.'

'I don't know.'

'You're lying, girl.'

Greenwood's face flushed to the colour of pickled beetroot and beads of perspiration stood out on his forehead. Irene stared at him nervously. If he carried on like this he would have a seizure and she did not want that on her conscience. She moderated her tone in an attempt to calm him. 'I'm sure Arthur will come home soon. He might even be there now and you'll find you've worried needlessly.'

'Worried!' Greenwood spat the word at her. 'I'm not worried – I'm furious. That blockhead is jeopardising his chances of passing his journeyman's examination. He ought to be at his bench, practising his craft and not gallivanting about town. Just wait until I get my hands on that young idiot.' He stormed out of the shop, slamming the door behind him.

Irene went to lock it, but as her fingers closed around the iron key she thought of Arthur. If he had spent last night and the best part of today in the cells, it would only be fair to warn him of what was awaiting him at home. She put on her bonnet and shawl and slipped out into the night, locking the door behind her. The streets were almost deserted now that the banks and businesses had closed. The bootblacks and costermongers were packing up and heading homewards together with a few harassed-looking clerks, who hurried, heads down, as if eager to reach the comfort and safety of home. This was the twilight hour when the bustling commercial heart of the City was lulled to sleep, and before the denizens of the underworld came to life.

She set off at a brisk pace along Cheapside, heading in the direction of the police headquarters in Old Jewry. There was a definite chill in the air and through a thin veil of chimney smoke she could see the stars, softened and blurred, like seed pearls on a bed of black velvet. A ragged old man lurched out of the shadows begging her for money. She was more startled than frightened but she quickened her pace. The man was probably harmless, but she had nothing to give him and she was not taking any chances. She ran the last hundred yards or so to the police station, but she stopped outside to catch her breath and compose herself before she went inside.

The desk sergeant was busy writing something in a large, leather-bound book, and although he must surely be aware of her presence, he did not look up. Irene cleared her throat. 'Excuse me, Officer.'

He raised his head, giving her a cursory glance. 'Wait a moment, young lady.' With maddening calm, he finished what he was doing and then he put his quill pen down. 'And what can I do for you, miss?'

'I want to know what's happened to Arthur Greenwood.'

The sergeant raised his bushy eyebrows. 'Do you now? And what is your business with the person in question? Are you his wife?'

Irene shook her head.

'His sister, maybe?'

'Look, mister. All I want to know is what's happened to my friend Arthur. I think he was brought here last night, but I need to know that he's all right. If he's here, I'd like to see him.'

'That won't be possible, miss.'

'Why not?' A wild vision of Arthur manacled in the hold of a convict ship flashed through Irene's mind, and she clutched the counter with both hands. 'What have you done with him? He's innocent, I tell you.'

'What's going on, Sergeant?' A familiar voice behind her made Irene spin round and she found herself face to face with Inspector Kent. He must have followed her in from the street, but she had been too absorbed in her conversation with the sergeant to notice. He took off his hat, meeting her gaze with a quizzical lift of his eyebrows. 'Miss Angel, we meet again.'

'What have you done with Arthur?' Irene demanded.

'That's no way to speak to the inspector,' the desk sergeant warned. 'I must ask you to leave, miss.'

'Or you'll do what?' Irene turned to glare at him. 'Arrest me for asking questions? Is that what you do to innocent members of the public?'

'Now, young lady . . .'

Kent raised a gloved hand. 'It's all right, sergeant. I'll deal with this.' He lifted a hatch in the counter and beckoned Irene to follow him along a narrow, poorly lit corridor. He opened a door at the far end and ushered her into an office lined with bookshelves which were crammed with files. In the middle of the room was a large desk neatly laid out with a silver inkstand, a blotter and two wooden filing trays piled high with documents. A fire burned brightly in the grate and a black marble clock with brass hands and numerals was placed in the exact centre of the mantelshelf. The office was clinically neat and without any personal touch that might have given a clue as to the nature of the man whose domain it was. Irene experienced a sudden desire to move the clock to one side, or to empty one of the filing trays on the floor, but she managed to control the impulse. Kent pulled up a chair and motioned her to take a seat.

She shook her head. 'I'd rather stand.'

'As you wish.' He peeled off his peccary-leather gloves and laid them in his top hat while he shrugged off his heavy greatcoat and hung it on a coat stand in the corner of the room.

Irene clasped her hands tightly behind her back, watching this well-practised routine with mounting impatience. 'Look, guv, all I want to know is what's happened to Arthur. What have you done with him?'

'Are we speaking of Arthur Greenwood?' Kent went to stand by the fire, warming his hands.

His casual manner fuelled Irene's resentment. 'You ought to know. It was you who arrested an innocent man.'

'You were both caught in an illegal gambling den.'

'Then why wasn't I arrested?'

'You were doing nothing. He was playing the tables.'

'Then you are holding him.'

'Not now. I believe he spent the night in the cells but he was released this afternoon.'

'Then where is he? What's happened to him?'

'No harm has come to your friend. Let's just say that he is helping me with my enquiries.'

'And what does that mean?' He was so maddeningly calm that Irene could have shaken him.

'It means that in return for receiving certain information, I am prepared to drop all charges.'

Suddenly, it all made sense. 'You've set him to spy on the Sykes gang.'

'He's gathering information.'

'Arthur is a boy,' she protested. 'He's just a

boy and the Sykes brothers will have him for breakfast.'

'I think you underestimate your friend, Miss Angel.'

'Don't play games with me, Inspector Kent. Everyone round here knows what happens to a nark if the gang catches him, and it ain't pretty. You'd have done better to lock Arthur up and throw away the key.'

'I'm dealing with this personally, and I can assure you that Mr Greenwood will be kept under surveillance at all times. The best you can do for him is to act normally and say nothing of this to anyone, not even your own father – especially your father.'

'Are you saying that my pa is in with the Sykes gang? Because if you are, then you're wrong, Inspector. My pa may be a lot of things but he ain't a gang member and never was.'

'Then the information I receive from your friend will be crucial in clearing your father of any suspicion that we may have, and you can help in this, Miss Angel.'

She stared at him in disbelief. 'Me? How?'

'Since you already know so much, you could act as go-between. It would draw suspicion away from Mr Greenwood and help to clear your father's name.'

'Are you asking me to spy on me own flesh and blood?'

'Not necessarily. If he's innocent you will be doing him a great service. I've been trying to smash the Sykes gang for years, but so far they have evaded the law. I believe that you could be instrumental in obtaining evidence that would lead to their arrest and conviction.'

'I told you before that my pa has nothing to do with the Sykes brothers, and Arthur don't go anywhere near them. He's just a silly boy who likes to gamble.' The thought of spying on Pa was too horrible to contemplate. Irene shook her head vehemently. 'No, I won't do it. You're asking too much.'

'I know that your father frequents the gambling hell in Blue Boar Court. He has been followed there on many an occasion and even if he isn't actually a member of the gang, he knows a great deal about them.'

'Ask him yourself then. I don't want nothing to do with this.'

She made for the door, but Kent moved swiftly to bar her way.

'Don't be afraid. I will do my utmost to protect your father, Miss Angel. Help me to crush the Sykes gang and you will make London a safer place in which to live.'

'No. You've got the wrong girl, Inspector. I'd never peach on my Pa. Now let me go.'

He stepped aside. 'You are free to leave if you wish, but I beg you to reconsider.'

'There's nothing to think about,' Irene said, pushing past him. 'I don't want nothing to do with any of this, Inspector Kent. I've got nothing more to say to you – we're on different sides, and always will be.'

Chapter Four

The police station and its officers represented everything that she had been brought up to dislike and distrust and Irene could not get away fast enough. She did not stop running until she reached the corner of Cheapside and Wood Street, when a painful stitch caused her to lean against the rough trunk of the plane tree. Holding her side she gasped for breath, but without any warning she was seized from behind and a hand clamped over her mouth.

'Renie, it's me.'

At first she thought she was hearing things, but the hoarse whisper certainly sounded like Arthur's voice and she froze.

'That's right, it's me. I'm taking my hand away so for God's sake don't scream.'

She nodded her head and was immediately released. She spun round to face him angrily. 'Arthur Greenwood, what d'you think you're playing at? You scared me half to death.'

'I'm sorry, Renie. I had to make sure you didn't call out. For all I know, they might be following me.'

'Who would be following you? I've just been down to the police station trying to find out what happened to you.'

'You shouldn't have done that.'

'You've got some explaining to do, my lad, and not just to me.' Irene moved out of the shadows, taking a quick look around to make sure that no one was about, and satisfied that the street was empty except for a couple of hansom cabs which clattered past without stopping, she beckoned to Arthur. 'Come into the shop. Ma's gone to Emmie's and Pa is out.'

Arthur hesitated. 'Are you sure there's no one spying on us?'

'Quite sure, you big baby. Come along.' Impatient now, Irene went round to the front of the shop and unlocked the door. She went inside and was about to light the gas mantle when Arthur scurried in after her. He closed the door, turning the key in the lock.

'Don't put the light on.'

'For goodness sake, Artie. Stop acting so mysterious and tell me what's going on.'

He slumped down on the chair, holding his head in his hands. 'I'm in trouble, Renie. I'm not up to this sort of thing. A bet or two at the tables or the race course is one thing, but getting involved with the Sykes brothers is another matter.'

'You'd better start from the beginning, Artie.

I've heard half of it from Inspector Kent, but what exactly has that man forced you into?'

Haltingly at first, but gaining momentum as he related the events of the past twenty-four hours, he told her how he had been carted off in the Black Maria with the rest of the punters from Potter's club. They had been kept in a cell for what seemed like hours before being taken out and interviewed one by one. It was then that Kent had offered him the choice of being charged with patronising an illegal gaming club, or being allowed to go free if he agreed to infiltrate the Sykes gang and spy on them.

'I didn't want my old man to find out about my gambling,' Arthur said, running his fingers through his already tousled hair.

'He was here earlier, and he wasn't too pleased with you then. Gawd knows what he'll say when you go home and tell him you spent the night in the police cells.'

'He'll kill me,' Arthur said gloomily. 'And if he don't, the Sykes brothers will.'

'I blame Kent for all this. He's so puffed up with his own self-importance that he thinks he's God.'

'I suppose he was only doing his job, and he's got a point. The Sykes brothers run this neighbourhood, and no one stands up to them.'

'You can't take them on single-handed. Kent

might have promised you police protection but that's not going to help if Vic and Wally discover that you're a copper's nark.'

'You're right, and I think I might have given myself away already,' Arthur said, rising to his feet and going to the window to peer out into the street. 'That's why I came here and didn't go straight home. I think I was followed, Renie. I went to Blue Boar Court, like Kent said, but he warned me not to play anything other than a game or two of billiards. I won a pocketful of money and then I saw Billy playing baccarat. He invited me to join them. I know I shouldn't have, but the temptation was too great and at first I was winning . . .' His voice trailed off miserably.

'Oh, Artie. You blooming idiot.'

'I know. I should have walked away, kept in the background and done what Kent told me, but I thought I was on a winning streak. Then I started losing, and I tried to get my money back, but I lost even more. I wrote one IOU, and then another. Then Wally turned up, and when he saw what was going on he threw me out. Told me I had to get the money right away or I'd end up at the bottom of the river. It wasn't meant to happen that way, Renie. What shall I do?'

'I don't know,' Irene said slowly. 'What a mess.'

'I was a fool, but it seemed too good a chance to miss. Now I've got Wally Sykes on my back as well as Kent.'

'There's only one thing for it, Artie. You'll have to tell your father. He'll pay up, I'm sure he will.'

'You don't know my dad. He'd sooner see me in prison than honour a gambling debt. He's a puritan when it comes to games of chance and the like.'

'Then you'll have to go and tell Kent what happened.'

'And end up in jail? I can't, Renie. I'll just have to leave the country.'

'Running away won't solve anything, and we're not going to cower here in the dark like scared rabbits.' Irene struck a vesta and lit a candle. 'I'll ask my pa what to do. Gawd knows he's been in enough scrapes in his life and wriggled out of them. He's well in with the Sykes brothers. Maybe they'll listen to him and give you a second chance.'

'I dunno, Renie. I don't think Billy has much time for me either. He'd probably say I deserve all I'll get.'

'Pa's not like that. You must stay here until he gets home, and then we'll tell him everything and see what he has to say.'

A glimmer of hope flickered in Arthur's eyes but then he shook his head. 'I can't stay here.

If Wally didn't have me followed then Kent almost certainly did. I'm a wanted man.'

'Wanted or not, you'll be safe here for tonight at least. I'm certain that Wally Sykes has bigger fish to fry than you, and Inspector Kent was probably bluffing. He was trying to scare you into doing his dirty work. He even tried to make me act as go-between.'

Arthur's eyes widened. 'No! Surely not?'

'Oh, yes, he did. But I told him where to go. I ain't playing his game. If he wants to make superintendent he'll do it without my help – or yours. Now cheer up, cully. There's a pie upstairs that needs eating before it grows legs and walks out of the shop. We'll sit and wait for my pa to come home.'

She led the way upstairs and made Arthur sit on her parents' bed while she rekindled the fire and hung the kettle on a hook over the flames. She cut the pie into three portions, and, saving one piece for her father, she gave a slice to Arthur with instructions to eat while she made the tea. Despite his obvious distress, he wolfed his share and washed it down with two cups of sweet tea. Irene tried to eat but the food stuck in her throat, and she gave what was left of her portion to Arthur, insisting that it would be criminal to waste good vittles. She sipped her tea, keeping an eye on the clock. The minutes passed and then the hours without a sign of Billy, and by two o'clock in the morning Arthur had slumped down on the bed and his even breathing indicated that he was asleep. Irene was too agitated to rest, and the fire had long since burned away to a pile of grey ash. The coal scuttle was empty and it was bitterly cold in the room. Rising to her feet, she went to the window and knelt on the small wooden chest where their clothes were stored with sprigs of dried lavender. She peered out through the bare branches of the tree in the hope of seeing Pa's familiar figure striding homeward, but there was still no sign of him.

By three o'clock she was getting desperate. The mere fact that he was out so late suggested that his luck was fickle to say the least. She was chilled to the bone and a sudden cramp in her leg made her stand up to rub her aching calf muscles. It was then that a germ of an idea came into her head. Forgetting her pain, she opened the chest and riffled through the neatly folded garments. At the bottom she found Jim's old nankeen breeches, a calico shirt and a corduroy waistcoat; clothes that had been outgrown even before he left home, but which Ma had stubbornly held on to, even though they would fetch a few coppers in the dolly shop.

An idea came into her head that shocked

her with its audacity, but Irene was never one to refuse a challenge. Keeping an eye on Arthur in case he should awaken suddenly, she took off her own clothes and dressed in the male attire. It felt strange to see her legs in trousers and Jim's old boots were a couple of sizes too large for her feet, but she shrugged on the coarse shirt and finally the waistcoat, which she hoped would disguise her feminine curves. Lastly, she crammed her hair into an old cloth cap, and a quick glance in the mirror was enough to satisfy her that in a poor light she could pass for a boy.

It was a daring plan, born out of desperation, but as she left the shop Irene was filled with nervous excitement. She strode along the pavements with a swagger in her step. So this was how it felt to be a boy. She gave a start as a feral cat sprang out from an alleyway in hot pursuit of a large rat, and somewhere in the darkness of a doorway someone moaned. Irene did not stop to investigate; she quickened her pace, putting her head down as she passed a couple of drunks who staggered along arm in arm as if in some bizarre three-legged race. If they noticed her they gave no sign of it, and Irene couldn't help smiling to herself. If she had been dressed in her normal clothes no doubt at least one of them would have propositioned her. Free for the first time from the constraints of stays and long skirts she felt that she was invincible.

When she reached Blue Boar Court, she took a quick look round, and satisfied that there was no sign of a bobby on the beat, she raised her hand and knocked three times on the door in rapid succession. She repeated the action, more slowly this time, allowing a heartbeat in between raps, just as she had seen her father do on so many occasions in the past. The door opened and she recognised the grizzled face of Jed Blacker, commonly known as Blackie, the ancient doorman who had protected the Sykes brothers since they were boys.

He held up a lantern, peering at her short-sightedly. 'Who are you?'

'I'm Billy Angel's boy, Jim. I must speak to my old man,' Irene said, lowering her tone to what she hoped sounded like a pubescent boy's voice.

Blackie stared at her, frowning. 'You run away to sea, you young devil. I remember it well.'

She had not expected him to remember that far back, but she must act out her part. She struck a pose, tucking her thumbs into her belt. 'I've come back.'

'And not a day older or an inch taller it seems.'

'Have you ever been to sea, mister?'

'No, of course I ain't.'

'Then you don't know what a hard life it is,' Irene said gruffly. 'Fed on dry biscuits with weevils in, and salt pork what makes you spew your guts up, it's no wonder I never growed very big. Now, are you going to let me see me dad, or not?'

'I suppose it won't hurt, but you mind your manners in here, boy. You'll keep out of Wally and Vic's way if you know what's good for you.'

'Ta, mister.' Irene hurried past him and made her way down the long, gloomy passage. That was a narrow escape, she thought, smothering a sigh of relief. It was just lucky that old Blackie was a bit slow on the uptake, or he might have worked out that Jim would be a man of twenty-four by now. She had never been inside the building and she had no idea where the gaming room was situated. She paused, straining her ears for the sound of voices. All was quiet on the ground floor, but as she ascended a rickety flight of stairs she saw a splinter of light beneath the door directly ahead of her. Taking a deep breath, she opened it slowly and was greeted by a wave of sound as she slipped unnoticed into the gaming room.

It was dimly lit and fogged with tobacco smoke. The pungent odour of strong spirits and male sweat assailed her nostrils. The click of billiard balls drew her attention to the tables at the far side of the room, where men in their shirtsleeves concentrated their full attention on the game in hand. At first she could not see any sign of her father, and she was beginning to think that she had missed him when she spotted Wally who was acting as banker at a game of baccarat. Seated next to him with his back to her was Pa. She made her way between the groups of men, who barely raised an eyebrow at the sight of a young boy in their midst. She was nervous now and her palms were damp with sweat as she went to stand behind her father. She prayed silently that he would not overreact, and she tapped him lightly on the shoulder. 'Pa, it's Jim. Can I have a word?'

Billy seemed to freeze for a moment and then he raised his head, turning very slowly to stare at her. 'Jim?'

Wally gave her a cursory glance. 'Tell the boy to go home where he belongs, Billy.'

'Jim?' Billy struggled to his feet, taking Irene by the shoulders and giving her a shake that rattled her teeth in her head. 'What are you doing here, boy?'

'I got a message for you from Ma.'

'What are you playing at?' Billy hissed in her ear.

'Call for Blackie and have him thrown out,'

Wally said, chewing on the end of a fat cigar and squinting malevolently at Irene through a column of smoke.

'Please, Pa,' Irene whispered. 'It's urgent.'

For a moment she thought that Pa was going to send her away with a flea in her ear, but then he seemed to think better of it and he scooped the pile of coins from the table in front of him into his hat. 'Family problems, Wally. I'll have to go now, but I'll be back.'

Wally took the cigar from his mouth and his eyes were like chips of granite. 'It ain't gentlemanly to leave with half the bank, Billy. See that you do return.'

'You know me,' Billy replied cheerily. 'I never could keep away from a good game.' He seized Irene by the collar and dragged her out of the gaming room and down the stairs.

Blackie was slumped in a chair by the door with a pint of ale in his hand. He looked up with an edentulous grin. 'So your boy's come home then, Billy?'

'Looks that way, don't it?' Billy opened the door and thrust Irene out into the dark court. 'What the hell d'you think you're doing?' Grabbing her by the arm, he led her along the alley and out into Friday Street.

'Let go of me, Pa. You're hurting me.'

Billy pushed her away from him so that she staggered against the window of a taxidermist's shop where stuffed animals stared at her glassy-eyed. She righted herself and moved away from the grisly sight. Who on earth would want to buy a stuffed stoat or a red fox with sharp pointed teeth? But then maybe someone like Wally Sykes might want a ferocious, but deceased, animal to adorn his home.

'Don't stand there daydreaming,' Billy said angrily. 'We're going home and I want an explanation for this wild behaviour. What will your poor mother say when I tell her I found you dressed in your brother's old clothes? D'you want to break her heart?'

Irene faced him with her temper rising to match his. 'No, Pa. It's you who've done that over and over again.'

Billy strode off with a snort and she had to run to keep up with him. He stopped at the shop door and fumbled in his pocket. 'Damnation, where is that bloody key?'

'No matter. I've got mine.' Irene stepped forward and unlocked the door. She stood aside as he stormed past her. She saw that he was about to go upstairs, and she called out to him. 'No, Pa. Please wait. I can explain.' It would be a disaster if he discovered Arthur sleeping in his bed before she had had a chance to tell him everything.

With one foot on the bottom step, Billy hesitated, turning to glare at her. 'This had better be good, and you can start by telling me what you're doing running round London in the middle of the night pretending to be that person we don't mention in this house.'

Irene was quick to hear the note of pain in his voice. 'Oh, Pa, when are you going to forgive Jim for running away to sea? It weren't all his fault.'

'I don't want to talk about him. It's you who've done wrong and I want an explanation.'

Slowly, picking her words with care, Irene explained why she had braved the Sykes brothers' gaming house. She told him about Kent and his hold over Arthur and the reason why she had insisted that he did not return to his own home that night. Billy listened with his head on one side, but Irene could tell that he was still furious. When she came to a stammering halt, he thumped his hand on the banister rail. 'That boy should have gone home and faced up to his punishment. Let's see what Clara has to say about all this.' He made as if to ascend the stairs, but Irene caught him by the coat tails.

'She's not here, Pa.'

'What?' Billy's thick eyebrows met over the bridge of his nose and his lips were white with anger. 'Where is she? Where's my Clara?'

'Don't you remember? I told you this morning that Emmie's in the family way and

Ma has gone to stay with her in Love Lane. Just for a while, you understand.'

'I'd forgotten,' Billy said slowly. 'That's what the drink does for a fellow. But I want her back, d'you hear me, Renie?'

'Ma isn't at all well. Her rheumatics are getting worse and she needs good food and a warm house, or she'll end up crippled. Can't you see that it's best for her?'

'Best for her? What about me? I need my wife to be here when I come home. She's my heart and soul, and I can't manage without her.'

'You're a selfish, selfish man, Pa,' Irene cried angrily. 'You never think of no one but yourself. Well, I'll tell you this for nothing. I'm glad that Ma ain't here to see the mess we're in, especially as you won't be the one to get us out of it.'

'I ain't staying to listen to this. I won't be spoken to like that by my own flesh and blood. You've put on your brother's clothes and now you're acting like him. You're a serpent's tooth, Irene, an ungrateful child.'

'That's not fair,' Irene protested, close to tears. 'At least give me back the money you took from the till.'

'I need to keep my stake intact, but I'll bring back a hundred times that amount,' Billy said, brushing past her to open the street door.

'It's a pity you have so little faith in me. I'm going back to where I'm known and respected.'

'Respected?' Irene shouted to his disappearing back. 'The Sykes brothers are bad men and the police will catch them, and you too if you ain't careful. Don't say I didn't warn you, Pa. And don't think I'll come visiting when they lock you up in Newgate.'

She ran to lock the door behind him and found that her legs were trembling so much that she could hardly stand. Tears burned her eyes but she brushed them away with an impatient hand. Really, men were more trouble than they were worth. First Arthur got himself into bother and now it was Pa who was giving her serious cause for concern. Kent, it seemed, was determined to smash the Sykes gang with or without Arthur's help, and if Pa was not careful he would go to jail with them. Vic and Wally were evil men. It was well known that they demanded protection money from small businesses in their territory, and that they were ruthless with anyone who defied or upset them in any way. Many a shopkeeper or owner of a sweatshop had been put out of business by the Sykes brothers, and some had paid with their lives for attempting to stand up against them. Pa might think life was all a game of chance, but Irene knew differently. She was frightened for him, and for Arthur who had clumsily stumbled into the dirty business of gang law.

She made her way slowly upstairs. Despite the sound of raised voices, Arthur was still sleeping peacefully. As if he had not a care in the world, Irene thought wryly. The first faint cawing sounds coming from the plane tree alerted her to the fact that it was almost daybreak, and soon the city would be coming back to life. There was no point in going to bed, and anyway she was too agitated to sleep. She changed into her own clothes and set about cleaning out the grate ready to light the fire, but then she remembered that there was neither coal nor kindling. Pa had not replaced the money that he had taken from the till and he had stormed off with his winnings in his pocket. She had not even the price of a loaf of bread for their breakfast. Scrambling to her feet, she went over to the bed and shook Arthur by the shoulders. 'Wake up, Artie.'

He opened his eyes. 'Renie?' He sat up, scratching his head as he gazed around the room with a puzzled expression on his face. 'What am I doing here?'

'Never mind that now. Have you got any money on you?'

He blinked owlishly and fumbled in his pocket, producing a handful of small change.

'That's all I've got. I lost nearly everything at the tables.'

She selected a few coins, just enough to buy some fuel and a loaf of bread. 'Artie, you've got to stop gambling or you'll end up like Pa.'

'I want to, but now I've got Kent breathing down my neck. If I don't give him information about the Sykes gang, he'll send me up before the beak and that would be the end of my career as a silversmith. My dad would never forgive me.'

'He might surprise you, Artie.'

'You don't know him as I do. As far as I can see the only thing I can do is to leave London as soon as possible.'

'But where would you go?'

'My Aunt Maude lives in Havering. It's a village in Essex, not too far from Romford. I was taken to see her when I was a boy, although she and Father don't really get on. I suppose I could go there until all this blows over.'

'I don't think that would solve anything, Artie. Go and see your dad. Tell him the truth and say you're sorry. I know he's a grumpy old codger, but you're his only son. He won't want to see you get into trouble with the police.'

'I dunno about that.'

'At least he won't break your legs or have

you beaten up so that your own mother wouldn't recognise you.'

Arthur paled visibly, and he shivered. 'I know what the Sykes brothers do to squealers, and it ain't pretty. That's why I must get right away from here.'

She took his hand and held it. 'Artie, think for a moment. If you run away Kent can't protect you, and if Vic or Wally gets to know why you've gone, they'll take it out on the next best person. How would you feel if they ruined your dad, or worse?'

'I wish to God that I'd never set eyes on the pair of them. If I hadn't gone with Billy that first time . . .'

'I know. My pa has a lot to answer for, but Kent has his eye on him too. If Vic and Wally go down they'll take Pa with them. We haven't any choice now but to cooperate with the cops. Much as I hate the man, I don't see any way out other than to help Kent put a stop to the Sykes gang for good.'

'You're certain you want to do this, Renie? You're just a girl. You don't have to get involved.'

She twisted her lips into a smile. 'I'll show you what a girl can do. I can be brave when my family is threatened, whether it's by the Sykes brothers or a ruthless cop.'

'You make me ashamed of myself,' Arthur

said, staring down at their entwined fingers. 'I'll stay, and what's more I'll go home right away and confess everything.'

'That's the spirit, but if I was you I'd give your dad a chance to get up and have his breakfast first. You stay here while I go to the bakery. You'll do better on a full stomach and so will I.'

'I'll fetch the water from the pump then.' Arthur released her hand and swung his legs over the side of the bed. 'I may be a coward but I ain't the type of fellow who lets a woman wait on him hand and foot.'

'Then it's settled,' Irene said with a nod of approval. 'We'll face up to this together. I'll agree to help Kent, if you'll spy on the Sykes brothers. We'll put an end to their gang, and keep my pa out of jail at the same time.'

'You're a brave girl, Renie. I always knew you had spirit, but until this moment I never realised just how much.'

'Stuff and nonsense. You're talking soft because you're hungry.' Despite her light-hearted words, Irene couldn't help feeling flattered. She went to the baker's shop with a warm feeling inside and a smile on her face. At least Ma was out of the way while all this was going on; she would be safe with Emmie in Love Lane.

* * *

An hour later, having breakfasted on fresh bread washed down by several cups of tea, Arthur went off to brave his father and Irene opened up the shop as usual, but her mind was occupied with thoughts far removed from selling pickled onions and chilli sauce. Somehow she would have to contact the inspector, but she did not want to be seen going into the police station in broad daylight. Vic and Wally had their spies everywhere – narks who would inform on their own mothers if they were paid enough. She was still wondering what to do when Yapp's cart pulled up outside and Danny leapt off the back and came shambling into the shop with a grin splitting his monkey face in two. 'Morning, miss. I come for your next week's order.'

'Now there's a thing, Danny,' Irene said more cheerfully than she was feeling. 'I'll need to restock, but I'm afraid I'll have to ask Mr Yapp for a bit of credit.'

Danny's face fell and he glanced nervously out of the window at Yapp, who was sitting on the driver's seat staring into space, with his pipe clenched between his teeth. 'He weren't best pleased when you couldn't pay up the last time, miss.'

'I know, but I did settle that account in full. It's just that business has been a bit slow, but it's only temporary.'

'I daresn't go out and tell him that you won't pay cash on delivery.'

'Can't pay, Danny. There's a big difference.' Irene hurried out from behind the counter. 'I'll go and tell him if you like.'

'Ta, miss. I really would appreciate it.'

Irene went out into the street with Danny following close on her heels. 'Mr Yapp, a word, please.'

He glared down at her, squinting through a haze of tobacco smoke. 'Eh? What's up?'

'I'll come straight to the point, Mr Yapp. I need to order more stock, but I'm afraid I'll have to ask for a week's credit.'

'You know I don't give credit and you was late settling up the last time.'

'But I did pay what I owed. All I'm asking is for you to be patient.'

'Well, I ain't a patient man, Miss Angel. You'll pay up the full amount on delivery or we don't do business.'

'My mother has dealt with you for twenty years and never let you down once.'

'That's as maybe, but I ain't joking. I'll give you a day to think about it, but you know the rules.' Yapp took the pipe from his mouth and spat into the gutter. 'Get on the cart, boy.' He flicked the reins and rammed his pipe back into his mouth. The old horse surged forward and Irene was left standing on the pavement, staring after them in dismay. She had thought that matters could get no worse, but now she realised that she had been wrong. If Yapp carried out his threat they would be ruined. Without stock she could not trade; if she could not trade then she would not be able to pay the rent. Without the rent, they would be homeless. Things had never looked so bleak.

Chapter Five

Trade was slow. By late morning Irene had taken less than a shilling and the rent was due the next day. She kept running to the door and glancing up and down the street in the hope of seeing her father sauntering home with enough of his winnings left to get them out of trouble. If he had done well he would be in excellent spirits and would have completely forgotten that they had parted on bad terms. Even if he did recall their heated exchange of words he would by now have seen the humour in the situation. One of Pa's saving graces was that he never bore a grudge; his temper might be explosive, but his fiery outbursts were soon forgotten.

There was little that she could do except wait, and she busied herself by sweeping the floor and polishing the counter until she could see her face in it, but all the while she found her thoughts straying to Arthur. She couldn't help wondering how his interview with his irascible parent had gone. She hoped she had done the right thing by insisting that he confess everything to his father, although lurking doubts unsettled her and made her even more anxious. When she had finished cleaning the shop she went outside to brush the pavement. The clock on the tower of St Michael's church struck twelve, and still there was no sign of either her father or Arthur. She leaned on the broom handle, frowning. She must do something, but what? Her stomach rumbled, but although she was hungry the thought of eating dry bread again made her feel nauseous. The crowds of people thronging the street did not seem unduly interested in stopping to purchase pickles or sauce, and feeling increasingly despondent Irene picked up the broom. She was about to enter the shop when footsteps behind her made her turn her head, but her hopes of serving an eager customer were dashed when she recognised the tall, slim figure dressed all in black.

Inspector Kent doffed his hat. 'Good day to you, Miss Angel.'

'What do you want?' Irene demanded ungraciously.

'May I step inside for a moment? Or would you rather we conducted our business out here on the street?'

Her good intentions dissipated like morning mist over the river. It went against the grain to cooperate with the law, and she glared at him mutinously. 'I don't have anything to say to you, mister.'

'About our conversation yesterday. Have you come to a decision?' Tucking his bowler hat under his arm, he followed her into the shop.

'You don't give up, do you?'

'No,' he conceded. 'I don't, but the choice is yours. I am not trying to coerce you into anything against your will.'

'Fine words, but they mean nothing. If I don't help you, it will be all the worse for my pa and Arthur.'

'They got themselves into this, but I'm giving you the chance to put an end to the gang who have caused so much pain and misery to so many innocent citizens.'

'And if I don't choose to help you? What then?'

'They will have to take their chances. I'm not blackmailing you, Miss Angel. I'm simply offering you the opportunity to help your father and your young man out of trouble.'

'He's not my young man.' She had not meant to blurt out the words with such passion, but Kent seemed to have the uncanny ability to draw the truth out of her. She tossed her head. 'Artie and me have known each other since we was nippers.'

'Then I'm sure you won't want to see any harm come to him or to your father.'

There was no arguing with the logic of this, and Irene knew that she was beaten. 'All right, I'll do what you want, Inspector, but only if you give me your word that you won't arrest Artie.'

'You have my word.' He put his hand in his pocket and took out a handful of coins. He selected a florin and a silver sixpence and laid them on the counter.

'What's this? Are you trying to bribe me?'

'Certainly not. I'd like to purchase a jar of piccalilli and a bottle of mushroom ketchup, if it's not too much trouble.'

She was not certain, but she thought that she had seen a flicker of amusement in his eyes and she suspected that he was teasing her. 'Is your wife a good cook, Inspector?' she said lightly as she turned away to select the items from the shelf.

'I'm unmarried.'

'Now why doesn't that surprise me?' Irene said, forcing her lips into a polite smile. 'No offence meant, but you don't strike me as the marrying kind.'

'I expect you're right.'

She picked up the sixpence but pushed the florin towards him with the tip of her finger. 'That's too much.'

'Call it an advance on expenses.' He turned to leave the shop, but she called him back.

'Inspector, you've forgotten your pickle and sauce, and you still haven't told me what you want me to do.'

He paused in the doorway. 'I'm on my way to court. I'll collect my purchases tomorrow and we'll arrange a meeting place then. You can tell Mr Greenwood from me that I expect him to pass on anything that he hears concerning the activities of the Sykes brothers, however trivial it may seem.' Setting his hat at a precise angle on his head he stepped outside onto the pavement, closing the door behind him.

Irene stared at the money on the counter. She had to decide whether to spend it on food and rent or to buy new stock. It was a difficult choice but she would not think about it now. If Pa repaid the money he had borrowed her problem would be solved. She tucked the florin into the top of her stays. She was not going to make the mistake of putting it in the till and risk losing it to Pa if his luck failed him yet again. There was no sign of any customers and she went upstairs to rekindle the fire and make a pot of tea and some toast.

She had just finished eating her frugal midday meal when the shop bell jangled and she ran to the top of the stairs. 'Pa,' she cried, running down to greet him. 'You've come home.'

Billy took off his hat and tossed it onto its peg with expertise of long practice. He shrugged off his coat and smiled. 'And where would I go, my poppet, except home?'

'You aren't still angry with me about last night?'

'Irene, my love, I have only myself to blame. I know that and I am sorry for shouting at you, and blaming you for your mother's sudden decision to abandon me. I can see now, in the rational light of day, that a little holiday with Emily will do her the power of good. I was being selfish, and I am a callous brute – a miserable wretch – for making my little angel unhappy.'

Irene eyed him suspiciously. 'What have you done, Pa? There's something you're not telling me.'

'Is there tea in the pot? My throat is so parched I can hardly speak.'

'I'll make a fresh brew as soon as you tell me why you are looking so pleased with yourself.'

He hung his coat on the peg next to his hat. 'Well, to be honest, my pet, I've had quite a good night . . .'

'And you can pay back the money you took from the till?'

'That and more, my darling. I'm off to make our fortune at Doncaster. I have a certainty running in the St Leger tomorrow and I'll be leaving as soon as I've changed my shirt and had a mouthful of tea.'

Irene stared at him aghast. 'But Pa, it will cost a small fortune to take the train to Yorkshire, and then you will have to find somewhere to stay for the night, and food . . .'

Billy patted his breast pocket with a triumphant grin. 'And I have the means here, my dove. By the time the race is over we will be rich. Your mother will never have to work again and we can get away from the stench of pickled onions and malt vinegar and rent a proper house where we can live like decent people.'

'But Pa, we need money to pay Yapp or he won't let me have any more stock.'

'And we won't need any more bottles of sauce and jars of pickle. I've just told you, darling. I've been given a hot tip for the St Leger; a French horse called Gladiateur; by tomorrow evening our money worries will be over. Now come upstairs and make me a nice cup of tea, and we'll finish off that pie you bought for supper last night.'

'We ate it, Pa. Arthur and me finished it off last night while we were waiting for you.'

'No matter, my pet. Tea and toast will do.

I'll take dinner on the train.' He took the stairs two at a time with Irene hurrying after him.

'But, Pa, I must speak to you about Inspector Kent.'

'Never mind him, Renie. As soon as I get my hands on my winnings, I promise you that my gambling days are over and done with. From tomorrow onwards I'm going to be a model husband and father. The Sykes brothers won't see my face at their tables and Inspector Kent will not bother us ever again. Come on, my angel, don't dawdle. I've got a train to catch.'

Irene held her tongue with difficulty as she followed him into the living room. There was no use talking to Pa when he was in this mood. She made tea and toast while he changed into a clean shirt.

'There's no butter or dripping,' she said pointedly. 'Couldn't you spare a few pennies, Pa? Just enough to keep me going until you return?'

'You know I would if I could, but it's just not possible. Why don't you go to your sister's house for supper? I'm sure they live like lords in Love Lane.'

'Pa, just listen to yourself. Have you any idea of the mess we're in?'

'You must have a little faith in your old pa, my little bird. Everything will be all right, I promise you.'

Irene was not going to give in so easily, but no matter how much she tried to reason with him, he would not listen. She cajoled, pleaded and finally lost her temper with her father, but he was adamant that his tip was solid gold and that Gladiateur could not fail to win the fabled St Leger. If the shop bell had not diverted her attention at that particular moment, Irene thought afterwards that she might have thrown something at Pa's head, preferably something heavy which would render him unconscious and unable to carry out his wild plan. Fuming inwardly, she left him to finish his tea while she went downstairs to serve the waiting customer.

'Hello, Irene? Having a nap, was you?' Sal Hawker rose from the chair and plumped her basket down on the counter. 'It's all right for some. You can do as you please, but I've got the old bitch up the road on me tail and if I don't get back with the goods she'll tan me hide.'

Irene assumed her best businesslike face. 'What can I do for you, Sal?'

'Cook wants a jar of pickled cucumbers and a bottle of relish. Oh, and some pickled beetroot too. I almost forgot.'

Irene selected the jars and bottle from the shelves. 'Anything else?'

'Oh my Lord, you look down in the dumps. What's up with you?'

'Nothing, Sal. I'm just a bit tired, that's all,' Irene said, hoping that Pa would not choose this particular moment to come into the shop. 'That will be one and ninepence three farthings, please.'

'Put it on the old cow's slate.'

Irene bit her lip. The silk merchant's wife was a good customer but a slow payer. Ma had always allowed her to run up an account and then patiently waited until the outstanding amount was paid. There was no time now for such politeness. She shook her head. 'I'm afraid it's cash on the nail or nothing.'

Sal's smile faded. 'But what shall I tell Cook?'

'I'm sorry.'

'The missis will go elsewhere.'

'I'd oblige you if I could, but it's impossible,' Irene said, replacing the jars on the shelf.

'I'll get it in the neck when I gets back to the house,' Sal said, pouting. 'Cook will blame me. She thinks with her rolling pin, that one. She'll clout me round the head as soon as look at me.'

Irene thrust the bottle of sauce into her hands. 'Here, take this to the old crow with my compliments. Since we're likely to be out of business soon, I don't suppose it will make much difference.'

'I bet it's all to do with them Sykes brothers,' Sal murmured, backing towards the door.

'It's well known that your old man is in with the gang.'

'You should watch what you say, girl.'

The sound of Billy's voice made Sal spin round to stare at him as he strolled down the stairs twirling his silver-headed cane. She eyed him nervously. 'I only speak the truth, mister. It's all round the street that you're in with the Sykes gang and the police are on your tail. I'd cut and run if I was you.'

Billy leapt the last three steps and making a growling noise deep in his throat he brandished his cane at Sal, who fled from the shop with a screech of fright. He laughed and hooked his top hat from the peg, tossing it in the air and catching it expertly on his head. In the past this trick had always made Irene laugh, but this time she was not at all amused. 'Pa, how could you? Now it will be all round town that you terrified poor Sal.'

'And maybe she will think twice before allowing her tongue to run away with her,' Billy replied calmly. 'I'll be off now. Don't worry about me, my dove. I'll be home before you know it and all our money worries will be a thing of the past.' He held out his arms. 'Come here and give your old pa a kiss for good luck.'

Irene hesitated but as usual his twinkling eyes and warm smile melted her heart and she crossed the floor to give him a hug. 'Oh, Pa. What am I going to do with you?'

He dropped a kiss on the top of her head and then extricated himself gently from her grasp. 'Trust me, Renie. I know I've let you and your mother down in the past, but this time it will be different.' He pressed a shilling into her hand. 'Spend it on food and coal, and don't give it to that bloodsucker Yapp. Tell him I'll settle up in full on my return from Doncaster.' Without giving her a chance to reply, Billy breezed out of the shop as if he had not a care in the world. Irene went to the door and watched with a sinking heart as he hailed a hansom cab. She had witnessed this scene so many times before that if she closed her eyes she could see the whole thing replayed to her like a bad dream. Tomorrow evening, or perhaps the following day, Pa would slink home like a whipped cur with his tail between his legs. He would have lost everything, possibly even his overcoat and the battered top hat which he wore with such aplomb. He would profess to be an older and wiser man and promise not to touch a bet again no matter how much he was tempted. By the same evening, he would have shaved, changed into a clean shirt and be off to the club in Blue Boar Court or some other gaming hell, where he would attempt to recoup his losses. In the past,

Ma would have cried a little, but she would have been so happy to have him home again that she forgave him unconditionally.

Irene had seen her mother endure all this with a brave smile and not a word of reproach, and she had been powerless to do anything to prevent Pa from repeating his actions over and over again. She was angry and she was upset, but this latest example of his feckless behaviour had served to convince her that Inspector Kent had been right. The only way to prevent Pa from tumbling even further into the abyss of a gambling addiction was to shock him out of his complacency. If the Sykes brothers were caught, convicted and sent to prison, or transported for life, it might just bring Pa to his senses.

She kept the shop open until seven o'clock, serving a few customers but not enough to make up the money that she needed to keep Obadiah Yapp sweet. The light was fading fast and she decided to lock up. There was still no news from Arthur, but she took this as a good sign. Perhaps his father had allowed him back to his bench in the workshop and Arthur was making up for lost time. She hoped so anyway. Artie might be irresponsible, but she loved him like a brother. She put on her shawl, let herself out of the shop and went up the street to fetch coal, candles and a box of vestas. She stopped on the way home to buy two steaming baked potatoes from the vendor on the corner of Cheapside, and she could not resist the tempting aroma of roasting chestnuts on a glowing brazier. She bought a poke and added it to the purchases in her wicker basket. Outside the door to the shop she was fumbling in her pocket for the key when she heard Arthur calling her name. She turned her head to see him limping towards her, and in the pale light of the street lamp she could see that his face was bruised and bloody.

'Artie! What happened to you?'

'The old man,' he murmured through a split lip. 'I told him the truth and he took it bad.'

She managed to find the key and with trembling fingers she unlocked the door. She hid her distress beneath a brusque tone of voice. 'Make yourself useful, Artie. Bring the coal in.' When he was safely inside she locked the door and slipped the bolt across. She had left a candle burning on the counter and she picked it up, holding it close enough to his face to inspect his injuries. 'Your dad did this to you?'

'It looks worse than it is. I'm afraid I lost my temper, Renie. I hit him back. For the first time in my life I lashed out at the old devil, and d'you know what? I enjoyed it. I got my own back for all the years he's beaten me and bullied me. I knocked him clean off his feet and bloodied his nose.'

'Oh, Artie! You should have walked away.'

'I know, but he caught me on the raw. He said things that I can't forgive and he's thrown me out of the house and my job. He said he wasn't going to have a gambler and a waster in the family. I'm never going back there, not in a million years.'

Irene picked up her basket and headed towards the stairs. 'Come on up. I'll clean your face and then we'll have supper.'

His footsteps echoed on the bare stair treads behind her. 'Can I stay here tonight? I'll look for something more permanent tomorrow.'

The fire in the living room was almost out and the wind whistled through the cracked windowpanes. Irene put the candle on the table and set about emptying her shopping basket. 'Of course you can. Pa's gone off to Doncaster and won't be back until late tomorrow night, if then. We have to have a serious talk, Artie. I mean really serious. I've had Inspector Kent here again today, laying down the law.'

Arthur dumped the sack of coal in the grate with a thud. 'If he's been making threats to you I'll go and sort him out right now.'

'Yes, and get yourself arrested for disorderly conduct.' In spite of everything Irene couldn't suppress a chuckle. 'Take a look at yourself in the mirror. You look like you've done ten rounds with a bare-knuckle fighter.'

He went down on his knees in front of the fire and began riddling the ashes. 'I've made a mess of things, Renie. I've nowhere to go and not a penny to my name. My mother will never forgive me for what I did to the old man, and I've lost whatever chance I had of becoming a silversmith.'

Arms akimbo, Irene glared at his hunched back. 'You won't get any sympathy from me, Arthur Greenwood. You brought this all on yourself by getting involved with the Sykes gang in the first place. You've got to be a man now, and make things right again.' A muffled sound that sounded suspiciously like a sob made her pause. She modified her tone. 'Cheer up, cully. You'll feel better when you've got some vittles inside you. It's lucky I bought two taters. I must have known you'd turn up on my doorstep.' When he did not answer she moved over to the fireplace and gently edged him out of the way. 'Here, you're useless, you are. Let me see to the fire while you clean yourself up. There's water in the jug on the washstand and there might even be a scrap of soap if Pa hasn't used it all up.'

Arthur scrambled to his feet, wiping his eyes on his sleeve. 'Ta. I won't forget this.'

'Don't mention it, boy. We'll see this thing

through together, like we did when we was nippers and got ourselves into bother.' Irene picked up the bellows and pumped them vigorously until tongues of flame licked around the fresh coals in the grate. 'A nice hot cup of tea and something warm in your belly, and you'll feel like a new man.'

'You make me ashamed of myself,' Arthur murmured, sniffing.

Irene sat back on her haunches. 'So you should be, you great booby. Now blow your nose, sit down, and have something to eat while I put the kettle on. You can stay here tonight, and who knows what's going to happen tomorrow, for I certainly don't.'

Next morning, soon after Irene had opened the shop, Yapp's cart drew up outside, but instead of Danny it was Yapp himself who burst through the door. 'Well, what is it to be, Miss Angel?'

Irene took the order book from beneath the counter and handed it to him. 'Next week's order, Mr Yapp.'

'You do understand that it's strictly cash on delivery?'

'I'll be able to pay,' Irene said, crossing her fingers behind her back. It had been a difficult choice to make, but she had used the little money she had to pay the rent and to buy food, coal and candles. She could only hope and pray that she would take sufficient money over the counter to pay for new stock.

Yapp shook his head. 'Not good enough. I want cash in advance this time.'

'Cash on delivery. That's the way it's always been. You said so yourself.'

'Your ma is a good businesswoman. I'll waive the advance if she gives me the order in person.'

'I'm afraid that's not possible. Ma is staying with my sister and I'm looking after the shop.'

'And your dad is helping hisself from the till, no doubt,' Yapp sneered. 'A nice state of affairs, I must say, and not one that gives me much confidence in getting me money on time.'

'You've no right to speak to me like that,' Irene cried angrily. 'We've been good customers to you all these years.'

Yapp sidled round the counter and before Irene had a chance to escape he seized her round the waist. 'Pay me in kind then, Miss Irene. I'm a reasonable sort of cove.'

His breath stank of salt fish and stale beer. Irene pushed him away, feeling her gorge rise. 'Get off me, you stinking old sod.'

He staggered against the counter, his face turning the same shade of purple as the jar of pickled beetroot on the shelf behind his head. 'You'll suffer for that, my girl.'

'Get out of my way.' She attempted to get past him but he caught her by the hair and pulled her closer.

'Not until I've had a kiss and a quick fumble. We'll call it a bit on account.'

'Leave her alone.'

A voice rang out from the shop doorway, causing Yapp to freeze. He turned his head slowly. 'Who says?'

Constable Burton strode into the shop. 'I say so. Now let her go.'

Irene jerked free from Yapp's clutching fingers and she moved swiftly out of his reach. 'Blimey,' she murmured. 'This is the first time I've ever been pleased to see a copper.'

'Well I ain't,' Yapp muttered beneath his breath.

Constable Burton drew himself up to his full height. 'That's enough of that. Get out or I'll arrest you for assault.'

'I'm a reputable trader, guvner,' Yapp whimpered, cringing visibly. 'This young person has been trying to cheat me.'

'Do you want to press charges, Miss Angel?'

Irene would have liked to see Yapp flogged with his own horsewhip, but she couldn't afford to offend him. She shook her head. 'No, Constable.'

'You're a lucky man. I suggest you leave before the young lady changes her mind.'

'Consider yourself struck off me list of customers, miss,' Yapp snarled, backing towards the open door.

'You can't mean that. You'll put me out of business.'

'Consider it done. I don't want nothing more to do with the likes of you and your father.'

'Good riddance to bad rubbish then,' Irene cried angrily. 'You're just a dirty old man.'

Swearing horribly, Yapp stamped out of the shop, slamming the door behind him.

'Were you in debt to him?' Constable Burton asked anxiously. 'I mean, I might be able to help you out if you're desperate – just a temporary loan, of course.'

Irene flashed him a grateful smile. 'No, ta. It's kind of you, but I can manage.'

Burton's face flushed scarlet above the collar of his tunic. 'Miss Angel, I don't know how to put this, but your father was seen boarding a train for Yorkshire last night. It doesn't take a genius to work out that he was on his way to Doncaster for the races, and it seems that he's left you short of money.'

So they were spying on her father as well as the Sykes brothers. Irene hid her chagrin by searching under the counter for the pickles and sauce that the inspector had paid for so generously. 'There's no need to worry on that score, Constable,' she said, putting them on the counter. 'Perhaps you'd be kind enough to give these to your boss to save him the trouble of collecting them himself?'

'If I spoke out of turn, I'm sorry,' Burton said hastily. 'The reason I came was to arrange a time and place for you to meet the inspector. I believe you were expecting to hear from him.'

Irene nodded her head. 'Yes, I was.'

'I won't let you do it, Renie.'

She looked up and saw Arthur standing at the top of the stairs. 'It's all right, Artie. I know what I'm doing.'

'So you were here all the time, hiding upstairs while Miss Angel dealt with that ruffian,' Burton said, eyeing Arthur with unconcealed contempt.

'I know what you must think of me.'

'Do you now?'

'You think I am a coward for not coming to Irene's aid.'

'No, Artie,' Irene said hastily. 'I'm sure that the constable thinks nothing of the sort. You did well to keep out of Yapp's way. I didn't want you involved.'

'No, Renie, he's right. I should have been here to protect you instead of licking my wounds upstairs.'

Burton eyed him curiously. 'Did the Sykes gang inflict those injuries on you?'

'No,' Arthur said, staring down at his once shiny but now scuffed and dirty patent-leather shoes. 'It was closer to home than that.'

Irene sensed her old friend's discomfort and she hurried round the counter to face Constable Burton. 'Just tell us what the inspector wants us to do, Constable, and we'll cooperate in any way we can.'

'Very well then. From now on he wants you both to go about your daily lives as usual. Mr Greenwood will visit the gaming house in Blue Boar Court and he must do nothing to raise their suspicions. The inspector thinks that the Sykes brothers are planning to start a gang war and he needs to know where and when they intend to strike, and which of the other street gangs are involved. You will give any relevant information to Miss Angel, sir, and she will then pass it on to the inspector.'

'I'll do what I can,' Arthur murmured sulkily.

Constable Burton pursed his lips in silent disapproval. 'I should hope so.'

'You can trust Artie,' Irene said firmly. 'Just tell me what I have to do.'

'The inspector will meet you in St Paul's churchyard at nine o'clock on Tuesday evening. He says you must never underestimate Vic and Wally Sykes. They are dangerous men and if they so much as suspect that they're being spied on they won't show any mercy.' Burton laid his hand tentatively on Irene's sleeve. 'You do understand that, don't you, Miss Angel?'

She could see genuine concern in his warm brown eyes, and she managed a tight little smile. 'I do, thank you, Constable.'

'I hope so, miss, I really do hope so.'

With a smart bow from the waist, Constable Burton strode out of the shop, leaving Irene and Arthur staring after him in stunned silence.

Chapter Six

'He forgot the pickles!' Irene said dazedly. Slowly she placed them back on the shelf. 'I knew that blooming inspector didn't really want them.'

'That man has ruined my life,' Arthur groaned. 'I can't do what he wants – it's too dangerous.'

'The only person who's ruined your life is you, Artie,' Irene said sadly. 'No one forced you to gamble or to get involved with the Sykes brothers. You saw what it had done to my pa and yet it didn't stop you. I'm afraid that you've got to take the consequences and so have I.'

'Vic and Wally will kill me if they find out I'm a copper's nark.'

'Then they mustn't find out. We're in this together, like it or not.'

'It's not fair that you should have to put yourself in danger.'

'There's nothing fair in life as far as I can see, Artie. If all things were equal, I'd be riding round in a carriage like me sister, wearing a silk gown and waiting for some bloke to marry me and keep me like a queen. But all I've got is a shop full of pickles and a father who gambles every last penny, not to mention a friend who drives me mad.'

This last remark made Arthur smile, but he winced with pain as his cut lip started to bleed. 'All right, Renie. I know I'm behaving badly, but I'm just scared.'

She moved swiftly to his side and gave him a hug. 'So am I, but we'll get through this together. You can stay here for as long as you like. I'm sure that Pa won't mind if you sleep under the counter until you find a room somewhere.'

'I can't sponge off you and your family. It wouldn't be right. I've just got to find work.'

She eyed him thoughtfully. This was a side of Arthur she had not previously seen. His normally ebullient nature seemed to have undergone a sudden change, leaving him serious and penitent. She patted his hand. 'Give your dad time to calm down, and maybe he'll take you back. After all, you've almost finished your apprenticeship; he must see that it would be a crying shame to lose a good silversmith because of a family row.'

'You don't know the old man.'

'Not very well, I must admit, but you won't

know until you try. If he's unhelpful then you'll have to look for work elsewhere.'

'I'm not trained for anything else, Renie.'

She angled her head as an idea struck her. 'Go and see Vic or Wally. Tell them that you had a row with your dad and he threw you out. Ask them for work, anything at all, even if it's running errands or washing glasses. If they take you on then you won't have to play the tables; you'll get information for Kent without even trying.'

A glimmer of hope lit Arthur's eyes, but then it faded into doubt. 'They're not stupid. They'll see through me.'

She snatched a jar of pickled cucumbers from the shelf. 'And this glass jar is going to come into contact with your head, Arthur Greenwood, if you don't stop feeling sorry for yourself and start acting like a man.' She had no real intention of causing him bodily harm but her action seemed to have the desired effect.

'All right, I'll do it. I'll go and see Wally right away.'

'Good for you, Artie.'

He took his jacket from the peg and put it on, wincing with every painful movement. 'Wish me luck,' he said with a glimmer of his old smile.

'Be careful. Don't take any unnecessary

chances.' She watched him leave the shop with mixed feelings. It was a relief that he was doing something positive, but he would be playing a dangerous game with battle-hardened adversaries. The Sykes brothers had ruled their empire unchallenged for as long as she could remember. She cast a look of loathing at the neatly stacked shelves. 'I hate you,' she said with feeling. 'I wouldn't care if I never saw another blooming pickled onion or cucumber again in me whole life.'

Trade picked up later that morning and continued to be brisk, giving her little time to worry about Arthur or to wonder how Pa's horse would do in the St Leger. She could only hope that his luck would be in and that he would bring home enough of his winnings to enable her to set matters right with Yapp. She did not expect Pa to put in an appearance until late that evening, but every time the shop door opened she glanced up hoping that it was Arthur returning with good news.

At closing time, having taken a few pennies from the till in order to buy supper, she put the rest of the takings into a leather pouch which she took upstairs and placed in the chest on top of Jim's old clothes. She fingered the coarse material of his jacket as she attempted to visualise his face, but she had only a misty memory of the elder brother whom she had loved and looked up to all those years ago. Jim would be a man now, and she might not even recognise him if he were ever to come home. After ten years with no word from him this seemed unlikely, but she knew that Ma still cried herself to sleep when she had been thinking of her long lost son.

Irene closed the chest and busied herself lighting the fire. She filled the kettle with water and hooked it over the flames to boil so that she could make a pot of tea. She was thirsty and her stomach rumbled suddenly, reminding her that she was extremely hungry. She decided to treat herself to a hot meat pie and some pease pudding from the shop further along Wood Street, and then she would sit and wait for Arthur and her father. She sighed. It felt as though she had spent her entire life doing just that – waiting passively for Pa, Jim and now Arthur to come home. Ma had been content to live this way, but Irene had always resented the restraints put on women by their men. Even if she was a wealthy heiress, a female was tied to her father until the time she married, and then she was similarly bound to her husband.

The water in the kettle began to bubble and she scrambled to her feet. She picked up a pot holder and poured boiling water onto the tea leaves in the pot, setting it down on the trivet to brew. If only she could make her own way in the world and win her independence; it was a wonderful thought, but as far from her reach as the stars twinkling in the blackness of the night sky.

She poured the tea, but when she went to add the milk she discovered that it was sour. She shrugged her shoulders and picked up her shawl. At least she had enough money to buy food for her supper and there was sufficient coal to take the bitter chill off the room. She had a roof over her head, which many less fortunate did not, but she could not help wanting more. One day she would have it all: a house of her own and money in the bank. She would eat chocolate every day of the week if she felt so inclined, and she wouldn't have to marry an old man like Josiah Tippet in order to make her wishes come true. She would wait until she found a man she could love and respect before tying the knot. She smiled, shaking her head at her own folly. Dreams were just that, and reality was an empty belly and the need to go out and buy food before she collapsed with hunger.

It did not take long to walk the short distance to the dairy and the pie shop, and with the first rush of the evening being over she was served quickly and returned home with the food still piping hot. She sat down to eat her meal alone, but with little enjoyment. She couldn't stop worrying about Pa and Artie. She did not really expect her father to return from Doncaster until late that night or even early tomorrow morning, but Artie was another matter. When midnight approached she was tempted to go out looking for him. Her imagination was running riot. Perhaps Vic or Wally had got wind of Kent's plans and had set their ruffians on Artie. Perhaps he was lying in the gutter somewhere, bruised and bleeding.

She had almost convinced herself of the worst when she heard someone banging on the shop door. Seizing the candlestick, she hurried downstairs to peer through the grime-smudged windowpanes. To her intense relief she saw Arthur standing on the pavement, blowing on his cupped hands and stamping his feet. She unlocked the door and let him in on a blast of ice-cold air. 'Artie, thank God you're safe.'

His teeth were chattering but he managed a weak grin. 'I did it, Renie. I convinced Vic that I needed work so badly that I'd do anything.'

'Come into the warm, and tell me all about it.' She locked the door and followed him upstairs to the living room. When he was settled by the fire with a cup of tea in his hands and a slice of pie on a plate at his side, she pulled up a stool and sat opposite him. 'Well, then. Tell me what happened.'

'I've spent the entire day cleaning out the privy in the back yard, crating bottles and scrubbing floors. Vic said I can stay on until the old man takes me back. He did offer to sort him out for me, but I said no thank you to that. I may hate the old sod but I wouldn't want any real harm to come to him, not on my account anyway.'

'Of course not. But did you hear anything that you could pass on to Kent?'

He took a bite of pie and shook his head. 'Nothing that would interest him. Maybe I'll do better tomorrow.'

When he had finished his supper, Irene gave him a blanket and a pillow from her parents' bed. 'You'd best try and make yourself comfortable under the counter in the shop, Artie.' She did not add that Pa might be easy-going in general and liberal minded, but he might jump to the wrong conclusion if he found Arthur sleeping in his bed.

Tucking the bedding under his arm, Arthur leaned over to kiss her on the cheek. 'Thanks for this, Renie. I won't forget what you've done for me.'

She gave him a playful shove towards the doorway. 'Get on with you, you soft thing. You'd do the same for me.'

As she curled up in a ball on her thin palliasse, Irene realised how much she missed her mother's calming presence. Ma would have dealt with Cuthbert Greenwood and Obadiah Yapp in her own quiet way. She had spent many years fending off creditors and she had dealt with punters who had lost small fortunes to Billy and then accused him of cheating. Irene had seen Ma face up to ugly brutes twice her size, sending them off shamefaced and apologising for the disturbance they had caused. She wished that she had her mother's tact and diplomacy, which, added to a sweetness of nature, could resolve the most difficult situation.

As she drifted off to sleep, Irene made up her mind to visit her ma and Emmie on Sunday. Perhaps Pa could be persuaded to put aside his dislike of his son-in-law and accompany her, which would please Ma no end. She would ask him tomorrow when he returned home from Doncaster.

But Billy did not come home the next day, or the next. By Sunday morning, Irene was convinced that something dreadful had happened to him. Arthur was still sleeping under the shop counter, leaving for work early in the morning and returning late at night. He continued to execute the most menial tasks for the Sykes brothers, but he had not learned anything that would be of the slightest use to Inspector Kent.

'I'll never get to know what they're doing while I'm cleaning out the privy or tapping barrels,' Arthur grumbled as he munched a slice of stale bread for his breakfast. 'The only way I'll get any information for Kent is to listen to the talk in the gaming room, but I can't play the tables without stake money.'

'And I can't give you any,' Irene said firmly. 'Surely they must pay you for your work?'

He hung his head. 'They gave me something yesterday, but it wasn't much.'

'Don't tell me you lost it at cards.'

Avoiding her gaze, he shook his head. 'I put it on a horse. It was supposed to be a sure thing.'

'Oh, Artie! What am I going to do with you?'

'I'm sorry, Renie. I really thought I was on a winning streak.'

She closed her eyes, biting back a sharp retort. She had heard that phrase time and time again, but then it had been her father making the same excuse to her mother. She bit back the harsh words that sprang to her lips. 'Go to work. Get out of my sight before I say something I'll regret.'

When she looked again he had gone and she heard his footsteps clattering down the stairs, followed by the grinding of the key in the lock and the thud of the door closing behind him. 'Men!' Irene shouted, shaking her fist at the noisy rooks in the plane tree. 'And you lot can shut up too.' She glared distastefully at the slice of stale bread that was her breakfast. There was no coal left to light the fire and there was no money in the old cocoa tin.

She turned to glare at her reflection in the mirror above the mantelshelf, and she scraped her hair back from her face, confining it in a knot at the nape of her neck. It was still early, but suddenly the walls seemed to be closing in on her and she simply had to escape from the confines of the tiny living room, even if it was just for the morning. She snatched her shawl from the back of a chair and made her way downstairs. Fractured beams of sunlight glittering with golden dust motes filtered through the small windowpanes, making a chequered pattern on the bare floorboards. Irene could not wait to get outside into the bright autumn morning. A walk to Love Lane was just what she needed. She would put her worries about Pa to the back of her mind, and try to forget that in two days' time she was expected to provide Inspector Kent with information that would help him smash the Sykes gang.

Although the sun shone from a clear azure

sky, there was a chill breeze blowing in from the east, bringing with it the stench from the tanneries, manufactories and the gasworks. Irene was used to the noxious smells, the dirt and the poverty that marched hand in hand with the affluence of the City banks and businesses, but today the differences seemed even more pronounced. Bare-footed urchins were scavenging in the gutters for anything that had the smallest value and could be sold or exchanged for food. Others hung round outside the church waiting for the congregation to leave, and doubtless hoping that the faithful might feel uplifted by the sermon and in a generous mood. Irene hurried past them, trying not to look at their grimy wizened faces and stick-like limbs. She had nothing to give them or to the old woman who slumped in the doorway of a closed shop with a tin cup on the pavement in front of her. Her tattered black skirt was damp with early morning dew and her lined face had a sickly pallor. She must have been there all night, Irene thought sadly as she hurried past. There was little or nothing that she could do for such people, but the sight of dire poverty and utter destitution made her realise that her situation might seem hard to bear, but she was much better off than some.

She reached Emmie's house just as the clock on a nearby church tower struck eleven.

She rapped on the gleaming brass doorknocker and waited. Moments later the door was opened by the young maidservant wearing a print dress and a starched white apron both of which were two sizes too large for her small frame. She pushed her mobcap back off her face and peered up at Irene with a disdainful expression that sat oddly on her young face. 'Tradesmen's entrance round the back.' She went to shut the door but Irene put her foot over the sill.

'I'm not selling anything, you silly girl. I've come to see my sister.'

'You've got the wrong house then.'

'Let me in at once. You know very well that I'm Mrs Tippet's sister.'

The girl did not look impressed. She tossed her head so that her mobcap slid down over her eyes again. She pushed it back with an irritable shrug. 'I don't remember you. I told you once and I'll not say it again. Tradesmen's entrance round the back.'

Irene put her shoulder to the door, sending the girl sprawling onto her back where she lay kicking her legs in the air and screeching. Irene stepped inside and was about to help the maid to her feet when the sound of heavy footsteps on the staircase made her pause and look up. Ephraim was bearing down on them with his sandy eyebrows drawn together so that they met over the bridge of his bulbous nose. He came to a halt and a look of recognition dawned on his pudgy face. 'Miss Angel, Irene, this is a pleasant surprise.'

Irene heaved the maid to her feet and gave her a shake. 'There now, you see, girl. Mr Ephraim recognises me.'

'Go about your work, Jessie,' Ephraim said, scowling.

'I didn't know who she was,' Jessie muttered, backing away from him. 'She don't look like the missis, and she don't dress like her neither.'

Ephraim raised his hand as if to strike her, and Jessie fled with a howl of fright. 'Emily should have sent that girl back to the workhouse,' he grumbled. 'She's not right in the head.'

'It wasn't really her fault,' Irene said hastily. 'She's only seen me once before and Emmie's much prettier than me. Since she married your dad she's always turned out like a duchess and I'm not exactly a fashion plate.'

'My stepmother pays altogether too much attention to fashion, and not enough to the smooth running of the household. You, on the other hand, appear to be a sensible, hard-working young woman with her mind on higher matters altogether.'

His censorious and pompous attitude irritated

Irene, but she forced her lips into a semblance of a smile. 'And how are you today, Ephraim?'

'I am well, thank you.' He cleared his throat, staring at her with his mouth working as if he were trying to speak but could not find the words.

'I've come to see Ma and Emmie,' Irene prompted. 'Are they at home?'

He nodded his head. 'Of course you want to see them. It's only natural.' He continued to stand in front of her, gazing at her with an unreadable expression in his dark eyes that reminded Irene of black boot buttons.

'Perhaps you could tell them I'm here?'

'Yes, of course. I'll do just that.' He crossed the narrow hallway in two strides and opened a door. 'If you would kindly wait in the morning parlour, I'll go and find them for you.'

She walked past him into a large, sunny room that faced onto the street. It had undergone a complete refurbishment since Irene had first seen it on Emmie's wedding day. She could only guess that the heavily patterned floral wallpaper, the crimson velvet curtains and the gleaming mahogany furniture upholstered in the same material had been chosen by her sister. Everything looked so new that she would not have been surprised to find the price tags still attached to the legs of the ornately carved chairs and sofas. The mantelshelf was crammed with china figurines, and an imposing black marble clock embellished with brass-topped Corinthian columns stood in the centre like a miniature cathedral. The contrast between this room and the poverty that lurked in the backstreets and alleyways was really quite shocking.

Irene turned with a start as the door opened and Ephraim ushered her mother into the room. 'My stepmother is still in bed,' he said, taking a gold watch from his waistcoat pocket and studying its face with raised eyebrows. 'I'll send Jessie to help her dress.' He bowed out of the room and closed the door behind him.

Irene flung her arms around her mother's neck. 'I've missed you, Ma. How are you?'

Clara gave her a feeble hug. 'Oh, Renie, I've missed you too.'

Gently disengaging her mother's arms, Irene led her to the sofa. 'Sit down, and tell me everything. Have they treated you well?'

'I can't complain, ducks. Emmie needs me and Josiah has been very considerate.' Clara patted the seat beside her. 'Sit down and tell me what's been going on at home. I thought maybe Billy might come and see me. Is he all right?'

'You know Pa,' Irene said lightly. 'He's always

in the best of health and nothing gets him down.'

'He hasn't complained then – about me leaving him to look after himself?'

'I'm there, Ma. We've muddled along, but it's not the same without you.'

'And he's kept away from the gaming tables?'

Irene hooked her arm around her mother's shoulders and was shocked by her increasing fragility. 'We haven't starved yet, and Pa will be along to see you very soon.'

'I hope so. I've got a feeling in me water that something is wrong. I know it's silly and you'd tell me if things wasn't going too well, but I can't sleep at night for worrying about my Billy.'

'It's all in your imagination, Ma. Everything is fine. Business is brisk and all the regulars have been asking after you. If trade keeps on increasing like it is, we'll need bigger premises.'

'You're lying, Renie. I can always tell, but just so long as you're managing, I'll try not to worry.' Clara glanced over her shoulder and smiled at Emily who had just breezed into the room. 'Hello, dear. Did you sleep well?'

'Hardly a wink, Ma. Josiah snores like a pig and takes all the bedcovers for himself. I think I shall insist that he sleeps in his dressing room from now until the baby comes.'

'You don't look too bad on it,' Irene said, chuckling. She couldn't help noticing that Emmie had yet another new gown, and if she had slept badly it did not show on her face. She looked quite blooming, in fact. Irene rose to her feet, taking her sister aside. 'I need to speak to you, in private.'

'What are you whispering about?' Clara demanded. 'Are you sure you've told me everything, Renie?'

'Quite sure, Ma. I was asking Emmie if I could see the nursery. You don't mind if we leave you for a moment, do you?'

'No, of course not, but don't be too long.'

As soon as they were outside the room Irene turned to Emily, lowering her voice. 'I don't want this to get back to Ma. Promise you won't say a word.'

Emily's face paled and her pretty mouth turned down at the corners. 'What's wrong? Is it Pa again?'

'He went off to Doncaster races and he hasn't come back. I've had no word from him for days and Yapp is being difficult about money. He's stopped our credit and I'm afraid I'll have to close the shop.'

'Oh, Gawd! Pa will be the ruin of us all. What will Josiah say?'

'I don't care what Josiah says, it's Ma I'm worried about. If anything has happened to

Pa she'll never get over it. She don't look too clever as it is. Have you been looking after her properly, Emmie?'

Emily bridled. 'Of course I have. She's got a lovely warm bed and three good meals a day. I can't help it if she pines for Pa, and no one can stop her worrying about that blessed shop. She hardly ever talks about anything else and it's so embarrassing when I have ladies round for afternoon tea.'

'My, haven't we become grand,' Irene said, throwing up her hands. 'You might stop thinking about yourself for once. Ma looks ill and I don't think she believed me when I said everything was fine.'

'Well, take a look in a mirror. You look a fright. No wonder Jessie thought you were a gypsy peddling her wares. She told me that Ephraim shouted at her, but I can see why she made such a mistake. You ought to take more pride in yourself, Renie. You can't expect to find a husband if you go round looking like a sack of old potatoes.' She paused, cocking her head to one side. 'That sounds like the dog cart. I told Tompkins to oil the wheels; one of them squeaks and makes everyone turn round to stare at me.'

'Perhaps they're just admiring your smart new clothes,' Irene suggested, smiling at her sister's inability to think of anything unless it was in relation to herself.

Emily shot her a suspicious glance. 'I know you're teasing me.' She pushed past Irene to study her reflection in a gilt-framed mirror that hung on the wall, and pinched her cheeks until they glowed with colour. 'Josiah will be coming through that door any moment. Don't mention a word of this to him. We'll just have to hope that Pa gets home soon and that he hasn't lost his shirt for the hundredth time.' The sound of the key grating in the lock made them both turn towards the front door as it opened to admit Josiah. Emily seized Irene by the arm. 'Remember what I said.' She went to meet him with outstretched arms. 'Josiah, my dear, look who has come to visit us.'

He took off his top hat and gloves, acknowledging Irene with a nod of his head as he planted a perfunctory kiss on Emmie's cheek. 'Yes, I see her. Good morning, Irene.'

'Hello, Josiah. I hope you don't mind my calling to see Ma?'

'Not at all. I consider it to be the duty of a daughter to show concern for an ageing parent.' He glanced over his shoulder at the young man who had come in after him and was standing in the open doorway staring at Irene with an appreciative smile on his face.

'Shut the door, Erasmus,' Josiah said testily. 'I can feel the draught cutting through me like a knife. After kneeling on the marble floor in that cold church I can feel a sore throat coming on already.'

Emily clutched his arm. 'Perhaps you had best spend the rest of the day in bed, Josiah?'

'Don't fuss, my dear.' He turned to his son. 'Well, boy? Are you going to stand there like a dummy or are you coming in to greet your stepmother's sister?'

With exaggeratedly slow movements, Erasmus divested himself of his top hat, gloves and muffler and tossed them onto the hall stand. 'Coming, Father.'

'I wasn't fussing,' Emily murmured.

'Come here,' Josiah said, scowling at his son. 'Where are your manners, boy? What have you to say to Miss Irene?'

Erasmus swept a mocking bow. 'Do I call you Irene or Step-aunt?'

'That's not what I meant,' Josiah thundered. 'You are an oaf, Erasmus. An ill-mannered jackass. Your mother would turn in her grave if she could see what a sorry fellow you've turned out to be.'

'A sorry fellow indeed,' Erasmus said lightly. He took Irene's hand and kissed it. 'You know me, I think, Irene. I can never take anything seriously, especially when I am being lectured by my worthy father.'

'Puppy!' Josiah snorted. 'I'll be in my study until dinnertime.' He moderated his tone.

His dark eyes seemed to disappear into his cheeks as he turned to Irene with a ghost of a smile. 'You will stay for luncheon? We eat at noon on Sundays.'

'Thank you, but . . .' A warning look from Emily made Irene hesitate. 'Yes, thank you, Josiah.'

With a muffled grunt, Josiah strode off, disappearing into the depths of the ground floor.

Erasmus struck a pose. 'There goes the worst-tempered man in London. Thank God I take after my sainted mother and not the old man.'

'You shouldn't tease him,' Emily scolded. 'You always get on his wrong side.'

'The old fellow hasn't got a good side as you'll discover, Stepmother, when he stops being polite to you and shows his true colours.'

'Don't say things like that to Emmie,' Irene said, frowning.

Emily tossed her head. 'Oh, I don't care. I take no notice of Erasmus; he's just a silly boy.'

'I'm five years older than you, dearest,' Erasmus said, tweaking a stray curl that had escaped from the coils of Emily's elaborate coiffure. 'I'd say you're wasted on the old goat, but then no one takes any notice of Erasmus Tippet, younger son and all that.' He turned to Irene with a winning smile. 'You and I are disadvantaged by our lack of seniority. My brother will inherit the business and you have been left to hold the fort, so to speak, while your father wastes his time on the gaming tables and your mother languishes in our magnificent but vulgar abode. Now I call that most unfair. What d'you think, Auntie?'

'I think you have too much to say for yourself. My father is worth ten of you.'

'I'm not staying here while you two bicker. I'm going to see if Ma wants anything.' Emily swept into the parlour, leaving Irene alone in the hall with Erasmus.

He angled his head, his dark eyes teasing her. 'Well, what shall we talk about now that my dear stepmother has left us?'

'Talk to yourself,' Irene said. 'You seem to love yourself above all others. I hope you and yourself will be very happy together.' She followed Emily into the morning room and closed the door, shutting him out.

Clara twisted round to give her a curious glance. 'Who was that you were talking to, dear?'

'It was Erasmus, Ma.'

'That boy will be the death of me,' Emily murmured. She slumped down on a brocaded chair by the fire and she tugged at the bell pull close by. 'I need a cup of hot chocolate and a piece of Cook's seed cake. Erasmus sends all my nerves into a jitter. He seems to enjoy aggravating my Josiah. One day he'll go too far and Josiah will explode.'

Irene could not repress a smile. That was a sight she would love to see, but she would not dare say so in front of Emily.

'It's not funny,' Emily scolded. 'Ras should follow Ephraim's example and show his father some respect. I do hope he will be on his best behaviour at the dinner table – I mean at luncheon. You know that in the best circles they have luncheon at midday, Renie, and dinner at night.'

'And I suppose we must ape the gentry now that we've come up in the world.'

'Don't you dare say such things in front of my Josiah,' Emily said, pouting. 'He's very conscious of his social position and we mustn't let him down.'

Irene opened her mouth to argue but a warning glance from Ma made her change her mind. She was beginning to wish that she had refused the invitation to stay for the family meal. It would be excruciating as always. The mutton would be tough, the vegetables either under-cooked or burnt, and the suet pudding stodgy, but at least she would leave the house with a full belly.

Clara cleared her throat nervously. 'Girls, please don't start arguing. I can't stand it and

I'm very worried about your father. I think there's something that you aren't telling me.' She turned to Irene. 'Where is he, Renie? What's been going on since I left home?'

Chapter Seven

There was no fooling Ma. Irene had hoped she could keep Pa's exploits a secret, but she had reckoned without her mother's acute intuitive powers, and now she had no choice other than to tell her everything, with the exception of her own unwilling involvement with Inspector Kent. To admit that she was planning to become a copper's nark would have been a step too far.

Clara listened and her pallor deepened to a sickly grey. 'So he's been gone for five days without a word?'

Irene exchanged worried glances with Emily and she nodded her head. 'Yes, Ma, five days. I didn't want to worry you.'

'Worrying about Billy comes naturally to me after all these years. I knew something was wrong the moment you walked through the door.'

Irene slid off the sofa to kneel at her mother's feet. She clasped Ma's hands and was startled to find them cold and clawed like the feet of a dead chicken. She chafed them vigorously, attempting to impart some of her youth and vitality into her mother's fragile body. 'Try not to worry too much. He's been missing for much longer in the past. I'm sure he'll turn up soon.'

'Yes,' Emily said earnestly. 'He's probably on a winning streak. He'll come home with a pocket full of money.'

'After five days?' Clara shook her head. 'It's more likely that he'll have blown the lot.'

Irene rose to her feet. 'Perhaps I'd better go home and see if he's there.'

'No, don't go,' Clara said, making an obvious effort to control her agitation. 'You're all skin and bone, Renie. Please stay and share a meal with us.'

'I am a bit hungry,' Irene admitted. 'Anyway, we mustn't worry Emmie in her condition. Let's talk about something pleasant.'

'Yes, of course,' Clara agreed. 'We must think about Emmie and my grandchild.'

Reluctantly, Irene returned to her seat and sat in silence while her mother and Emily chattered about things related to babies. Somehow Irene could not summon up much interest in an unborn child, and despite her attempts to sound positive she could not forget Yapp's threat to put them out of business. Then there was Inspector Kent who was expecting her to bring him information that Arthur did not have, but most important of all there was Pa, who might be dead in a Yorkshire ditch for all she knew. She was startled out of her own personal nightmare by Jessie barging into the room and announcing that dinner was on the table, and Cook said they'd best sit down quick before it got cold. Emily scolded her for her lack of decorum, but Clara murmured excuses, declaring that the poor child was so recently released from the workhouse that they must not expect too much of her, and Emily must have more patience.

With a petulant scowl marring her pretty features, Emily raised herself from her chair and flounced across the hall to the wainscoted dining room. Ephraim and Josiah were already seated at the table with their napkins tucked into their collars.

'We've been waiting for five minutes at least,' Josiah said, taking a half-hunter watch from his pocket and staring pointedly at its face. 'When you ladies get talking there's no stopping you, but Emily knows that I demand punctuality at mealtimes.'

'Yes, Josiah, dear,' Emily said sweetly. 'So where is Erasmus?' She took her seat at the opposite end of the dining table with Clara seated on her left, leaving Irene no choice other than to sit next to Ephraim.

'We won't wait for him,' Josiah said, rising

to tug at the bell pull. 'If he cannot come to the table at the correct time then he will have to go without.'

Ephraim nodded his head. 'You're quite right, Father. Ras needs taking down a peg or two. He's too cocky by half.'

'He takes after his mother,' Josiah said sententiously. 'She was a flighty, empty-headed chit of a girl when I married her.'

'She is dead, Josiah.' Emily snatched a bread roll from a basket in front of her and she tore it in half, frowning. 'I don't think your late wife is a fit subject of conversation for the dinner table.'

Josiah had the grace to look embarrassed and he managed a sheepish smile. 'You are quite right, my dear, and I'm sorry. But I've told you before, it's luncheon at midday, not dinner.'

There was an awkward silence, but at that moment Jessie staggered into the room bearing a large soup tureen. Josiah beckoned to her and helped himself to a generous portion, licking his lips as if in anticipation of a great feast. Irene raised her eyebrows; she didn't know much about manners, but Pa had always taught her that it was ladies first. She glanced at Emily who, despite having consumed a cup of hot chocolate and a large slice of cake less than half an hour ago, was now stuffing bread and butter into her mouth as if she had not eaten for a week. Clara sat silently, staring down at her plate and twisting her table napkin between nervous fingers. Irene sighed inwardly. The soup smelt greasy, and as Ephraim ladled it into his bowl she could see globules of fat floating on its grey, glutinous surface. Her empty stomach heaved, but she was too hungry to refuse when Jessie thrust the tureen under her nose.

Irene was no cook, but when the next course was presented and Josiah was hacking at a leg of mutton surrounded by root vegetables, she could only guess that the revolting soup had been the broth in which the meat had been boiled, to which very little in the way of seasoning or flavouring had been added. As she had anticipated, the mutton was tough and stringy and the vegetables were overcooked so that they were an undistinguishable mush on her plate. Neither Josiah nor Ephraim seemed to find any fault with their meal and they gobbled their food with apparent relish. Emmie also ate ravenously, gulping down mouthfuls of meat and potatoes as if this was her last meal on earth. Clara merely toyed with her food, apologising to Josiah for her lack of appetite. He waved his fork at her with a carrot wedged in its tines. 'No wonder you're pale and sickly, Mother-in-law. You must eat or you will never be strong enough to go home.'

Ephraim muttered something beneath his breath and washed his meal down with a draught of porter. Irene sipped a glass of water and pushed her plate away. She had eaten as much as she could force down; if she took another mouthful she was certain she would disgrace herself by being sick. Josiah frowned ominously, and seemed about to comment on her lack of appetite, but was forestalled by the timely entrance of his youngest son.

'Oh, dear,' Erasmus said, chuckling. 'It seems I've missed one of Cook's bloody awful Sunday dinners. What a crying shame.'

Josiah wiped the gravy off his plate with a hunk of bread. 'Mrs Peabody is a fine cook. I won't have you saying otherwise, Erasmus. And don't assume you can join us for pudding, because I won't have it. You either turn up on time for meals or you go without.'

'Then it's just as well that I took myself off to Ned's chophouse in Finch Lane, where I had an excellent meal,' Erasmus said, eyeing the food left on Irene's plate and winking at her. 'You should have come with me, Miss Irene. I would have enjoyed your company and you would have made a decent meal, instead of putting up with Cook's slop.'

Josiah tore his napkin from his neck and rose

to his feet. 'Leave the room at once, boy. I won't have you parading your bad manners in front of guests.'

Erasmus leaned against the door jamb and stuck his hands in his pockets. 'Come now, Father, Miss Angel is family. The poor girl is one of us by marriage, God help her.'

'That's no way to speak to our father,' Ephraim said stiffly. 'You should apologise, Ras.'

'I speak only the truth, and I won't apologise for that. Anyway, I'll leave you to enjoy one of Mrs Peabody's leaden puddings.' Erasmus turned to Emily, who was staring at him open-mouthed. 'Eat well, Stepmother. You have to think of the child: yet another half-brother to add to Father's collection. I always think that we are like hunting trophies. In fact, I shouldn't be at all surprised to come home one day and find Ephraim's head mounted on a shield, glaring down at me from the wall.'

'Erasmus!' Josiah thundered. 'You will apologise to your stepmother for such rudeness, and then leave the room.'

Burying her face in her table napkin, Emily burst into tears, and Clara rose from the table to go to her. 'That was uncalled for, Erasmus,' she said, wrapping her arms around Emily's shaking shoulders. 'You are a bad boy.'

Before Erasmus had a chance to respond,

Irene had risen from her seat and she made her way swiftly round the table to face him. 'Outside! Now.'

He stared at her in surprise and his dark eyes twinkled mischievously. 'Why, Miss Irene, what could you want with the likes of me?'

She gave him a push that caught him off balance and sent him staggering out into the hallway. She followed him, closing the door on the outraged occupants of the dining room. 'I suppose you think you are very clever, but you are not. You've upset my sister and Ma, and I won't have it. D'you hear me, Erasmus?'

His smile returned and he shook his head. 'Ras, please. I hate the stupid name Erasmus.'

'A stupid name for a stupid boy,' Irene cried hotly. 'All right, the food is terrible and your brother is a pompous idiot, but that doesn't give you the right to embarrass the rest of us.'

'Er, you've left my father out,' Erasmus said, angling his head with a quizzical smile. 'How would you label him?'

'You don't want to know, and I'm not going to give you the satisfaction of telling you.'

'I think I can guess, and it wouldn't be flattering.'

'What I think of Josiah is unimportant,' Irene countered angrily. 'You've upset Emmie and made Ma feel uncomfortable. I can't forgive that.'

His smile faded and a look of genuine concern flickered across his handsome features. 'For that I do apologise. Emmie's all right, and it's not her fault that the guvner is a bastard.' He held his hands out, palms uppermost. 'Pardon my language, but he drives me mad. I can't believe that I'm his son.'

Irene felt her anger dissipating into something like sympathy. She laid her hand on his arm. 'Even so, you shouldn't take it out on Emmie. It's not fair.'

'No,' he conceded. 'But I find it hard to believe that she has genuine feelings for the old goat, or that she didn't marry him just to get away from the pickle shop.'

He looked so much like an angry little boy that it made Irene smile. 'Wouldn't you, in similar circumstances?'

He threw his head back and roared with laughter. 'I like you, Step-aunt.'

'Well then, if we're to get along I think you should come back into the dining room and apologise to Emmie and your dad.'

'No! Not that!' Erasmus pulled a face. 'I never apologise for anything.'

Irene took him by the arm. 'Then it's time you did.' She attempted to drag him across the hall, but he was a good head and shoulders taller than she, and sturdily built. It was, she thought, like trying to uproot an oak tree.

She was rapidly losing patience when the doorbell jangled, echoing deep in the bowels of the house, and Jessie appeared as if from nowhere, wiping gravy from her chin on a corner of her apron. She shot them a curious look as she hurried to answer the impatient caller who was now rapping on the doorknocker.

'Hold on,' she cried. 'I'm coming as fast as me legs will carry me.' She wrenched the door open and was thrust aside by Billy, who breezed into the house as if he had not a care in the world.

'Irene, my little star, I guessed that you would be here.' He swept her off her feet in a fond hug that almost took her breath away.

She struggled free. 'Pa! I've been worried sick. Why didn't you come home sooner?'

He took off his curly-brimmed bowler hat, which Irene noticed immediately was brand new, as was his suit of clothes in a smart brown and white check. His smile was at once apologetic and disarming. 'My little pickle, what a thoughtless brute I am, but as you see I have come home now with a pocketful of winnings and now everything will be all right.'

'Good for you, sir,' Erasmus said enthusiastically. 'I'm not a gambling man myself, but that doesn't mean I don't enjoy a flutter every now and again.'

Ignoring him, Irene held her hand out to

her father. 'Let me see, or I won't believe you haven't squandered the lot on that new get-up.'

Billy shrugged his shoulders. 'Don't put me on the spot, darling. I have enough to get us by for a while, and I've come to take my Clara home. Now where is she?'

Erasmus crossed the hall in two long strides to open the door leading into the dining room. 'Father, we have a visitor.'

Tucking his hat under his arm, Billy swept into the dining room. Irene followed him and was in time to see her mother's face suffused with a delighted smile at the sight of her errant husband. She attempted to rise, but Billy hurried to her side and dropped a careless kiss on the top of her head. 'Rest awhile, my dear, and then I'll take you home.'

Emily jumped to her feet. 'Really, Pa. You disappear for days on end and then you waltz in here as if you owned the place. It won't do.'

'I agree with my wife,' Josiah said stiffly. 'We are in the middle of our dinner, Father-in-law. I suggest you take a seat and wait until we have finished.'

Billy flicked him a careless glance. 'You always were a pompous fool, Josiah. Nothing has changed.' He held out his hand to his wife. 'Come, Clara. I'm taking you home now.'

'Pa,' Irene said, laying her hand on his arm. 'Think about this.'

'Yes,' Emily added, bristling. 'How dare you speak to my Josiah in that way? It's not fair. He's been very kind to Ma and me.'

'I should hope so,' Billy said calmly. 'He's your husband, and if he don't treat you right I will want to know the reason why.'

Clara struggled to her feet. 'Billy, that's enough. I won't have you upsetting Emily in her condition, and she's quite correct in what she says. Josiah has been very good to me and I am comfortable here.'

Billy eyed her with surprise written all over his face. 'What are you saying, my dove?'

'That I will come home when the time is right. Emily needs me more than you do, and I won't desert her. Irene will look after you, won't you, dear?'

Irene nodded her head and she tightened her grip on his arm. 'Of course I will. Come along, Pa. Let's go home.'

Ephraim had been sitting silently all this time but he stood up suddenly, clearing his throat. 'I think you should leave, sir.' He made for the door but found his way barred by his brother. 'Stop grinning like a fool, Ras. Get out of the way.'

'I don't see why I should. I haven't been so

entertained since you slipped on the ice outside the shop and broke your leg.'

'Idiot!' Ephraim pushed him aside and he beckoned to Billy. 'Come, sir. Allow me to show you the door.'

Irene felt her father's muscles tense beneath the tweed material of his jacket. 'We should go now, Pa.'

'Yes, my dear,' Clara said firmly. 'I will stay on for just as long as necessary. You must manage without me for a while.'

Billy frowned and he shook off Irene's restraining hand. 'I see how it is. You have been won over by all this luxury and comfort. Our home is not good enough for you now. I will leave, but with sorrow in my heart.'

'That's not fair, Billy,' Clara murmured with tears in her eyes. 'But you won't change my mind. It's a mother's duty. I'm staying with Emmie until the baby comes.'

'Please, Pa,' Irene entreated, tugging at his arm. 'Come with me.'

'A fine welcome home,' Billy muttered. 'I return with ample funds and I am greeted with coldness and disdain.' He made to leave the room with a dramatic flourish of his arms. 'I have restored the family fortunes and this is how I am treated.'

Irene kissed her mother on her thin cheek. 'Don't worry, Ma. I'll look after him.'

Clara watched her husband stalk out of the room and she sighed. 'I know you will, ducks. He'll come round, I know he will.'

Josiah tapped his spoon on the tabletop. 'Let us finish our meal like civilised people.'

Ephraim hesitated in the doorway. 'Shall I see them off the premises, Father?'

'Sit down, boy,' Josiah said, shaking his head. 'I think my father-in-law can find his own way out. Goodbye, Irene. You are welcome to call whenever you feel you must.'

'Ta, Josiah. I'll remember that.' Irene hurried past Ephraim and almost bumped into Erasmus, who was waiting outside the door.

'He's gone,' Erasmus said casually. 'He walked out of the house without so much as a backward glance. I'll escort you home to the pickle shop.'

She shot him a suspicious look. 'I don't think a draper's son should look down on them as sells pickles and sauce for a living. We're both in trade. You'd do well to remember that, and I can find my own way home, ta very much.' She swept past him, snatching her bonnet and shawl from the hall stand and she let herself out of the house. She hesitated for a moment, standing on the pavement and glancing up at the elegant façade of the draper's house. If she were to be completely honest, part of her envied Emmie living as she was in such a grand dwelling, although the price she was paying for her rise in status was perhaps too great. She turned in the direction of home and caught a glimpse of Pa's nattily dressed back disappearing round the corner into Wood Street. She set off after him, breaking into a run. If she did not stop him, he would most likely head straight for Blue Boar Court or some other gaming house and lose what was left of his winnings.

As she had feared, Billy strode past the shop and turned into Cheapside. She caught up with him just as he reached Blue Boar Court. 'Pa,' she cried breathlessly. 'Don't go in there and gamble it all away.'

Billy's angry expression softened and his lips curved in a smile. 'Don't worry your pretty head about me, darling. I'm on a winning streak. I can't lose.'

She clutched his hand. 'At least give me some of it so that I can buy in more stock. We need food, and Arthur is—'

Billy's brow darkened. 'What about Arthur?'

'His dad threw him out of the house and he's been sleeping under the counter in the shop.'

'What? Are you telling me that you've spent nights alone with him?'

'No, Pa. You don't understand. Artie is just a friend. He wouldn't lay a finger on me.'

'He's a man and you're a pretty girl. I won't have it, Renie. I'll do worse to him than his father did if I catch him hanging round you, and that's the truth.'

'Artie's working for Vic and Wally. Please don't say anything, Pa. If you make a fuss they'll send him on his way or they'll set their toughs on him. He doesn't deserve that.'

'He's a fool, and he should keep away from the gaming tables. He's got himself into this spot of bother and I won't have him involving you. He'd best not bother you any further, Renie, or he'll have me to deal with.' Billy rapped on the door and waited, tapping his foot. The door opened a crack and a clay pipe stuck out, exuding puffs of blue smoke. 'Who's that knocking? State your name and business.'

'It's Billy Angel. Let me in, Blackie.'

The door opened just wide enough to allow a man of Billy's size and stature to pass. He paused on the threshold, taking a leather pouch from his pocket and extracting a golden sovereign which he pressed into Irene's hand. 'There, poppet, that will keep us going for a while, and when I double my money I promise to buy you a new gown and a bonnet with scarlet ribbons.' He blew her a kiss and disappeared into the narrow passageway. The door closed with a bang, leaving Irene standing on the cobblestones staring at the gold coin in the palm of her hand. It would be enough to restock the shop and pay the rent, but it was frustrating to know that Pa had taken at least this much and probably double the amount to squander on the gaming tables. She did not have much faith in winning streaks, and she knew from experience that sooner or later Pa's luck would run out.

She closed her fingers around the coin and set off for home. As she trod the all too familiar path from the gaming house to the corner of Wood Street, she tried to think of a way to shock Pa out of his complacency. She was painfully aware that his addiction to gambling was out of control, and if he continued this way she was certain he would end up in prison. His involvement with the Sykes brothers was becoming too intense for him merely to walk away, and now Arthur seemed to be heading down the same path. By the time she reached the shop, Irene had made up her mind to have it out with Pa the moment he returned home. She would force him to face reality; if he did not stop gambling they would lose their livelihood and their home, and Ma would have no alternative other than to live in Josiah Tippet's house as a permanent poor relation.

Billy did not return home that night or the next, and neither did Arthur. Irene paid Yapp, who seemed disappointed that he had no excuse to close her down. Danny on the other hand had a wide grin on his face as he brought in fresh stocks of pickles and sauces. He left Irene with a cheerful wink and he waved to her through the window as he loped off behind Yapp's cart.

She opened the cash box and counted out the remaining coins. There was enough to pay the rent and she would be able to purchase food, coal and candles for a few days, but only if she was careful. She drummed her fingers on the counter as she waited for the customers to trickle in through the door. The shop in which Ma had worked so diligently for as long as Irene could remember had kept them from starving when Pa had failed to bring home any money, but the profits were small and there was not enough space to allow for any expansion of trade. Life with Pa had always been a see-saw of ups and downs. Luck, she decided, was a fickle mistress. Suddenly the familiar surroundings closed in on her like a prison from which she feared there was no escape, and tonight she would have to face Inspector Kent, with absolutely nothing to tell him.

In the shadow of the great cathedral of St Paul's, the churchyard was dark and forbidding. It was a moonless night and Irene could barely make out the pathway. She moved silently between the looming shapes of shrubs which swayed in the wind and made rustling sounds as though someone was hiding behind them, ready to pounce. Surrounded by warehouses on the south side and large business premises to the north, the churchyard was a green oasis in the daylight, but an altogether different place on a dark night. It would be so easy to imagine that restless spirits rose from their graves to walk the gravel paths bemoaning their loss of life. Within reason, Irene had never been afraid of the living, but the uneasy dead were another matter altogether, and now she was on tenterhooks, jumping at the slightest noise.

She could just make out a bench close to the wall and she went to sit down before her knees gave way beneath her. The hairs on the back of her neck stood up with each unfamiliar sound, and she caught her breath as she heard the unmistakeable crunch of approaching footsteps on the gravel. She drew her shawl around her head, covering her face so that only her eyes remained exposed as she pressed herself back against the hard wooden slats of the seat. As the figure drew nearer she breathed a sigh of relief. There was no mistaking the determined stride and upright silhouette of Inspector Kent.

'Miss Angel.' He took off his top hat and sat down on the far end of the seat, leaving a space between them.

'Yes, Inspector.'

'Have you anything for me?'

'No, not yet.' She stole a sideways glance at him as he sat ramrod stiff, staring straight ahead of him into the darkness. She could just make out his stern profile with his dark hair swept back from a high forehead, emphasising an aquiline nose and a resolute chin.

He turned to stare at her as if sensing her close scrutiny, but his expression was drowned in the deep shadow. 'Nothing at all?'

'I haven't seen Arthur since he went to work for the Sykes brothers. He hasn't come home.' She paused, realising how that sounded. 'I mean, he's been staying at the shop, sleeping under the counter, because his father threw him out.' She bit her lip. Why was she explaining this to him? He was almost a complete stranger, so what did it matter if he got the wrong impression about her relationship with Arthur? He probably thought she was no better than she should be anyway.

'Do you think he has run away?' He spoke in a conversational, almost matter of fact manner, and Irene was shocked to realise that this was exactly what she had been thinking.

'I don't know.'

'But you think that it might be true?'

'It's possible,' she admitted reluctantly.

'If he has we will find him,' Kent said in a low voice. 'It will not go well for Greenwood.'

'I don't think he would leave without telling me.'

'I hope for his sake that he has not, but this isn't a game, Miss Angel. I want to put the Sykes brothers behind bars before they initiate gang wars that will inflame the whole of the East End. I want information and I need to have it soon. If Greenwood has absconded I will have to enlist the help of someone else who is known to be close to the Sykes brothers.'

'I hope you don't mean my pa. He may be a gambler, but he's not a criminal and he won't peach.'

'He mixes with the gang members and that puts him very definitely on the wrong side of the law.'

She rose to her feet. 'You're so wrong. My pa is a good man at heart. He wouldn't hurt a fly and he isn't involved with Vic and Wally.'

Kent remained seated, his face a pale oval in a shaft of moonlight that had filtered through a ragged tear in the clouds. 'You seem to be on familiar terms with them.'

'I'm not. I mean, everyone round here calls them by their first names. I grew up knowing them as Vic and Wally; it don't mean that we're bosom friends.'

He stood up. 'Keep it that way, Miss Angel.'

'So what now? You haven't told me what you want me to do. Wasn't that the sole purpose of our meeting?'

'It was, but with Greenwood gone there is nothing further for you to do.'

He was about to walk away but she caught him by the sleeve. 'You can't leave me in suspense. I want to know what you're planning.'

He paused, eyeing her coldly. 'That is police business.'

'It's mine if it concerns Pa. What are you going to do? Please, you must tell me.'

Chapter Eight

'Go home, Miss Angel. There is nothing more you can do.' Kent strode off along the path heading towards Old Change Lane.

Following him, Irene broke into a run. 'You can't leave it like that.'

He stopped, turning his head to give her an inscrutable look. 'I should never have involved you. I have no further need of your services.'

'What! You dragged me into this and now you say you have no use for me?'

'Do you mean to tell me that you want to be a copper's nark?'

She shook her head vehemently. 'No. I never said that. Don't twist my words, Inspector. You're wrong about Arthur running away; he'd never do nothing like that.'

He did not look convinced. 'My men are on the lookout for him. He might have given us the slip, but he will be found and then he will be charged and sent before the magistrates, who will decide his guilt or innocence.'

'He is innocent; I'm telling you that for nothing. But it's my dad I'm worried about.

If you point the finger at him the Sykes brothers won't show any mercy. My pa will end up at the bottom of the river with a lead weight tied round his neck.'

'Then it's up to you to persuade him to keep better company. Goodbye, Miss Angel. I'm sorry we had to meet under such dire circumstances.' He strode off leaving Irene standing alone in the shadow of the great dome of St Paul's, staring after him. His tall figure disappeared into the gloom and the sound of his footsteps died away, leaving an unearthly silence to close round her.

Irene balled her hands into fists. What a rude, insufferable man he was to be sure; officious, arrogant and cold-hearted. He was like one of those automatons that she had seen in shop windows, with a heart made out of coiled steel. She doubted whether he had ever felt a human emotion in his whole life. If Kent had ever cared about anyone other than himself he would realise that she loved her pa. He might not be perfect, but he was a warm and loving father and he had never been part of the Sykes gang. Irene stifled a sob of sheer frustration. The distant chiming of a church clock brought her back to the present and she started off towards Wood Street and home. She must warn Pa about Kent's plan to catch the Sykes brothers red-handed. She would tell him everything, even though it meant revealing Arthur's part in the whole sorry business, which would confirm Pa's poor opinion of him. Poor Arthur, she thought sadly; everyone was against him.

Once safely inside the shop she locked the door behind her. 'Arthur,' she called, hoping for a response. 'Are you here?'

Her voice came back to her in an echo, but it was obvious that there was no one in the shop.

The living room was similarly deserted. In the pale moonlight shafting through the windowpanes, Irene could just make out the shape of her parents' bed and the wooden chair by the fireplace where Ma had spent so many hours waiting for her man to return home. The room seemed so quiet and empty now, but once, not so long ago, it had been filled with love and laughter. Of course there had been the inevitable arguments, followed by Ma's gentle but firm reprimands. These family squabbles nearly always ended in tears of regret, hugs and apologies. There had been good times, when Pa was flush with money and there had been abundant food on the table and coal for the fire. There had been hard times aplenty, when they were cold and hungry and barely able to subsist, but these paled into insignificance now as Irene recalled only the happy events in her years of growing up in the room above the shop.

The bare branches of the plane tree scratched at the window above her bed, sounding eerily like sharp fingernails being drawn across the glass. The curtains had long since shredded into tatters and there had been no money to spare for replacements. The irony of the situation struck her forcibly. There was her sister married to a wealthy draper, and Ma did not even possess a decent pair of curtains to keep out the winter cold and dark. Irene sat down on her bed and took off her boots. She huddled, fully clothed, beneath the coverlet and closed her eyes, but sleep evaded her. She found herself listening for the grating of the key in the lock, and Pa's heavy tread on the staircase, or the sound of Arthur shuffling about in the shop below as he made up his bed beneath the counter. Eventually she drifted into a fitful sleep, but when she awakened next morning nothing had changed.

A thick white mist had crept up the Thames and it hung in a damp cloud over the city. Irene went out to fetch water and almost immediately her hair was pearled with tiny droplets of moisture. She managed to dodge Sal's inquisitive company by going to the bakery and then the dairy where she had her jug filled with a pint of milk. At least when

Pa did eventually turn up she would have breakfast waiting for him. When he was in a good mood it would be time for them to talk seriously. As she left the dairy, Irene was pleased to see that Sal had latched on to one of the scullery maids from the Mitre pub, further along Wood Street. They were deep in conversation and did not notice her as she hurried past them to draw water from the pump. She struggled home with the heavy bucket, and was attempting to fish the key from her pocket when the sound of approaching footsteps made her glance over her shoulder. 'Pa! Thank goodness you've come home.'

Taking the key from her hand, Billy grinned as he opened the door. 'Don't I always turn up like the proverbial bad penny, my little flower?'

'Don't soft soap me, Pa. You know it won't work.' Irene stepped over the threshold and set the heavy pail of water down carefully so as not to spill a drop. She turned to him, concealing her relief with a frown. 'I suppose you've only come home now because you've run out of funds.'

Billy tossed his hat onto the peg, followed by his muffler. 'Not entirely, my pet.' He tapped the side of his nose and winked at her as he made for the stairs. Irene knew that there was no use scolding him when he was in this ebullient mood. 'What do you mean by not entirely, Pa?' She followed him upstairs to the living room.

'I mean exactly that, dumpling. I lost some and I won some, and then I lost some more, but Vic has got a job for me which will pay ten times what I lost at the tables.'

'What job would that be?' She spoke more sharply than she had meant to, and she tempered her words with an attempt at a smile.

Billy perched on the edge of his bed and began to unlace his boots. 'Just a job, sweetheart. Nothing bad, I can assure you, so don't worry your pretty head about that.'

'But I do worry, Pa. You know that Inspector Kent has been asking questions.'

'You didn't tell him anything, did you?'

'How could I, when I don't know what's going on?'

'And that young idiot Arthur, did Kent speak to him too?'

Irene knelt down to riddle the cinders in the grate. 'Why didn't you ask him yourself? You must have seen him at the Sykes' place.'

'Not a sign of him, the lazy young devil. I daresay he's gone crawling back to his father.'

She sat back on her haunches, eyeing him suspiciously. 'You didn't have a row with Artie, did you, Pa?'

'I told you, ducks. I haven't seen the boy, and I wouldn't waste my breath on him if I had. Unless he'd been making improper advances to you, and then I'd tan his hide.'

'He hasn't done anything of the kind. I've told you that Artie isn't like that.'

'Likes boys better than girls, does he? I've always had my suspicions about that fellow.'

'Don't be cruel, Pa. He's just an ordinary bloke, but he's sensitive and his dad is a bully. I think Artie might have run away.'

'Bah!' Billy threw himself back onto the bed and closed his eyes. 'I've no patience with the fellow. Wake me when my breakfast is ready, love.' He opened one eye and raised his head. 'And I don't want tea and toast. I'll have a pork pie with a good dollop of mustard pickle on the side and a pint of porter to wash it down with.'

Irene scrambled to her feet. 'And where is the money coming from for this feast, Pa?'

Billy thrust his hand in his pocket and pulled out a crown. He tossed it to her. 'Get yourself something better than a slice of bread and scrape. There's more where that came from. Soon we'll be rolling in money and I'll have your mother back home where she belongs.'

Fear clutched at Irene's heart. 'Promise me that you haven't got yourself mixed up in anything bad.'

Billy folded his hands on his chest and groaned. 'How many times must I tell you not to worry? Now go and get those vittles before I die of starvation.'

There was little that Irene could do other than humour him, and when she had a good fire blazing up the chimney she went out to purchase the food and drink that he had demanded. Billy demolished his meal with obvious enjoyment and did not seem to notice that she contented herself with a slice of bread and a thin scraping of butter. She intended to use what was left of the money he had given her to buy new stock, and now she could pay the old villain Yapp in advance as he had demanded.

Billy went to bed as soon as he had finished his meal, instructing Irene to wake him at noon. She went downstairs to open the shop but she could not rid herself of the fear that something awful might have happened to Arthur. Supposing that either Vic or Wally had discovered that he was spying on them? They would show no mercy to an informer and their vengeance would be swift and deadly. Somehow she managed to get through the morning, and having dutifully awakened her father at midday she waited until he had left for Blue Boar Court, saying nothing about her intention of closing the shop for as long as it took to visit the Greenwoods' house in Bread Street. If Arthur had gone home without telling her, she would want to know the reason why, but if he had not then she would be really worried.

Irene did not recognise the maidservant who answered her urgent rapping on the door-knocker, but she was hardly surprised. The servants in the Greenwood residence never seemed to stay for any length of time. Mr Greenwood was a notoriously hard task-master and Mrs Greenwood was possessed of a volatile temper. Living in their house, Irene thought, must be like dwelling on the edge of an extremely active volcano.

'The master is at the shop in Silver Street.' The maid was about to close the door but Irene was too quick for her and she put her foot over the sill.

'I meant Mr Arthur Greenwood.'

'Haven't seen him for days, miss.'

'Then I would like to see your mistress. Please tell her that Miss Irene Angel would like to speak with her.'

The maid blanched visibly. 'Mistress is having her midday meal, miss. I daresn't disturb her.'

'Oh, for goodness sake let me in,' Irene exclaimed, pushing past the astonished girl and heading towards the dining room. Although she had never been formally invited into the Greenwoods' establishment, Irene was familiar with the general layout of the house. She had often sneaked in with Arthur when they were younger, and he had smuggled her up to his room on the third floor where they had played war games with his lead soldiers. The four-storey house had always seemed like a palace to the young Irene, but now, by comparison with Josiah Tippet's mansion, the house in Bread Street did not seem quite so large or so grand. The wallpaper in the hallway was slightly faded and there were chips off the plasterwork on the high ceiling. The black and white marble floor tiles were crazed and worn down in places by the passage of feet over the course of two centuries, and the atmosphere was one of faded elegance and pervading melancholy.

'You can't go in there, miss,' the maid cried, running after Irene and catching her by the arm. 'She'll skin me alive.'

'I'm sorry, but this won't wait. I'll take the blame for my bad manners.' Shaking her off, Irene opened the door and stepped into the dining room.

Mrs Greenwood, resplendent in purple, with her dark hair severely scraped into a bun and crowned with a white lace cap, looked to Irene like a rather poor imitation of her majesty the Queen. Drusilla Greenwood raised her slanting black eyebrows so that they formed a triangle over the bridge of her sharp nose. 'What's all this? How dare you burst in on me like this?' She lifted a lorgnette and peered myopically at Irene. 'Is that you, Irene Angel?'

'I'm sorry to disturb you, ma'am,' Irene said, bobbing a curtsey. 'But I'm worried about Artie. Has he come home?'

Mrs Greenwood turned on the maid. 'This is all your fault, Ethel. How dare you disobey my orders?'

'I'm sorry, missis. She pushed past me. I couldn't stop her.'

'Get out of my sight, you stupid girl.' Mrs Greenwood rose to her feet, shaking her fist at the maid who fled sobbing from the room.

'There was no need for that,' Irene said angrily. 'It wasn't her fault. She tried to stop me, but I needed to see you urgently.'

Mrs Greenwood subsided onto her seat, clutching her bosom. 'I'm having one of my turns. Fetch the sal volatile.'

Irene looked round helplessly. 'I don't know where it is.'

'In my reticule, you fool.' Mrs Greenwood pointed to the chiffonier where a small black beadwork bag lay on a silver salver. 'Bring it to me.'

Irene passed it to her and waited until Mrs Greenwood had inhaled the pungent fumes from a silver vinaigrette, coughing and spluttering and then wiping her eyes on a scrap of lace handkerchief. 'All I asked was if Arthur had come home,' Irene murmured. 'I didn't mean to upset you.'

'Upset me? You encourage my only son to leave home and live in sin with you in that pickle shop, and you say you didn't mean to upset me.'

'No, ma'am. You've got it all wrong. It's not like that. Arthur and me are just friends, as we've always been. It was Mr Greenwood who threw him out on the street. Artie had nowhere else to go.'

Mrs Greenwood eyed her beneath lowered lids. 'It seems he's found somewhere else now then, for the worthless boy has not returned to the bosom of his family. He has abandoned his apprenticeship and broken his father's heart, and mine too. Was there ever such an ingrate as he?'

Irene opened her mouth to defend Arthur, but Mrs Greenwood had turned away from her and was attacking a plateful of roast lamb as if the poor animal was still alive. She stabbed at the meat with her knife and forked large portions into her mouth, followed by a whole roast potato and then a carrot. Irene backed out of the door, closing it softly behind her. It seemed that Arthur's mother was more concerned with her belly than with her son's fate. Poor Artie, no wonder he sought solace in drinking and gambling whenever he had the chance. She hesitated for a moment in the hallway. The last thing she wanted was to linger in this gloomy and unhappy house, but there might be a clue as to Arthur's whereabouts in his bedroom. She cocked her head, listening for sounds of movement, but all was quiet except for the solemn tick-tock of a long-case clock at the foot of the staircase. She reasoned that at this time of day, unless summoned by the master or mistress, the servants would be downstairs in the basement having their midday meal.

She headed for the back stairs and made her way up to Arthur's room, where she discovered that almost nothing had changed since she was last here. There were no toy soldiers in evidence now, but the chintz curtains were the same, if rather faded, and the coverlet on the narrow iron bedstead was similar to the one that had been there when they were children. In fact, it was a child's room still, with no indication as to the personality or taste of the adult occupant. Perhaps Arthur liked living in a monk-like cell? Maybe he didn't even notice the austerity of his surroundings. Irene did not stop to wonder why he had not demanded a little more comfort from his well-off parents. She set about methodically going through the drawers in the tallboy but it did not look as though he had come home to collect any of his clothes, and this was borne out by a portmanteau and a valise sitting on top of the wardrobe.

She closed her eyes, trying to remember his exact words when he had threatened to run away. He had mentioned an aunt living in Essex. Aunt Maude, who lived in a place called Havering which was fairly near a town called Romford. Irene had no idea where that was. It would not be difficult to find out, but she needed the full address. She gazed round the room in desperation and then she spotted Arthur's old school desk tucked away in a corner and half hidden under a pile of discarded clothing. She crossed the floor and threw the garments onto the bed. Lifting the lid she discovered a leather-bound notebook buried beneath a jumble of sealing wax, pen nibs and scraps of paper. She flipped through the pages of notes and designs for silverware and jewellery and at the back, written in Arthur's untidy scrawl, she found some names and addresses including that of Miss Maude Greenwood, The Round House, Havering-atte-Bower, Essex. Committing it to memory, she put everything back in its place and opened the door just wide enough to make certain that there was no one about. The corridor was empty and there was no sound to be heard apart from the odd creak of ageing timbers. Breathing a sigh of relief, Irene crept down the backstairs and let herself out of the house.

When she arrived home, she was horrified to find the shop door open. At first she thought that someone must have broken in, but there was no obvious sign of forced entry. She stepped inside. 'Hello?'

'Is that you, Renie?'

She breathed a sigh of relief at the sound of her father's voice. 'Yes, Pa.'

He came thundering down the stairs and for a moment she thought he was going to upbraid her for closing the shop, but he wrapped his arms around her in a bear-like hug. 'Pack some clothes, enough for a day or two. You're going to your sister's until I get back.'

'What do you mean? Why am I to go and stay with Emmie?'

'I have to go away on business, my duck. You'll be safer in Love Lane than you would be if I left you here on your own.'

'What sort of business?' Irene watched him shrug on his greatcoat. He seemed to be avoiding meeting her gaze and she was instantly suspicious. 'You're not doing a job for the Sykes brothers, are you, Pa?'

He shot her a quick glance and then turned away to ram his bowler hat on his head. 'Never you mind, Renie. The less you know the better.'

'You promised you wouldn't get involved with their goings-on.' Irene caught him by the coat sleeve. 'Please don't do this, Pa. I'll use the money you gave me to restock the shop and we can live on the takings, just like we used to.'

'You don't understand, poppet. I owe Vic a small fortune, and it's the only way I can pay him off. I want you to trust me, Renie. Do as I say, there's a good girl.'

Irene bit her lip. 'You know that Inspector Kent is having the gang watched. He's just waiting for a chance to arrest them all, and that will include you if you're not careful. Please don't do this.'

He dropped a kiss on the top of her head. 'Lock the shop up, ducks. Go to Emmie's and I'll come for you as soon as it's all over.'

'As soon as what is over, Pa? What have you got yourself into?'

'Nothing for you to worry about, my angel, but if things go wrong I want you to look after your mother.' He moved swiftly to the door and wrenched it open. He paused for a moment, glancing over his shoulder.

'You know I'd never do anything really bad, don't you, Renie?'

She nodded silently as she watched him walk out of the door. She had a terrible feeling that she might never see him again, and yet she knew that it was useless to try to dissuade him from his purpose. Billy Angel was a stubborn man. She ran to the door in time to see him disappearing round the corner into Cheapside. Suddenly he seemed to her like one of Artie's lead soldiers, marching into battle; a gallant figure but very much misguided and doomed to be on the losing side.

She brushed tears away from her eyes with the back of her hand as she stood, undecided as to what to do next. Should she run straight to Inspector Kent at Old Jewry and tell him that the Sykes brothers were planning something desperate? She abandoned the idea almost immediately. To do so would immediately incriminate her father, and she had no definite information to give Kent. Her instinct was to remain in the shop and await Pa's return, but there was Artie to consider. The police were already searching for him, and it would not be too long before they traced him to Essex, if indeed that was where he had gone.

A cold east wind sent a shower of copper and gold leaves tumbling from the plane tree, and something startled the rooks into an angry protest of cawing and flapping wings. Irene closed the shop door and went upstairs to pack a few necessities into a canvas bag, but the plan forming in her head did not include a visit to Love Lane. She paused by the oak chest and then knelt down to open it. Jim's old clothes lay on top where she had left them. For all she knew, Kent's men might be keeping a watch on her as well as Pa, and she had no intention of leading them to Arthur.

Half an hour later, feeling horribly self-conscious to be dressed like a boy in broad daylight, Irene left the shop, locking the door behind her. She had emptied the till and she reckoned she had enough money for her train fare to the station closest to her destination and possibly for the hire of a cab to Havering. She hitched her pack over her shoulder and adopted a boyish stride as she headed into Cheapside, where she caught an omnibus to Shoreditch station. Her heart was thudding away inside her chest as she walked up to the ticket office. The rheumy-eyed representative of the Eastern Counties Railway blew his nose on a piece of oily-looking rag, sneezed several times, and informed her that Romford was probably her best bet. She purchased a return ticket and following his instructions, given between racking coughs and wiping his nose, she went to the platform where an engine was hissing steam like a giant prehistoric monster.

The third class compartment was almost full but Irene eventually found a seat squashed between a ruddy-cheeked man wearing a billy-cock hat, moleskin trousers and gaiters who kept dozing off and leaning on her shoulder and a middle-aged countrywoman who clutched an empty wicker basket and seemed unwilling to put it on the rack above their heads. Every time the train lurched over the points or rounded a bend, they swayed against her, almost crushing the breath from her lungs. In her boyish persona, Irene merely grinned and did not complain. The woman appeared to have taken a liking to her and chattered incessantly, boasting that she had taken a basketful of eggs to market and earned two shillings, which judging by her gin-tainted breath she had already spent in the pub. Having run out of things to say about herself, she then turned her attention to Irene, firing questions at her. How old was he? What was his destination? And what were his parents thinking in allowing a young lad to travel alone by train? Was anyone meeting him? Irene answered in a series of monosyllables and grunts, praying silently that the nosey old woman would either get off at the next station or fall asleep like the man on her right, who was now snoring loudly and grunting like a stuck pig.

After suffering almost an hour of this, Irene was only too glad to alight from the train at Romford. She was carried out past the ticket collector on a surging crowd of travellers eager to reach home, but just how she was going to get to Havering she had no idea. The white face of the station clock showed half past four and it was already dark. A smoky haze hung above the bare branches of a hawthorn hedge, dimming the light from the street lamps to a yellowish glow. The air smelt of hot cinders and damp earth, and the ground shook as the great iron beast shunted off towards its final destination. Her fellow passengers had vanished into the gloom, leaving Irene standing alone and wondering what to do next when a horse-drawn box wagon trundled to a halt outside the station entrance. The driver climbed down from his seat, barely giving her a glance as he hefted several heavy-looking sacks off the wagon and into the station.

When he returned after depositing the last of his load he paused for a moment, staring hard at Irene. 'What? You still here, boy?' His voice was gruff and his accent was strange to Irene's ears, but he did not sound unfriendly.

'I got to get to a place called Havering-atte-Bower, mister. Are you going that way, by any chance?'

The man tipped his cap to the back of his head. 'That's a fair way, young man.'

'I can pay.' Irene put her hand in her breeches pocket and jingled the few coins that were left after paying her train fare.

'What's your name, son?'

'I'm Jim . . .' Irene hesitated for a moment. 'Jim Smith.'

'I go by the name of Farmer Mason, but you can call me Gaffer.' He eyed Irene thoughtfully. 'You're powerful young to be travelling alone.'

Irene did not like the way the conversation was going. She had always thought that country people were slow on the uptake, but this old bloke seemed to be all there and back again. He seemed to suspect that something was amiss, and he was probing for answers. She raised her chin and looked him straight in the eye. 'Either you can give me a ride to where I want to go or not.'

'All right. No need to get in a state. I can take you as far as Noak Hill. That's where my farm is.' He climbed onto the driver's seat and held out his hand. 'Hop up beside me, and you can keep me company.'

Irene hesitated for a moment, but then she realised she had very little choice. This was not London. There were no hansom cabs or hackney carriages tooling around looking for custom, and she did not want to be stranded all night at the station. She took his hand and flinched at the touch of his work-roughened skin.

'You've got hands like a girl,' Farmer Mason said, chuckling as he helped her clamber up beside him. 'I'll bet you've never done a hard day's work in your whole life, boy. Are you running away from home then?'

'No, I ain't.' She settled herself as comfortably as she could on the hard wooden seat. 'I'm going to visit my aunt in Havering. She lives at the Round House. D'you know it, mister?'

'No, can't say I do, but I don't often go that way. What's her name?'

'Miss Greenwood.'

'Now I have heard of that lady. A bit eccentric she is by all accounts. I seen her in Romford market selling day-old chicks and bantam eggs. Dresses like a bloke she does, and smokes a clay pipe. And her supposed to be a lady too.'

Irene digested this in silence. She had not given much thought to Arthur's Aunt Maude until now. But what did it matter if the old lady was a bit strange? If she had taken Artie in, then she could act as weird as she liked.

Irene clamped her hand on her cap as the sturdy shire horse plodded forward at the flick of Farmer Mason's whip. Her hair was a sure giveaway, and to lose her cap would be a disaster. As they turned into the main market-place, the stallholders were just packing up for the day. Their voices rang out above the deep lowing of cattle being driven from their pens and the grunting of pigs as they were loaded into farm carts. The smell of animal dung and damp straw filled the frosty air, and naphtha flares sent bright pools of light flooding onto the cobblestones.

Farmer Mason acknowledged shouts and friendly insults from his fellow farmers with a cheery wave of his hand. They left the town behind them, plunging into the darkness of the country road. Here and there along the way there were groups of cottages with pale shafts of light streaming from their windows. Curls of smoke billowed into the night sky and above them countless stars twinkled with jewel brightness. Irene tucked her cold hands into the jacket pockets and wished she had her shawl to wrap around her shoulders.

'How far now, Gaffer?' she asked, making an effort to control her chattering teeth.

'A couple of miles. Old Tom will start to pick up a bit when he thinks he's near to home.' Farmer Mason stuck a clay pipe between his teeth and handed the reins to Irene. 'Hold him steady while I light up.'

She took the leather straps nervously. She had never held reins before but perhaps the old horse would not realise that she was a complete novice. She glanced sideways at Farmer Mason as he filled his pipe from a baccy pouch and struck a match on the side of the wagon. It flared and then hissed as it ignited the tobacco. Fragrant plumes of smoke puffed into the air and he emitted a satisfied sigh as he took the reins from her hands. 'You've never done that afore, I'll warrant,' he said conversationally. 'What sort of life have you led, boy?'

'Not your sort, that's for certain. I'm London born and bred. I ain't sure I like the country-side that much. It's dark and it's cold, and it smells funny.'

Farmer Mason's great gust of laughter caused Old Tom to prick his ears, and he quick-ened his pace to a near trot. 'That's good country air you can smell, son.'

'Maybe, but it's awful cold here. It's much warmer in the city.'

'It is a bit chilly. What we need is something to warm our bellies. We'll stop at the Ship Inn for a hot rum toddy. You can treat me by way of payment for the ride, if you feel so inclined.'

Irene fingered the coins in her pocket and

was about to make an excuse, but she was too late. The horse seemed to know his way, and obviously this was a normal stopping place. The wagon drew to a halt outside a black and white timbered inn, and Farmer Mason climbed down with surprising agility. 'Stay, Tom,' he murmured as he placed a nosebag over his horse's head. 'Good boy. I won't be long.'

'You'd think the animal understood,' Irene said as she leapt to the ground.

'Old Tom knows every word I say. Now come along, Jim. I can taste that toddy already.'

Inside the pub, the low beamed ceiling was yellowed with many years of tobacco smoke and a log fire crackled in the inglenook where men sat chatting over their pints of ale. Irene fingered the coins in her pocket and reluctantly handed over a silver sixpence to her travelling companion. He pointed to an oak settle by the window and told her to take a seat while he went to the bar. Two men leaning against the counter greeted him like an old friend. They exchanged a few jocular words, slapping each other on the back and guffawing loudly, and then one of them shot a curious glance at Irene. 'Hey, Gaffer. You haven't been picking up waifs and strays, have you?'

Farmer Mason grinned and shook his head. 'Just giving the lad a lift as far as my place.

He's on his way to Havering to see his Aunt Greenwood. You know, the odd lady who lives in the Round House.'

The landlord placed a foaming tankard on the counter. 'That's the second time today I've heard her name mentioned.'

'I'll have two hot rum toddies,' Farmer Mason said, placing Irene's sixpence on the bar counter. 'And who was that then, asking about the lady in question?'

The landlord slid the sixpence into the till and reached for the rum bottle. 'It was the police. It seems they're looking out for one of her relations. A bad lot, I'm told. One of them gangsters from the East End.'

There was a sudden silence, as all eyes turned on her and Irene leapt to her feet. 'They ain't looking for me, mister. Honest, I'm no gangster.'

Chapter Nine

She hesitated, poised for flight, but the silence was broken by a bellow of laughter from Farmer Mason. 'Just look at him standing there all white and shaking like a girl. Is that your idea of an East End villain?'

A murmur ran through the taproom followed by a ripple of amusement. Farmer Mason slapped his hands on his thighs and tears of mirth ran down his cheeks. 'Sit down, boy. No one could mistake you for a gangster unless they was deaf, dumb and blind.'

Irene's knees gave way beneath her and she collapsed onto the settle. She managed a weak smile. 'I should hope not, Gaffer.'

The laughter died away and Irene found herself largely ignored as the men's conversation turned to topics more close to their hearts.

A young barmaid brought her a rummer filled with hot toddy. 'So you're the boy from London. Do you know any of them bad men up there?'

'Nah! Not me.'

'Oh, you're no use then.' The girl flounced

off to collect empty tankards, leaving Irene to sip the heady brew in peace, but her heart was still thumping against her ribs. If the police had traced Arthur to Miss Greenwood's house, she would be too late. He might already have been arrested and taken back to London. She swallowed the drink in a couple of gulps, and as the strong spirit warmed her stomach she began to feel more optimistic. She might still be in time, but she would have to make haste. She was about to ask if anyone might be travelling as far as Havering-atte-Bower when Farmer Mason put his glass down and said goodnight to his friends. He strode over to the door, beckoning Irene to follow him. 'C'mon, lad. We'd best be on our way. I think there's a hint of snow in the air.'

Half an hour later Old Tom pulled the wagon into the farmyard. It seemed to Irene that they had been travelling for hours and it must be close to midnight, but when Farmer Mason ushered her into the kitchen she saw by the clock on the wall that it was just half past seven. Mrs Mason, a thin scrawny little woman with a neck like a plucked chicken, was ladling soup into bowls from a black pan resembling a witch's cauldron. Seated round the table were six children ranging in age from a toddler of about two to a strapping lad of fifteen or sixteen.

'You're late, husband,' Mrs Mason said angrily. 'The children have almost finished their supper. I was thinking that you must have suffered a broken axle or something of the kind, but I can tell by stink of your breath that you stopped off at the pub.'

Ignoring this accusation, Farmer Mason pushed Irene forward. 'This here is Jim. He's on his way to Havering but I said he could stay here tonight since it's too far to walk and with snow threatening.'

Mrs Mason cast an accusing look at Irene. 'I hope you wasn't imbibing strong liquor, my boy. It's the work of the devil.'

'No, ma'am.'

'Well, take a seat at the table then,' Mrs Mason said, pointing the ladle at a vacant chair.

Irene sat down next to a scruffy little girl who sniffed the air like a bloodhound. 'You was telling whoppers, boy. I can smell rum on your breath.'

'Shut up, Cora.' The girl seated on Irene's left scowled at her younger sister. 'Take no notice of her, Jim. She's only ten. I'm fourteen.' She fluttered her eyelashes.

Cora poked her tongue out. 'You're not fourteen until January, Hilda.'

Irene crammed a hunk of bread into her mouth. It was hot from the oven and spread thickly with farmhouse butter. It tasted good and she was starving. She applied herself to eating the savoury soup, ignoring the children's chatter. Most of them had finished eating and she could feel six pairs of eyes staring at her.

'You should take you cap off indoors,' Mrs Mason said, sniffing. 'It's bad manners to keep it on. Didn't your mother teach you that, boy?'

'I'm an orphan,' Irene said, keeping her head down. 'And I got a bald spot. It might be catching. I have to keep me cap on or I'll die of lung fever.'

'What nonsense. George, don't stare.' Mrs Mason clipped her son round the ear and she glared across the table at his younger brother, who had begun to giggle. 'Don't think I can't reach you, Ronald Mason, because I've got a long arm and a strong hand.' She looked round the table. 'If you've all finished you can go into the yard and wash your hands and faces ready for bed.'

The younger children rose in silence and marched out into the farmyard, leaving Hilda and the eldest boy to clear the table. Irene gave up her plate reluctantly. She would have welcomed another helping of soup but she did not like to ask anything of the fierce woman sitting opposite her. Farmer Mason ate his meal in silence and with a good appetite. He seemed unperturbed by his wife's sharp manner and quick temper, or perhaps he simply found it easier to let her vent her feelings without comment.

Irene cleared her throat. 'Thank you for my supper. It was very good.' She rose from her chair. 'If you could just tell me how to get to Havering from here, I'll be on my way.'

'You'll never find your way in the dark,' Farmer Mason said, glancing up from his plate. 'Best wait until morning.'

'Ta, but I really need to get there tonight.'

Mrs Mason rose to her feet. 'My husband is right. You'd be lost before you'd walked a hundred yards. You can sleep with the boys and leave first thing in the morning. We're early risers.'

'Ta very much.' Irene struggled to think of a plausible reason for not sharing a bed with the boys, but perhaps it was safer than doubling up with Hilda and Cora. It would be almost impossible to keep her secret from the girls. Hilda would have the cap off her head and the rest of her clothes too, if her flirtatious glances were anything to go by. Irene surmised that the boys would barely notice if she kept her head covered. She managed what she hoped was a grateful smile. 'You're very kind, missis.'

'Get along with you and your London ways.' Mrs Mason rose from the table, flapping her apron at Hilda and George. 'Clear the table and take Jim with you to the pump. Nobody goes to bed dirty in my house.' She shooed them out into the yard where the younger children were crowded around the trough, splashing and flicking water at each other seemingly impervious to the cold. Irene was reluctant to join in but Cora flapped a wash rag at her. 'Let's see your bald patch then, Jim.'

'You'll catch the disease,' Irene said gruffly.

'Leave him be.' Hilda gave her sister a shove that send her tumbling backwards into a pile of wet straw. 'Serves you right, you pest.'

Cora began to howl and George bent down to pull her to her feet. He shot a withering look at Hilda. 'Say you're sorry, or I'll tell Mum.'

Hilda hid behind Irene. 'Shan't.'

Irene was tempted to bang their stupid heads together, but she managed to restrain herself. What would Jim have said in similar circumstances? She ruffled Cora's curls. 'No harm done, eh?'

Cora wiped her nose on her sleeve, leaving a snail-trail of mucus on the thin cotton. 'She's a bully.'

George slapped Irene on the back. 'Sisters! Who'd have 'em?'

'Yeah! They're nothing but trouble.' Irene nudged him in the ribs, chuckling and deepening her voice. 'Hey, it's blooming freezing. Do we have to stay out here all night?'

George curled his lip. 'You London folk are soft. You'd best go into the house then, city boy, while me and Ronnie go and lock the hens up for the night.'

'Lock the hens up?'

George thrust his face close to hers. 'Or the foxes will get them. Don't you know nothing?'

Irene bit back a sharp retort. 'I never been in the countryside afore, but I bet you wouldn't be so cocky if you was on your own in London with sewer rats the size of dogs and cutthroats lurking round every corner.'

George shrugged his shoulders and stomped off in the direction of some wooden outhouses with Ronnie trotting after him.

Hilda linked her arm through Irene's. 'C'mon, Jim. I'll show you where you're going to sleep tonight.'

Irene pulled her arm free with a grunt. 'It ain't bedtime yet.'

'It's near eight o'clock. We always goes to bed at eight, and gets up at five. Don't you do that in London?'

'Nah!' Irene said, swaggering towards the kitchen door with her thumbs tucked in her belt. 'We goes to bed at midnight or later if we feels like it, and don't get up until dinnertime.'

'I'd like that,' Cora said enthusiastically. 'Maybe I'll come to London and see you one day.'

'Don't pay no heed to her,' Hilda said, elbowing Cora out of the way. 'She's just a kid. You and me is grown up compared to her, Jim.'

Irene would have loved to cut and run at that point, but sleety rain had begun to fall and the air was so cold that each breath she took was like swallowing shards of ice. She had no alternative but to follow the girls into the welcome warmth of the farmhouse kitchen. As soon as the boys returned from securing the livestock Mrs Mason packed them all off to bed, and Irene followed the children up a narrow flight of stairs to a room beneath the eaves.

In the light of Hilda's candle stub, Irene was mortified to discover that the brothers and sisters shared this space, which was little more than a draughty loft. She could see chinks of moonlight filtering through gaps in the roof tiles and a cold wind whistled around her ears. It appeared that the boys slept top to toe on one straw-filled palliasse and the two girls shared another.

'You can sleep with me and Cora if you want,' Hilda said with an arch smile. 'You'll not get a wink of sleep crowded in with our smelly brothers.'

'That's all right,' Irene replied, edging away from her. 'I'll sleep on the floor. I don't care.'

'Suit yourself.' Tossing her head, Hilda began unlacing her boots. 'Get into bed, Cora, and warm my side up or I'll pull your hair.'

Cora uttered a cry of fright and dived into bed, pulling the covers over her head.

Hilda sloughed off her print frock like a snake shedding its skin and she slithered beneath the thin coverlet, patting the space beside her with an inviting smile. 'There's room for you here, Jim?'

Irene shook her head. 'No, ta. I said I'd sleep on the floor.'

'Well, you ain't coming in with us,' George said firmly. 'You city folk have fleas and lice. If she wants to cuddle up to you that's Hilda's business, but I'd rather sleep with the pigs than share her bed.'

Irene did not respond to his insult or the suggestion that she might sleep with the girls. She leaned against the wall and slid to a sitting position, wrapping her arms around her knees. The candle had guttered and gone out but at least the almost complete darkness hid the fact that she was still wearing her cap. She was cold and cramped and she longed to stretch out in a warm bed. Judging by the rhythmic sounds of the Mason children's breathing, they had all fallen asleep almost as soon as their heads touched their pillows. The temperature seemed to be dropping still further, and she could hear strange rustlings in the exposed rafters above her head. It could be mice or rats, Irene thought, peering nervously into the gloom. Or even worse, it could be bats. When something skittered across the floor passing just inches away from her she had finally had enough. Forgetting all about Hilda's suggestive behaviour, she crawled into bed beside her and curled up in a ball.

When Irene opened her eyes it was still dark and for a moment she thought she was back in her own bed at home, but as the mists of sleep cleared from her brain she remembered where she was. Someone was breathing down her neck and she could feel a warm hand caressing her belly. It took her only a few seconds to realise that Hilda was awake and it was her hand that was sliding downwards to where she expected to find Jim's manhood. 'Leave me be,' Irene hissed as she rolled out of bed almost taking Hilda with her. 'What d'you think you're doing?'

Hilda made a futile attempt to grab her hand. 'Don't go. I know how to pleasure a fellow; I done it a dozen times or more in the barn with Davey Tanner.'

'I'm not like that.' Irene clambered to her feet. She straightened her cap, which had come askew in the night but luckily had stayed on her head, and she rearranged her clothes. 'You'll end up in trouble, my girl,' she said severely.

'I might be already for all I know.' Hilda pulled her shift up to expose her bare legs. 'Davey will have to marry me, so what's the difference if I does it with someone good-looking like you?'

Irene backed towards the doorway, praying silently that George was a heavy sleeper and would not wake up to defend his sister's maidenhood, although judging by Hilda's performance that had been lost long ago. Ignoring the soft pleading sounds from the bed, Irene let herself out of the room and tiptoed down the stairs to the kitchen. Mrs Mason was on her hands and knees riddling the ashes in the range. She looked up, frowning. 'What are you doing creeping about the house this early, boy?'

'I must be on my way, missis.'

'You was going to rob us. I've heard all about the goings-on in London town. Mr Mason told me that one of them gangsters has come this way and the police are searching for the villain.'

'No, truly I wasn't. As a matter of fact I was going to leave some money for my bed and board.' Irene took a threepenny bit from her pocket and put it on the kitchen table.

Mrs Mason scrambled to her feet and picked up the coin. 'Well, that's only fair. You'd best get going then.'

'If you could just point me on my way?'

'Turn left at the farm gates and walk to the main road. Turn right and keep on for a couple of miles or so, then take the next right turn. You can't go wrong.'

After walking for over an hour there was still no sign of dawn, and Irene had stumbled into so many potholes overflowing with ice-cold water that she had lost count. She was thankful that the snow had held off, but her boots were thick with mud, and she had to stop every now and again to scrape off the sticky matting of wet earth and rotting leaves. She came across the main road eventually, although it was little more than a country lane overhung by trees with their interlaced branches forming a dark tunnel. She was not entirely sure that she was going in the right direction for Havering, and she had not seen anyone who might be able to tell her the way. She trudged onwards for what seemed like hours. Her feet were sore, and although there was not much more than a change of clothes in her canvas bag it seemed to grow heavier by the mile.

At last she came to a right hand turn and she almost cried with relief when in the first streaky green light of dawn she saw a signpost pointing to Havering-atte-Bower. At least she was on the right track now, and she stopped by the roadside to munch the crust of bread that Mrs Mason had seen fit to give her when she left the farmhouse. It was a bit stale, but tasted good and she was too hungry to be fussy. As soon as she had eaten, she started off again. The stormy night had given way to a pearly dawn and a mist hung over the neat hedgerows and fields. Cows chewed the cud as they lined up at a farm gate, their hides steaming in the cold air as they waited for the cowman to collect them for milking. The air was sharp with the unfamiliar country smells of cow dung and damp earth, but it was not altogether unpleasant.

In the distance Irene could hear sounds of the village coming to life: the striking of a church clock, the clip-clopping of horses' hooves and the rumble of cartwheels. There were a few scattered cottages now, and wisps of smoke from their chimneys curled upwards into a sky that was the colour of a duck's egg. She could hear the creaking of a handle as an unseen person lowered a bucket into a well, and the muffled splash as it hit the water. A cockerel was strutting about on the roof of a barn, stopping every now and then to flap its wings and screech cock-a-doodle-do.

Somewhere in the distance someone was chopping wood. She could hear the rhythmic blows of the axe and the splintering of wood.

At last, rounding a sharp bend in the lane, she saw what could only be Miss Greenwood's home, the Round House. Set in neat gardens on three sides, the house was more hexagonal than round, but it was impressive nonetheless. The white stucco walls glowed pink in the rays of the rising sun, and the small-paned sash windows glinted and winked at her like an old friend smiling a greeting.

Irene stopped for a moment to catch her breath, and was about to cross the road to knock on the blue-painted front door when a strange-looking person strode round the side of the house. At first Irene thought it was a workman or a farm labourer, but on closer inspection she realised that although the curious apparition wore breeches, gaiters and boots, it possessed a deep bosom and had long grey hair escaping from a battered felt hat. The person was definitely female even though she walked like a man and had a clay pipe clenched beneath her teeth. It was then that Irene recalled Farmer Mason's description of the eccentric Maude Greenwood.

'Excuse me,' Irene called. 'Miss Greenwood?'

'Who wants her?' The voice was gruff, but feminine for all that.

'Miss Greenwood, I am looking for Arthur.'

'He's not here. I told the police that yesterday. I don't know who you are, boy, but I'm advising you to be on your way or I'll set the dogs on you.'

Irene looked around and could not see anything larger than a robin perched on a nearby branch, singing its little heart out. She cleared her throat, speaking in her normal voice. 'I'm not a boy. I'm Artie's friend, Irene. If he's here I must see him.'

Miss Greenwood took the pipe from her mouth and exhaled a puff of smoke from her thin lips. 'Come closer. I can't see you properly from that distance.'

Irene hurried across the lane and stood by the gate. 'Is he here? Please tell me.'

'You say you're a girl and a friend of my nephew's, but you could be a police spy for all I know. Take your cap off.'

Irene dragged her cap off her head and shook out her hair. 'There, you see. Just because I wear breeches doesn't make me any more of a boy than you are a man.'

For a moment she thought she had offended the strange lady, but Miss Greenwood threw back her head and roared with laughter. 'So you're Irene. Arthur's told me all about you and that rascally father of yours. Come inside.' She unlatched the gate and held it open, allowing Irene to walk past her into the neatly kept garden with box hedges surrounding beds of late-flowering bronze chrysanthemums and clumps of misty-mauve Michaelmas daisies. A pair of small brown and white Jack Russell terriers came hurtling round the side of the house, barking furiously until a word from their mistress silenced them. They approached Irene cautiously, sniffing her boots and staring up at her with button-bright eyes. She bent down to pat their heads. 'Good dogs.'

'The boys like you,' Miss Greenwood said gruffly. 'That's good enough for me.' She strode off in the direction from which she had first appeared, leading the way round to the back of the house where a half-glassed door had been left ajar. She went inside and Irene followed her into a small room lined with shelves on which scarlet geraniums sheltered from the onslaught of winter. Muddy boots, pattens and galoshes lay in a pile on the floor, together with yellowed newspapers and an assortment of small garden tools.

The smell of hot bread wafted through from the kitchen and Irene could just make out a plump woman wearing a white pinafore, with her sleeves rolled up as she pummelled dough on the scrubbed pine table. Miss Greenwood entered the room with the dogs trotting at her heels. She turned to Irene and beckoned to her. 'Don't loiter in the doorway; I won't bite. That's a job for my boys, but they only go for policemen and people they don't like. Come in and Martha will give you some breakfast. I expect you're hungry. Boys are always hungry. Oh no, sorry, you're a girl. Well, come in anyway.'

'Who is this?' Martha demanded, glaring suspiciously at Irene.

'Never you mind, you nosey old crow,' Miss Greenwood said sternly. 'Feed the girl and give her a cup of tea while I finish what I set out to do and see to the livestock.'

Irene stood by the door, clutching her cap in her hands. 'I'd like to see Artie first if you don't mind.'

'She could have been sent by the police,' Martha said, thumping the dough with her floury fists. 'She's not from round these parts.'

Miss Greenwood clapped her hands slowly. 'Go to the top of the class. Of course she's not from here, you silly woman. She's a Londoner. The world doesn't stop at Romford, you know.'

'Really, I would like to see Arthur,' Irene said hastily. The relationship between the two women seemed so volatile that she was afraid the argument might escalate into outright war. 'If it's no trouble.'

Miss Greenwood went to the fire and knocked the ash from her pipe. 'He's not well, you know.' Taking a tobacco jar from the mantelshelf, she proceeded to fill the bowl of the pipe and lit it with a spill from the fire. In between puffs she stared thoughtfully at Irene. 'He went down with a chill on the first night here, but it's nothing to worry about.'

'Says you,' Martha murmured darkly. 'I'd send for the doctor if it was my nephew out of his head with fever.'

'Well he ain't,' Miss Greenwood said tersely. 'Go and see him, girl. He'll perk up I'm sure when he sees a friendly face. One look at Martha's vinegar features and the milk turns sour.'

'Haven't you got anything better to do than bait me, Miss Maude?' Martha demanded, punching the lump of dough.

'I'm going, you old warhorse,' Miss Greenwood retorted amicably. 'I'll leave you to look after Arthur's young friend.' She left the kitchen with the dogs trotting at her heels.

Martha seemed to have forgotten Irene's existence, or else she was deliberately ignoring her, and Irene struggled to curb her annoyance. 'Er, Miss Martha, if you could just tell me where to find Artie, please? I won't trouble you no further.'

'I still say that he needs the doctor. You might be able to convince the stubborn old fool, but she won't listen to me.'

'Just tell me where he is.'

'Hiding him in the cellar when the police came wouldn't have done him much good. I told her she should turn him over to them. If he's done wrong he should be punished, but she says he's her own flesh and blood and anyway she can't abide the police. She don't take to people and they don't take to her. I reckon I'm her only friend. We get along fine.'

Irene wasn't going to be drawn into this and she forced her lips into a smile. 'I'm sure. Now Arthur is – where?'

Martha jerked her head in the direction of a doorway on the far side of the kitchen. 'Through there, up the stairs to the second floor and it's the door facing you. Don't be surprised if he don't recognise you. I don't think he'd know his own mother right now.'

Following her directions, Irene left the kitchen and found herself in a hallway with a cantilevered staircase rising in a spiral through the centre of the house. She could see up to the top floor where light flooded down from a domed window in the roof. The polished oak stair treads echoed to the sound of her footsteps as she ran up two flights of stairs to the galleried landing. She entered the room, blinking as her eyes grew accustomed to the darkness. A glimmer of light shone through the curtains and she went over to the window to draw them back. The pale November sun flooded the small room, which was sparsely furnished with a brass bedstead, an oak washstand and a tallboy. She moved closer to the bed, where Arthur lay tossing and turning and muttering feverishly. His dark curls clung damply to his forehead and his skin was pearled with beads of sweat.

'Arthur,' Irene whispered. 'Artie, can you hear me?' When there was no response, she went to the washstand and tipped water from the jug into the bowl. Taking a flannel from the towel rail, she dampened it and went back to the bed to bathe his face. It was obvious that he was very poorly indeed, and Martha had been quite right: Arthur was in desperate need of professional attention. She did not want to leave him in this state, but she had little alternative. She thought of ringing the bell for Martha, but decided against it. The contrary old woman would probably ignore any summons, however urgent.

Irene retraced her steps and returned to the kitchen, where Martha had cleared the table and was setting it for breakfast. She looked up as Irene entered the room. 'Well? What did I tell you?'

'You were quite right, Martha. He is very sick and needs a doctor.'

Martha's crab-apple faced cracked into a

triumphant smile. 'I knew I was right. She wouldn't believe me because she's a stubborn woman who's never had a day's illness in her whole life. Now me, I'm a martyr to me bunions and me delicate stomach. Any upset and I'm up all night with bellyache something chronic, so I know what it's like to suffer.'

'I'm sorry to hear it, but we must send for the doctor at once. Tell me where to find him and I'll go, now.'

Martha shook her head. 'Best not. You'd cause a stir in the village and no one is supposed to know that the young gent is here. If the local constable finds out he'll have his mates round here like flies round a dog turd. I'll go and you can tell her when she comes home that it was all your idea.' She waddled over to a wall rack hung with hats and outdoor garments. She selected a thick woollen shawl and wrapped it around her shoulders. 'Sit down and have some food. There's porridge in the pan on the hob and tea in the pot. If Miss Maude comes back afore I do, make sure she gets some vittles inside her. She forgets to eat unless I tell her to.' With that, Martha stalked out of the kitchen, leaving the door swinging on its hinges. Irene had little alternative but to follow her instructions and, despite everything, she enjoyed a hearty breakfast.

She had just scraped the bowl clean when Miss Greenwood breezed into the kitchen, tossing her hat onto its peg with a deft stroke. 'Where is the old crone?'

Irene rose to her feet. She was not sure how to take Maude Greenwood. She had begun to realise that her bark was definitely worse than her bite, and that her relationship with her servant was not the one portrayed by their constant sniping at each other, but she did not want to upset the lady. 'I asked her to fetch the doctor for Artie. I know I took a lot on meself, but he's really sick, Miss Greenwood. I'm afraid he might die.'

'Die? Nonsense, girl. Don't talk rubbish. We Greenwoods are made of sterner stuff than that. It's just a chill and he'll be up and about in a day or two. I don't want word to get about that he's here or we'll be swamped with policemen, poking their noses in where they don't belong.'

'Martha knows that, ma'am. She wouldn't let me go for the doctor for just that reason.'

'Oh, well, it seems that the old fool does possess a modicum of sense after all.' Maude sat down at the table and reached for the teapot. 'I expect this is stewed and undrinkable. Do you know how to brew tea, missy?'

Irene nodded her head. 'Yes'm.'

'Then please do so, and you can help me to

a bowl of porridge. If I don't eat something it will upset the old dragon and she'll nag me all day.' Maude stared at Irene, frowning. 'I like you, girl. You may call me Miss Maude.'

Irene accepted this honour with a nod of her head, and busied herself making a fresh pot of tea and serving Miss Maude with her breakfast. She kept glancing at the clock but the hands seemed to be stuck in the same position while she waited for Martha to return with the doctor. When she eventually walked through the door, followed by a small man dressed all in black, Irene could have cried with relief.

'Dr Joliffe has come,' Martha announced unnecessarily.

Maude pushed her plate away from her and rose slowly to her feet, glowering at the unfortunate physician.

'Good morning, Miss Greenwood,' he said, clearing his throat nervously. 'And what can I do for you today?'

'You can keep your own counsel about what goes on in this house for a start.' Maude leaned towards him so that her face was close to his. 'Do you understand me, you old pill-peddler?'

'You offend me, madam. I never divulge anything to anyone concerning my patients.'

'Not even if this one was on the wrong side of the law?'

Irene held her breath as the doctor hesitated for a moment.

'So it's true what they're saying in the village? You are harbouring a felon.'

Moving swiftly, Maude grabbed him by the scruff of his neck and shook him. 'Say that again and I'll take the horsewhip to you. No Greenwood was ever involved in anything illegal. D'you understand me, doctor?'

'There's no need for violence, Miss Greenwood,' he said, staggering a little as she released him. 'Lead me to the patient, Martha. I'll not stay a moment longer in the room with a madwoman.'

'Grrrrr.' Maude made a growling sound like one of her dogs and the doctor fled from the room.

As she followed Martha and the doctor up the stairs Irene was torn between concern for Arthur and amusement at Miss Maude's tactics. It seemed that Artie's aunt was not afraid of anyone or anything, and Irene felt a sneaking admiration for the tough and unconventional woman. She put all such thoughts out of her mind as they reached the sickroom and she waited anxiously while the doctor examined Arthur. Martha hovered in the doorway as if afraid of catching something, but Irene moved close to the bed. She had to swallow a lump in her throat at the sight of Arthur's hollow cheeks and waxen skin. He opened his eyes but he did not seem to recognise her.

'Tell me, doctor,' she whispered. 'Is he going to get well?'

'That I cannot say with any degree of certainty, miss.' Dr Joliffe eyed her curiously. 'Are you related to Miss Greenwood by any chance?'

Irene had almost forgotten her boyish garb, and if the situation had not been so serious she might have smiled. As it was she merely shook her head. 'No, doctor. I am Arthur's friend from London. Is there anything you can do to make him better?

He shook his head. 'Not very much, I fear. He must be kept quiet and given sips of water if he will not take anything else. I'll bleed him, and then we will have to wait until the fever breaks. It could go either way, so you must be prepared. Now I suggest that you ladies leave the room while I apply the leeches. I don't want either of you swooning over my patient.'

Chapter Ten

After the doctor had left, Irene and Martha returned to the kitchen where they found Maude pacing the floor with a clay pipe clenched between her teeth and the dogs at her heels. 'Well?' she demanded, coming to an abrupt halt and taking the pipe from her mouth. 'What did the doctor say?'

'Arthur is very poorly,' Irene said gently. 'The doctor bled him.'

'And he left by the front door,' Martha added. 'You frightened the poor man to death with your antics.'

'Joliffe is a silly old fool, but I suppose he knows what he's doing.' Maude stamped her foot and the dogs backed away, showing the whites of their eyes. 'Hell and damnation! I blame my brother for Arthur's condition. If he hadn't been so hard on the boy, forcing him into a trade that he had not the heart for, none of this would have happened.' She glared at Irene. 'You will stay and nurse him back to health, of course.'

It was a statement rather than a question

and it took Irene off guard. She had not thought past the simple act of warning Arthur that Kent's men were looking for him, and even in that she had been too late. 'I – I suppose I could stay for a day or two, if you don't mind.'

'Whether I mind or not doesn't matter. I'm no good in the sickroom and Martha has too much on her hands already. Arthur needs proper care.'

Martha had followed Irene into the kitchen, and was silent for once as she took the hot loaves from the oven. Maude rounded on her. 'Have you nothing to say on the matter? It's not often that you are lost for words, Martha Marchant.'

'So you do remember my name then?' Martha said, curling her lip. She cocked her head on one side, addressing herself to Irene. 'It's usually "you old crow" or "hey, you".'

Irene glanced nervously at Miss Greenwood, half expecting a row to ensue, but to her relief Miss Maude seemed to find Martha's words amusing and she chuckled. 'Shut up, you old crow. You know I rely on you entirely.'

'It's not always this pleasant in the Round House,' Martha said, winking at Irene, 'but if you're willing to stay, you can make up the bed in the dressing room next to young Arthur.'

'No!' Maude said firmly. 'It's too small and cramped. Where are your manners, Martha? The young lady will have the rose room while she's a guest in my house.'

Martha opened her mouth and then closed it again, and her eyes rounded in apparent astonishment. 'The rose room – are you sure?'

'For the Lord's sake, woman, haven't I just said so?'

Shrugging her shoulders, Martha turned to Irene. 'So you will remain here until the boy is out of danger?'

Irene hesitated. She had not expected to be away for long, nor had she thought to leave a note telling Pa where she had gone. If he returned and found her missing he would in all likelihood go to Love Lane expecting to find her there. Her prolonged and unexplained absence might start a panic, but Artie's life hung in the balance – she could not think of deserting him now. 'I'll stay until Artie is over the worst, but I must get back to London soon.'

'That's settled then,' Maude said. 'Now I've got work to do. I'll leave you two to sort things out.' She plucked her coat and hat from the rack and was gone, leaving a trail of pipe smoke in her wake.

'I'll show you to your room then,' Martha said, assuming a brisk and businesslike manner. 'But I don't go upstairs any more than I have to, not with my bunions, so don't go ringing the bell every time you want something.'

* * *

The room that Irene had been given was bright and airy. The wallpaper blossomed with pink cabbage roses entwined with a tracery of green foliage, and the curtains were made from matching material. The delightful summer garden effect was continued in the pink and green Chinese carpet with a soft pile that made Irene feel as though she were walking on air. Despite her grumbles, Martha had hefted a scuttle filled with coal up the stairs, and a fire burned brightly in the grate, its dancing flames reflecting off the highly polished brass bedstead. The rosewood dressing table and clothes press gleamed with lavender-scented beeswax polish and oil lamps with cranberry-glass shades adorned the bedside tables. Irene could imagine their rosy glow illuminating the room after dark.

This was a room fit for a princess and as she caught sight of her reflection in the cheval mirror she felt grubby and out of place in such feminine surroundings. Stripping off her boyish garments Irene went over to the wash-stand and filled the china washbowl with warm water from the jug she had brought from the kitchen. Blowsy pink roses stared up at her from the bottom of the bowl and a cake of soap had been provided for her use. The sweet scent of it filled her nostrils, making her feel quite dizzy, and as she washed away the grime from two days on the road she began to feel more human.

She dressed in her own clothes and folded Jim's coarse breeches and shirt in a bundle, ready to be washed. Brushing her hair with a silver-backed brush Irene stared into the large mirror on the dressing table, revelling in the luxury of being able to see the whole of her face at one glance. The shard of looking glass on the mantelshelf at home only revealed a fraction of her features at a time, and it was fortunate that vanity was not one of her besetting sins. She had always considered herself to be the plain one in the family. Why couldn't she have been a beauty like Emmie, with silky blonde curls and a rosebud mouth?

A groan from the room next door brought her plummeting back to earth. What did her personal appearance matter when her best friend might be on his deathbed? She hurried into Arthur's room and was dismayed to find him considerably worse. His skin was the colour of parchment and he was raving wildly in his delirium. She bathed his forehead and bare torso with a damp flannel. She held his hand and talked to him in a low voice. When she found that he seemed to respond, she kept up a running commentary, saying anything that came into her head until she was hoarse and in danger of losing her voice. She left him only to go downstairs and replenish the jug with water, but Martha insisted that she sat down at the table and ate a bowl of stew. 'How is the boy?' she asked as she buttered a slice of bread and handed it to Irene.

Irene swallowed a mouthful of the delicious mutton broth. 'He's very poorly. He's out of his head with fever. I don't think that the bleeding did him much good.'

'I never trust pill-peddlers,' Martha said grimly. 'There's a wise woman who lives a mile or two outside the village. She's the one I go to when my aches and pains gets too much to bear. She makes medicine with herbs and roots and she don't charge as much as old Dr Joliffe.'

Irene was not convinced but she did not want to offend Martha. 'If he's no better by morning we might give her a try.'

'If we leave it until then it might be too late. I'll go and see her as soon as the mistress has had her dinner.'

'I – I haven't much money,' Irene said hesitantly.

'Old Biddy Thorne would sell her soul for an ounce of baccy or a poke of snuff. Don't you worry about paying, miss. Herself has ample funds but she's usually too mean to spend it. However, this is an emergency so I'll just take some of the housekeeping money and we'll argue about it later.'

Later that afternoon Irene was almost at her wit's end as Arthur grew steadily worse. His eyes were wide open as he thrashed about on the bed, but the terrifying sights which made him scream with fear were visible to his eyes alone. It was all that Irene could do to prevent him from throwing himself out of bed, and she could have cried with relief when at last Martha appeared carrying a brown glass bottle which contained a decoction of herbs from Biddy Thorne. Martha pulled the cork from the bottle with her teeth and she poured a measure into a teaspoon, handing it to Irene.

'Biddy said give him one teaspoonful every hour until the fever breaks.'

Irene eyed the thick brownish-black liquid with suspicion and she sniffed it cautiously. It smelt bitter and yet there was also a hint of liquorice and black treacle in the mixture, together with just a suspicion of brimstone.

'I'll hold his head,' Martha said, grabbing Arthur by the shoulders. He bucked and wriggled, but Martha had weight behind her and he had little strength left. 'Quick,' she urged. 'I can't hold him for long.'

Somehow Irene managed to get the spoon between his lips and most of the fearsome brew went into his mouth. He swallowed automatically and she mopped the trickle of liquid from his chin. 'There, Artie. That will make you better in no time at all.' She glanced up at Martha's set face and a shiver ran down her spine.

'I seen many go like this,' Martha said gloomily as she laid him down on the pillows. 'Once the lung fever gets them there's not much hope.'

'He's not going to die. I won't let him.' Irene took Arthur's limp hand in hers and she chafed it gently. 'See, Martha. The medicine is beginning to work. He's quieter already.'

'Or on his way out.' Martha waddled to the door. 'Just keep giving him Biddy's medicine and pray. There's nothing else we can do for him.'

Irene did pray. She had never set much store by religion, but now she prayed to whatever god there might be up in heaven to save Arthur's life. He was not a bad fellow, just a bit weak and easily led. If his father had not been such a bully, and his mother a cold and ambitious woman, maybe he would have turned out differently. She blinked the tears from her eyes and swallowed hard. Giving way to despair would not help Artie get well. She settled herself on the chair and watched him as the drug lulled him into an uneasy sleep.

She must have dozed off herself as she awakened with a start and found the room in almost total darkness. Spikes of moonlight slanted through the windowpanes, giving just enough light for her to find the box of vestas on the bedside table. She lit the oil lamp and peered anxiously at Arthur. Was it her imagination, or did he really look a little better? She laid a tentative hand on his forehead and he did not seem to be quite as hot as he had been previously. She forced another spoonful of medicine between his lips and bathed his face. He did not respond, but at least his delirious ravings had ceased. Whatever Biddy Thorne had put in her decoction, it seemed to be having some effect.

Irene left his bedside to go to the kitchen for a bite of supper and a cup of tea, after which she returned to the sickroom. She spent the night taking catnaps in the armchair by the fire, waking at the slightest sound from the bed and rising hastily to check on Arthur's progress. She tried to keep awake, but this proved more difficult than she had anticipated, and when she opened her eyes after what she had thought was a short nap she was shocked to see the first cold grey light of dawn filtering through the half-closed curtains. She rose stiffly and went over to the window to draw them and allow daylight into the room. Glancing over her shoulder, she realised that there was no movement from the bed and her heart missed a beat. Holding her breath, she crept over to the bedside, fearful of what she might find. All manner of imaginings ran through her mind. Supposing Arthur had cried out to her in the night and she had not heard? What if he had breathed his last and she had been sound asleep?

He was lying on his back with his face turned away from her, and he was very still. For a moment she was convinced that he was dead, and her hand flew to her mouth to stifle a moan of despair. Then, as if by a miracle, Arthur moved. He turned his head slowly towards her. His eyelids fluttered and opened.

'Artie. Oh, thank God. I thought you was a goner.' She laid her hand on his brow and tears flooded down her cheeks as she realised that the crisis was past. His skin was cool and his breathing regular.

'Is that really you, Irene?'

'It is me. Yes, it is.' Her voice hitched on a sob and she grabbed his hand, holding it to her cheek. 'You gave us such a fright, you silly boy.'

'Why are you crying then?' Arthur stared at her, frowning. 'Where am I? This isn't the pickle shop and it isn't my room at home.'

'Don't talk, Artie. Save your strength.' Assuming an air of authority and busying herself by straightening his tumbled bedclothes,

Irene hid her relief beneath an air of authority. 'You must rest. You've been very poorly but thank God you're on the mend now.' She plumped his pillows energetically. 'I'm going to give you another dose of medicine and then I'll go downstairs and make you a nice hot cup of tea.'

When Dr Joliffe came to see his patient, he was cautiously optimistic about Arthur's chances of making a full recovery, but he shook his head and tut-tutted when he saw the bottle of elixir that Biddy Thorne had prescribed. 'Foolish and dangerous nonsense,' he said angrily. 'Who knows what she puts in her nostrums? She might have poisoned the boy.'

Irene listened politely, but she was certain that if anything had helped to pull Arthur round it was Biddy's potion. Still mumbling into his starched shirt points, Dr Joliffe said that he would call again in a day or two and in the meantime his patient must stay in bed and rest.

Having left Arthur propped up on his pillows gazing drowsily out of the window Irene went downstairs to the kitchen. She found Miss Maude standing in the middle of the room with her hands on her hips. 'Pompous little pill-pusher. I can't abide doctors. Never could.' She turned to Irene and her eyes were still blazing. 'I won't be lectured by any man, let alone someone as self-opinionated as that old fool. He virtually accused me of using witchcraft to cure my nephew – the damn cheek of him.'

Martha stopped rolling out pastry for a piecrust. 'He was just put out because old Biddy is a better physician. The boy might have died if it wasn't for her medicine.'

'I'm glad Arthur is better, of course, but I can't stand around all day gossiping,' Maude said dismissively. She turned to Irene, giving her a hard stare. 'You will stay until he is completely recovered, won't you?'

'I must go home soon, Miss Maude. My family don't know where I am and they will be worried about me.'

'Send them a letter then. Martha will post it for you in the village.' Maude picked up her battered felt hat and rammed it on her head. 'I'll be at the smithy all afternoon. Parson needs shoeing and there's a ploughshare needs straightening out. Damn fool of a boy went over a rock the size of Canvey Island. I don't know if he's half blind or stupid, but you just can't rely on anyone these days.' She made for the back door and the dogs yapped a greeting as she stepped out into the cold November afternoon.

Puzzled by Miss Maude's last remark, Irene

turned to Martha. 'The parson needs shoeing? What does that mean?'

'Well, it ain't the vicar,' Martha replied, chuckling. 'Parson is her horse, named after the last incumbent at the vicarage who got on her wrong side. Miss Maude don't like clergymen nor doctors.'

'She doesn't seem to think much of men in general.'

'Nor most women neither.' Martha laid the pastry over a dish of meat and potato and she trimmed off the excess with deft strokes of a knife. 'You're lucky she took a fancy to you straight away. That don't happen too often, I can tell you.'

Irene's curiosity was aroused. She had thought that Miss Greenwood was simply a grumpy old woman, and rather eccentric, but now she wanted to know more. 'Why doesn't she like people, Martha? And why is she so bitter when she has a lovely home and everything she could possibly want?'

'She had a disappointment in love and a younger sister who betrayed her.'

'What happened?'

'It's something we don't talk about.'

Irene digested this in silence, watching Martha as she brushed the piecrust with beaten egg before placing the dish in the oven.

'There,' Martha said, wiping her brow with

the back of her hand. 'That's done. Hadn't you better get back to the sickroom?'

'Yes, of course, and I don't want to pry into Miss Maude's business, but did my room once belong to her sister?'

'Yes, that was Miss Dora's room. She was a lovely girl, full of life and pretty as a picture. It wasn't surprising that Miss Maude's old sweetheart fell in love with her when his first wife died.'

'That sounds like a story from a penny novelette. What happened?'

'I've said too much already. It was a long time ago and best forgotten. You mustn't mention a word of this to Miss Maude; she'd be mortified if she knew I'd told you this much.'

'I won't, I promise,' Irene said reluctantly. 'I'll take some of that broth upstairs to Artie. He might be able to manage a few mouthfuls.'

'My beef tea has been known to work miracles,' Martha said, beaming as she ladled the savoury-smelling liquid into a bowl. 'We'll soon have him back on his feet. And if you write that letter I'll take it to the post this afternoon.'

'Maybe it's not such a good idea after all,' Irene said thoughtfully. 'If the police start asking questions and they find out I'm here, they'll come back for Artie. I don't want that to happen.'

'Well, you're stuck then, aren't you? She won't let you go until young Mr Arthur has recovered, so you'd best make the most of it. Now take him that beef tea before it gets cold.'

Arthur's recovery was slow. Irene was torn between the desire to return to London and the need to make certain that he did not suffer a relapse, which Dr Joliffe warned was quite possible, especially after the patient had been dosed with goodness-knows-what, which might eventually prove to have fatal consequences. In the old days, he added darkly, Biddy Thorne would have been burned at the stake or put in the ducking stool and drowned in the village pond.

After three days, Arthur was well enough to sit in the chair by the fire for an hour or two each afternoon. It was now almost a week since Irene had left London and she was desperately worried. She could not imagine what Pa might be thinking and Ma would be worried sick if she had discovered her missing. She simply had to go home, and now that Arthur was out of danger there was really nothing to keep her here. It was almost four o'clock and Irene had brought a tray of tea to the sickroom with some of Martha's fairy cakes to tempt his appetite. She set it down on a table beside his chair and she poured the tea.

She placed one of the delicate bone china cups in his hand, and went over to the window to draw the curtains. Outside, the sky was the colour of old pewter and a heavy drenching rain was beating against the windowpanes. The lawn below was rapidly turning into a huge muddy puddle.

'Are you all right, Renie?' Arthur asked tentatively. 'You're very quiet.'

She turned to him, forcing a smile. 'I can't fool you, can I, Artie? As a matter of fact I've been wondering how to tell you this, but I really must go back to London.'

'I thought that was it, but I was afraid to ask.'

She was quick to hear the tremulous note in his voice and she hurried over to kneel by his side. 'You're well on the mend now. I wouldn't leave you if I didn't think you was over the worst, but I've left the shop all shut up and I didn't have a chance to tell Pa where I was going. Goodness knows what sort of state he'll be in by now.'

'If he's even noticed,' Arthur said with a hint of his old spirit. 'He goes away for weeks on end without a word. It'll do him good to have a taste of his own medicine.'

'Maybe, but I don't want him telling Ma that I've disappeared, or Emmie come to that.'

'And there's Inspector Kent. What will you say to him?'

'Nothing about your whereabouts, that's for sure.'

'But you were supposed to be passing on information I'd given you. He'll be wondering where you are. I don't want you getting into bother with the police because of me. I've let him down badly, and you too.'

She squeezed his fingers. 'Don't talk soft. Drink your tea and try one of Martha's cakes. They're very good.'

Arthur took one, crumbling it between his fingers and frowning. 'You must go when you please, Renie. I'm getting better all the time.'

'Are you sure, Artie? I don't want you going and having one of them relapses that the doctor talks about.'

He flashed her a weak smile. 'I'm well on the road to recovery, and you've done enough for me. I'll never forget it. I mean that.'

'Don't be daft. You'd do the same for me. We're mates, aren't we?'

'Yes, mates. I suppose that is all.'

She stared at him, angling her head. 'What does that mean?'

'Nothing. Don't take any notice of me. It's the weakness talking, and I'm just being selfish, wanting to keep you here. You go home tomorrow, Renie.'

'I will, and you'll follow me as soon as you're strong enough.'

He shook his head, avoiding her eyes and staring into the fire. 'I won't be coming back to London, Renie. There's nothing there for me now. I've missed my chance of taking the journeyman's examination this year and I'm not even sure I want to be a silversmith. Perhaps I never did and I just let the old man talk me into it. But I won't let him do that any more. In fact, I think I'd like to stay here in the country and help Aunt Maude on the farm.'

Irene sat back on her haunches, staring at him in astonishment. 'What? You working on a farm, Arthur Greenwood? You'd miss London and all its excitements too much to bury yourself in the country.'

He turned his head slowly to meet her gaze. 'If I go back to London I'll only end up like Billy. The gambling fever got into my blood and it makes me afraid. If I stay here there won't be the temptations that there are in the city, and I'll be safe from the Sykes gang.' He reached out to grasp her hand. 'You could stay here too, Renie. Send word to London and tell Billy that you've had enough of slaving away in the pickle shop, and stay here with me.'

She thought for a moment that he was joking, but there was no hint of humour in his eyes. 'There now, that's a pleasant thought, Artie, but what would your Aunt Maude say to it?'

'She must like you or she wouldn't have let you have Aunt Dora's room. My family rarely speak of her, but Mother told me the tale years ago.'

'Miss Maude has been good to me, but I can't stay. I'm a London girl through and through and this sort of life ain't for me. I must go, Artie. You do understand, don't you?'

He released her hand and his lips curved in an attempt at a smile, but his eyes were bright with unshed tears. 'I do, but if you change your mind you can always come back. We could have a good life here, girl.'

She did not pretend to misunderstand, but she hoped that his dependence on her had been brought about more by illness than a deeper emotion. She rose to her feet and, leaning over, she kissed him on the cheek. 'It wouldn't do, but I'll always love you as a friend, you know that.'

'I don't know how I'll manage without you. Stay with me. Marry me and live here in comfort and safety.'

'You know I can't do that, Artie.'

'Go back to London then. Spend the rest of your life keeping Billy out of trouble and trying to keep one step ahead of the police. It's not what I'd choose for you, but I know I can't change your mind once it's made up. I never could, but my offer is still there.'

She sensed the hurt beneath his harsh words

and she longed to give him a hug. She wanted to comfort him as she would have done when they were children, but she knew that one wrong word might give him false hope, and that would be cruel. 'You mustn't overtire yourself,' she said briskly. 'I'll leave you now so that you can get some rest, but I'll be up again later with your supper.'

She left the room without giving him a chance to argue. She needed time alone to think and restore her equilibrium. Instead of returning to the kitchen where Martha was preparing the evening meal, Irene went to her room. A waft of cold air enveloped her as she opened the door and the room was in darkness. She moved swiftly to the fireplace and went down on her knees to set a match to the kindling. Orange and crimson flames licked round twigs and dry sticks, snapping and crackling and sending sparks up the chimney. When the coals began to glow, Irene raised herself to sit in the chair by the fireside, holding her hands out to the warmth.

She glanced round the room where the flickering firelight sent shadows dancing on the walls and ceiling, and she felt a sudden strong empathy with Dora Greenwood. She wondered if that young woman had sat in this same chair all those years ago, agonising over her future as she did now. Dora had had to make a choice between her sister and her lover and that must have been heart-wrenching indeed. Irene would have liked to know more, but it seemed that the passage of time had not healed the wounds inflicted on Miss Maude and she was afraid to enquire further.

Staring into the flames, she thought about Arthur's sudden and unexpected proposal. Although she had never for a moment considered him in that light, it would be so easy to accept his offer of marriage and to stay here in the safety of Miss Maude's lovely old house far away from the stews of London, but she did not love him as he wanted to be loved. He was like a brother to her and always would be. And yet, the thought of a quiet life in the country had a certain appeal. There would be no more long hours spent behind the shop counter, or worries as to where the next meal was coming from. She would not have to worry about Pa's involvement with the Sykes brothers or his addiction to gambling, nor would she have any further contact with the City of London Police. All she had to do was to change her mind and accept Artie's proposal.

Chapter Eleven

Irene arrived home after a long and tedious journey. Miss Maude had driven her to Romford station in the farm cart, and she had paid the extra money needed to enable Irene to travel first class to Shoreditch. Touched by this generosity, Irene had been moved to give Maude a hug and a kiss on her leathery cheek. Although Miss Maude had backed away as if she had been stung by a wasp, she had not seemed too put out and had gruffly repeated her invitation to visit the Round House whenever Irene felt like a stay in the country. She had shaken Irene's hand and stomped off along the platform as the train wheezed to a halt.

Irene was tired after the long walk from Shoreditch to Wood Street. The cold smoky smell of the city filled her nostrils and clogged her lungs in sharp contrast to the fresh country air that she had left just a few hours previously. It was almost dark by the time she reached the shop and she fumbled in her pocket for the key, but when she tried to insert it in the lock she found to her horror that it did not fit. A notice had been pasted to the inside of the door, and she moved closer to read the spidery scrawl. *Under new management. Shop closed until further notice.* She took a step backwards and was horrified to see that the window was boarded up. She tried the lock again but to no avail.

She stood on the pavement, clutching the bag containing her few possessions and staring helplessly at her former home. It was as if she had awakened from a nightmare only to find that it was actually happening. She looked around, hoping to spot a familiar face, someone who might know what had been going on in her absence, and on the far side of the street she saw a constable patrolling his beat. Her first thought was to run from the law, but then she recognised the friendly face of Constable Burton. She ran across the road, dodging in and out between horse-drawn vehicles and only narrowly avoided being run down by a messenger on horseback. 'Constable Burton, stop.'

He paused, glancing over his shoulder, and a gleam of recognition lit his eyes with a warm smile. 'Miss Angel, is it you?'

She hurried to his side. 'Yes, it's me. I need your help.'

He puffed out his chest and the buttons on his uniform glinted in the light of the gas lamp. 'Happy to oblige, miss. What can I do for you?'

'Do you know what's happened to my shop? Why is it shuttered and under new management? I never agreed to such a thing.'

'Don't you know, miss?'

'I wouldn't be asking you if I did.' Irene hesitated, seeing his face fall at her sharp tone. 'I'm sorry, I didn't mean to be rude, but I've been in the country for a few days and now I've come back to find I'm locked out of my own home.'

'I'd like to help you, but it's not my place to say. Perhaps you'd best speak to the guvner about it.'

'If you know anything, please tell me.'

'I can't tell you much, but Billy – I mean, Mr Angel – was arrested last week. Like I said, miss, you'll have to see Inspector Kent if you want to know more.'

Irene stared at him in horror. 'My pa's been arrested?'

Burton ran his finger round the inside of his collar and his brow puckered with consternation. 'Like I said, miss, it's not up to me to give you that information. Is there somewhere you can go for the present? A relative or a close friend who could put you up for a while?'

'No. I mean, yes. But that doesn't matter. I must find out what's happened to my father.'

'They might be able to tell you at the police station,' Burton said reluctantly. 'I'd take you there myself but I can't leave my beat.'

Despite her agitation, Irene could not help but be touched by his obvious concern for her. She patted him on the sleeve. 'Don't worry about me, Constable. I know me way to Old Jewry.'

He looked as though he would like to say more, but he saluted her and strode off at a measured pace with his hands clasped behind his back.

Irene stared after him, stunned by the shocking news. Her father's parting words came back to her like a hammer blow and she could only hazard a guess that he had been caught red-handed doing a job with the Sykes gang. If that were true, he was in terrible trouble. As Constable Burton had said, there was only one person who could put her straight. She did not relish the thought of seeing Inspector Kent, but she had no choice. She made her way along Cheapside to the police station in Old Jewry.

The desk sergeant raised his eyebrows when she demanded to see his superior. 'I'm afraid that's impossible, miss.'

'But I must see him,' Irene insisted. 'It's a matter of life and death.'

A grim smile flickered across the officer's craggy features. 'I don't think so, miss. Tell me what the problem is and I'll see if I can help you.'

'Please, Sergeant,' Irene said with what she hoped was a persuasive smile. 'I really do need to see Inspector Kent. If you would just tell him that Miss Irene Angel is here and must see him urgently.'

'Even if I was so inclined I couldn't do that. The inspector ain't here. Put your question in writing if you must, but that's all I have to say to you.'

'But I've got to speak to him today. Please tell me where to find him.'

'I've already told you that it's out of the question, miss.'

Irene had never had hysterics in her life, but now she could feel a bubble rising in her throat which threatened to erupt into a scream. With difficulty, she forced herself to remain calm, and she fluttered her eyelashes. 'I wouldn't ask if it wasn't really important. Just tell me where he lives and I'll put a note through his door. He won't mind, honest! We're working together, you might say. He relies on me for information.' She had the satisfaction of seeing a flicker of uncertainty in the sergeant's grey eyes.

'I'd lose my job if I gave out such information, miss.'

Irene moved a little closer to the desk. 'I won't tell and it really is urgent.'

He shook his head as he scribbled something

on a sheet torn from his notebook. 'I can see I won't get rid of you until you get what you want, but if you breathe a word of this to anyone . . .'

'I won't, I promise,' Irene said, snatching the paper from his hand. 'Cross me heart and hope to die.' She reached across the counter and kissed his whiskery cheek. 'Ta, ever so. You're a darling.' She did not wait to see his reaction and she left the police station at a run, just in case he should change his mind and send one of his constables chasing after her. She did not stop until she was certain that no one was following her, and she leaned against a lamp-post, peering at the scrawled note. *6 Robin Hood Court, Robin Hood Passage, Milk Street.* She breathed a sigh of relief; it was not far away. She quickened her step with a burst of energy borne out of desperation. Kent was the only person who knew where her father was and why he had been arrested. She wouldn't put it past the ambitious police inspector to set Pa up if only to get closer to the Sykes gang. She was angry now as well as worried, and her dismay on finding the shop closed was as nothing compared to her fear for her hapless father.

She knew Milk Street well, and although she must have passed the narrow entrance to Robin Hood Passage many times before, she had never noticed it until now. The dark alleyway opened out into Robin Hood Court, which proved to be a small square surrounded on three sides by modest red-brick houses. These were the type of dwellings that might be inhabited by respectable persons of limited means such as bank clerks, printers and junior lawyers. Irene found number six easily enough and rapped on the door knocker. At first she thought that there was no one in, but as she stepped aside to peer through the window she could see the glow of a coal fire burning in the grate and there appeared to be a small figure lying on the sofa. She knocked again.

'Come in.'

The voice was faint but Irene needed no second bidding and she stepped into a narrow hallway. A steep flight of stairs rose immediately opposite the front entrance and to her left the door to the front parlour was ajar. She did not like to barge in and she tapped on the wooden panel, waiting for a reply.

'Come in.'

It was a girl's voice, light and slightly tremulous, and Irene entered cautiously, wondering if she had been given the wrong address. She found herself in a moderate-sized room with a high ceiling and one tall window overlooking the court. It was simply furnished with a dresser set against the far wall, a table and four chairs beneath the window, and a sofa drawn up close to the fireplace. Reclining on it was a fair-haired girl with a pale, heart-shaped face and bright blue eyes. She smiled apologetically. 'I am afraid I cannot get up to greet you.'

Irene cleared her throat nervously. 'I – I'm sorry to disturb you. I think I may have come to the wrong house.'

The girl's smile faded. 'Oh, I do hope not. I was longing for company and then you appeared as if by magic. Won't you sit down for a moment and tell me who you have come to see? If it is my brother, I am afraid he is not at home.'

'Your brother?'

'Yes, Edward, or rather Inspector Kent of the City of London Police. I'm his sister Alice, and you are?'

'Irene Angel.' Irene sat down rather more abruptly than she had intended on the nearest chair and she put her canvas bag on the floor, flexing her cramped fingers. 'Inspector Kent is your brother?'

'Yes, indeed he is,' Alice said, chuckling. 'Beneath that stern exterior there is a real human being, I can assure you.'

Virtually speechless, Irene could only nod her head and murmur an apology. 'I – mean I didn't . . .'

Alice threw back her head and her laughter filled the gloomy room. 'Don't apologise. I know what people think when they meet Edward but he is a dear really, and he is so good to me. As you see I am a cripple – there is no denying the fact. I cannot walk more than a few steps, and then only with the aid of crutches. I am always falling over but he picks me up without ever saying a harsh word. He is the best of brothers. I just wish he was not quite so dedicated to his job, but then he has to support us both. I am such a burden to him.'

'I'm sure you are not, and he is lucky to have a sister who thinks so highly of him. I doubt if my brother would speak so well of me. In fact, I don't suppose he would even recognise me if we met in the street.'

'Really?' Alice's face was alight with curiosity. 'That is sad indeed. Do tell me about it. I rely on people to bring me news of the outside world. But perhaps you ought to start by telling me why you need to see Edward.'

'It's a long story,' Irene said hesitantly.

'I have all the time in the world. Won't you take off your bonnet and shawl and make yourself comfortable? He shouldn't be too long now, and you can tell me all about yourself while you wait.'

'I do need to see him urgently. Are you sure he will return soon?'

Alice nodded her head emphatically. 'Oh, yes. He comes home in time to give me my supper, but if he should be delayed by work he sends word to our neighbour, Mrs Priest, who has been like a second mother to me. It's amazing how kind people are to someone in my circumstances.'

'Were you always . . .' Irene hesitated. She did not want to upset Alice, but now she had started she simply had to go on. 'I mean, how did this happen?'

'It was a stupid riding accident. We grew up on a farm in Essex. Our mother died when I was seven and I am afraid I ran wild, doing much as I pleased. One day I took Edward's horse although I had been told not to ride him because he was too mettlesome for me. Anyway, I disobeyed my father and Edward and I was thrown, injuring myself seriously. The doctor said I had broken my back. They thought I would die, but I'm made of much stronger stuff than they reckoned with, and I recovered, but my legs wouldn't work.'

'I'm so sorry,' Irene murmured. 'But living here in London is a far cry from being brought up on a farm. Is there no one at home who could look after you?'

Alice shook her head and her ringlets glinted gold in the firelight. 'Father remarried when I was eight and everything changed. Edward is ten years older than me and his heart was never in farming, so he went away to London to join the police. Our stepmother was kind enough, but she never quite regained her strength after the birth of her baby boy, and I'm afraid I was of little use to her. I pined for Edward, and when he came home one day and saw how unhappy I was he brought me to London and has looked after me ever since. He is so good to me, and I am so fortunate to have such a brother. Now tell me about yourself, Irene.'

After hearing Alice's story it was impossible to refuse her request, and Irene found herself relating her life history from the moment Jim had stormed out of the house to the present day.

Alice listened wide-eyed, and when Irene had finished she clapped her hands. 'Oh, my! What a tale you have to tell. I can't believe that you actually dressed like a boy and went searching for your friend Arthur. And he loves you.' Alice's eyes brimmed with tears. 'Poor young man, he must be so sad to have lost you.'

'I'm sure he'll get over it,' Irene said dismissively. 'Don't waste your pity on Artie; he brought most of his troubles on himself by gambling and getting involved with one of the worst street gangs in London. However,

I would like to ask your brother if he still intends to have Artie arrested, and I am desperate to find out what happened to my pa.'

Twin dimples played on either side of Alice's pretty mouth, and her eyes sparkled mischievously. 'This is so exciting. It's like being in one of the penny dreadfuls that I so love to read. Mrs Priest smuggles them in for me beneath her apron. Edward wouldn't like it if he knew that I read such frivolous tales, but they are such a wonderful escape from boredom and loneliness.' She reached across to lay her hand on Irene's arm. 'And that isn't a plea for sympathy. It's merely a statement of fact, and I have so enjoyed our chat, Irene. Would it be too much to ask you to come again to see me? Your life sounds so very exciting, and I wish I could visit the pickle shop and meet Gentle Annie and Fiery Nan. They seem such colourful characters.'

Irene shook her head. 'It might be best if you don't mention them to your brother. I don't think he'd approve of your knowing about that sort of woman.'

'No, I suppose you're right. Edward is quite strait-laced, but what he doesn't know won't hurt him. You can tell me all about the Sykes brothers and gambling and street women, and it will be our secret.'

Irene was about to demur when a footstep

in the hallway made them both turn with a guilty start as Inspector Kent entered the room.

'Edward, look who's come to see you,' Alice said, with an adoring smile. 'We've had such an interesting chat.'

Irene rose to her feet. 'I'm sorry, Inspector. I know I shouldn't have come to your home, but I had to see you.'

He acknowledged her presence with a curt nod. 'Perhaps we should speak in private?'

'No, don't take her away yet,' Alice cried. 'Irene has told me everything; do let her stay for a while longer, and please tell her what has happened to her father. The poor girl is desperate to know.'

Irene stared in amazement as she saw Kent's harsh features soften. A tender smile curved his lips as he leaned over Alice to drop a kiss on her fair head. 'All right, you minx. If Miss Angel doesn't mind, we will have our conversation here, but it must wait until after you've had your supper. I won't have you fainting from lack of nourishment.'

'Irene can join us,' Alice said happily. She turned to Irene with a pleading look in her eyes. 'You will stay and eat with us, won't you? I would love that.'

Irene glanced at Kent and met his cool gaze with an uplift of her chin. 'I wouldn't want to impose on you, Inspector.'

A ghost of a smile lit his eyes. 'It would be our pleasure if you would stay and have supper with us, Miss Angel.' He made for the doorway and paused. 'Our neighbour, Gladys Priest, cooks a meal for us every day. I'll just go and fetch it.' He left the room and Irene heard the front door open and close behind him.

'Gladys's son Danny runs errands for me. He works for a dreadful man who makes pickles,' Alice said, pulling a face. 'Perhaps you are acquainted with the odious Mr Yapp, since you are in the same line of business?'

'Unfortunately yes, and I do know Danny; he's a good boy.'

'He makes me laugh,' Alice said, chuckling. 'And he's extremely obliging. I only have to ask him to do something for me and it's done.'

'That sounds like Danny,' Irene replied, smiling at Alice's boundless enthusiasm. She glanced around the tidy room, feeling suddenly guilty for her own good health. 'Is there anything I can do to help?'

'There are plates on the dresser and cutlery in the drawer. We usually sit by the fire to eat, but as we've got company it would be nice to sit at the table.'

Irene busied herself by laying the table and setting out the chairs, and she had just completed her task when Kent returned carrying a steaming saucepan. He placed it on the table and from his greatcoat pocket he produced a loaf of bread. 'Miss Angel, perhaps you would like to serve while I help Alice to her chair?'

Irene did as he asked, and her stomach rumbled with hunger as she ladled the boiled beef and carrots onto the plates. She waited while Kent divested himself of his coat and jacket. In his shirtsleeves he looked so much more human and approachable that it was hard to see him as the enemy. He lifted Alice from the sofa as easily as if she had been a featherweight, and he set her gently down on a chair at the table. She smiled up at him. 'Thank you, Eddie.'

'Miss Angel, won't you take a seat?' He pulled out a chair.

'Really, must you be so formal?' Alice said, chuckling. 'We aren't at the station now. Can you not call her Irene?'

As Kent helped her to her seat, Irene was suddenly conscious of his nearness, and she was aware of his capable, workmanlike hands as they held her chair. She was rapidly reassessing her former opinion of him and it was unnerving. It was easier to imagine him as the aloof, cold-hearted foe than as a loving and caring brother whom Alice plainly worshipped. He seemed quite unaware of her confusion as he took his seat opposite and cut thick slices from the loaf, serving her first.

'This is most pleasant,' Alice said, smiling. 'We so seldom have guests for supper and I've really enjoyed our chat, Irene. I do hope you will come again.'

Irene almost choked on a mouthful of meat and gravy. She glanced warily at Kent expecting to see censure in his expression, but to her annoyance he was eyeing her with something akin to amusement. It might please him to play a game of cat and mouse but she wanted answers. 'I don't know,' she said. 'It depends on your brother.'

'I'm not the ogre you seem to think me, Miss Angel.'

'Then will you kindly put me out of my misery and tell me what has happened to my father, Inspector Kent?'

'No, this won't do,' Alice said, frowning. 'We are eating together as friends, and I can't allow you to be so formal. You must call my brother by his Christian name, and he must do the same. Otherwise it will make me most uncomfortable.'

Kent reached across and tweaked one of her fair ringlets. 'You are a spoilt little madam, Alice. But I'm sure that Miss Angel would not want to upset you, and neither would I.'

'No, of course not,' Irene agreed. 'But I

would be grateful if you would tell me what has happened to my father – Edward.'

His smile was apologetic and seemed genuine as he met her anxious gaze. 'I'm sorry to tell you that he is awaiting trial in Newgate prison. He was caught with the Sykes gang as they fought with their rivals from Spitalfields. Unfortunately the ringleaders got away.'

'My father isn't and never has been a member of the Sykes gang.'

Kent inclined his head. 'I believe you, but all the same he was caught in the middle of the fray.'

'Pa hates violence. He must have been in the wrong place at the wrong time. What will happen to him?'

'It will be up to the judge at his trial, but it will almost certainly mean a custodial sentence.'

Irene pushed her plate away, staring at him in horror as the truth dawned on her. 'You knew what was going to happen, didn't you? You couldn't get my pa to peach on the gang so you had him followed.'

'I can't comment on police matters. But perhaps if your friend had done what I asked of him and not run away, things might have been different.'

Kent's tone was cold and his face had assumed the shuttered look that Irene had begun to know only too well. She rose to her feet. 'I'm sorry, but I've lost my appetite. If you will excuse me, Alice, I should go now.'

'Oh, no, please don't leave like this,' Alice said, casting a pleading glance at her brother. 'Can't you do something, Edward?'

Irene snatched up her bonnet and shawl. 'I'm sorry,' she said, reaching for her canvas bag. 'I should not have come here.'

Kent pushed his chair back and stood up. 'I understand that you are upset, but it was inevitable that Billy would be caught. Anyone who gets involved with the Sykes brothers must know where it will lead.'

'My pa can't help himself when it comes to gambling; it's like a fever in his blood. Vic and Wally prey on men like him. They've used Pa and now he's paying for his folly. Are you satisfied?'

'I was just doing my job. Billy Angel is a grown man and he broke the law.'

'But Arthur is little more than a boy,' Irene countered, too angry now to care whether or not she upset Alice. 'You hounded him and he almost died as a result of it. Are you going to seek him out for trial by jury also?'

'He is of no interest to me now.'

'You used him,' Irene cried passionately. 'You used him and you used me for your own selfish ends. Well, I hope you get your promotion on the broken backs of my family and Arthur's ruined career.' She turned to Alice and was smitten by guilt at the sight of her white, tear-stained face. 'I'm sorry to bring my troubles to your door, Alice. Forgive me.' Irene pushed past Kent and ran from the house into the pouring rain.

'Miss Angel – Irene – wait. Please stop.' Kent caught up with her before she had taken more than a couple of steps across the wet cobblestones. He gripped her by the arm, and when she tried to pull free he tightened his grasp. 'What are you going to do?'

She was shaking with suppressed anger. 'Let me go.'

'You cannot go running about London on a night like this. I know that the shop has been boarded up and that you have no home to go to.'

'And whose fault is that?' Irene glared up into his pale face illuminated by a shaft of light from the parlour window.

His fingers dug into her soft flesh. 'You could have stayed and paid off your debts, but instead you chose to run after your sweetheart,' he said grimly. 'Don't blame the law for your mistakes.'

'You made me think that you were going to arrest him, and that was why I risked everything to warn Artie.' She wrenched her arm free. 'I think you planned it. You wanted me out of the way so that you could entrap my father as well as the Sykes brothers.'

'That isn't the case at all.'

'Well, I believe it is. My father told me never to trust a copper.'

'I can see that you've made up your mind, but you are wrong.'

'Just leave me alone.'

'But where will you go now?'

'That's none of your business,' she answered defiantly, but she was seized by a sudden feeling of panic. She had not thought that far and her options were strictly limited. He was staring at her with a perplexed expression in his eyes. His shirtsleeves and waistcoat were soaked with rain, and his dark hair was plastered to his forehead, but Irene felt no sympathy for the man who had sent her father to jail. She wrapped her sodden shawl a little closer around her body and it was only then that she realised that she too was soaked to the skin. She shivered convulsively, clenching her teeth to prevent them from chattering. 'Tell your sister that I'm sorry I won't be able to call on her again. I'm really sorry, because I would like to have known her better, but hear this, Inspector Kent, I won't never lift a finger to help you again. You could be on fire and I wouldn't waste my spit on you.' She turned on her heel and broke into a run, but the cobblestones in the court were wet and she slipped, stumbled and would have fallen if he had not been at her side and caught her before she fell to the ground. 'Let go of me,' she cried, lashing out at him with her bare hands.

He righted her and released her immediately. 'You can't wander the streets on a night like this. You'll end up dead in a shop doorway or worse.'

'And cause your lot a bit of inconvenience, I suppose? Well, don't worry, I won't clutter up the dead house tomorrow morning. I've got somewhere to go, and it really don't concern you.' She retrieved her bag from a muddy puddle and marched off with her head held high. It was only when she was safely away from Robin Hood Passage that she relaxed enough to realise that her teeth were clattering together like a busker playing the spoons and she was trembling from head to foot. She felt abandoned and lost, with no home to go to. It was the old nightmare returning to claim her – but this time it was real.

Rain was tumbling down from the sky and huge puddles glistened in the light of the street lamps. Passing cabs and carriages sent up waves of muddy spray, soaking Irene's skirts, and her boots were letting in water so that her feet squelched with every step. On the corner of Wood Street a hot chestnut vendor huddled beneath a sacking cape and rivulets of rain-water poured off his wide-brimmed felt hat every time he moved his head. Steam rose from his clothes as he stood close to the glowing brazier and the smell of roasting chestnuts filled the damp air. Irene's stomach rumbled and she thought longingly of the supper that she had tasted but left on her plate in Kent's house. Another mouthful would have choked her, but she was ravenous and there was only one place that she could go now.

Jessie opened the door with her customary surly expression. 'Oh, it's you, miss. What d'you want at this time of night?'

Irene was in no mood for pleasantries and she pushed past her. 'Is my sister in the drawing room?'

Jessie closed the door with a thud. 'Here, you can't walk in without me announcing you. The mistress would skin me alive.'

'Then announce me and be done with it. Can't you see I'm wet through and in danger of catching a fatal chill?'

Jessie sniffed and stomped off towards the staircase. 'Follow me then, my lady.'

As she passed one of the many wall mirrors in the entrance hall, Irene saw her reflection with a feeling of dismay. No wonder the maid had looked as her askance; she did indeed look like something the cat had dragged in. Her hair hung in wet strands around her face and shoulders and there were smuts on her cheeks and nose. Her bonnet had lost all its stiffening and had crumpled into a soggy mess at the back of her neck, and her clothes were sodden and mud-spattered. Glancing down at the carpet she saw to her dismay that she had left a trail of muddy footprints all along the new runner in the hall and on each of the stair treads. Emmie would kill her, Irene thought gloomily, and she could only hope that Erasmus was out for the evening. He would tease her mercilessly if he were to see her now, and as for Ephraim – well, he would be shocked beyond belief.

Irene entered the drawing room without bothering to knock, but Jessie was close on her heels.

'I'm sorry, ma'am,' Jessie whined. 'She pushed past me like a mad thing.'

Emmie had been reclining on the chaise longue but she sat upright, staring open-mouthed at her sister. Clara rose stiffly from an armchair by the fire and came hobbling over to greet Irene, laughing and crying at the same time. 'Oh, Renie. Where have you been, you bad girl? We've heard nothing from you for well over a week.'

Irene dropped the bag in the doorway and hurried over to her clasp her mother's hands, holding her at arms' length. 'Don't touch me, Ma. I'm soaked to the skin and I'll make you wet.' She glanced at Emmie and smiled. 'Hello, Emmie.'

'I hope no one saw you enter the house in that state,' Emmie said peevishly. 'What have you been doing all this time and why are you here?'

'I've come to ask a favour.'

'If it's money you want, I have only a little left of my allowance,' Emily said, pouting. 'I've had to spend a fortune at the dressmaker's. I don't think my waistline is ever going to stop expanding, and I doubt if I'll ever see my feet again.'

'Come and sit by the fire, ducks,' Clara said. 'Jessie, please fetch a bowl of hot water and mustard powder, and a towel.'

'Yes'm.' Jessie bobbed a curtsey and backed slowly from the room.

Irene went to sit by the fire, ignoring the fact that she would make a wet patch on Emmie's brand new velvet cushions. Billows of steam erupted from her wet skirts and the odour of damp wool and mud containing particles of the stinking detritus from the streets wafted round the room.

Emily wrinkled her nose. 'For heaven's sake,

Renie. What a state you're in. You look and smell like – well, I don't want to say what, but it's not nice. Couldn't you have tidied yourself up before you came to my house? I do hope you came in through the tradesmen's entrance.'

'No, I came in through the front door, and I'm sorry if I've upset the neighbours, but there's something I have to tell you both. You obviously have no idea what's been going on.'

Clara slumped down on the chair opposite Irene. 'It's your father again, isn't it? We haven't seen him since you were last here, and I've been out of my mind with worry.'

'You should be used to it after all these years, Ma,' Emily said irritably. 'All this fuss isn't good for baby. He's kicking me something awful tonight. I don't think he likes oysters. I must tell Mrs Peabody not to put them in the steak and kidney pudding until after he's born, although my Josiah won't like it, because he's particularly partial to oysters.'

'Oh, shut up, Emmie,' Irene cried, driven almost to screaming point. 'Don't you ever think about anything other than yourself?'

Emily's eyes filled with tears and her bottom lip trembled. 'Don't be horrid. You know I mustn't be upset in any way. Why did you have to come here tonight and spoil everything?'

'I'm sorry,' Irene said more gently. 'I don't want to alarm you, but I'm sorry to say that we are ruined. Pa has somehow got himself involved in a gang fight between the Sykes brothers and the Spitalfields mob, and he's in prison awaiting trial.'

Clara uttered a low moan and covered her face with her hands. 'I knew something dreadful had happened. Oh, Billy, what am I to do with you?'

Irene gave her a hug. 'Pa will be all right. You mustn't upset yourself.'

'Yes,' Emily agreed, nodding her head. 'Pa will be fine, but what will Mr Tippet say when he finds out? I wish Pa was here so that I could give him a piece of my mind.'

Irene shot her a warning glance. 'Never mind that now.'

Clara produced a handkerchief from her sleeve and blew her nose. 'You're right, Emmie. My Billy has been through worse.' She gave Irene a watery smile. 'But where have you been all this time, ducks?'

'Arthur ran off to his Aunt Maude in Essex and I had to go chasing after him to warn him that the police were on his trail. I came back today to find that the landlord has changed the locks and let the shop to someone else; most probably to one of those strange people who actually pay the rent.' Irene stopped for breath just as Jessie staggered into the room carrying a foot bath.

'Where shall I put it, ma'am?'

'Where do you think, you silly girl?' Emily clambered to her feet, holding her swollen belly with both hands. 'Put it down by my sister and get out.'

Jessie dumped the bowl in front of Irene and fled the room, slamming the door behind her. Irene glanced anxiously at her mother, who was silent and deathly pale.

'What will my Josiah say?' Emily sank back onto the chaise longue, fanning herself with her hand. 'This is all your fault, Renie. I blame you more than I blame Pa. You were supposed to be looking after him and you didn't. You ran off after that useless idiot Arthur Greenwood.'

'You don't understand—' Irene began, but Emily cut her short.

'You'll have to marry him now, you know. You've ruined your reputation and ours too. Josiah will be so angry. He won't want you in the house, Renie. You'll have to go back to your lover and beg him to make an honest woman of you. You can't stay here. I won't have disgrace brought on the house of Tippet, so when you're warm and dry, off you go. I mean it, Renie. Go away and leave us in peace.'

Chapter Twelve

'No, Emmie,' Clara cried angrily. 'I won't allow you to treat poor Renie so. You can't turn her out on a night like this without even giving her a chance to tell us how she came to be in such a pickle.'

It was far from funny, but the mention of the word pickle made Irene giggle. Perhaps it was simple hysteria that was making her laugh uncontrollably, but in the face of destitution and disaster the allusion to their former trade could not have been more inappropriate. 'Oh, Ma, I wish you could have thought of something other than onions and cucumbers swimming in vinegar. Our whole lives have been in a pickle if you ask me.' She paused for breath as she realised that Emmie was not at all amused and that Ma was weeping into a cotton handkerchief, which came almost certainly, Irene thought inconsequentially, from Josiah's shop. It was probably not of the best quality; the hankies made of fine lawn trimmed with lace would have been reserved for his richer customers. She was suddenly serious. 'Don't look at me like that, Emmie. You don't know the whole story, but I can tell you for sure that there's nothing funny going on between me and Artie. We are good friends and that's all.'

'Then why did you go running after him? And if there wasn't anything in it, why did you stay away so long?' Emily reached for a silver vinaigrette that was strategically placed on a table by her side and she sniffed the aromatic fumes, closing her eyes and coughing delicately.

Irene ignored this piece of theatre and she put the steaming bowl of mustard water aside in order to kneel at her mother's feet. 'Don't upset yourself, Ma. If Emmie doesn't want me here, I'll find somewhere else to stay.'

Clara gulped and sniffed. 'No, you won't. You'll stay here even if I have to go to Josiah and beg him on bended knees.' She turned to give Emily a hard stare. 'And you, miss, I'm ashamed of you, putting your own feelings first. Let Renie tell her story and stop thinking about yourself for a moment.'

'I'm sorry, Ma.' Emily's cheeks flooded with colour and she hung her head. 'I'll hear you out, Renie, and I daresay I can persuade Josiah to let you stay for a night or two, just until you've sorted matters with the landlord. But you must understand that I have to put my husband first. Just think what it would do to his trade if it got out that his father-in-law was in prison, and his wife's sister was no better than she should be.'

'Oh, Emmie,' Irene said with a reluctant smile. 'You should get together with Inspector Kent. I'm sure he would agree with you about my character.'

'Just let me speak to that person,' Clara said angrily. 'I'll give him a piece of my mind all right. Your father would still be a free man if it wasn't for that Inspector Kent.'

'Don't worry, Ma. I'll be keeping well out of his way in future. That fellow has a heart of stone.' Irene hesitated as she recalled the tenderness that Kent had shown his crippled sister, and she felt obliged to qualify her statement. 'He might not be so bad to others, but there is no common ground between us. We're as different as mint sauce and Worcestershire relish.'

'Will you forget the wretched shop for a moment and tell us everything,' Emmie said, frowning. 'And be quick about it before Josiah and Ephraim return from stocktaking. If you must stay then I'll get Jessie to make up a bed in the room next to hers on the top floor.'

Clara stared at her in horror. 'You can't put your sister up in the attics with the servants, Emmie. What will they think?'

'Perhaps you're right, Ma. Well, you can

have the back bedroom on the floor below, Renie, but you must understand that this is just a temporary measure.'

'That's settled then,' Clara said with a satisfied smile. 'Have you eaten, Renie? If you're hungry I'm sure that Cook could make up a supper tray for you.'

'A bit,' Irene replied, thinking wistfully of the tasty meal she had rejected at the Kents' house. 'But I don't want to put Cook out as well as Jessie.'

'The servants will do as I say.' Emily closed the vinaigrette with a decisive snap. 'If you want food it shall be brought to your room. Now, tell us what put you and Arthur on the wrong side of the law.'

Half an hour later, after answering all Emmie's questions, Irene followed the flickering light of Jessie's candle as they made their way up the stairs to the third floor. Jessie paused on the landing, pointing to the door immediately opposite them. 'That's Mr Ephraim's room.' She continued on her way, stopping outside a door further along the corridor. 'That's Mr Erasmus's room. He's inclined to wander in the night, if you get my meaning. I should lock my door if I was you, I know I do and so does Cook, although I can't see that Mr Ras would want to tumble an old besom like her.'

'Thank you, Jessie,' Irene said tiredly. 'I don't think I want to hear any more.'

'Suit yourself, but don't say as how I didn't warn you.' With a disdainful sniff, Jessie walked off to open a door at the end of the long, dark passage. 'I suppose you'll want the fire lit?' she said grudgingly.

'Y-yes, I w-will,' Irene murmured through chattering teeth. She was shivering violently as her damp clothes absorbed the chill in the room, which looked as though it had not been used for some time. The furniture was covered in white dust sheets that seemed to shift like restless spirits in the flickering light of Jessie's candle.

'And I've got to bring supper up all them stairs too,' Jessie grumbled, half to herself as she lit two candles strategically placed on the dusty mantelshelf. 'I can't make up the bed and light the fire as well as carrying a heavy tray up from the basement. What does she think I am? A blooming slave?'

At this point, Irene was too tired to argue and too cold and hungry to care about the manners of a servant girl. If she were to tell the truth, she quite sympathised with young Jessie. She could see that the girl was much put upon, and it was obvious that Josiah was not a generous employer, expecting too much from one skinny maidservant who was little more than a child. He probably paid her in buttons too.

'I'll fetch the clean linen first,' Jessie said, moving towards the door. 'It's in the cupboard just down the passage.'

'No, you've got enough to do,' Irene said. 'Just tell me where it is. I can make up my own bed.'

'You won't tell the missis, will you? She'll be angry with me if I don't do exactly as I'm told.'

'I won't say a word, but I would be grateful for a fire and some hot food, if it's not too much trouble.'

'Well I never did!' Jessie stared at her wide-eyed. 'Are you sure that you're her sister? You don't act like her, and you don't even look much alike.'

'Get on with you before I change my mind.'

'All right then, miss. The linen cupboard is two doors down on the right.' Jessie backed out of the doorway. 'I'll fetch the coal first.' She disappeared into the darkness and her footsteps echoed on the bare treads of the back stairs.

Irene picked up a candlestick and went in search of the linen cupboard, but a sudden cold draught of air extinguished the candle, leaving her in the dark, and she had to feel her way along the wall, counting the doors as she went. She opened the one she thought Jessie had said was the linen cupboard, but to her horror she found herself staring at Erasmus's bare legs as he hopped about on one foot in an attempt to put on his trousers. He stared at her open-mouthed and a dull flush suffused his face. Irene did not know whether to laugh or to cover her eyes. 'I'm so sorry. I thought this was the linen cupboard.'

'Wait a moment.' He turned away to fasten his breeches, glancing at her over his shoulder with a slow smile. 'I say, old girl, you caught me with my trousers down.'

'It was a mistake – the maid must have given me the wrong direction. I'm sorry.'

'I had no idea that you were paying us a visit, and I can't think why a guest in my father's house should be searching for the linen cupboard.'

'My candle went out. I picked the wrong door. Excuse me.' Irene backed towards the door. 'I wasn't expected – the maid went downstairs to get coal for the fire . . .' She knew it sounded lame, but she was so taken aback that she was for once lost for words.

Erasmus turned to give her an appraising stare. 'You do look a bit bedraggled, if you don't mind me saying so, Aunt-in-law. Won't you come in and make use of my fire until the girl has made your room habitable? We can't allow guests to wait on themselves; it wouldn't do at all.'

'Don't laugh at me, Erasmus,' Irene said, recovering just enough to feel angry rather than nonplussed. 'I know I look a sight, but then so would you if you'd spent half the day travelling and arrived to find yourself homeless.'

'And your father locked up in Newgate. Not a good state of affairs, I'm afraid. Take a seat by the fire and tell me all about it.'

Irene was so cold that she had lost all feeling in her hands and feet, and the button-back armchair by the hearth looked warm and comfortable. It was an offer too good to refuse. She perched on the edge of the seat, holding her hands out to the blaze. 'How did you find out about Pa?' she demanded. 'Emmie didn't know and neither did Ma.'

'Word gets round.' Erasmus tapped the side of his nose. 'Especially in the sort of establishments I frequent. I believe it was your friend Gentle Annie who told me, or it could have been Fiery Nan.' He rubbed his jaw and smiled. 'I can still feel the punch she once gave me. She had a right hook equal to that of the celebrated Tom Cribb.'

'Do you think that the news has reached your father?' Irene asked anxiously.

'Not so far as I know.'

'Then keep it to yourself. Please, Ras, for

Emmie's sake don't say anything until she's had time to break it gently to Josiah.'

'What's it worth?' he demanded, grinning. 'I'd expect a hug at least, or maybe a kiss.'

Irene jumped to her feet. 'I'm not in the mood for joking.'

'I can see that, and I'm too much of a gentleman to press my point, but remember that you owe me something for keeping quiet about your pa's sad plight.'

'You'll get what you deserve,' Irene said with a touch of her old spirit. 'A clip round the ear is what you'll get for your cheek, my boy. I may be tired and grubby but I ain't stupid.'

'You women! You burst into a fellow's bedchamber, catching him in a state of undress, and then you act all coy and modest.'

It was impossible to be angry with him, and in spite of everything Irene chuckled at his expression of mock outrage. 'You're a rogue, Ras Tippet.'

'Takes one to know one,' he retorted, following her to the door and opening it for her. 'Now you know where my room is, you can call on me any time of the night or day, especially the night.'

Irene gave him a gentle slap on the cheek. 'That's for nothing; see what you get for something.'

'I can't wait, Irene my angel. Let me take

you out for supper tomorrow night, followed by the theatre, or a penny gaff if you'd prefer something a bit livelier.'

'One Angel sister involved with the Tippet family is quite enough, ta very much. Goodnight.' Irene started off in what she thought was the direction of her own room, but he called her back.

'You'll end up giving Ephraim the fright of his life if you go that way.'

She turned on her heel, changing direction. 'Don't worry, Ras. I never make the same mistake twice.'

'The linen cupboard is the second door on the left,' he called after her.

'Ta, I'll remember that.'

She found the linen cupboard, and was amazed to see piles of sheets, pillowcases and blankets, all neatly folded and the shelves labelled as to their size and colour. It was the draper's version of a treasure chest. There were definite advantages, she thought, in being married to a linen merchant. She selected what she needed and made her way back to her own room, where Jessie was on her knees attempting to light the fire.

'You took your time, miss. Was you lost?'

'You can go now. I'll see to the fire.'

Jessie scrambled to her feet. 'I got to make the bed, miss.'

'I can do that. I'm not entirely helpless. Anyway, it's time a girl of your age was tucked up in her own bed. Off you go.'

'Well, if you're sure . . .' Jessie blinked at her in astonishment. 'Your supper's on the table by the window, although it's probably cold by now.'

'Never mind that. I'm sure it will be fine, thank you.'

Jessie left the room, closing the door softly behind her.

'Poor little bitch,' Irene murmured, going down on her knees and taking the bellows to the fire. 'I'd rather be a pure finder than have her job.'

Next morning, despite their crumpled and grubby appearance, Irene had little choice other than to dress in the clothes she had worn yesterday. It was either that or Jim's shirts and breeches and she did not think that to appear at breakfast in boy's clothes would go down too well with the family. Ras would probably hoot with laughter and think it extremely funny, but he would be alone in this. She pulled on her skirt, which was stiff with mud and still damp, and then her cotton blouse, which was badly creased and travel-stained. She pinned her hair into a bun at the nape of her neck and smoothed the sides over her ears. A quick glance in the dressing-table mirror was not encouraging. She looked like a dishevelled scullery maid, but unless she wanted to spend the day in her room there was nothing for it but to go downstairs to the dining room and hope that she could snatch something to eat before anyone else was about.

The house was eerily silent, and the only sound she could hear as she descended the stairs was the ticking of the long-case clock in the entrance hall. Irene entered the dining room to find Josiah seated at the head of the table with his napkin tucked into his collar as he attacked his breakfast of bacon, kidneys and buttered eggs. His round cheeks pouched in surprise when he saw her and he swallowed convulsively. 'Good Lord! What a sight you look, Irene. Your sister told me you had arrived last evening, but she failed to mention that you were in such a terrible state.'

'I'm sorry, Josiah. I have nothing else to wear. There appears to have been some misunderstanding while I was out of town and the landlord has changed the locks on the shop door.'

'Mrs Tippet gave me a garbled account of your actions but I cannot say that I approve of them. It's not right for an unmarried young woman to go traipsing about the country on her own, let alone to chase after a young man wanted by the police.' He lifted his hand as

Irene opened her mouth to defend her actions. 'No, don't say a word. My wife has told me that your father is temporarily out of circulation. I can't bring myself to name the place where he is incarcerated, but if this piece of news should get out it will seriously damage my trade and my standing in the community. You know that I am hoping to stand for alderman next year, I suppose?'

Irene nodded her head. 'I do.'

'And yet you still act rashly and without a thought as to the effect such behaviour might have on your family. Shame on you, Irene! Did you never stop for one minute to consider your sister's delicate condition, or your mother's poor health? No, I can see that you did not. I shudder to look at you now, my girl. Your behaviour is quite shocking. D'you hear me?'

'Yes, Josiah, I hear you, but—'

'No buts, young lady. You are in no position to argue or even to plead your case. You have thrown yourself on my mercy, and it is fortunate for you that I am a fair man. Mrs Tippet tells me that you have nowhere to go, and it is my duty to honour her wish that you should be allowed to remain here for as long as necessary. However, while you are under my roof you will obey my rules. You will behave with decorum, and that means that you will not go running about the city like a common street girl.'

Clenching her hands behind her back and digging her fingernails into her palms, Irene bit back angry words. She longed to tell Josiah exactly what she thought of him, but she was in no position to argue. She had no money, and until she could find a situation that allowed her to support herself she would have to rely on her brother-in-law's charity.

'Do you understand me, Irene?' Josiah raised his voice to a shout and his face was suffused with an unattractive shade of purple.

Irene stared down at her feet. 'Yes, Josiah.'

'Now go to your room before anyone sees you looking like a Billingsgate fishwife. I will speak to Mrs Tippet and she must find you some garments that are suitable for a guest in a house such as this.'

Irene's stomach rumbled as she glanced at the table set for breakfast. The aroma of fried bacon and hot toast made her mouth water, but she was not going to beg Josiah for food. She would rather starve. 'I don't want your charity, Josiah. I could work in your shop and earn my keep.'

'That's out of the question. Tongues would wag.' Josiah picked up his coffee cup and slurped a mouthful, choking on the hot liquid and scowling at Irene over the rim as though it was her fault that he had burnt his tongue.

'I don't see why,' Irene said, unwilling to

give in so easily. 'Your sons work for you, so why can't I? I could sweep floors or dust shelves. You seem to forget that I am used to working in a shop.'

'A shop! You call my emporium a shop and compare it with that – that cupboard at the bottom of Wood Street where your mother sold pickles?'

Josiah's eyes bulged over his fat cheeks and for a moment Irene had a vision of them popping out altogether, like the stopper from a ginger beer bottle. His breathing was erratic and she was afraid that he was going to have an apoplectic fit. She backed towards the doorway. 'No, of course not. It was just an idea and I'm sorry if my presence here embarrasses you, but I won't stay a moment longer than necessary. You have my word on that.' She had the satisfaction of seeing him momentarily bereft of speech, and she marched out of the dining room with her head held high.

She was halfway up the second flight of stairs when she met Ephraim coming down. He stopped and stared at her, looking her up and down. 'Good heavens, Irene. What a sight you look.'

'If anyone says that to me once more, I'll scream.' She pushed past him and ran up the remaining stairs to her room. Once safely inside, she shut the door and flopped down on her bed. Wild plans of escape ran through her mind. She could put on Jim's clothes and beg in the streets, or sell matches or bootlaces. She could go down to the docks and find a shipmaster who would take her on as a cabin boy and she would search the world for her brother. Or she could beg Emmie to give her the money for the train fare to Romford and return to the peace and quiet of Miss Maude's house in Havering. Perhaps life in the country would not be such a bad thing after all. But in her heart she knew that she was a city girl born and bred, and that country life would soon pall. She would miss the sights and even the smells of London, and in particular she would miss the hurly-burly and excitement of each day in the throbbing heart of the capital. She could not desert Pa, who would need her to make a home for him when he was released from prison, as he must surely be when the jury found him innocent of any crime other than being in the wrong place at the wrong time.

Once again, she had no choice. She must put up with Josiah's ranting and self-righteous condemnation. She would have to bite her tongue and act like a meek and dutiful sister and sister-in-law, not to mention being a support to Ma, who must hate having to be dependent on Josiah's charity. Poor Ma.

She was the one who had suffered the most, and she was not in a fit state of health to endure much more.

Irene rose to her feet as someone tapped gently on her door. 'Come in.'

'Let me in, Renie. Me hands is full.'

Irene opened the door and found her mother standing in the passage with her arms piled high with garments. 'You shouldn't be doing this, Ma,' she said, taking them from her. 'You should be resting.'

'I ain't an invalid, and Emmie didn't want that nosey maidservant to find out what was going on.' Clara entered the room and stood for a moment looking around, tut-tutting and shaking her head. 'It's better than the attic, I suppose, but not much. Really, ducks, I don't like to speak ill of your sister, but this is little more than a boxroom. My bedchamber is bigger than this, and the girl lights my fire first thing every morning.'

Irene laid the clothes out on the bed, staring at the tumble of delicately coloured fabrics from the finest cotton poplin to mousseline and silk taffeta. 'Hmm,' she murmured. 'At least there are some advantages in being married to an old stick like Josiah.'

'Don't be unkind, Renie,' Clara said, smothering a chuckle. 'Emmie is very fond of him and he worships her.'

'I should hope so, but she didn't need to turn out so many of her fine clothes. A blouse and a skirt would do for me.'

'Now listen to me, love,' Clara said, sinking down on a chair by the empty grate. 'Take what's on offer. With your pa in jail we can't afford to be choosy.'

Irene moved swiftly to her side and wrapped her arm around her mother's thin shoulders. 'You've been so brave about it, Ma. It must cut you to the heart to know that Pa might be facing a long prison sentence.'

'I've always known it would come to this one day and I feared that we'd end up on the street, but at least I know where my Billy is now, and that he's safe from the Sykes brothers. It's small comfort, but when you've lived with worry for so many years it's almost a relief when the worst happens.'

Irene hugged her and dropped a kiss on her mother's grey hair. 'I wish I was more like you, Ma.'

'No, ducks. You are fine as you are and I'm proud of you, even if I don't tell you so very often.'

Irene blinked hard and swallowed the lump in her throat that threatened to make her bawl like a baby. 'I love you, Ma, and I don't say that often enough either.'

'What a pair of sillies we are to be sure,'

Clara said, sniffing and fumbling in her pocket for her handkerchief. 'But we must put up with things as they are until your Pa gets out of jail and we can begin again. It's just lucky that Emmie showed good sense in accepting Josiah. At least one of my girls is settled, and quite handsomely too. Now all I've got to worry about is you.'

'You mustn't, Ma. You concentrate on getting yourself fit and well. I can look after meself, and one day we'll have a nice house to live in, just like this or better. I can't do much about it at present, but give me time and I'll get us back on our feet, you'll see.'

'I believe you, love,' Clara said, mopping her eyes and becoming brisk and businesslike. 'But first things first. Let's see you in one of Emmie's cast-offs. She said she don't want any of them back, and at the rate she's eating for two, I doubt if she'll ever get into them again anyway.'

The gown of fine merino wool in a shade of dark blue fitted Irene's slender figure as if it had been made for her. On Ma's instructions, she piled her hair high on her head and fastened it with two tortoiseshell combs that Emmie had also thoughtfully provided. Irene was not ungrateful, but she realised that this apparent generosity on her sister's part was fuelled by the need to keep Josiah happy. Irene had sensed from the moment she first met him that Josiah Tippet was a social climber, and now she was to be included in his outward display of familial respectability, which must never be tarnished by scandal. It was going to be a hard part to play, but for the time being she must try to act like a lady.

Downstairs in the morning parlour, Irene discovered Emmie sitting by the fire with her head bent over an embroidery hoop and her tongue gripped between her teeth as she stabbed the linen with a needle. She looked up with a start as the door opened and yelped with pain. 'Ouch! You made me prick my finger,' she mumbled, sucking her injured digit.

Ignoring this ungracious welcome, Irene did a twirl. 'How do I look?'

'Very nice,' Emmie said, examining her finger for traces of blood. 'It's not fair to remind me that I wore that gown just months ago.'

'And you will again, love.' Clara hobbled over to the sofa and sank down onto the crimson velvet which was stretched over the horsehair stuffing like the skin of a drum.

'I shan't ever wear it again. When baby is born I intend to make Josiah buy me a whole new wardrobe, which is the least he can do for me after I've gone through all this hideous discomfort. Anyway, what's the use of being married to a draper if I can't have new clothes every season?' Emmie tossed her embroidery aside and reached for a copy of a fashion journal. 'He likes me to look smart, and I intend to be a credit to the name of Tippet.' She glanced up at Irene, frowning. 'And you're not to let us down, d'you hear me, Renie? Don't even think about paying Pa a visit in prison, and you must keep away from anyone and anything that has to do with that dreadful Sykes gang. We're respectable people now; just you remember that.'

'I don't think anyone is going to let me forget it,' Irene said, sighing. 'But I'm going out this morning to look for work and then I'll be off your Josiah's hands for good.'

'What?' Emily paled alarmingly. 'No, you can't go out alone. Josiah would have a fit. You've got to behave like a young lady now, and anyway I want you to stay and keep me company. I'll be big as a whale soon and I won't be able to go out at all.'

'Stuff and nonsense, Emmie,' Clara said with a touch of asperity. 'You've a while to go yet and if you are growing fat it's because you stuff chocolates and cream cakes all day. When I was carrying you I worked long hours in the shop and almost gave birth to you under the counter.'

Emily fanned herself with the magazine.

'Ma, please. That's not a fit subject to speak of in front of Renie.'

Irene hooted with laughter. 'Stuff and nonsense. I've spent enough time in the company of Fiery Nan and Gentle Annie to know what goes on in the world. You may pretend to be a delicate flower, Em, but I'm as common as the old plane tree on the corner of Wood Street. We were born and raised in the city and our feet are planted firmly in the dirt, so you can just stop talking like a silly bitch and let me get on with things in me own way.'

Clara clutched her hand to her forehead. 'Girls, don't fight, please. My poor head is aching from listening to you.'

'There now,' Emily said, pulling a face at her sister. 'You've upset Ma with your coarse ways. Keep what company you like, but don't let Josiah catch you, and don't go roaming the streets on your own. If you do anything to bring disgrace on this house I'll never speak to you again.'

Irene had had enough. She might be dressed like a lady but she was still the same person inside, and she was already feeling like a caged tiger. She could see that Ma was close to tears, and not wanting to upset her further she bit back a sharp retort, schooling her features into what she hoped was a meek expression. 'I promise that I won't show you or your precious Josiah up in any way. I'll act the lady in company and no one will see me walking out unattended.'

'There, you see, that wasn't so hard now, was it?' Emily's smile was so smug that Irene could almost hear her purring.

'I'm proud of you, Renie,' Clara said, sighing with relief. 'That couldn't have been easy for you to say, ducks.'

No, Irene thought, bowing her head so that they could not see the gleam of excitement in her eyes. It wasn't easy to curb her rebellious spirit, but she had just thought of a way to get round Josiah's stupid rules: however, it wouldn't do to let either Ma or Emmie in on her plans. She rubbed her temples with her fingers. 'I think I'll go to my room and have a lie down. I'm a bit tired after all the travelling I did yesterday.'

'Of course you are, love,' Clara said sympathetically. 'You go upstairs and have a rest.'

Emily flicked through the pages of the magazine. 'Luncheon is at one o'clock sharp. You know that Josiah hates people who are unpunctual.' She looked up, giving Irene a hard stare. 'You'd better not be planning anything rash, Renie.'

'Who, me? As if I would.' Irene left the room with a swish of starched moreen petticoats.

Chapter Thirteen

Half an hour later, Irene crept barefoot down the back stairs with Jim's boots clutched in her hands. She had discarded her unaccustomed finery for her brother's cast-off clothing, and with her hair tucked up in the peaked cap she was satisfied that she would not excite anyone's curiosity on the city streets. She was confident now that she could stroll along, hands in pockets, and melt into the crowd as she had done before; but first she had to get past Cook and Jessie and anyone else who happened to be slaving away in Josiah's kitchen. She stopped at the foot of the stairs to put on the boots and lace them up. Having done this she crept along the flagstone passage hardly daring to breathe.

She passed closed doors conveniently labelled *Broom Cupboard, Flower Room* and *Larder*, but the door at the end of the passage had been left ajar and clouds of steam gusted out into the cold air. The mixed aromas of frying onions and roasting meat made her mouth water, but she put aside her hunger and peeked round the door. She could see a thin woman enveloped in a mobcap and a large white apron standing at the table chopping herbs. Luckily she had her back to the door and Jessie was too busy stoking the range to pay attention to anything that was going on around her. Irene slipped past unnoticed and she smothered a sigh of relief when she found that the half-glassed door leading into the area was not locked. Luckily the kitchen window was steamed up on the inside, enabling her to ascend the steep area steps unseen and escape through the wrought-iron gate onto the pavement.

She took a deep breath of frosty air, ignoring the stench of boiled cabbage that wafted from the basement kitchen of the adjoining house and the unmistakeable odour of cat's piss that made her eyes water. Nothing could spoil this moment. It had been all too easy. She was free and it felt wonderful, but as she stepped out with long masculine strides she remembered that there were some drawbacks to wearing breeches: the coarse material chafed the soft skin of her inner thighs, but it was a small price to pay for regaining her liberty, even if it was only temporary. Her first stop was to be Newgate prison, and she cut through a narrow passage between the houses which led from the mews into Love Lane. She walked at a brisk pace, adding a slight swagger to her gait just for the fun of it. She went unrecognised by those in Wood Street who would have known and greeted Irene Angel, and she made her way to Cheapside. No one seemed to be interested in a shabbily dressed youth; she might as well have been invisible. It was most encouraging.

She hurried along Newgate Street, which was little more than a lane that ran beneath the grim smoke-blackened walls of the prison, and she threaded her way between market stalls selling anything and everything from potatoes to silver plate. Judging by the villainous-looking characters who hung around the place, a great many of the items on the stalls were stolen property. The whole area had the sordid atmosphere of a lawless twilight world just beyond the reach of the Court House in Old Bailey. Irene would not normally have set foot in this place, but in her male guise she felt supremely confident and unafraid. The only person who accosted her was a snot-nosed urchin who accused her of stealing his pitch when she stopped for a moment to get her bearings. He shoved his grubby face close to hers, and the smell of his unwashed body made her want to retch. She was not in the mood for arguing and she pushed him out of the way, receiving a mouthful of foul invective that seemed to impress one of the costermongers who tossed the boy an apple.

Irene hurried on past the debtor's door where public hangings took place with depressing regularity. These never failed to attract huge crowds of spectators who, she had been informed on good authority, watched the gruesome spectacle as if it were a sport akin to bear baiting or cock fighting. There were those who actually paid huge sums to watch the grisly proceedings from upper windows in the prison itself. Irene had never wanted to see such dreadful sights but no one could live in the city without being aware of what was happening on their doorstep.

She made her way to the main gate and rang the bell. A small hatch in the door flew open and a gaunt, unshaven face peered out at her. 'What's your business here?'

Irene lowered her voice to what she hoped was a more masculine tone. 'I want to visit a prisoner.'

'No visits allowed.' The voice was firm, but the beady eyes stared out at her as if expecting something in return for this information. She had no money with which to bribe the screw and so she tried another tack.

'If you please, mister. You got me dad in there and us twelve children is close to starving. Let me see him just for one minute, please.'

'Can't be done. Clear off.'

'I would pay you, but I ain't got no money.' A sudden idea flashed into her mind and Irene moved closer to the grille. 'I knows Vic and Wally Sykes. They'll see you right if you'll turn a blind eye and let me in.'

'I am an officer of the law and not open to bribes,' the man said stiffly, but Irene was quick to note a sly look flicker across his face.

'Vic and Wally think the world of me dad,' Irene said, pressing home her advantage.

'I'm known for me tender heart, young 'un, and I might just be persuaded to pass a message to your dad. What's his moniker?'

'Billy Angel, guv. He shouldn't be in prison. He ain't no criminal.'

'They never are, boy. What's the message?'

'We want to know if he's been up before the beak, and if he has then how long is he in for?'

'You say that he's a mate of the Sykes brothers?'

Irene nodded her head emphatically. There had to be some advantage in Pa's mixing with notorious criminals.

'What's your name then, boy? I need to know it if I'm going to speak to your dad.'

'It's Jim.'

'Wait here, Jim.' The hatch snapped shut and

there was nothing that Irene could do other than wait and hope that the screw kept his word. It was cold and getting colder. Above her the sky was the same granite-grey as the prison walls and a bitter wind was blowing from the north, threatening snow. She stamped her feet and cupped her hands over her mouth, breathing on her fingers in an attempt to keep them warm. She had no idea of the time, but the wait seemed like hours rather than minutes as she paced up and down outside the prison gates. She had just about given up when the hatch flew open and the same pair of beady eyes peered at her through the grille. 'Come here, boy.'

Obediently she moved closer. 'You've spoken to me dad?'

'He don't seem too fond of you. He went quite pale when I spoke your name and he said you was a great disappointment to him, but you was to take care of your ma and sisters since he's going to be in here for the next six years. Now clear off. I've done me bit.'

Shocked to the core by this harsh sentence, Irene walked away, barely knowing where she was headed. How would she break the news to Ma and Emmie she was at a loss to know. Perhaps it would be better to keep this piece of information to herself as it would only upset them, and if they realised that she had been roaming the streets dressed as a boy there would quite literally be hell to pay. There was nothing for it; she had to get back into the house unseen and keep her own counsel. With her head down, Irene pushed and shoved with the rest of the crowds in Newgate market, ignoring angry accusations that she had jostled a fat woman or had trodden on someone's big toe.

When she reached the corner of Wood Street she saw Yapp standing on the pavement outside the pickle shop. He was hammering on the door and shouting. She could not hear his exact words, but he was obviously extremely angry. She caught sight of Danny standing in the road, holding the horse's reins, and she crossed the street to speak to him. 'Hello, Danny.'

He stared at her, uncomprehending.

'Don't make a fuss, but it's me – Irene.'

He stared at her for a moment and then his face cracked into a grin. 'Miss Irene, what are you doing dressed up like that?'

'It's a long story and I don't want Yapp to recognise me.' She glanced over her shoulder, but Yapp was fully occupied in his attack on the shop door. 'Why is he banging on the door like a madman? He must know we aren't there any more.'

Danny eyed Yapp nervously. 'Of course he

does, miss. He's making out you owe him money so that he can reclaim the stock to cover the money he says you owes him.'

'But I paid him in advance, you know that.'

'He'd skin me alive if I was to say anything. I can't afford to lose me job.'

'I understand, Danny.' Irene laid her hand on his arm with a sympathetic smile.

He eyed her curiously. 'But the outfit, miss. Why?'

'It's a long story and it would take too long to go into it now, but I want you to do something for me, Danny.'

'Just name it, miss.'

'I believe that you live next door to Alice Kent.'

'I do,' Danny said, his eyes widening with surprise. 'I didn't know you was friends with Alice.'

'Will you give her a message from me? Tell her that I am very sorry for leaving so abruptly, and that I am safe.'

'I'll do that, of course I will, but supposing she wants to send you a message? Where will I find you?'

'At my sister's home in Love Lane,' Irene whispered. 'Josiah Tippet's house. Anyone will direct you there.'

'You can trust me. I'd do anything for you, miss,' Danny said, blushing.

Irene resisted the temptation to plant a kiss on his freckled face, and instead she gave him a hearty slap on the back before hurrying off in the direction of Love Lane.

She arrived in the mews just as the poulterer's boy was delivering a tray of game. Leaning nonchalantly against the railings of the adjoining property Irene waited her chance, and when the boy had left she slipped into the house unnoticed. Judging by the sound of raised voices emanating from the kitchen, Cook harboured suspicions that the purveyor of game and poultry had short-changed them. She could hear Jessie's plaintive voice protesting that it was not her fault, followed by the slap of a hand connecting to soft flesh and a loud howl. Poor Jessie, Irene thought as she ran up the stairs two at a time. No wonder she was a surly little beast if that was the way she was treated.

As she changed back into the clothes donated by Emmie, Irene thought long and hard about what she would do next. She must find a way to earn her own living, but the drudgery of service in a household such as this was less than appealing. She did not have a good enough education to teach in a school or to put herself up as a governess, and her lack of experience with small children made it unlikely that anyone would employ her as a nanny. She could, perhaps, get a job serving in a shop, but that would not provide her with the necessary accommodation. She toyed with the idea of working in the blacking factory or picking oakum or even washing bottles in the brewery, but again she would have nowhere to live. Josiah would be so thunder-struck by the notion of his sister-in-law doing menial work that she would never be allowed over the threshold again. She sat down at the dressing table and brushed her hair until it glinted with golden lights. She studied her features critically and sighed. She was fair enough, but hardly a ravishing beauty. If her face was not her fortune then she would have to live by her wits. She sighed as she coiled her hair into a knot at the nape of her neck, securing it with the tortoiseshell combs.

The knowledge that Pa was to be locked up for six years hung over her like one of the pot-bellied snow clouds that she could see from her window. Ma and Emmie would find out in time, of course, but for now it was best that they remained ignorant of the truth. She had not a hope of raising enough money to pay a lawyer to appeal against the sentence, and the only person in authority who knew that Billy Angel was not a member of the Sykes gang was Inspector Edward Kent. Hell would freeze over before she would beg him for help.

* * *

The threatened snow began to fall in earnest that evening and it continued night and day for a fortnight. Irene found herself virtually a prisoner in her sister's home. Ma and Emmie would not venture out for fear of slipping on the icy pavements or catching a chill in the bitter cold. Irene had to content herself with remaining indoors and occupying her time as best she could. She found a sudden interest in reading, and when she tired of listening to her mother and sister chattering endlessly about the baby she would retire to her room and curl up on the bed with a novel. Josiah had filled his study with books bought by the yard, but on the shelves Irene found volumes by Jane Austen, Mrs Gaskell and Charles Dickens, which she devoured avidly. These stories opened up a whole new world to her, far removed from selling pickles in Wood Lane or the seedy gaming establishments that Pa used to frequent. Reading made life just a little less dreary, and enabled her to put a brave face on dull mealtimes with Josiah presiding at the head of the table and Ephraim watching her, ready to draw attention to any lapse in her manners. Erasmus rarely ate with the family and even managed to time his breakfast so that everyone else had long finished and his father and brother had already left for the emporium.

'How do you get away with it?' Irene asked

one morning when he bowled into the dining room just as she was about to leave.

He paused with a silver serving spoon hovering over the last of the devilled kidneys in the salver. 'Get away with what, my dear Aunt-in-law?'

'You know very well what I mean, Ras. You flout every rule in the house and you go to work late and finish early. I wonder that your pa doesn't send you packing, or at least force a good day's work out of you.'

Erasmus piled sausages onto the kidneys, followed by a golden mound of buttered eggs. 'Blast, they've eaten all the bacon and the toast is stone cold.' He reached for the bell pull and gave it a tug before taking his plate to the table, where he seated himself in his father's place at the head. 'I'm the master here for the moment,' he said, chuckling. 'Sit down and keep me company, Aunt-in-law.'

'Stop calling me that. I'm not your aunt, and you haven't answered my question. Why do you get special treatment in this house? The rest of us have to behave like little mice when your pa is around, and yet you seem to do as you please.'

'I do, don't I?' Erasmus bit the end of a sausage and chewed it thoughtfully. 'I've never bothered my head with such a question, but now I come to think of it, perhaps the old man has just given up with me. I have been a bit of a trial to him, I suppose.' He shrugged his shoulders and attacked the kidneys with relish.

Hesitating for a moment, Irene tossed up between joining Ma and Emmie in the morning parlour and listening to a discussion about clothes for the expectant mother and the infant's layette, or talking to Ras and discovering how he managed to do exactly as he liked. She took a seat at the table and sat with her chin resting on her cupped hands. 'Go on then, tell me how you do it.'

Ras chewed thoughtfully and swallowed. 'Well,' he said, waving his knife in the air as if to emphasise the point, 'I just do it. I don't give a fig what the old man says and he knows it. No matter how many times he tanned my hide when I was a boy it didn't make a scrap of difference, whereas he only had to glower at poor old Eph and he collapsed in a quivering heap like a pink blancmange. As to the emporium, well now, Papa knows that I can charm the bloomers off the ladies.' He winked and grinned. 'Sometimes quite literally.'

'You're disgusting,' Irene said, stifling a chuckle.

'But charming, you must admit.' Ras polished off the remainder of his meal and pushed his plate away. 'Now what can I do for you, sweet Irene? You look a little down in the mouth to me. Aren't you enjoying your stay in Tippet's Castle?'

'I'm bored out of my mind, if you must know. If I hear the word baby mentioned once more, I think I'll scream. I'm used to working, not lazing around like some kept woman.'

'What you need,' Ras said slowly, eyeing her with his head on one side and a thoughtful frown, 'is to be taken out of yourself and I know the very thing.'

'Oh, yes, and what is that? A trip to a penny gaff with you and a quick grope in the hansom cab on the way home when, I should add, I would have to slap you round the chops for your cheek.'

'Nothing so vulgar. You've spent too much time dragging your pa out of cheap gaming houses and mixing with the wrong sort, old girl. No, I meant the Christmas Ball at the magnificent premises of the Drapers' Company in Throgmorton Street. It is next week, as it happens, and I haven't arranged to escort any particular young lady. I'm sure that Emmie would want you to go if only to keep her company.'

'A ball?' Irene shook her head. 'Crikey! Me going to a ball with all them toffs. Anyway, it's out of the question. I can't dance and I haven't got a ball gown. It's not for me.'

'Rubbish! I'll teach you a few dance steps,

and as to the rest you just smile and copy what everyone else is doing. Emmie will lend you a gown. I daresay she has a wardrobe bursting with frocks for every occasion, judging by the yards and yards of fine materials that have been sent home from the shop. Come on, Renie. Say you will and turn a dull event into a romp.'

'I'll think about it,' Irene said, rising from her seat. 'And now I'd best put in an appearance in the morning parlour before Ma and Emmie send out a search party.'

Ras sprang to his feet and barred her way. 'Say yes or I'll keep you prisoner in the dining room until you do.'

'Move aside, you fool.'

'I mean it. Be my partner for the evening and save me from utter boredom.'

She found that she could not resist the wicked twinkle in his blackberry-bright eyes and the thought of getting out of the house, if only for one evening, was irresistible. 'Oh, all right then. I suppose it might be interesting to see how the toffs amuse themselves.'

Emily was only too pleased to loan one of her splendid gowns for the coming event. She said she had been going to ask Irene to accompany her anyway, but what with the baby and everything it had quite gone out of her head. It would be her last chance to dance in public before her confinement in April, and she wanted to make the most of it. If she put her top hoop a little higher and wore the Brussels lace shawl that Josiah had given her for her birthday, her condition would scarcely be noticed. Irene bit back a sharp retort. Women had babies every day in Wood Street and Cheapside and they went about their business until they were about to give birth. Emmie might aspire to be like the pampered wives of the rising middle classes, but she was still an East End girl at heart. However, it would be mean to spoil her enjoyment and excitement over the preparations for the social event of the year in the drapery world.

The corsages were ordered and a private carriage had been hired for the evening. Josiah, it seemed, was sparing no expense. Irene guessed that this sudden burst of generosity had more to do with his desire to be made alderman than a change in his parsimonious nature, but she kept that thought to herself. She was looking forward to getting out of the house for an evening of music and dancing, but on the day of the ball disaster loomed in the shape of Emmie's expanding waistline. When she tried on her new gown, it did not fit. There were screams and hysterics and an urgent need to have the garment taken to the dressmaker in order for the necessary alterations to be made. Irene offered to go, seizing the chance to get out of the house even if it was only for an hour, but Emmie was afraid of what Josiah would say if he found out that Irene had been allowed out unchaperoned.

'This is awful,' she cried, pacing the floor and wringing her hands. 'I can't send that stupid girl, Jessie. She would get the instructions all muddled up, and there's no one else to go. They've all gone to the shop to supervise the Christmas rush, even Ras, so there's no one I can send.'

'Oh, for God's sake, Emmie. Stop being so dramatic. I'll go,' Irene said crossly. 'I'm sick of being shut up in this house anyway, and a walk will do me the world of good.'

'I suppose you could go, just so long as Josiah doesn't find out . . .'

'Just tell me where the woman lives and how much you want let out and I'll go now. I'll be back well before Josiah returns for his midday meal.'

Emily turned to her mother who had been sitting in silence throughout. 'What do you think, Ma?'

'I think that Renie has been a good girl for staying cooped up in the house, and it's high time she was allowed a bit of freedom. Let her go, Emmie, and stop fussing. You won't do the baby no good by getting all of a dither.'

'Yes, you're right as usual, Ma. But I'll only agree if you take a hansom cab there and back, Renie.' Emily reached for her reticule and took out a silk purse, which she tossed to her sister. 'There should be more than enough to pay for everything, but I want the change. Josiah doesn't mind spending money on clothes and furniture and things that show his rise to wealth, but he doesn't give me much pin money.'

Irene caught the purse deftly and put it in her pocket. 'I'll be there and back before you know it, so don't worry about anything.'

Minutes later, dressed in a fur-lined mantle borrowed from Emily and a matching fur hat that was said to be a copy of the latest Paris fashion, Irene pulled on a pair of kid gloves and, with Emmie's gown wrapped in butter muslin, she set off for the dressmaker's rooms in Bread Street. It had stopped snowing but a freeze had set in and the pavements were as slippery as a skating rink. She looked for a cab but each one that sped past was taken, and she decided that it would be quicker to walk. After all, it was not too far to Bread Street and it seemed a crying shame to waste good money when she was fit and healthy and longing for some exercise.

She walked to the end of Love Lane and turned left into Wood Street, but she had to tread carefully, and every now and then she slipped and had to grab at some railings to prevent a fall, although she was more concerned about the ball gown than for her own safety. She knew that her smart outfit made her stand out from the crowd and that she was attracting the stares of passers-by, but she did not care. It was wonderful to be out walking again, and to get away from the stultifying atmosphere of Tippet's Castle, as Ras ironically dubbed it. She made her way down Wood Street and crossed Cheapside, heading in the direction of Bread Street where she found the dressmaker's basement room without any difficulty. After a brief discussion, and having extracted a promise from the woman that she would do the necessary alterations immediately and return the gown to the house by evening, Irene was free to return home at a slower pace. The hard frost on top of the fallen snow had chilled and purified the air, almost eliminating the city stench and carpeting the filthy streets in a fluffy white blanket. The plane tree on the corner of Wood Street had lost all its leaves and its stark branches were iced with snow like frosting on a cake. The rooks were strangely silent as they perched, huddled and sulky-looking, like exclamation marks on the branches. They glared at Irene with beady eyes, as if they were taking the inclement weather as a personal insult.

She walked past her old home, and saw to her dismay that the window was now empty of jars and bottles. It looked as though Yapp had got his way after all; not that it made much difference to her, but she couldn't help wondering what had happened to their personal possessions. She would have paid a visit to the landlord, but as they owed him several weeks' rent she knew he was within his rights to sell their belongings, although they would fetch hardly anything at auction. She walked on, determined not to pine for a few old clothes and odd sticks of furniture. At least Artie was safe from arrest, and although Pa was incarcerated in Newgate, he was free from the clutches of the Sykes gang at least for the present. Perhaps if she put his case well, Josiah might be persuaded to pay for a lawyer who would appeal against the harsh sentence, and maybe, just maybe, Pa might come out a wiser man and give up gambling.

She had almost reached Love Lane when she heard the sound of running footsteps and someone calling her name. She stopped, glancing over her shoulder just as Danny skidded to a halt at her side. 'I thought it was you, miss. Although the fancy duds put me off a bit, and then I seen your face and I knew it could be no other.'

'What is it, Danny? I'm in a hurry.'

'It's Miss Alice. I found her collapsed on the floor in their parlour when I went in to see to the fire. I think she took a tumble, but Ma's out doing her washerwoman work and I don't know where to find her. Please come, miss.'

He was so breathless that it was difficult to understand what he was saying and Irene was confused. 'Have you tried to find her brother?'

Danny nodded emphatically. 'He's in court and they wouldn't let me in to see him. I left a message, but she needs someone to help her now.'

Irene could see that he was desperately worried and although the Kent's house was the last place on earth she wanted to visit, she could not bear to think of Alice all alone and possibly badly hurt. She may have the misfortune to be a copper's sister, but that was not her fault. Despite her reluctance to become involved, Irene knew that she could not simply walk away. 'All right, I'll come with you. At least I can stay with her while you fetch the doctor.'

Danny's face split into a grin of sheer relief. 'I knowed you wouldn't let me down, miss. Hold on to me and we'll get there in two ticks.'

With her hooped skirts swaying, Irene

clutched his arm and they hurried off in the direction of Milk Street. When her feet went from under her, he held her up with surprising strength and within minutes they had reached Robin Hood Court. Danny opened the front door, but he did not cross the threshold. 'You go in first, miss. I'm afeared she might be a goner, and I can't stand the sight of a dead 'un.'

Irene did not waste time in remonstrating with him. 'Make yourself useful then, Danny. Go and fetch the doctor and tell him to be quick.' Without waiting for his reply, she entered the house. The door to the parlour was wide open and Alice lay spread-eagled on the floor by the sofa. Irene moved swiftly to kneel beside her and she could have cried with relief when she discovered that Alice was still breathing, although deathly pale with a livid bruise on her forehead. Irene did not attempt to move her. She covered her with a crocheted rug from the sofa, and sat on the floor beside her, whispering words of comfort in the hope that Alice might be able to hear.

The ticking of the brass clock on the mantelshelf seemed to get louder and louder as she waited, although the hands barely appeared to move. The fire had almost burnt to nothing and it was bitterly cold in the room. Irene rose stiffly to her feet; there was little she could do for Alice until the doctor had examined her and deemed her fit to be moved, but she could do something to relieve the chill. She piled coal onto the dying embers and worked the bellows until tongues of golden flame licked up the chimney. When she was certain that the fire was burning satisfactorily, Irene took a spill from the jar on the hearth and lit the candles on the mantelshelf and on the dining table. She checked Alice again and was relieved to see a little colour returning to her pallid cheeks. 'Alice,' she said softly. 'Can you hear me?' There was no response and Irene was close to panicking, but the sound of footsteps crunching on the frozen snow in the court made her hurry to the window. To her intense relief she saw Danny, followed by the familiar figure of Dr Drummond, who was Ma's old physician. She went to the door to meet them. 'Thank goodness you've come, doctor. I done what I could but I'm afraid she's badly hurt.'

'Wait in the hall, Danny,' Dr Drummond said firmly. 'I might need you to go to the apothecary to fetch some medicine.'

Irene could see that Danny was close to tears and she patted his hand. 'You did well to find the doctor so quickly.' She hurried into the parlour to find the doctor on his knees beside Alice. He looked up and gave her an encouraging smile. 'Nothing broken, although I fear she might have a mild concussion from the blow to the head. Fetch the boy in, Irene, and we'll lift her onto the sofa. Perhaps you would go to the scullery and see if there is any arnica to put on that bruise.'

The scullery was small and the walls were lined with shelves. A window looked out onto a back yard with a pump and a privy close to the back fence. Jars and tins were ranged neatly on the shelves and there was bread in the crock on the table beneath the window. Irene searched a cupboard for arnica but found only a pitcher of milk and several brown paper packets containing tea, sugar and cocoa. She found a clean towel hanging on a hook and she took it outside to hold it under the pump, wringing as much water out of the wet material as she could before returning to the living room. She was relieved to discover that Alice had regained consciousness and was lying on the sofa.

'I couldn't find any arnica so I brought this instead,' Irene said, handing the damp cloth to Dr Drummond.

He placed it on Alice's forehead. 'A cold compress usually works wonders and I don't think there's any lasting harm done, but she must rest. It is very hard to make Alice follow instructions. She is not a model patient.'

His tone was severe but Irene saw a twinkle

in his grey eyes and Alice did not seem upset by this remonstrance. She managed a wobbly smile. 'I'm sorry to be such a trial to you, doctor.'

'So you should be. You must not over-exert yourself, Alice. There are plenty of people around who are only too willing to do things for you.'

Irene saw Alice's bottom lip quiver and she gave her an encouraging smile. 'Don't be too hard on her, doctor.'

'It was my fault,' Alice said humbly. 'I wanted to read my book but it was too dark to see. I tried to get to the table in order to light the candle, but I must have fainted or simply fallen. I don't remember anything else.'

'You could have fallen on the fire,' Danny muttered. 'You might have set yourself alight. You only had to wait for me to come in, miss.'

'I know. I'm sorry to cause so much fuss.' Alice's blue eyes filled with tears and she fumbled in her pocket for a handkerchief.

'It was an accident,' Irene said, shooting a warning glance at Danny. 'No lasting harm has come from it.'

Dr Drummond picked up his medical bag. 'There's nothing more I can do at the moment. You must rest now, Alice. I've no doubt that Mrs Priest will be back soon and she will look after you until your brother returns. I'll call in again tomorrow, but if you should need me sooner, just send the boy.'

'Thank you, doctor,' Alice said meekly.

'Mind you follow my instructions, young lady,' Dr Drummond said, allowing his stern countenance to crack into a smile. He left the room, beckoning Irene to follow him into the hall. 'Perhaps you could stay here until her brother arrives home,' he said in a low voice. 'I don't think she ought to be left alone until we are certain that there are no adverse effects from the fall.'

Irene hesitated. She did not relish the idea of facing Kent after their last stormy meeting, and Josiah would be returning home soon for his luncheon. There would be an almighty row if he discovered that she was missing.

Chapter Fourteen

'Come now, Irene,' Dr Drummond said with an impatient twitch of his shoulders. 'Surely I don't have to ask you twice? You are not unused to caring for the sick and infirm. Why do you hesitate?'

She tried to think of a plausible excuse, but Dr Drummond was regarding her with a steely look in his eyes. The parlour door had been left slightly ajar and she could see Alice lying as pale and limp as a rag doll on the sofa. Irene struggled with her conscience and lost. 'I'll be glad to sit with Alice.'

'I knew you wouldn't let me down.' Dr Drummond's expression lightened just a little and he snatched up his bag, seeming eager to be on his way. He let himself out of the house and a gust of ice-cold wind blew in from the court bringing with it a flurry of snow. Irene closed the door and hurried back into the parlour where she found that the draught had extinguished the candles, leaving trails of blue smoke rising to the ceiling and a strong smell of hot candle wax.

'That's what happened,' Alice said wearily. 'When Gladys left this morning the candles went out. I had to light them or else I would have been in semi-darkness until she returned.'

Irene took a spill from the jar and held it in the fire. 'There you are,' she said, relighting the candles. 'Now you can see to read.'

'My head aches,' Alice said, rearranging the cold compress. 'I think I would rather talk to you, if you don't mind.'

It was no use looking at the clock, although Irene was aware that it must be well past noon. Emmie would have to make up an excuse for her absence from the table or face her husband's wrath for breaking one of his cast-iron rules. Irene pulled up a chair and sat down beside Alice. 'I don't mind at all and I've all the time in the world. What would you like to talk about?'

Alice smiled. 'I know you parted on bad terms with my brother. It grieves me and I'd like to say a word in Edward's defence. You see, I love my brother. He is so good to me.'

And that is why he leaves you on your own all day without proper care, in a dark and dingy room with so little cheer that it would make the most optimistic person want to cut their throat? The words went through her head, but Irene managed to bite her tongue. 'I'm sure he is,' she said in as mild a tone as she could manage. 'Tell me how you fill the long day? You said you were reading. What books do you like?'

Alice peeled the compress from her forehead. 'This is making me shiver. Do you think it would be all right if I left it off?'

Taking it from her, Irene tossed it onto the table. 'You must do as you please, Alice. I think you spend too much time being concerned for others. You should be a bit more selfish – like me.'

That made Alice giggle. 'I don't believe you are selfish at all. Just look at you, Irene. All dressed up like a lady and you obviously have much better things to do than simply sitting here with me.'

'I haven't,' Irene said truthfully. 'And these clothes aren't mine. They belong to my sister, Emily, who has married a pompous boor of a man who is middle-aged and fat but has plenty of money.'

Alice's eyes opened wide with interest. 'Really? That sounds just like one of the novels that I've been reading. Have you read Mr Thackeray's *Vanity Fair*? The heroine, Becky Sharp, is so determined to better her position in life that she will do almost anything. I don't think she marries a much older man, but I haven't quite got that far. Although,' she added hastily, 'I didn't mean to liken her to your sister. I'm sure she married for love and not for money.'

Irene let this pass and she settled herself more comfortably on the chair. 'I've only just begun reading novels. I haven't had that much education, but Josiah, my brother-in-law, has scores of books in his study. I've read some of them, although I am a bit slow, and sometimes struggle with the long words.'

'I do admire you for that. We were lucky, I suppose. Although we grew up on a farm, our mother was an educated lady and she made certain that we could both read and write at a very young age.'

'You must miss her.'

'I do. She was a wonderful person; so sweet and loving. She taught us herself until she fell ill and then she made certain that we attended the village school. Our lives would have been so different if she had lived. But everything seemed to go wrong after she died, and then I had the accident. If Edward had not brought me to London I tremble to think what sort of life I would have led on the farm, for I am very little use to anyone.'

'You must not think like that,' Irene said hotly. 'It's quite obvious that your brother thinks the world of you and quite rightly too.'

Alice sighed. 'Yes, Edward is so patient with me. He never complains.'

And he is hardly ever here, Irene thought angrily. If he spent a little more time with his sister and lot less time chasing promotion, he might be a better person.

'He is a good man,' Alice insisted as if sensing Irene's disapproval. 'And he's very good at his job too.'

Irene could see that an answer was expected and she said the first thing that came into her head. 'I believe he works very hard.' She did not add that Inspector Kent had been instrumental in putting her own father behind bars and had sent her childhood friend into exile. To wilfully hurt Alice would be like pulling the wings off a fragile butterfly. Irene glanced at the clock again. It was half past one and by now Ma and Emmie would be frantic with worry. Her stomach rumbled, reminding her that she had not eaten since breakfast.

'You keep looking at the clock,' Alice said softly. 'Please don't stay here on my account. Edward will come as soon as he can and Gladys should be back from delivering her washing any moment now.'

'Do you always have to wait for her to get your meals?'

'I'm used to it, and I don't have much of an appetite.'

Irene put her hand in her pocket and felt the reassuring jingle of coins in Emmie's purse.

She rose to her feet and slipped on the fur-lined mantle. 'I'm starving even if you're not. There's a pie shop on the corner of Milk Street; it won't take me more than five minutes to walk there and buy us some food. Will you be all right if I leave you alone for that long, Alice?'

Alice nodded and smiled. 'Of course, but please don't put yourself out for me.'

Irene fastened the military-style frogging across her chest and pulled on her gloves. 'I'm not. This is for me, pure and simple.'

It was a relief to leave the dreary house and she was tempted to keep going, but she could not let Alice down. Irene trudged on, driven by loyalty as well as hunger, and she purchased two hot meat pies, pease pudding and mashed potato. The bundle wrapped in a copy of yesterday's newspaper warmed her hands as she made her way back to the house.

'That was quick,' Alice said, sniffing appreciatively. 'It smells so good. I think I might be hungry after all.'

Putting aside all thoughts of facing Inspector Kent and the embarrassment it would cause, Irene served the food and settled down to enjoy her meal. She couldn't help noticing that Alice ate less than half of what was on her plate before declaring that she could not manage another mouthful.

'I've eaten much more than usual,' she said apologetically. 'I don't need much food, sitting about all day as I do.'

'Do you never go outside these four walls?'

'Not very much at all in the winter, but in the summer Edward hires a Bath chair and we go down to the river where I watch the ships and barges. That is my favourite place. I love the river and I try to imagine it from its source to the sea and all the sights it must pass on its way. Sometimes I wish I could sail away on the tide and let the river take me to some of the far-flung places that I read about in books.'

Irene swallowed the last of her pie, feeling quite guilty that she enjoyed the best of health while poor Alice was forced to live a life of dreams. She hid her feelings by taking the plates to the scullery. She was on her way back to the living room when she heard footsteps on the frosty cobblestones and the doorknob rattled. She held her breath, drawing herself up to her full height in the expectation of facing Kent, but it was Mrs Priest who burst into the hall with a worried expression deepening the lines on her face into ridged furrows. 'Oh, miss, my Danny told me that you were here. Hasn't the inspector come home?'

'Obviously not,' Irene said more coolly than she had intended to. Her relief on seeing Mrs Priest instead of Kent was so great that she was quite breathless. 'I stayed to keep Alice company until someone came to look after her.'

'How is she, dearie?'

'She doesn't seem any the worse for her fall, other than a bump on the head and a large bruise. The doctor said he will call again tomorrow.'

Mrs Priest clutched her hand to her bosom and her eyes were moist. 'I love that poor girl as though she was my own, and I feel terrible that she suffered an accident. I'm so grateful to you for everything you've done, miss.'

'I did what anyone would do in the circumstances, but now I really have to go. Will you stay with Alice until her brother returns home?'

'I'll look after my little pet; you don't have to concern yourself on that score.'

'Then I'll just collect my things and say goodbye to Alice.'

Irene fully expected to walk into a scene of near hysteria when she returned to the house in Love Lane at half past three, but Jessie admitted her without comment.

Irene made her way upstairs to the drawing room, pausing outside the door and she braced herself for a barrage of accusations and questions. She opened it quietly and stepped inside, but the scene that met her eyes was anything but stormy. Ma was seated on one of the elegant damask-covered sofas smiling proudly as Emily paraded around in the ball gown, which now fitted her perfectly.

Emily spun round to face Irene and she was laughing delightedly. 'Isn't this just wonderful? The seamstress has done a superb job and she returned the gown just half an hour ago. I'll definitely give her more custom in the future.'

'It's lovely,' Irene murmured. 'Er, has Josiah seen it?'

'No, he didn't come home for luncheon. With Christmas so close they are so frantically busy in the shop that neither he nor the boys could get away. Still, that means more money coming in and more new gowns for me. I think I shall ask Josiah for a carriage and pair as a present when the baby is born. After all, he can hardly expect his wife and child to use public transport. It wouldn't do.'

Irene breathed a sigh of relief. It seemed that they had not missed her after all, although it was a bit galling to think that she might have been the victim of an attack, or had a fatal accident, and no one had even noticed that she was missing. She glanced at her mother, who gave her a reassuring smile. 'We knew you was on a mission of mercy, Renie. Yapp's boy, Danny, came to the door and told us that you'd gone to that copper's house to look after his crippled sister. I call that a noble act on your part, considering the hurt that man has done our family.'

'More likely she did it to get in well with the police,' Emily said, tossing her head so that her diamond earrings glinted in the candlelight. 'I hope Inspector Kent was grateful to you, and maybe he'll put in a good word for Pa.'

'I'm sure the judge will be lenient,' Clara said wistfully. 'After all, my Billy hadn't done anything really bad and it was his first offence. I expect they'll let him out soon, but I've been too afraid to make enquiries.'

'And I'm certain that a good lawyer could get him off,' Emmie said confidently. 'I'm waiting for the right time and then when Josiah is in a particularly good mood I'll ask him if he will hire a brief. After all, it would be in his best interests to have Pa released from prison.'

Irene had not the heart to tell them that Pa had already been tried and convicted. They would learn the truth of his harsh sentence soon enough. 'I think I'd better go to my room and start getting ready for this evening.'

'Yes, of course, ducks. You need to be fresh and lovely for the ball. I can't wait to see you dressed up in them fine feathers of Emmie's.'

'Yes, and make sure you're ready on time,'

Emily said, doing another twirl and admiring her reflection in the huge gilt-framed mirror that hung over the ornate mantelpiece. 'You know that Josiah doesn't like to be kept waiting.'

Irene had never imagined that one day she would be arriving at the grand entrance of the Drapers' Company in Throgmorton Street in a hired carriage, or that a liveried footman would assist her onto the red carpet which covered the slushy pavement. She had to struggle with the voluminous skirts of pale pink mousseline, frilled and draped in the latest fashion and drawn back to form a train. She must remember to take tiny steps or else she would be in danger of catching her toes in the wire cage of the crinoline, which made her feel like a trapped canary. She would have preferred to stride about unnoticed in Jim's breeches than to be an object of admiring glances in her borrowed finery. Erasmus was at her side in a moment, proffering his arm, and she accepted gratefully, although as she was relieved of the velvet cloak by one of the minions inside the great entrance hall she saw Ras's eyes wander to the décolletage and she felt the blood rush to her cheeks. He looked up and laughed. 'What a modest little violet you are, dear Aunt.'

'I'm more of a stinging nettle, Ras Tippet, as you will find if you try to take liberties. And I am not your blooming aunt.'

This remark elicited a guffaw of laughter that made those nearest to them turn and stare with looks of marked disapproval, but Ras appeared to be unabashed and he chuckled. 'Come on, let's show these jumped-up shopkeepers that we don't give a fig for their stuffy conventions.' Without waiting for her answer, he led her along the red carpet, cutting a swathe through the respectable merchants and their wives who patiently waited their turn to be announced and ushered into the great hall. Irene did not know whether to laugh or to remonstrate with him, but to have a fight in such a public place would only draw more attention to them, and Josiah, Emmie and Ephraim were not too far behind. 'Excuse me, sir, I believe we are next,' Ras said, pushing past a portly man whose florid jowls overlapped a stiff white collar which threatened to sever his head if he moved too quickly.

The man's eyes bulged and his face turned from crimson to puce as he spluttered a protest, but Ras ignored him and went to the head of the orderly queue, giving their names to the major-domo, who duly announced them in a clear bell-like tone. Irene stifled a nervous giggle, gazing around and barely able to take in the splendour of the great chamber. For a moment all eyes were on them, but then the orchestra struck up and couples began to take the floor.

'Will you honour me with this dance, Miss Angel?' Ras said, bowing from the waist and grinning at her with a mischievous sparkle lighting his eyes. The air was filled with the scent of hothouse flowers, and the smell of hot wax from hundreds of candles mingled with the perfume and pomade worn by the guests.

'Thank you, I will, but I warn you now that I can't dance.'

'Nonsense,' Ras said confidently as he slipped her hand through the crook of his arm. 'There's nothing to it; just follow me. It's the grand march first and all we have to do is prance about the floor like a pair of thoroughbred horses at Tattersalls, then it should be a waltz to follow. I look forward to that above all.'

The guests of honour had taken the floor and to Irene's relief Ras waited respectfully until it was their turn to join in the dance. Josiah led Emmie onto the floor and Irene experienced a rush of pride and affection to see her sister looking so radiant and happy to be out in company. Even though she could not in her heart acknowledge Josiah as the best husband in the world, Irene had to concede that Emmie was more than content with her lot.

'Don't look so serious, Irene,' Ras said, squeezing her fingers. 'This is supposed to be fun.'

'I'm concentrating on my feet.'

'And very pretty feet they are too, just like the rest of you.'

'I hope you're not trying to flirt with me, Ras.'

'I am flirting quite outrageously, my dear, as would all the men in the room who are not in their dotage.'

'You are a bad lot,' Irene said, smiling.

His eyes strayed once more to the swell of her breasts and he grinned. 'I admit it, but at least I'm not made of wood like your friend over there.'

Following his gaze, she saw Edward Kent standing in a group of important-looking bewhiskered gentlemen. At his side was a pretty young girl who was talking animatedly, fluttering her eyelashes and smiling coyly up at him. There was an instant spark of recognition in Kent's eyes as Irene sailed past him on Ras's arm, but she did not acknowledge him. How selfish men are, she thought grimly. He is here most probably to further his career in some way regardless of the fact that his sister is left alone and injured. He had better not speak to me, for if he does I shall have to give him a piece of my mind and tell him a few home truths which he will not like one bit.

'You look cross,' Ras said, laughing. 'I know I haven't stepped on your toes, so what has made that lovely mouth droop into a pout and creased your alabaster brow in a frown?'

'I am fine, thank you, Ras.' Irene withdrew her hand from his arm as the grand march ended, and she made for the table where Ephraim was seated looking distinctly grumpy. 'Aren't you enjoying yourself, Ephraim?'

He half rose to his feet and then slumped down again as Ras drew out a chair for Irene. 'Not particularly. This type of do doesn't appeal to me at all, but the guvner insists that we all put in an appearance.'

Irene angled her head. 'Wouldn't you like to dance? There are some young ladies who look as though they are dying to be asked.'

'The pretty ones are all taken. I ain't here to fuss over plain girls doomed to be wallflowers.'

'Now with that I agree,' Ras said heartily. 'And I want you to put my name against every dance on your card, Irene; especially the last waltz.'

'What I would love is a glass of punch,' Irene said, fanning herself vigorously. 'I never realised that dancing was such hard work – I'm parched.'

Ras winked at his brother. 'A girl after me

own heart. You won't get a partner at all if you show that miserable face to the world, Eph. It's enough to curdle the milk. Have a drink and cheer up for God's sake.' Without waiting to see if his barb had struck home, Ras sauntered off towards the table at the end of the room where a small crowd of gentlemen hovered around a silver punchbowl like wasps gorging on a squashed plum.

'You want to watch him,' Ephraim said, scowling. 'He's a young libertine. Our father would take a horsewhip to him if he knew half the things that my dear brother gets up to.'

'Well, he won't get up to any mischief with me. I've got his measure,' Irene replied, smiling.

'May I have the pleasure of this waltz, Miss Angel?'

She turned her head and found herself staring up into Kent's face. For a moment, she was so flustered that she couldn't think how to refuse him without appearing downright rude. She had not expected him to single her out, let alone ask her to dance. Couples were already taking the floor for a waltz and the men had their arms around the ladies' waists in a very familiar fashion. Irene glanced at Ephraim, who was staring at the inspector open-mouthed. She looked for Ras but he was too far away to claim that she had promised him the next dance, and, unable to think of a plausible excuse, she rose to her feet. 'Yes, thank you,' she murmured.

Without saying a word, he swept her into the midst of the swirling couples and led her into the fluid movements of a Viennese waltz. Irene had to concentrate hard on following him at first, but soon they were whirling around the room as if they had done this a thousand times in the past. Her heart was thudding against her ribs and it was not just from exertion. To her intense astonishment, being held in Kent's arms was like the embrace of a tiger – exciting and just as dangerous.

'I heard what you did for Alice today,' he said in a low voice. 'I can't thank you enough.'

She met his eyes and realised that he was sincere. 'It was nothing. I only did what anyone would have done for anyone in similar circumstances.'

'Even someone who has as much reason to dislike me as you do?'

'I dislike what you stand for,' Irene replied evenly. 'But Alice is another matter.'

A smile transformed his harsh features. He was not exactly handsome, she thought, but had he been anyone else she might have considered that he was really quite nice-looking in a marble-statue kind of way. She stiffened her shoulders, drawing a little further away from him. She must not allow the romance of the evening to beguile her into dropping her guard; she must always remember that they were on opposing sides. Never trust a copper; that's what Pa always said. If he was being nice to her he must have an ulterior motive.

'My sister is an angel,' Kent said, twirling her round in a breathtaking turn. 'She never complains. Sometimes I wish that she would.'

Irene had been concentrating on her feet during the complicated movement, but something in his voice made her look up, and she was shocked to see a look of genuine pain in his eyes. 'Is there no cure for her?'

He shook his head. 'The doctors don't think so. They say that she is lucky to be alive and that there is nothing more they can do. She will remain a cripple for the rest of her life.'

Once again, Irene forgot that this man was her enemy. She could sense and sympathise with his genuine anguish. 'I am truly sorry.'

He inclined his head, but he did not meet her gaze. It was almost as if he were afraid of revealing too much of his inner self. They continued in silence, and she realised with a guilty feeling of pleasure that she was dancing just like the ladies who had been taught the art from an early age. She allowed herself to float in his arms to the magical strains of the

Viennese waltz; and it was only when the music stopped that she came back to earth with a bump. Kent released her with a polite smile and escorted her back to her table. 'Thank you, Miss Angel.' He bowed from the waist and walked away.

With mixed feelings, she watched his tall figure vanish into the crowd. The orchestra might have ceased playing but she could still hear the music in her head.

'I thought you were saving that dance for me.'

She turned with a start to see Ras standing behind her. He had a sulky scowl on his face which made him look like a petulant schoolboy. Irene forced a smile. 'You weren't here and I decided to keep in well with the law.'

'With a father like yours that seems very sensible,' Ephraim muttered.

Irene turned on him angrily. 'I won't have a word said against my pa.'

Ras slipped his arm around her waist. 'Come now, old girl. Eph didn't mean anything by it. He's a tactless clod if ever there was one. Why don't you sit down and take a sip of punch?'

Irene was too angry to be placated by words and wine, and she shook her head.

'Then let's dance,' Ras said, taking her hand in his. 'It's a quadrille, quite slow and simple; just follow my lead.'

The quadrille was followed by a schottische, then a lively polka and some country dances which Irene struggled to perform. Emmie on the other hand was seemingly tireless and danced every dance. She even managed to persuade Ephraim from his seat for the lancers, which Josiah chose to sit out. Irene was not short of partners; even so she found herself scanning the company in an attempt to catch a glimpse of Kent, but it seemed that he did not choose to dance with anyone else. She was unaccountably pleased, and was immediately ashamed of her own vanity in thinking that he had singled her out above all the females present. He had chosen her simply to thank her for looking after his sister; that was the truth of the matter, but she couldn't help feeling just a little smug.

She looked for him at supper, but he was nowhere to be seen. Perhaps he had gone home early to keep Alice company. Irene hoped so, anyway, but when she returned from the dining room she spotted him conversing with the same distinguished-looking gentleman as before. She turned to Ras. 'Who is that man talking to Inspector Kent?'

He shrugged his shoulders. 'I couldn't say for certain but I think he's the Commissioner of Police. It seems that your friend is here to further his career. Personally, I can't stand cops.

They'll arrest a fellow as soon as look at him, as I found out to my cost some years back when I was a green youth.'

Irene felt disappointment and anger roil in her stomach. So Kent was everything that she had thought him to be and more. What a fool she had been to allow herself to be persuaded otherwise simply because he had partnered her in a waltz. She had always prided herself on being above silly girlish fancies, but in a moment of weakness she had allowed simple physical attraction to cloud her judgement.

She was startled out of her thoughts by Ephraim, who suddenly leapt to his feet. He moved to her side and executed a nifty bow from the waist. 'I know this one, Irene. Would you do me the honour?'

Taken completely by surprise, Irene could not think of a valid excuse and she allowed him to lead her onto the floor. It was a complicated country dance and she had to concentrate hard on following the patterns set by the other couples, which involved changing partners many times. With a sinking heart she saw that Kent had partnered the young lady with the copper-coloured ringlets and rosy cheeks who had been so anxious to attract his attention earlier in the evening. Irene could only hope that she would be spared dancing with him a second time, but it was not to be.

'Are you enjoying yourself, Miss Angel?' Kent asked as the complicated pattern of the dance united them once again.

'I am, and it would seem that you are too. You appear to have done your duty. Shouldn't you be going home to your sister, Inspector?'

'She is well cared for.'

'That wasn't the case earlier today. I suppose you were just doing your duty when Alice needed you most.'

'Now you are just being difficult, Miss Angel. Are you trying to pick a fight with me?'

They were separated for a moment by the dance, but when they came together again Irene stopped, refusing to move another step. 'Work comes first and foremost with you, doesn't it, Inspector Kent? Your career means everything to you and you don't care how you go about gaining promotion or who gets hurt on the way. You had my Pa arrested and thrown into jail because you couldn't catch the real criminals.'

'For God's sake keep your voice down,' Kent said in a low voice. 'You're making a scene.'

'I don't care,' Irene cried, too distraught to care that all eyes were upon them.

He took her by the hand, clasping it to his chest so that she could not move. 'You don't know what you're saying.'

White lines edged his mouth and his eyes

were dark expressionless pools in his pale face. Irene knew she had gone too far but she could not stop herself. 'Leave me alone. I don't want anything more to do with you.'

'You can't accuse me of these things and not hear me out. We will settle this once and for all, in private.' Kent released her hand only to take her by the elbow in an attempt to lead her off the dance floor.

Panic-stricken, she twisted free from him and raising her hand, she slapped him hard across the face.

There was a gasp from the onlookers followed by a stunned silence and Irene fled.

Chapter Fifteen

'What were you thinking of, Renie?' Emily demanded, mopping her eyes with her handkerchief.

'He made me angry,' Irene said, turning away to peer out of the window as the snow-covered city streets flashed past. The carriage wheels clattered over the icy cobblestones and the metallic sound of the horses' hooves shattered the silence that hung in a pall over the shuttered business heart of the City.

'He made you angry?' Josiah spluttered. 'You made a spectacle of us tonight, Irene. You behaved outrageously and I won't stand for it.'

Emily laid her gloved hand on his arm. 'Please don't be cross, Josiah. I'm sure that Renie is very sorry and will apologise to everyone concerned.'

'You mustn't upset yourself, Mrs Tippet,' Josiah said gruffly, covering her hand with his. 'It's not good for you and the unborn infant, and that makes your sister's behaviour even more despicable. I can see my position as alderman fading into the distance and all because of her.'

'I am sorry, Josiah,' Irene said with a sigh. 'I acted on the spur of the moment. I didn't think . . .'

'No, you didn't think. You behaved liked a harridan. I don't know how I shall face my business colleagues after this. It only needs for the news to leak out that my father-in-law is a common criminal in league with the notorious Sykes brothers, and I will be ruined. What respectable man would send his wife to shop at an emporium run by people associated so closely with the underworld?'

'Oh, no, dear,' Emily said, sniffing and dabbing her eyes with her hanky. 'Don't say that.'

'I do say it and I mean it. In future, Irene will not accompany us to any of the festive season functions, and she will stay within doors until this latest scandal blows over.' Josiah leaned across the swaying carriage to put his florid face close to Irene's. 'Do you understand me, miss?'

'Yes,' Irene muttered, almost choking on the word. She had to agree if only to save Emmie further distress, but she was damned if she was going to obey Josiah. It would be worse than being locked up in Newgate.

'You will stay by your sister's side, Irene,'

Josiah continued, wagging his finger at her. 'You will keep her company and look after your mother. If I find that you have disobeyed me, I will throw you out onto the streets where I think you truly belong, with the rotten cabbage leaves and turnip tops from the costermongers' barrows.'

'Oh, Mr Tippet,' Emily sobbed. 'Please stop.'

'I'll say no more, but your sister will do as I say, or she will leave our house.' Josiah glared at Irene. 'Don't think I will relent. I mean every word.'

Irene discovered to her cost that Josiah was unshakeable in his decision to keep her indoors and out of sight. She was confined to the house. She had no money and no means of escape. She had once made an attempt to get out, but she had found the front door was firmly locked and Jessie had been put in charge of the key. It was insufferable that a servant should be placed in such a position of power, but Emily could do nothing to alter the situation, and Ma's entreaties to Josiah fell on deaf ears.

Matters were made worse by Ephraim, who made it clear that he considered Irene had been dealt with quite leniently under the circumstances; and Ras seemed to think the whole sorry affair was a joke. He offered to smuggle Irene out of the house, but only if she promised to accompany him on one of his forays into the less reputable parts of the East End for a night of gambling and carousing. She might once have been tempted, but she did not entirely trust him. She had heard him staggering along the corridor to his bedroom in the early hours of the morning often enough, and seen him at breakfast, bleary-eyed and obviously suffering from the effects of over-indulging in cheap grog and opium. No matter how many times Josiah remonstrated with his son, Ras let it all wash over him like the waves on the foreshore. Irene would have found it amusing if it had not been so frustrating. If only she were a man. They got away with murder. Quite literally in some cases, as Vic and Wally Sykes were free to roam the streets while Pa was locked up in jail. There was no justice in this world, she thought bitterly, but she was not going to stand for being treated like a wayward child a moment longer than was absolutely necessary.

Christmas came and went and Irene tried to put a brave face on her continuing lack of freedom, if only for Ma's sake and to keep Emmie from fretting. To alleviate the tedium of the long winter days, she read every novel in Josiah's possession and her thoughts often strayed to Alice, who was doomed to this sort of existence for the rest of her days. She even went so far as to ask permission from Josiah to visit Alice so that she might apologise to her at least for the embarrassment she had caused Kent, but Josiah refused point-blank. 'You will stay indoors until my wife has given birth,' he had said. 'After that I might allow you to accompany her in the carriage, but you will not roam the streets alone as you have done in the past. My one hope for you, Irene, is that I can find a respectable man to marry you and take you off my hands. To that end, once Mrs Tippet has recovered from her confinement, we will invite eligible bachelors to our home and pray that one of them might consider you worthy of an offer of marriage.'

Irene had been left speechless and also furious. She had retreated to her room and locked herself in until she could face Ma and Emmie without giving vent to her feelings. In the cold confines of her cheerless bedchamber she decided that she simply must escape from Josiah's house, and the sooner the better. She had to face the fact that she would not be able to exist alone on the streets; it would be different if Pa was free to earn a living of sorts, even if it was from gambling. Together they could find rooms and maybe even persuade their old landlord to give them another chance to run the shop. She could do nothing unless Pa was released from prison, but perhaps the very people who were responsible for his plight might be the ones to secure his early release. Gradually she formulated a plan. Despite her hatred of gambling and everything that the Sykes brothers stood for, she decided to brave the evil ones in their den and put her case to them. But first she had to escape from the house without being accosted by a power-crazed Jessie or Cook brandishing a rolling pin.

The next day, after breakfast, she went to her room pleading a sick headache. Half an hour later, wearing Jim's old clothes, she hid on the back stairs waiting her chance to escape through the tradesmen's entrance. For several days now, she had watched from an upstairs window and timed the arrival of the various deliveries so that she knew almost to the minute when the butcher's boy would call. He was the one who lingered longest, and even though she could not see her, Irene guessed that it was Jessie who was the unlikely recipient of his amorous intentions. Today was no exception, and she crouched on the staircase listening to his cheeky banter and Jessie's coy responses. An impatient shout from the kitchen brought their flirtation to an abrupt end and Jessie scuttled off, carrying the tray of meat.

Irene could have cried with relief when she discovered that Jessie had forgotten to lock the outside door. It opened easily on well-oiled hinges and Irene made her escape. It was so good to be outside that she could have taken off her cap and thrown it in the air, but she forced herself to walk slowly without drawing attention to herself. The icy grip of winter had eased and there was a hint of mildness in the damp February air. Huge grey clouds hung ominously overhead, ready to spill rain on the city below, but at the moment it was dry and once she had reached the comparative safety of Wood Street she strode off with a determined lift of her chin and a spring in her step. She went straight to Blue Boar Court and knocked on the door.

After a moment or two she heard shuffling footsteps on the flagstones inside and the door opened just enough to reveal Blackie's beady eye peering at her. 'What d'you want, boy?'

'You must remember me, Mr Blacker, sir. I'm Jim Angel, Billy's son. I come to see Vic or Wally, whichever one of them is about.'

'They ain't interested in a sprat like you. Push off.'

He was about to close the door but Irene had been ready for this and she gave it a mighty shove, catching him off guard. She slipped past him. 'Sorry, mister, but this won't wait. Don't bother to show me in. I knows the way.'

His large hairy hand reached out to grab her, but Irene was too quick for him and she scuttled along the narrow passage ignoring his tirade of threats as to what he would do if he caught her. She ran up the stairs and barged into the main saloon. The pungent smell of stale cigar smoke and the fumes of strong spirits assailed her nostrils and she almost tripped over the inert body of a punter lying on the floor with his legs under one of the card tables. She thought at first that he was dead, but he groaned and she could tell by the foul stench of his breath that he was dead drunk. She stepped over him.

'Hello.' Her high-pitched voice echoed off the smoke-blackened ceiling and the glasses behind the bar tinkled a response. 'Is anyone about?'

She heard a door open at the far end of the room and she spun round to see Vic Sykes, the younger of the brothers, standing in the doorway, staring at her. 'Who the devil are you and what do you want here?'

Irene took a deep breath. Her legs were shaking but she forced her dry lips into a grin and approached him with an attempt at a confident swagger. 'Am I speaking to Mr Vic Sykes?' she asked, feigning ignorance.

'Never mind that. Answer my question, boy. Who are you?'

'I'm Jim Angel, Billy's son.'

Vic's scowl lightened to a frown. 'So you

are. I reckon I saw you here one night with the old codger. How is your dad?'

'Bearing up, mister, but he shouldn't be in jail.'

'That ain't how the beak saw it, young 'un. Your dad got caught and that was his fault, not mine.'

'I got a sick mother to support, mister. We've lost the shop because we couldn't pay the rent. I know you could get my pa out of prison if it suited you. I've heard that Vic and Wally Sykes can do anything.'

He perched on the edge of the billiard table, eyeing her thoughtfully. 'How old are you, boy?'

'Fourteen, mister. I don't expect something for nothing. I'm stronger than I look and I'm prepared to work for you to pay off the favour.'

'You look younger and you sound like a girl. Come back when your voice has broken and you got a bit more flesh and muscle on your bones. Maybe I can find you work then.'

'You got friends in high places, so they say,' Irene said, determined not to be put off so easily. 'My pa needs a good mouthpiece to get him off the hook.'

'Lawyers cost money, kid. Why would I want to fork out for a tuppeny-ha'penny gambler like Billy?'

'I thought you was his friend,' Irene said angrily. 'Some mate you are.'

Vic moved with panther-like swiftness and he grabbed her round the throat. 'Cheeky little bastard, ain't you? Well, listen to me, boy. If you want to live to see your dad released from Newgate you'd best keep out of my way. And you can tell Billy from me that he'd best serve his time and keep his trap shut or it'll be the worse for him and his family. Got it?'

His fingers tightened on her windpipe and Irene struggled to breathe. Her eyes were watering and she could only nod her head in response. He released her with a violent shove that sent her crashing into one of the tables. It tipped over and she fell to the ground in a shower of gaming chips.

'Get out of here,' Vic snarled. 'I won't be so gentle next time.'

Although she was bruised and slightly dazed from the fall, Irene's first thought was for her disguise, and her hands flew to straighten the cap that had slipped over one eye and was in danger of coming off to reveal her long hair. She scrambled to her feet and staggered from the room to the sound of Vic's derisive laughter. Spots of light danced before her eyes as she made her way down the stairs to the passage below.

Blackie eyed her with contempt. 'Give you

a good hiding, did he? Don't say I didn't warn you, boy.' He strode to the door and opened it. 'Get out while you can. You know what will happen if you cross the Sykes brothers. Take my advice and keep well out of their way.'

Irene stumbled out of the building. She had known all about the Sykes brothers' reputation for violence. Pa had always seemed to get on well with them, but Vic's vicious treatment had shaken her to the core. She made her way to Cheapside but as she crossed the busy thoroughfare her mind was elsewhere, and she only narrowly avoided being run down by a brewer's dray, to the obvious annoyance of the driver who swore at her and shook his fist. She was too shocked to retaliate but she managed to get to the far side without further mishap.

She had set so much store on the old adage *honour amongst thieves*; it had not occurred to her that the Sykes brothers would abandon her father so completely. Unable to think clearly, she found herself walking in the direction of Robin Hood Court. It was only then that she realised how much she wanted to see Alice and to apologise for the humiliating scene at the Drapers' Company ball. Irene cared little for Kent's feelings, but she knew how devoted his sister was to him, and she would not upset Alice for all the tea in China. It hurt her pride to acknowledge it, but Irene was beginning to think that Kent might have been right in his estimation of the Sykes brothers; in fact she was slowly coming round to his way of thinking, but she would have died rather than tell him so.

She found Alice in her customary place on the sofa, reading a copy of *Pride and Prejudice*. Her eyes rounded in surprise as she gazed at Irene's clothes. 'Oh, my goodness. Is it really you, Irene?'

'I'm afraid it is, Alice.'

'I thought that girls dressing as boys only happened in penny novelettes.'

'It was the only way I could get out of the house. I've been imprisoned in that wretched place just like one of the unfortunate females in popular novels.'

'Then do sit down and tell me all about it,' Alice said, setting her book aside. 'You know how I love stories, and this one will be true to life and not from the pages of a book. I'm so happy to see you, but I was afraid that you might not want to visit this dull place again.'

'It wasn't that, Alice.' Irene pulled up a chair and sat down. 'I wanted to see you, but it's been difficult, and I wasn't certain that you would want me to call again after what I did to your brother at the drapers' ball.'

'What did you do? Edward never tells me anything.'

Irene had gone too far to stop now. She could have played down her part in the unfortunate scene, but the truth lay heavily on her conscience and admitting her folly to Alice was the nearest she could get to apologising to the man who had become the bane of her life. Taking a deep breath, she launched into a detailed description of the events that had led up to her abandoning Kent in the middle of the dance floor. Alice listened wide-eyed and enthralled, as if Irene was reading a chapter from one of her favourite novels. 'My goodness,' she exclaimed as Irene came to an abrupt halt. 'Poor Edward. He must have been so embarrassed.'

Irene hung her head. 'I know and I'm truly sorry, but it seemed to me that he had deserted you when you needed him the most.'

'Gladys was with me all evening. She put me to bed like a child and then waited until Edward returned home. I'm never left alone for long.'

'I don't know what came over me,' Irene said humbly.

'You mustn't be too hard on yourself. You have suffered abominably at the hands of others and you needed someone to blame. I am just sorry that it was my brother.'

Irene reached out to grasp her hand. 'I'm sorry too. I've had plenty of time to mull it over while I've been locked up in my sister's house. I know that Edward – I mean, Inspector Kent – was just doing his job, and it was very wrong of me to say those things in public. I can't believe that I slapped him; it was an awful thing to do.'

'Perhaps he understands more than you think,' Alice said gently. 'He has never breathed a word of it to me, and I expect he has forgotten all about it by now.'

Somehow this did not please Irene as much as she might have expected. She did not relish the idea that Kent could put her out of his mind so easily, when he was constantly in hers. 'It's very warm in here,' she said, in an attempt to change the subject.

'You are still upset. Think no more about it, my dear. Edward is not a vengeful man and I am sure he would understand why you acted as you did if you were to tell him everything, just as you have explained it to me now.'

Irene shook her head. 'No. I think not. We are on opposite sides of the law, Alice. My father is a convicted felon and I can't forgive your brother for putting him in jail. I'm sorry if this causes you pain, but it is a fact.'

'Please don't say that, Irene. Edward and I have few friends other than dear Gladys and Danny. People round here are wary of having anything to do with a police officer or his family.'

'I'm truly sorry, but I can understand why, and it makes it difficult for us to remain friends.'

'Don't let the law come between us. You bring life into this dull house and I truly value your friendship. If there is any way that I can help you, then I will. Perhaps I could speak to Edward—'

'No,' Irene said emphatically. 'No, please don't. Thank you for the thought, but I must manage alone.'

'What will you do?'

'I don't know, but I will have to return to Love Lane and hope to sneak into the house unseen or Josiah will have my guts for garters . . . begging your pardon, Alice.'

'No need to worry on my account,' Alice said with an irrepressible chuckle. 'I was raised on a farm where I heard far worse language than that. I'm not a delicate flower, Irene. I used to be a real tomboy until the accident that left me crippled. In fact I can see a lot of myself in you, and that cheers me immensely. I know that things are bad for you at the moment, but sharing your troubles is a great adventure for me. I'm beginning to feel alive for the first time in years. Don't abandon me now that I've found a true friend.'

Irene felt tears burning the backs of her eyes and she went down on her knees in front of Alice, taking her small hands in hers and squeezing them gently. 'I am your friend, and I'm grateful to you for not judging the way I have dealt with your brother. I know you love him, as I loved my brother before he ran away to sea.'

'Perhaps he will return one day.'

'He could be dead for all I know.'

'You must not lose hope. He might turn up on your doorstep having made his fortune abroad. It happens.'

'Only in books, I'm afraid.' Irene rose to her feet. 'I must go, Alice.'

'You will come again, though? Please say you will. You can go anywhere dressed like that.'

'I must admit that wearing men's clothes gives me a wonderful sense of freedom. I can stride down the street without anyone giving me a second glance. I expect I could walk right past your brother without being recognised.'

'Oh, I think he would know it was you, Miss Angel.'

The sound of Kent's voice made Irene spin round to stare at him. 'How long have you been standing there?'

He eyed her coolly. 'Long enough to know

that you enjoy parading round town in that outlandish garb. Why are you here?'

'She came to apologise for her behaviour at the ball,' Alice said hastily. 'And to see me, Edward. I want Irene to be my friend. You shan't send her away.'

'There, there, my dear. Don't upset yourself,' Kent said gently. 'I won't throw Miss Angel out on the street, but I would like to speak to her in private, if you don't mind.'

'You won't be hateful to her, will you, Edward?'

'I won't, if she'll promise never to humiliate me in public again.'

Irene managed a weak smile. 'I promise.'

'If Edward says anything to upset you, I will be very angry,' Alice said with spirit. 'You will come again soon, won't you, Irene?'

'If your brother has no objection to your mixing with the daughter of a common criminal, then I will be glad to come and visit you as often as I can.'

'She is free to come and go as she pleases,' Kent said, ushering Irene from the room. 'I'll only be a moment, Alice, and then we'll have something to eat.' His smile faded as he followed Irene into the hallway. He closed the door, leaning against it with his arms folded across his chest. 'Well, what have you to say for yourself?

What was your real reason for calling on my sister?'

'I wanted to see her, and I owed you an apology for my behaviour the other evening.'

'And this is your apology?'

'If you care to accept it.'

'I do. As a matter of fact I think I can understand what drove you to behave as you did. I was in part to blame.'

Irene stared at him in surprise. She could tell nothing by his carefully controlled expression and his tone was certainly not conciliatory. 'You were?'

'I should have been plain with you from the outset. I believe that your father was foolish to allow himself to be taken in by the Sykes brothers, and now he is paying the price for that folly, but I will say that I think the sentence was too harsh. Vic and Wally have robbed, murdered and wrecked many more lives than yours, which must not go unpunished. So far they have evaded the law, but that will not continue. You have my word on it.'

'That won't help my father.'

'I am afraid there's nothing more I can do for Billy Angel.'

'You could have spoken up for him at his trial. You said yourself that he is not a criminal.'

'I did what I could.'

'I won't rest until he is released. I will make the Sykes brothers pay for what they have done to my family.'

Kent's hand shot out and he seized her by the arm. 'Don't be stupid. They would slit your throat as soon as look at you. This isn't a game, Irene. Leave the Sykes gang to the police and go back to your brother-in-law's house where you belong. The streets of London are no place for a girl like you.'

'Now you listen to me for a change, Inspector Kent,' Irene cried angrily, shaking off his restraining hand. 'I will do as I see fit, and neither you nor the City of London police force will stop me.' She wrenched the front door open and was about to storm out but she hesitated, glancing at him over her shoulder. 'I will continue to visit Alice, if you have no objection.'

He inclined his head, unsmiling. 'I can't stop you, but I don't want my sister involved in your scheming, which I'm very much afraid will end badly for you.'

'Why would you care what happens to me?'

He hesitated for a moment. 'I don't know,' he said slowly, 'apart from the fact that I admire your loyalty and your tenacity. You are a stubborn, maddening young woman but you have courage. I wouldn't want to see you brought down by a pair of sewer rats like the Sykes brothers. Take my advice and steer clear of them. Allow the law to take its course.'

Irene left the house without dignifying his warning with a reply. There was something about Kent that both annoyed and disturbed her and she realised now that the feeling was mutual. She wanted to hate him, but she could not find it in her heart to do so. She knew that he was right to warn her of the dangers of getting involved with the Sykes gang, but she resented his interference. They had but one thing in common, and that was Alice. In the short time that she had known her, Irene realised that she had formed a deep attachment to the young woman who bore her affliction with such bravery and good humour. Irene was only too aware that her own impatient nature would not have borne up so well under such trying circumstances. She strode along in her boyish clothing, careless of the rain beating on her face and the cold wind whipping strands of hair from beneath her cap. She revelled in her last moments of freedom before she reached the house that she was forced to call home.

She tried the door to the tradesmen's entrance and found it locked. She toyed with the idea of ringing the bell and abandoned it almost immediately. Jessie would be only too pleased to catch her out, and Cook would not dare risk offending her employer by allowing Irene into the house unannounced. She lingered in the mews for a while, hoping that someone might arrive with a delivery of bread or groceries, but commonsense told her that it was too late in the day. It was raining even harder now and she was soaked to the skin. There was nothing for it but to go round to the front of the house and hope that Ras would be the first to return from the emporium. He would think it a huge joke to find her in such a state, but he would not tell his father; of that she was certain.

She hung about in the street, walking up and down in an attempt to keep warm, which was almost impossible with sodden clothes and rainwater trickling between her breasts and running down her back. The lamplighter was doing his rounds when Ras arrived, as expected, the first to arrive home from work. He paid off the cabby and was about to mount the front steps when Irene leapt out of the shadows and caught him by the sleeve. 'Ras. It's me.'

He stared at her in astonishment. 'Renie? Good grief. Just look at you. What a state you're in.' He threw back his head and laughed. 'I'd give a year of my life to see the old man's face if he were to come along now.'

'I pray that he won't,' Irene said, her teeth chattering. 'You've got to get me into the house without being seen.'

He angled his head. 'What's it worth?'

'Anything, just get me into the house before I catch my death of cold.'

'I'll hold you to that, young sir,' Ras said, chuckling. He rang the doorbell. 'Leave it to me.' He took off his cloak and wrapped it around her shoulders. 'Give me your cap. Be quick, I hear the sound of Jessie's flat feet.'

Irene did as he asked and shook out her hair just as the door opened.

Jessie stepped backwards to allow them to pass. She stared open-mouthed at Irene who, in spite of everything, had to suppress a giggle.

'What are you staring at, girl?' Ras demanded, peeling off his gloves and handing her his top hat. 'Miss Angel and I got caught in the rain, as you see. Take hot water to her room and plenty of towels at once.'

'Yes, sir,' Jessie murmured, bobbing a curtsey. 'At once, sir.' She scuttled off towards the back stairs.

Irene uttered a sigh of relief. 'Thank you, Ras. You've saved my life.'

'And you owe me a debt of gratitude, Renie. One that I will be eager to collect.' He drew her to him and kissed her on the lips before she had a chance to turn her head away. 'Tonight,' he whispered. 'You will come to my room. I can't wait.'

Chapter Sixteen

'Don't be an oaf, Ras,' Irene said, breaking free from his amorous grasp. 'That's not funny.'

He struck a pose. 'Do I look as though I'm joking?'

'You must be. You don't want me. You could get what you want from any of the women in the places you frequent.'

He took her hand and raised it to his lips. His dark eyes gleamed with lust. 'But you are different, my pet. I've wanted you from the first moment I saw you, and I mean to have you.'

'Under your father's roof? Are you so depraved?'

'I'm afraid I am,' he said, smiling. 'And I assure you that you will enjoy your first time. I assume it will be your first.'

'I won't have this conversation with you.' Irene went to pass him but he held on to her hand, gripping it so hard that she winced. 'Let me go.'

He drew her nearer, placing his lips close to her ear. 'Come to my room at midnight.'

She could see by the steely expression in his eyes that he meant what he said, and she was desperate to escape to the privacy of her room. 'I'll think about it,' she said, forcing her lips into a smile. 'Now let me go or I'll scream.'

'I don't think you will, my pet. If the old man discovered that you had gone against his wishes, you would be flung out on your pretty little ear.'

'It would be your word against mine.'

'And who do you think my father would believe? Now go to your room and make yourself presentable.' He released her so suddenly that she stumbled and only saved herself from falling by clutching the newel post at the foot of the stairs.

'Go to hell,' Irene muttered furiously.

Ras took a menacing step towards her and he was not smiling now. 'I mean what I say. Come to me when the household sleeps or I will tell Father that I caught you dressed in those outrageous garments, openly flouting his orders. Take your choice, my pet.'

Wrapping his sodden cloak more tightly around her, Irene raced up the stairs and did not stop until she reached the relative safety of her bedchamber. Once inside she turned the key in the lock and tore off the offending garment. The scent of Ras's expensive pomade lingered in her nostrils even after she had undressed and put on her wrap. A fire had been lit in the grate and she huddled on the hearthrug, folding her arms around her knees and rocking herself to and fro as she struggled with her emotions. She had thought that matters could get no worse but she had been mistaken. She had also been wrong in labelling Ras as a good-natured rattle brain. She had accepted his flirting at face value: just a bit of fun not to be taken seriously. How wrong she had been.

A knock on the door startled her from her dismal thoughts and Irene scrambled to her feet. 'Just a moment.' She patted her damp hair into place before unlocking the door to a disgruntled Jessie, who stomped into the room carrying a ewer filled with hot water and a large towel. She glared accusingly at Irene, saying nothing as she filled the jug on the washstand and hung the towel over its rail. She left the room without a word, ignoring Irene's murmured thank you. Perhaps Jessie is right, Irene thought miserably. She recognises me for a fraud. I am no lady and she knows it. I am no better than she is. Emmie might have risen in the world by marrying a prosperous merchant, but I am the cuckoo in the nest. As she towelled her damp hair, Irene caught sight of her reflection in the mirror and she pulled a face. 'I will never be a lady.' She sighed, shaking her head. 'But I am no slut. I will call Ras's bluff. I don't believe for a moment that he will carry out his threat. After all, it would be his word against mine. Josiah has a low enough opinion of his son already. Ras wouldn't risk losing his job and his comfortable home. At least, I don't think he would.'

Dinner that evening was an uncomfortable meal for Irene. Ma and Emmie obviously thought that she had spent the day in bed with a sick headache and were most solicitous. Josiah and Ephraim eyed her nervously, as if fearing that she might have an attack of the vapours at any moment, and Ras kept winking at her in a most salacious manner. By the time they reached dessert, Irene was itching to throw a jug of cold water over him, but somehow she managed to contain her annoyance at his suggestive behaviour. She noted that he was drinking more than usual, and that did not bode well. He had a reckless look in his eyes and she could only hope that he would imbibe enough wine to make him virtually insensible. Whatever happened, she was not going to his room. She would lock her door and pretend to be asleep. After all, what could he do? If he made a noise it would rouse the whole household and it would be Ras who was in trouble.

'Are you sure that you are all right now, dear?'

The sound of Ma's voice brought Irene back to earth with a bump. 'Oh, yes. I'm sorry, Ma. I was miles away.'

'Not too far, I hope,' Ras said, grinning. 'We would miss you if you left us, Renie.'

'What sort of talk is that?' Emmie scolded. 'Renie is here to stay, at least until after my confinement. I don't want to hear talk of her leaving.' She rose from her seat. 'But I suggest that we ladies go to the drawing room and let you gentlemen enjoy your port and cigars, which is what I believe they do in the best of households. Come, Ma. And you too, Renie.' She swept from the room, blowing a kiss to Josiah, who was steadily munching his way through a plate of Stilton and celery. He half rose to his feet and then sat down again to cut himself another slice of cheese.

Renie was glad to escape from Ras's covert glances and sly winks, but she hesitated outside the drawing room. 'Ma, Emmie, if you don't mind I think I'll go to bed.'

Clara's brow puckered with concern. 'My dear, are you sure you are not sickening for something? Perhaps we should send for the doctor?'

'No, Ma. Really, I am just a bit tired. I'm sure I'll be better for a good night's sleep.'

'You go on then,' Emmie said. 'We can't have you falling ill so close to my time. I'll need all the help I can get then. Goodnight, dear.'

Irene climbed the stairs to her room and locked herself in. The fire had been made up and her bedcovers turned down. Jessie would not return until morning when she brought hot water for the washbowl and coal for the fire. Irene was too tense to think of sleep and she busied herself by hanging Jim's still damp clothes over the back of the chair, and setting his boots before the fire to dry. Having accomplished this, she undressed and climbed into bed, settling down to read a copy of Mrs Gaskell's *North and South*, which she had borrowed from Josiah's library. She read for a while, but all the time her eyes kept straying to the clock on the mantelshelf, and as midnight drew inexorably nearer she found it hard to concentrate. The words began to dance before her eyes and the letters swam about on the page like tadpoles. It was a good story and she had been enjoying it until now, but in the end she had to admit defeat. She put a bookmark in place and laid the novel on her bedside table.

She lay back against the pillows, watching the patterns made on the ceiling by the flickering firelight as she listened to the sounds of the household preparing for sleep. She heard footsteps above her head as the servants went to their attic rooms. Doors closed and bedsprings creaked and then there was silence except for the occasional crackle from the dying embers of the fire and the gentle ticking of the clock. Minute by minute the hands crept closer to midnight. Irene pulled the coverlet up to her chin and lay stiff as a corpse in her bed as she waited.

Five minutes passed and then ten. Irene began to relax. Perhaps Ras had been teasing her, or maybe he had passed out on his bed under the influence of alcohol. She closed her eyes and was drifting into the sleep of sheer exhaustion when someone tapped on her door. She snapped upright, her heart thudding against her ribcage. She did not answer when she heard Ras's voice calling her name. The knocking became more insistent and she covered her ears with her hands. She could see the doorknob turning and the key rattled in the lock.

'Irene, open the door.' His voice grew louder and more demanding.

'Go away,' she cried. 'Leave me alone.'

A great thud made her leap from her bed as the door panels shook. 'Stop it, Ras. You'll wake the whole household.' Irene unlocked the door and opened it just enough to peer out at him. 'What do you think you're playing at? Go away.'

Ras pushed past her and staggered into the room. 'I think I've broken my bloody shoulder, thanks to you, you silly tart.'

'You're drunk. Get out and leave me alone.'

He made a grab for her but she managed to dodge him.

'You promised you'd come to me. I will have you, Renie. Here and now, whether it pleases you or not.'

She managed to avoid his grabbing hands, putting the width of the bed between them. 'We'll talk about this in the morning.'

He vaulted the bed and caught her round the waist. 'No. We'll settle this matter now. You've been teasing me ever since you arrived. There's a name for girls like you.' He tore at her nightgown so that it fell open to the waist, exposing her breasts.

She kicked and struggled in an attempt to break free. 'If you don't let me go, I'll scream and bring the house down on you.'

He stopped her mouth with a drunken kiss. His breath reeked of wine and garlic and as she drew breath to cry for help he forced his tongue between her parted lips. He cupped her left breast in his hand, teasing her nipple until it formed a hard peak which seemed to excite him all the more. Irene scratched and fought, and it was only when she managed to bite his tongue that he released her with a howl of pain and rage. She stumbled free from his grasp and ran to the door, almost colliding with Ephraim.

'What in heaven's name is going on?' Ephraim demanded. He glanced in horror at Irene's state of undress and he looked away quickly, turning his attention to his brother. 'I might have known that you would have something to do with this. What have you got to say for yourself, Erasmus?'

Ras assumed an air of injured innocence. 'My dear Eph, I came to Irene's aid when I heard her cry for help.'

'What?' Irene spun round to face him. 'That's a lie.'

'Come, my dear,' Ras said smoothly. 'You know very well that you were entertaining a gentleman in your room. I suppose matters got out of hand or you would not have protested so loudly.'

'That is just not true. You are the culprit here.' Clutching her torn nightgown over her naked breasts, Irene turned to Ephraim. 'You know your brother only too well. Who do you believe – him or me?'

Ephraim frowned, shaking his head. 'If there was a man, where is he now?'

'In Erasmus's imagination,' Irene said bitterly. 'He tried to seduce me and now he is seeking to put the blame on me.'

'Hold on, my dear,' Ras said, strolling across

the floor to take Jim's damp breeches and jacket from the chair by the fire. 'These are not my garments, nor yours, I presume.' His eyes glittered with malice. 'I would say that there is a young gentleman running down the road half naked and desperate to remain undiscovered.' He held up the clothes, waving them at his brother. 'What do you say, Eph? Pretty damning evidence, don't you think?'

Ephraim paled visibly. 'Outrageous. I can hardly believe it of you, Irene. Father will hear of this, first thing in the morning.' He beckoned to Ras. 'I never thought I would say this, brother, but I see that I have misjudged you. Come, we'll leave Irene to think about her behaviour.'

Ras walked past Irene, giving her a triumphant glance. 'You can't cross me and get away with it, sweetheart,' he whispered.

'Wait,' Irene cried as Ephraim took the key from the lock and was about to follow Ras from the room. 'Those clothes are mine, or rather they belonged to my brother. I was wearing them when Ras found me in the street outside the house. He smuggled me in. Jessie can vouch for that. There never was a man in my room, other than Ras, and he was not here by invitation.'

'Rubbish,' Ras snorted. 'A tissue of lies from start to finish.'

'Just ask Jessie,' Irene insisted. 'Get her from her bed and then we'll see who is telling the truth.'

Ephraim shook his head. 'We'll sort this out in the morning, and Father will be the judge. We will keep this from the servants so that there will be no hint of a scandal. But I have to say that I am most disappointed in you, Irene.' He closed the door in her face and she heard the key grate in the lock.

'Silence!' Josiah boomed, shaking a finger at Irene. 'I've heard enough. You've been nothing but trouble ever since you arrived here, miss. I won't have you in my house a moment longer.'

Irene stood frozen with outrage. Ras was standing behind his father, openly smirking, and Ephraim sat on the edge of his chair with a sanctimonious expression on his face. If he had risen to his feet and given a sermon on wanton women she would not have been surprised. She licked her dry lips, momentarily bereft of words. She had admitted leaving the house and flouting Josiah's orders. She had told them that the clothes belonged to Jim, but she had been met with cold disbelief. She had begged Josiah to allow her mother to see the garments and vouch for the fact that they had once belonged to her son, but Josiah had refused point-blank.

'You will leave this morning,' he said, pronouncing his sentence in the tones of a High Court judge. 'I don't want Mrs Tippet upset in any way and so you will not see her or your mother. It is best if they know nothing of your disgraceful behaviour.'

Irene recoiled as though he had slapped her across the cheek. 'You can't do that, Josiah. What will they think? Let me see them at least to say goodbye.'

'No. I'll make up some tale that will satisfy their curiosity, but they must never know the truth. If one word of this should leak out we will have a monumental scandal on our hands and my business will be ruined, let alone my chances of becoming an alderman.'

'That's right, Father,' Ephraim said, nodding his head. 'We must preserve our good name at all costs.'

Irene glared at Ras. 'This is all your fault. You put me in this position. Admit it like a man.'

'She's desperate, Father,' Ras said lazily. 'You can see guilt written all over her face. She's a sly little temptress and totally lacking in morals. You do right to send her on her way. She can earn her living on the streets.'

'And how will that look when your stuck-up customers discover that your wife's sister is nothing better than a common harlot?' Irene demanded. She had the satisfaction of seeing that her crude speech shocked both Josiah and Ephraim, but Ras laughed.

'There, sir. She's showing her true colours now. A woman of the streets is what Irene Angel has turned out to be. She's just like her father and will end up in prison with her own kind.'

'Nevertheless, there is some truth in what she says,' Ephraim murmured, running his finger around the inside of his starched collar. 'We don't want any of this to come out in public, Father.'

Josiah scowled at Irene, leaning forward in his chair. 'I will give you enough money to pay for lodgings until you find work. Have you any friends or family who reside out of town? I want you as far away from here as possible.'

The atmosphere in the small study was stifling and Irene was beginning to feel faint. It was still early in the morning, long before either Emmie or their mother would have risen from their beds. Irene had not had breakfast or even a cup of tea and she had spent a sleepless night, pacing the floor in her room and trying in vain to think of a way out of her predicament. She had pinned all her hopes on Jessie corroborating her story, but Josiah had taken heed of Ephraim's advice not to involve the servants and he had refused to question the girl.

'Well, miss, have you lost your tongue as well as your morals?' Josiah thumped his hand on his desk, scattering a sheaf of papers.

Irene was about to shake her head when she thought of Artie and Miss Maude. 'There is someone who would welcome me into their house,' she murmured. 'But I would need my train fare for the journey to Essex, and money for a cab from the station.'

'Ephraim, fetch the strongbox.' Josiah leaned his elbows on the desk, steepling his fingers. 'You will go to the country and stay there. I don't want to see you again.'

'That suits me,' Irene retorted hotly. 'But I demand to see my mother and sister before I go. I'll tell them something – anything but the truth, if that's what you want. But you must see that sending me away without allowing me to say goodbye will distress them both.'

'Don't listen to her, sir,' Ras said, a flicker of anxiety wiping away his self-satisfied smirk. 'She is not to be trusted.'

'Maybe not, but she has a point,' Ephraim said, hefting an iron strongbox from a wall cupboard and placing it on the desk in front of his father. 'I don't think Irene would do anything to distress my stepmother or Mrs Angel.'

Josiah took a bunch of keys from his pocket and unlocked the box, taking out a leather pouch. He opened it and frowned, fingering the coins as if he could not bear to part with any of them. He selected two golden sovereigns and four half-crowns, which he slid across the tooled leather desk top. 'Here, take this, but don't expect me to give you more when it is spent.'

Irene would have loved to fling the coins in his face, but she must be practical and she pocketed them. 'I beg you to let me see Emmie and Ma before I leave here, Josiah. My sudden and unexplained departure would upset them both.'

'What will you tell them?' Josiah demanded.

'I will say that Miss Greenwood has invited me to stay, and that since I have already offended you by my behaviour at the ball, I feel it best for everyone that I accept.'

Ras chuckled. 'She's a born liar, Father. Irene has convicted herself from her own lips.'

'Be silent,' Josiah thundered. 'You are hardly in a position to be judgemental, Erasmus. Anyway, it's time that both of you went to the emporium. I will stay here and make certain that Irene leaves the house.'

'And I will be able to see Ma and Emmie first,' Irene insisted.

'You may say your farewells, but I will be

present to make certain that you do not go back on your word. Now go to your room and remain there until I send for you. Pack your things and be ready to leave as soon as you have said goodbye to your mother and sister.'

An hour later, with Ma and Emmie's entreaties to stay still ringing in her ears, Irene stood on the pavement outside the house with her canvas bag in one hand and her reticule in the other. The coins made it feel reassuringly heavy and she looked about for a cab. Two pounds ten was not a fortune, but it would get her to Havering and give her time to formulate a plan of action. She had no intention of remaining long in Essex, but she needed somewhere to go and she knew that Artie would be pleased to see her. She walked to the end of Love Lane and hailed a passing hansom cab on the corner of Wood Street.

'Where to, miss?'

Irene travelled third class in order to save money and the train was packed from Shoreditch to Romford. It was market day in the town and she had to tramp the streets for an hour before she found a cabby who was willing to undertake the journey to Havering, and he only agreed when she promised to double the usual fare. It was late afternoon and the winter sun had plummeted below the skyline, leaving the countryside to dissolve slowly into a grey and misty dusk.

It was quite dark by the time they reached Havering and Irene was both exhausted and chilled to the bone. As the cab drew to a halt outside the garden gate, she was relieved to see a welcome glimmer of light emanating from one of the downstairs windows. She paid the cabby, but when he held his hand out for a tip she shook her head. 'I've paid over the odds, mate. You ain't getting a penny more.' She picked up her bag and let herself in through the garden gate, allowing it to swing back on its hinges as she trudged up the path and round the side of the house to the back door. It was unlocked and Irene entered the porch which was, as usual, crammed to overflowing with muddy boots, damp coats and empty buckets. A pair of Miss Maude's muddy gloves lay on the floor with the fingers clenched like a pair of disembodied hands. The smell of wet dog permeated the small room and light from the kitchen shone through the half-glazed door.

Irene turned the knob and her heart gave a flutter of apprehension, but she need not have worried. Martha looked up from ladling stew into large white bowls and her plump face creased into folds as she smiled a welcome. 'Miss Irene! What a surprise.'

Maude was seated at the table with her back to the door, but she turned her head and on seeing Irene, she pushed her chair back and rose to her feet. 'Well look at you – all done up like a lady. I hardly recognised you.'

'I – I wondered if I could stay for a while,' Irene said nervously.

Martha put down the saucepan and waddled across the flagstone floor to envelop Irene in a motherly hug. 'You look frozen stiff. Those fancy clothes won't keep the cold out on a night like this.'

Irene's fingers trembled as she untied the ribbons of her bonnet. 'It's so good to see you both again. I'm sorry to turn up on your doorstep unannounced.'

Maude resumed her seat and she smiled. 'Don't be silly, Irene. You're more than welcome. Now sit down and have some supper. You look famished as well as chilled to the bone.'

'Aye, sit down,' Martha said, bustling over to the dresser to fetch another soup bowl. 'There's plenty to go round. I always cook enough for an army, or so she says.' She ladled out a generous portion of the stew and placed it on the table. 'There, now I want to see a clean plate and then you can tell us everything.'

Irene was only too glad to sit down. The

warmth from the range was already seeping into her bones and her stomach growled with appreciation at the sight and smell of the appetising food on her plate. Maude speared a chunk of bread on a knife and slipped it expertly onto Irene's side plate. 'Not another word until you have eaten, my girl.'

Irene swallowed a mouthful of the delicious rabbit stew and she glanced anxiously at the empty place set at the table. 'Where is Arthur? I was afraid that he had returned to London and that I had missed him.'

'I said no talking,' Maude said with mock severity. 'He's at the smithy, if you must know, but he'll be home soon for his supper. Martha's turned him into a real trencherman with her cooking. When he first came here he was as thin as a rake and just pecked at his food.'

'Now he's got the appetite of a lion,' Martha said proudly, taking her place at the table. 'And there's meat on his bones. He's not a skinny-malink now.' She laughed heartily as she tucked into her food.

Irene shot an enquiring glance at Maude, who had finished her meal and was sitting back in her chair watching her every mouthful with nods of approval. 'That's a good girl. At least you haven't lost your appetite.' She took a clay pipe and a tobacco pouch from her pocket. 'And I know what you're going to ask next. What is Arthur doing at the smithy? Well, I can answer that. He is learning the trade.'

Irene almost choked on a piece of potato. 'Arthur is learning to be a blacksmith?'

'It's working with metal. Not quite the same as being a silversmith but it seems to suit him much better. I believe he enjoys the work and is proving to be quite adept at it already, according to Bligh the blacksmith.'

'And Bligh has a young daughter,' Martha added with a mischievous chuckle that made each of her chins wobble in unison. 'Betty Bligh is probably the prettiest girl in the village. I think young Artie has taken quite a shine to her.'

'Martha,' Maude said, frowning as she filled the pipe with tobacco. 'You don't know that for certain.'

'It's all right, Miss Maude, I don't mind in the least.' Irene broke off a piece of bread and dipped it in the soup, safe in the knowledge that no one in this house would upbraid her for bad manners. 'There never was anything romantic between me and Artie, not on my part anyway.'

'I'm glad to hear it.' Maude rose from the table to light a spill. 'I thought perhaps there was some longstanding attachment between you.'

'Not at all. We were childhood friends and

no more, but I am very fond of Artie and if he is happy then I am too.'

'Well said, my dear,' Maude said, sucking at the pipe stem and allowing a trickle of smoke to escape from the corner of her mouth. 'Now perhaps you feel able to tell us what has been happening to you, and the reason for your unexpected visit.'

A sound in the porch made Irene turn her head and she jumped to her feet as Arthur burst into the kitchen. He came to an abrupt halt and a slow smile spread across his features. He held out his arms. 'Renie! By God, this is a wonderful surprise. When did you arrive?'

She rose from her seat and was enveloped in an embrace which almost robbed her of breath. 'Artie, you look so well. I hear that you have changed your trade.' Extricating herself from his grasp, she surveyed him critically and was delighted by the change in him. He had looked so poorly after his illness but now his face was tanned by wind and weather and he had put on several pounds in weight.

He ran his hand through his already tousled hair, which was longer than usual and curled wildly round his head, giving him a gypsy-like appearance. He grinned ruefully. 'Yes, the old man won't be best pleased when he hears what I've done, but I find working at the forge much more satisfying than sitting hunched up over some intricate piece of silverware. I like the open air and I feel happier living in the country than I ever did in London.'

'Sit down and eat your supper, boy.'

Maude spoke sternly, but Irene noticed that her eyes smiled indulgently.

Arthur shrugged off his damp corduroy jacket and was about to drop it on the floor when a daggers look from Martha sent him scurrying back into the porch to hang it on a hook. He returned to the table and sat down with an apologetic grin. 'Actually, Renie, I'm very glad you're here because there's something I must share with you all.'

Irene knew that look of old. Arthur could never keep a secret or hide his guilt when he had done wrong.

Chapter Seventeen

'Never mind your secrets, Arthur,' Maude said, tapping ash from her pipe into the fire. 'Have you locked the hen house, and did you notice if Albert had finished in the milking parlour as you passed by?'

'Oh, really, Miss Maude,' Martha said impatiently. 'Can't you let the boy tell us his news before you start on at him about the farm? He's all of a dither about something; anyone can see that.'

'My livestock is more important to me than any goings-on at the smithy. But I suppose I'll get no peace until you've told us this wonderful piece of news. What is it that can't wait, Arthur?'

He puffed out his chest. 'I'm betrothed to the sweetest, loveliest girl in the whole of Essex. Miss Betty Bligh has consented to be my wife.'

Irene stared at him in shock as she digested the news. She was pleased for him, of course, but even so she was inexplicably hurt to think that he had transferred his affections so quickly and with such apparent ease. She opened her mouth to congratulate him but the words stuck in her throat.

'Well, Renie? Have you nothing to say?' Arthur demanded, frowning. 'Aren't you happy for me?'

'Congratulations, Artie,' she murmured with a half-hearted attempt at a smile.

Maude shook her head. 'It's a bit sudden, Arthur. You've only known the girl for five minutes and she's little more than a child.'

'Marry in haste, repent at leisure,' Martha added sagely.

Arthur's smile faded and he cast a pleading look at Irene. 'I thought you at least would be happy for me, Renie.'

'Of course I'm pleased for you, Artie. If you're happy, then I must be too. Only . . .'

'Only what?' His mouth drooped at the corners. 'What's wrong? I thought you at least would wish me well.'

'I do. I mean you haven't known the girl for long. Perhaps you ought to have waited for a while, especially if she is as young as Miss Maude says she is.'

'Betty is seventeen, quite old enough to know her own mind. It was love at first sight for both of us.'

Martha ladled a generous helping of stew into his bowl. 'That don't mean it will last. It's spring fever that's got into your blood a bit early this year, young man.'

Maude flicked a scornful glance in her direction. 'Don't talk nonsense, you old fool. The boy is clearly besotted, but he won't thank you or me for telling him so.' She strode into the porch and took her waxed coat from its peg. She slipped it on with a martyred expression. 'I'm going to see to the hens and make sure that Albert hasn't left the lantern burning in the milking parlour.'

'He's getting past it, if you ask me,' Martha said gloomily. 'The old fool almost set fire to the barn last week.'

'Why keep him on then?' Irene asked, steering the conversation away from Arthur's announcement. She would speak to him later – in private.

'Because he has worked on the farm since I was a girl,' Maude said, ramming her felt hat on her head. 'Albert Perkins has been a good and faithful servant and he'll stay in the tied cottage until he breathes his last.'

'Let's hope he doesn't burn it down then,' Martha muttered just loud enough for Maude to hear.

'I'm ignoring that remark.' Maude opened the back door, letting in a draught of cold air. 'You eat your supper, boy. Never mind me. I know I come a poor second in your affections now that you've found a lady-love. Although for a time I thought your heart was pledged elsewhere. However, it seems I was badly mistaken.' She disappeared out into the darkness, slamming the door behind her.

'I'm afraid you've upset her, Artie,' Irene said anxiously.

Martha busied herself by clearing the dirty crockery from the table. 'She'll get over it. She's a tough old bird and it would take more than Mr Arthur getting himself engaged to young Betty to put Miss Maude out of countenance for long. She's worried because Albert is past his prime and she can't afford to hire a younger man. Anyway, she don't like change.'

'It's my fault,' Arthur mumbled through a mouthful of food. 'I should have seen to it, but I forgot.'

It was Irene's turn to feel guilty. She had come here uninvited and with little money to pay for her board and lodging. 'Perhaps I could help round the farm?'

Arthur almost choked on a mouthful of tea. 'I'd like to see you milk a cow or muck out the stables.'

'I could if I put my mind to it.'

'Leave her alone, Mr Arthur,' Martha said, flicking him with the dishcloth. 'Eat your vittles. I don't want to spend the whole evening at the sink.'

Arthur looked up from his plate and grinned. 'This is one of your best stews, Martha. I'd marry you if I was ten years older.'

Martha's chubby cheeks flooded with colour. 'Get on with you, you bad boy. I'm old enough to be your mother and you know it.' She hurried to the sink and applied herself energetically to the pump handle.

Irene stifled a giggle. 'Don't tease her, Artie.'

He managed a chubby-cheeked smile, but his mouth was too full of food to allow him to respond.

Irene waited in silence until he had finished his meal. Her heart was as heavy as lead in her breast. She had not come here with any romantic notions as far as Arthur was concerned, but now that he had made himself a new life in the country and found himself a new love, she realised that he had no need of her. It was a sad fact, but no one needed her. She felt as though she had lost her way. Smothering a sigh, she rose slowly to her feet. 'Can I do anything to help you, Martha?'

'Not in them clothes you can't. That dress alone would cost more than my year's wages. You're a guest in this house, Miss Irene, so you just leave everything to me. There's a fine blaze roaring up the chimney in the parlour so you two can go in there and finish your chat while I do all the work – as usual.'

'Come on then, Artie,' Irene said, holding out her hand to him. 'Let's do what Martha says, and I'll tell you why I left London in such a hurry.'

When they were seated on either side of the fireplace in the parlour, Arthur put his feet up on the brass fender. 'Go on then, tell me what brought you here all of a sudden. It must have been something bad to make you leave London. Come on, Renie, out with it.'

Haltingly at first, but gaining confidence as she related the events that had driven her from home, Irene told him everything that had occurred since she returned to town. Although he listened patiently, she could tell by the faraway look in his eyes that his thoughts were wandering. It was not hard to guess who occupied them so completely. 'So you see,' she concluded, 'I had no choice but to get on the train at Shoreditch and throw myself on Miss Maude's mercy until I think of a way to support myself.'

Arthur was suddenly alert. 'Surely you're not thinking of going back to London?'

'I have to, Artie. I won't rest until I have seen Pa released from jail and the Sykes brothers brought to justice. I'm not going to give in without a fight.'

His generous lips formed a tight little circle

as if he had just been sucking a particularly sour lemon. 'Oh, no, Renie. I can't allow you to do that. You must steer clear of Vic and Wally. They wouldn't think twice about having you permanently silenced, if you get my meaning.'

'And that is my point exactly. Unless someone puts a stop to them they will just go on and on, bullying, murdering and terrorising the population. I can see that now, and it's the one thing that I have in common with Inspector Kent.'

'Don't tell me you are changing your opinion of the worthy inspector?'

'No, of course not. He is arrogant and so stiff-necked that he might as well have swallowed a poker. I don't know how he came to have such a sweet sister who thinks the sun rises and sets at his command.'

'Maybe he is not as bad as you first thought,' Arthur said, chuckling.

Irene plucked the cushion from her chair and threw it at him, narrowly missing his head and knocking a china figurine from the mantelshelf. With a quick reaction that Irene noted would have been impossible a few months ago, when he had been drinking heavily, Arthur caught the porcelain shepherdess in his left hand. At the same moment the door opened and Maude walked into the room. She opened her mouth as if to remonstrate and then a slow smile lit her face. 'Children, behave yourselves.'

Irene jumped to her feet. 'I'm sorry, Miss Maude. Won't you come and sit by the fire?'

Maude did not argue. She sat down, holding her hands out to the glowing coals. 'It's raw outside tonight.'

'I should have seen to all that, Aunt Maude,' Arthur said apologetically. 'I'm sorry.'

She stretched her stockinged feet out to warm them on the hearth, and her bare toes wiggled through gaping holes in what appeared to be a pair of men's socks. Maude saw that Irene was staring at her feet and she chuckled. 'As you can see, I'm not much of a one for darning, and Martha's eyesight isn't what it was.'

'I'm no good with a needle or I'd offer to mend them for you,' Irene said, smiling. 'I'm all fingers and thumbs when it comes to sewing.'

Arthur winked at her. 'You should have been a boy, Renie. You and Aunt Maude have a lot in common and you both look well in breeches.'

'You may not believe this, young man, but I was young once and considered to be quite handsome,' Maude said sternly. She sighed. 'I can remember what it is like to be in love.'

Irene pulled up a footstool and sat down

beside her. 'But you never married, Miss Maude.'

'My father said that the man I loved wasn't good enough for me and he forbade the match.'

'It sounds as though Grandfather Greenwood was just like my old man,' Arthur muttered. 'Bad-tempered and unreasonable.'

'I suppose there must be a similarity,' Maude agreed, staring dreamily into the dancing flames. 'But Papa expected me to marry into my own class. Eddie was a farmer and that was quite unacceptable.'

'Tell us about him,' Irene said gently. 'Was he very handsome?'

'No, not exactly handsome, but he had the bluest eyes I've ever seen, and dark hair that waved back from a high forehead which made him look more like a poet than a farmer. He was tall and slim, not at all the physique one might expect of a man who worked the land for a living.'

'Well, Aunt, I'm sorry to hear it,' Arthur said with apparent sincerity.

Irene eyed him curiously. This was a new and very different Arthur from the careless, pleasure-seeking young man she had known since childhood. There could be little doubt that his heightened sensitivities had been brought about by his feelings for the lovely Betty Bligh. She turned her attention to Maude.

'And you never found anyone to take his place?'

'No, my dear, for me there could only be one man. There was never another who came even close to Edward Kent.'

The breath hitched in Irene's throat. 'Edward Kent?' Alice had told her that their father was a farmer and that the family came from Essex, but surely this must be a coincidence.

'Edward Kent!' Arthur repeated slowly. 'Damn me! It can't be the same family.'

'Language, Arthur,' Maude said, frowning. 'You may be working with labouring men but don't bring their bad habits into my home.'

'Sorry, Aunt, but – well, I mean to say.'

'It's all in the past,' Maude said, rising to her feet. 'I don't want to talk about it and I'm very tired, so I'll bid you both goodnight.'

'Goodnight, Miss Maude,' Irene said automatically.

Arthur stood up dutifully, but his attention was fixed on Irene and as soon as the door closed on his aunt he slumped back on his seat. 'Hell's bells, can you believe that, Renie?'

'No,' she said slowly. 'It doesn't seem possible.'

'What a laugh. I'll ask old Bligh if he knows Farmer Kent and his family.'

'I think it's best left in the past,' Irene said, smothering a yawn. 'I'm a bit tired. I might go to my room if you don't mind, Artie. It's been a long day.'

'Of course, you must be worn out. I should have realised that before I started jawing about Betty, and then Aunt Maude had to throw that in about her long lost love. I never associated the old girl with anything so romantic, which just goes to show that one should never make judgements about others.'

'No, and we don't know for certain that Miss Maude's farmer is related to the person we know in London.'

'No,' Arthur said, frowning thoughtfully. 'But it explains why she won't have anything to do with her sister. I was told that Aunt Dora married Maude's old flame and that was why they hadn't spoken from that day to this. Wouldn't it be funny if we discovered that this was a skeleton in the inspector's family cupboard?'

'Yes, I suppose so, Artie.' Irene leaned over to kiss him on the cheek. 'Goodnight. I'll see you in the morning.'

He seized her hand and squeezed it. 'You won't go dashing back to London before we've had time to talk more, will you?'

'No, I won't. Cross my heart and hope to die.'

'Good. I'm glad we've settled that.' He raised her hand to his lips and kissed it. 'You always were my best friend, Renie, and you always will be.'

'That goes for me too. Now let me go or I'll be blubbing like a baby.'

It was not until she reached her bedchamber that Irene allowed herself the luxury of a good cry. She flung herself down on the soft feather bed and gave vent to a maelstrom of emotions which both shocked and confused her. She had always thought of herself as being strong-minded and self-possessed, and yet here she was sobbing into her pillow like a baby for reasons which it was hard to define. When at last the tears dried on her cheeks, she rolled onto her back and stared up at the flickering shadows dancing on the ceiling. The burning coals made companionable crackling and snapping sounds. Outside, the wind whistled through the bare branches of the trees and rain lashed the windows in a relentless downpour. Irene shuddered to think she might have been living rough on the streets for all Josiah cared.

The room was bathed in the rosy glow from the oil lamps and she was warm and comfortable, but she couldn't help wondering how Pa was faring in his cold prison cell with little or no hope of imminent release, and her heart ached for him in his ordeal. He was a good man really; just a little weak and easily led. Her determination to procure his release hardened. She must think of a plan that would enable her to return to London and earn her own living while she sought justice for him. She would see the Sykes brothers caught, tried and condemned to jail, even if it meant throwing her lot in with the police. She sat upright, staring into the glowing coals. She must not give in now. There must be a way to achieve her goal, even though the outlook at present was bleak.

She slithered off the satin coverlet and undressed slowly in front of the fire, slipping on the white lawn nightgown that Martha had thoughtfully laid out for her. She turned down the wicks in the bedside lamps until the flames guttered and died, leaving the room in semi-darkness, with only the soft light from the fire to keep her company. She slipped between the starched cotton sheets and lay back against the soft pillows. She closed her eyes and allowed herself to drift into the pleasant state between waking and sleeping. Tomorrow, she thought dreamily, I will come to a decision.

Weeks passed and Irene still had not formulated a definite plan of action. She had considered asking Miss Maude for a loan in order to set herself up in rented rooms in London while she tried to secure Pa's release, but she soon came to realise that the Greenwood fortune had been eaten away over the years. Maude worked the land from necessity and the farm brought in just enough money to keep the house going, but with little to spare. Arthur worked long hours at the smithy and to Irene's surprise he proved eager to turn his hand to anything about the farm, from mending a ploughshare to milking the cows if Albert was laid up with a bad chest.

Irene did what she could. She helped in the dairy and fed the chickens and pigs, but she pined for London. She yearned for the noise and excitement of the city, and if she were to tell the truth, she found life in the country deadly dull. She missed Ma and she worried about Emmie, whose time was drawing near. She wrote letters to them every week, struggling with the grammar and spelling, and received the occasional reply written in Emmie's spidery scrawl, which were almost entirely about the trials of her condition and quite brief. Irene read these blotted missives with a lump in her throat. She might have argued and sometimes quarrelled with her sister but she was fond of her for all that.

It was not only those closest to her who were uppermost in her thoughts. Irene was still struggling to come to terms with the idea that Edward Kent's father might once have been Miss Maude's sweetheart. If it were true then it seemed like the weirdest of coincidences, and the knowledge that his family possibly lived just a few miles away from Havering made it seem even stranger. She had attempted to write to Alice on several occasions just to let her know that she was safe and well, but somehow she couldn't find the right words and her efforts had ended up in the fire.

As the days lengthened and a hint of spring warmed the air, Irene grew even more restless. She saw little of Arthur these days. He came home for his supper, but when he had eaten and changed out of his dirty work clothes he took himself off to pay court to Betty. He had brought her to the house on several occasions, and despite her initial misgivings Irene had to admit that Arthur's fiancée was a sweet girl and an ideal mate for him. Under Betty's influence he had given up drink, except for the odd pint of beer every now and again, and he had lost his desire to gamble unless it was on a game of shove-halfpenny in the village pub or playing the old men at dominoes, and then the stakes were farthings rather than pounds. Arthur was a happy man, there was no doubt about that, and Irene rejoiced for him, but his love for Betty had stirred longings in herself that she found hard to define.

With the improvement in the weather, Irene began taking long walks when her chores were done. She discovered a whole new world in the burgeoning hedgerows, which were now alive with birdsong and the rustling sound of small mammals scurrying through the dead leaves as they hunted for grubs and insects to feed their young. The bare branches of the blackthorn were studded with tiny white flowers and catkins dangled from hazel and willow trees, waving in the breeze like tiny foxtails while clusters of yellow primroses and cowslips made pools of instant sunshine on the grassy banks. Having grown up in the brick and concrete canyons of the city, Irene was constantly amazed by the ability of the natural world to regenerate itself after the apparent slow death of winter.

She might often be bored and lonely, but she was aware that her health had improved with good food and exercise. When she looked into the mirror on her dressing table, she realised that her complexion was as fresh as any milkmaid's and her eyes were clear and bright. Her hair, which Martha washed for her in soft soap and rinsed with an infusion of camomile, now shone with golden glints and her cheeks were rosy. And yet her old life called to her and she still yearned for the dirt and smoke of London; she could not abandon those whom she loved the most. She would even be civil to Inspector Kent if she ever found a way to return home, but only for Alice's sake, of course.

On a pleasant April morning, Irene was feeling particularly ill at ease. She put her edginess down to the fact that Emmie's confinement was imminent, but she knew in her heart that this was only a small part of the cause. The enforced inactivity was driving her to a point beyond endurance. She felt as though her life had come to a complete standstill, and she needed to do something constructive. Martha and Miss Maude had gone to market in the gig and would not be home until late afternoon, and Arthur was at work. Irene had finished her tasks early and she found the prospect of spending a whole day alone in the house daunting to say the least. Acting on the spur of the moment, she put on her bonnet and shawl and set off for a walk.

Without planning her route, she found herself heading in the direction of Navestock. In one of her chatty moods, Martha had been only too eager to talk about Farmer Kent, who kept himself to himself and was not a popular man. By dint of tactful questioning, Irene had found out the exact whereabouts of the Kents' farm. She had not planned to go there, but she was curious to see the man whom the young Maude Greenwood had loved so desperately. Navestock was several miles away, but the sun was warm on her face and she had a sudden overwhelming desire to visit the farm that might once have been home to the young Edward Kent and his sister Alice.

The sun was high in the sky by the time she reached the farm and she was both hungry and thirsty. She had a few pennies in her purse and she decided to knock on the door and enquire if she could purchase a glass of milk and some bread and cheese.

The half-timbered farmhouse was surrounded by single-storey red-brick outbuildings. Irene paused by the gate in the picket fence, taking in all the details of the rutted and muddy yard with hens busily pecking at the ground. A desultory-looking sheepdog was chained to its kennel and it wagged its tail, uttering a feeble woof which seemed more like a greeting than a threat. She let herself into the enclosure, taking care to close the gate behind her, and she stopped to pat the dog. It licked her hand and whined when she walked away to knock on the farmhouse door. She waited for a while but there did not seem to be anyone at home. The yard was deserted, although she could hear the sound of voices coming from one of the outhouses. She picked her way between the fowls and avoided deep puddles as she headed towards a brick building, which turned out to be the dairy. Inside with his back to her was a tall, thin man who was berating a freckle-faced boy of eleven or twelve.

'Excuse me, mister,' Irene said, clearing her throat. 'I don't mean to intrude but I was out walking and I wondered if I might buy a glass of milk and something to eat.'

The man turned his head to stare at her. She could see the resemblance immediately and it was so marked that she caught her breath.

'This is private property, young woman,' he said coldly. 'It's not an inn. I suggest you go down the road where you'll find a public house. I'm sure they will oblige you.'

Irene was not going to give in so easily. She had come this far and she was convinced that this must be Farmer Kent, but she could not leave until she was certain. 'Thank you, but I really would appreciate a cup of milk, if you could spare one, Mr – er . . .'

'Farmer Kent is the name, young lady,' he muttered, turning to the shame-faced boy. 'Fetch the lady a cup of milk, Arnold, and mind what I just told you.'

'Yes, Father.' The boy hurried to the back of the dairy and dipped a half-pint measure into a churn. He scuttled back, handing it to Irene before making his escape through the open door.

Irene took a mouthful of the warm, creamy

liquid. She eyed Farmer Kent warily. 'Thank you, mister. How much do I owe you?'

He dismissed her question with a wave of his hand. 'Nothing. You're welcome to it, but I'll ask you to leave as soon as you're done.' He made to follow his son but Irene called him back.

'Farmer Kent, I believe you have a son and daughter living in London.'

He stopped, shoulders hunched and hands clenched at his sides. 'You are mistaken.'

Irene stared at his rigid back and she sensed that he was lying. 'I don't think so,' she said boldly.

He spun around to face her, his expression grim. 'Are you calling me a liar?'

'No, mister. I just thought—'

'Why did you come here, young woman? What right have you to snoop on me and my family?' He took a step towards her, his dark eyebrows meeting in a scowl over the bridge of his aquiline nose.

There was no getting away from the physical resemblance between the farmer and the police inspector. Although, she decided, taking an involuntary step backward, Edward at his worst was no match for his ill-tempered sire. 'All right,' she said hastily. 'I admit that I came here out of curiosity. Alice is a dear friend of mine and I have a slight acquaintance with her brother.'

'Who sent you here?'

'No one. I came of my own accord entirely, but I can see that I've offended you and I'll bother you no further.' With a defiant lift of her chin, Irene walked past him and out into the yard, but she had not gone more than a few paces when she slipped on the mud and tumbled to the ground, twisting her ankle. She lay in a crumpled heap, gasping with pain.

'You stupid girl, you should take more care.' Farmer Kent yanked her roughly to her feet. 'Can you walk?'

She attempted to put weight on her ankle but the pain was too intense and she leaned against him, shaking her head. 'It hurts.'

'Of course it does.' He hitched her arm around his shoulders. 'I'll help you to the house and my wife will see to you. Lean on me.'

There was nothing she could do other than allow him to assist her over the rough ground to the farmhouse. In the kitchen the aroma of freshly baked bread mingled with the fragrance of herbs hanging in bunches from the blackened oak beams. Hams hung in the smoky inglenook above the fire and a kettle was bubbling and singing on the hob. A pale, tired-looking woman was standing at the large pine table, slicing raw meat ready for the pot. She looked up as they entered the room and her eyes widened as Farmer Kent dumped Irene on a chair as if she had been a sack of potatoes.

'Dora, stop that and help this young person. She took a fall and twisted her ankle. I don't think it's anything more than a simple sprain, but you must take a look at it. See to her and then send her on her way.' Without waiting for his wife's reply, he turned on his heel and strode out into the yard.

'I'm sorry to put you to any trouble, missis,' Irene said apologetically, but despite her pain and embarrassment she couldn't help staring at Dora Kent. She must have been quite pretty when she was a young woman, but now her small features were etched with wrinkles and dark smudges of fatigue underlined her large brown eyes. She was swaddled in a large calico apron with her hair tucked up beneath a mobcap, but the shabby garments could not disguise an indefinable air of gentility.

She knelt at Irene's feet and began to unlace her boot. 'I hope I'm not hurting you, miss.'

Irene winced but she bit her lip and shook her head. 'It's all right, Mrs Kent. You've got a gentle touch.'

A fleeting smile crossed Dora's face. 'I haven't seen you round these parts before. What's your name?'

'Irene Angel. Ouch.'

'That's the worst of it over.' Dora eased Irene's boot off and examined the ankle closely. 'It's only a bit swollen. A cold compress should sort it out, but I'm afraid you won't be able to walk on it for a day or two.' She scrambled to her feet and crossed the flagstone floor to take a clean cloth from a drawer in a large oak dresser. She dipped it in the stone sink and wrung it out. 'Have you come far today, Miss Angel? We don't see many strangers around these parts.'

'From Havering,' Irene said, wincing as Dora wrapped the cold, wet cloth around her ankle. 'I am staying there with friends.'

Dora raised her head and a shadow passed across her features. 'From Havering, you say?'

'Yes. I'm staying at the Round House with Miss Maude Greenwood.'

Dora's pale face blanched to ashen and she sat down heavily on the nearest chair. 'How is she? Is Maude well?'

Irene nodded. 'Your sister is in good health.'

Dora's eyes widened. 'H how did you know we were sisters?'

'Martha Marchant told me a little of your story.'

'My sister hasn't spoken to me since I married Eddie,' Dora said, sighing. 'She has never been able to forgive me for marrying her old sweetheart. We haven't passed so much as the time of day for thirteen years.'

'Perhaps if you went to see her . . .' Irene began, but the expression on Dora's face stopped her in mid-sentence.

Dora rose to her feet in an obvious state of agitation. 'No – that would be impossible!'

Chapter Eighteen

'I never wanted to fall out with her so completely. I really thought that she would come round when she grew accustomed to the idea of my marriage to Eddie, but she is a stubborn woman.'

'But it all happened so long ago and you have a son – don't you want him to know his aunt?'

'The rift between us is too great to be breached.' Dora moved to the range and busied herself making a pot of tea. She left it to brew while she fetched blue and white willow-pattern cups and saucers from the dresser. 'Maude is my senior by ten years. I would have been the youngest of five had not two of our brothers died in infancy, which left Maude, Cuthbert and myself. I was little more than a child when Eddie was courting my sister, and I liked him well enough then, but that was all. I do remember how upset she was when our father forbade the match, but it was many years later when I met Eddie again. I was almost thirty-nine and had long given up hope of marriage and children, and he was a widower with two children. I snatched my last chance of happiness, but Maude cannot forgive me.'

'I'm sorry,' Irene murmured helplessly. 'That is so sad.'

'The tragedy is that she cannot put the past behind her,' Dora said, pouring the tea. 'Do you take milk and sugar?'

'Milk and one sugar, if you please. Do go on, if you feel you can. Alice has told me a little about you, but not very much.'

'How do you know Alice?' Dora's hand shook as she handed the cup and saucer to Irene.

'It's a long story, but I must confess that my friendship with Alice and her brother is one of the reasons why I came here today. When Miss Maude mentioned that she had once been in love with a farmer whose name was Edward Kent I was curious to discover if he was Alice's father, or if it was just a coincidence.'

Dora sank down on a chair at the table. 'I think it was difficult for my stepson to accept another woman in his mother's place. He did not feel that I was a fit person to care for Alice, whom he adored.' She picked up a spoon and stirred her tea, as if concentrating on the repetitive movement helped her to put her thoughts into words. 'I know that I was not the best stepmother in the world, but I did try to make them like me.'

Irene tried to imagine herself in Edward's place, and she experienced a sudden overwhelming sympathy for him in his predicament. How would she have felt if Ma had died and Pa had brought another woman into their home? 'It could not have been easy for any of you,' she said, thinking out loud.

'No, indeed. But if I had not accepted Eddie's proposal I would more than likely have died a spinster. Maude and I had very little in common; the difference in our ages and temperaments was too great, but I wish we could have remained friends.'

'Couldn't you tell her that yourself?'

'I tried in the beginning, but she was obstinate and I was desperate to make a success of the marriage that had come to me so late in life.'

'You have a fine son,' Irene said gently. 'I saw him in the dairy.'

Dora nodded and smiled. 'Yes, I have a son. Very soon after our marriage, and to my great surprise, I found that I was in the family way. I had thought that I was too old to bear children and you can guess my joy when I discovered that I was to have a child of my own to love and care for. I had a difficult confinement, and for a while the doctors thought that both Arnold and I would die, but somehow we survived. I confess that I gave all my attention to my boy, and in my anxiety to nurture him I'm afraid I neglected Alice. I am not proud of that fact.'

Irene was at a loss as to what to say in the face of such an admission. 'I'm sure you did your best,' she murmured.

'I tried, but I haven't the strength of character that my sister possesses, and I'm ashamed to say that it was a relief when my husband's son decided to take Alice to London. Perhaps I should have prevented it, but I thought that she would be much happier with young Edward.'

'She adores him,' Irene said simply. 'And he is very good to her.'

'I'm glad. Edward is a fine young man but he was not cut out to be a farmer, any more than my son is. Arnold helps his father on the farm, but I'm afraid he has no liking for the life. My husband insists that he must learn to work the land and take over from him when the time comes.'

'And how do you feel about that?'

'I want anything that will make my son happy.' Dora wiped her eyes on her sleeve and sniffed. 'But I am afraid he will never settle for rural life. He's never met my brother Cuthbert, but one day I must tell Arnold that he has relatives in London. I have a feeling that as soon as he is old enough to leave home he will want to go to London to seek his fortune, and then he will have need of Cuthbert's protection and guidance.'

Irene pitied any young fellow who had to rely on Arthur's parents for guidance, but she kept her thoughts to herself on that score. 'It might comfort you to know that your nephew, Arthur, has come to live in Havering with Miss Maude. He hated being an apprentice silversmith and got himself into all sorts of scrapes in town. He is now learning the blacksmith's trade and plans to marry his employer's daughter, so you see the wheel has come full circle.'

A reluctant smile lit Dora's eyes. 'I have not seen Arthur since he was in petticoats and I think it highly unlikely that anyone told him about Arnold. I would like to meet Arthur again, but I fear that Maude would object.'

'Perhaps,' Irene replied thoughtfully. 'But surely it would be worth trying to heal the rift between you?'

'I don't know about that. I think matters have gone too far.' Dora broke off with a guilty start as the door opened and Farmer Kent strode into the kitchen.

'So you're still here,' he said, scowling at Irene. 'Do you think you could walk on that ankle?'

Dora rose to her feet and fetched another cup. She filled it with tea, adding liberal quantities of milk and sugar, and she passed it to her husband. 'She cannot walk home with a sprained ankle, my dear,' she said mildly. 'Why not allow Arnold to drive her home in the trap?'

'He could, but it's very inconvenient.' He finished his tea in two large gulps. 'All right, you may call the boy and tell him to make the trap ready, but I want him back here as soon as possible. I need his help ditching this afternoon.'

'Would you like him to collect the ploughshare from the smithy, Eddie?' Dora asked innocently. 'It would save you a trip to the village.'

He hesitated, as if the decision was a momentous one, and then he nodded his head. 'I suppose the boy could be trusted to carry out such a simple task unaided. Very well, but tell him not to use it as an excuse to loiter.' He shoved the empty cup into her hands and left the kitchen without a backward glance.

As the door closed on him, Dora turned to Irene with a conspiratorial smile. 'I want Arnold to meet his cousin. Even if Maude wants nothing to do with us, there is no reason for my boy to be kept apart from his own flesh and blood.'

'I agree with you. And perhaps Miss Maude is not quite as unfeeling as you seem to think.'

'Why do you say that?'

Irene was touched by the eager look on Dora's face and she gave her an encouraging smile. 'I believe that the bedchamber where I sleep might have once been yours. I was allowed to use it on my previous visit to Havering and it struck me then that it was like no other room in the house. I don't think that a thing has been changed in it since you left home all those years ago, but it has been kept clean and aired as if in readiness for your return.'

'Is it a room overlooking the garden?' Dora asked with a tremor in her voice. 'Are the curtains and coverlet patterned with roses, and does the afternoon sunshine flood the room with light?'

'Yes,' Irene said, smiling. 'It is exactly like that.'

Dora's eyes misted and her lips trembled. 'Thank you for telling me, Irene. Perhaps, deep down, Maude has forgiven me after all. You don't know how happy that makes me.'

An hour later, after an uneventful ride in the somewhat rickety trap behind an aged carthorse with no apparent ambition to go faster than a snail, they arrived at the village smithy. Irene had suggested that Arnold, a boy of few words, might like to go there first. Dora had already told him that he was to meet his cousin from London, but Arnold had not appeared to be particularly interested. Irene could only hope that Arthur might be a little more enthusiastic when she introduced him to his young relative. Perhaps under Artie's influence, the rather surly and taciturn Arnold might turn out to be a totally different boy. It was worth a try.

'Here we are, Arnold,' Irene said cheerfully as they approached the smithy.

'I've been here before,' Arnold muttered, shooting her a pitying look, as if to imply that all women were scatterbrained creatures who must be tolerated but otherwise ignored. 'You are the stranger round here, not me.'

Arthur emerged from the forge and was heading towards them. 'And that is your cousin Arthur,' Irene said, ignoring his rudeness.

'This is a surprise, Renie,' Arthur said, casting a curious glance at her companion. 'I didn't know you had a gentleman friend in the neighbourhood.' He winked at Arnold, who turned his head away with a disdainful sniff.

'I won't get down, Artie. I've hurt my ankle and Arnold is going to drive me home when he has done an errand for his father, Farmer Kent.' She gave Arthur a meaningful glance, jerking her head in Arnold's direction.

'Farmer Kent's son?' Arthur stared at her with a puzzled frown. 'I don't understand.'

'Artie, I want you to meet your cousin, Arnold Kent.'

'My cousin?' Arthur looked at Arnold and then back to Irene. 'I still don't understand.'

'I never asked to meet you. It was Ma's idea and my dad says that all women are simple-minded.' Arnold shot a scornful look at Irene. 'If you ask me, this one ain't no better than the rest.'

'Here, boy, don't talk to Miss Irene like that,' Arthur said angrily. 'Show some respect.' He drew Irene aside, lowering his voice. 'Is this true, Renie?'

'Yes, and it explains a lot. It was Dora, Miss Maude's sister who married her old sweetheart.'

'Damn me!' Arthur said, staring at Arnold in amazement. 'No wonder the old girl was upset. Are you certain?'

'I met Dora at the farm. There's no doubt that she is Miss Maude's sister.'

'Stop whispering.' Arnold stood up in the well of the cart. 'What are you saying? I want to know.'

'It's up to you to sort this out, Artie,' Irene said gently. 'I've done my bit.'

A shadow of doubt crossed Arthur's face, but he stepped up to the cart and held out his hand. 'How do, old chap? I'm pleased to meet you.'

'I have to collect a mended ploughshare,' Arthur said stiffly, ignoring Arthur's outstretched hand. 'We deal with Bligh, not his apprentice.'

Arthur's smile faded. 'Do you now? Well, young man, I'm sorry but the gaffer is busy at present, and I think I can be trusted to find the article in question. Would you like to hop down and give me a hand?'

'No, I would not. Just do as I ask and be quick about it, my man.'

With a swift movement, Arthur hoisted his surly cousin from the driver's seat by the scruff of his neck and the seat of his breeches. 'Blood relative or not, you don't speak to anyone in that tone of voice, young 'un.'

Irene smothered a giggle at the sight of Arnold's red face and flailing limbs as Arthur dangled him above the ground. 'Don't be too hard on him, Artie. He's just a boy.'

'And a rude one at that,' Arthur retorted, releasing Arnold so that he landed on his hands and knees in the mud. 'Get up and help me find the ploughshare. I'm sure you wouldn't want to take the wrong 'un home to your pa.'

Arnold scrambled to his feet, brushing the

mud off his knees. 'You did that on purpose, you big bully.'

'I did it to teach you to mind your manners, cousin,' Arthur said amicably. He held out his hand. 'You and I should be friends and not foes. Come, shake on it.'

Arnold backed away. 'How do I know that we really are cousins? You could just be saying that to make a fool of me.'

'It's time someone told you a few home truths, young man. Come with me and I'll tell you a bit about your mother's family. Then you can decide whether or not you want to get to know the Greenwoods.' Arthur strolled away from the cart and disappeared into the fiery interior of the smithy.

Arnold hesitated and he glanced nervously at Irene. She smiled and nodded. 'Go on. You'll like Artic when you get to know him, and you might find you have more in common with him than you imagine.'

For a moment she thought that he was going to refuse, but then he seemed to think better of it and he trotted after Arthur like an obedient puppy. Irene sighed. Her ankle was throbbing painfully and her head was beginning to ache. She was glad that she had been able to introduce Arthur to his cousin, and maybe in time the breach between Miss Maude and her sister would be healed, but all this only served to remind her that she was far from home and family. Meeting Edward's father had unsettled her even further, but it had made her realise that she should stop looking for answers in the safety of the countryside. She must return to London where she truly belonged.

Rainclouds had gathered and the sky had darkened ominously. She called out to Arthur to hurry and was relieved to see him returning with Arnold helping him to carry the heavy ploughshare. They loaded it in the trap and Arnold leapt up beside her with the agility of a young monkey. He took the reins and released the handbrake.

'Goodbye, young 'un,' Arthur said, ruffling his hair.

'Do you promise to come and see me at the farm?' Arnold asked plaintively. 'You won't forget, will you?'

'I will come on Sunday. I don't hold with family feuds and I look forward to meeting your ma and pa.'

Arnold nodded his head and grinned. 'Walk on,' he said, clicking his tongue against his teeth.

Irene shot a grateful look at Arthur and he responded with a wink and a smile. 'See you later, Renie.'

She blew him a kiss as the horse started off at a steady plod, and she turned to Arnold with a smile. 'That wasn't too painful now, was it?'

He hunched his shoulders and grunted.

She took this for assent and they lapsed into silence for the rest of the short drive to the Round House. As Arnold slowed the horse to a halt outside the gate, Irene prepared to climb down.

'Do you need some help?' Arnold murmured with a half-hearted attempt to rise from his seat.

'I can manage, and you'd best get home before it starts to rain or you'll get drenched.'

She winced as she attempted to put weight on her injured ankle. 'Maybe I could use a hand,' she admitted reluctantly.

'Someone's coming down the path,' Arnold said, peering over her shoulder. 'And he's bigger and stronger than me.'

Irene turned her head and her heart lurched against her ribs. For a moment she couldn't catch her breath. Hope and fear of disappointment merged into one as he drew nearer, and the blood pounding in her ears threatened to deafen her. He vaulted the gate and came to stand by the cart. Even in the half-light she would have known that familiar face. It might be ten years since she had last seen her brother, but there was no mistaking Jim's grin, which spread from ear to ear as he looked up at her.

'Strewth, girl, I hardly recognised you.' He lifted her down from the trap and held her at arm's length, staring at her in wonderment. 'You've changed so much, Renie. What happened to that little kid who was bawling her eyes out because I was leaving?'

'Jim – after all this time. I – we thought you might be . . .' Her breath caught on a sob as she gazed at him through a veil of tears. The boy was now a man; his round boyish features had been sculpted by maturity but the eyes were still the same. 'I c-can't believe it. Is it really you?'

'It's me all right. I've come to take you home, ducks.'

'How did you know where to find me? Oh, Jim, I think I must be dreaming.'

'I'm off then,' Arnold said sulkily. 'Seems you don't need me any more.'

Irene gave him a watery smile. 'Ta for bringing me home, Arnold.'

Jim took a coin from his pocket and tossed it to Arnold. 'That's for your trouble, boy.'

Arnold caught it deftly but he tossed it back at Jim and the coin landed on the soft ground at his feet. 'I don't want your money, you great oaf.' He flicked the reins. 'Walk on.'

'You've hurt his feelings,' Irene said, torn between tears and laughter as she watched the cart disappearing into the gloom.

'Never mind him,' Jim said, glancing up at the leaden sky. 'We've got ten lost years to catch up on, so let's get you indoors before the heavens open.'

Irene gazed up into his suntanned face. 'I can't believe it's really you. Pinch me or I'll think I'm dreaming.'

He pinched her arm. 'Is that real enough for you?'

'Ouch! That hurt,' Irene said, laughing. 'There's so much I want to know.' She had almost forgotten her injured ankle but it reminded her now with a sharp stabbing pain as she attempted to walk and she reached out to grasp Jim's arm.

'What's the matter, Renie? Are you hurt?'

'It's nothing – just a twisted ankle.'

He swept her up in his arms. 'Same old Renie,' he said, chuckling. 'You was always getting into scrapes as a nipper. You may look like a lady, but you haven't changed a bit.'

She clung to him, scarcely able to believe that her long lost brother had really come home. Despite the tingling sensation where he had pinched her, she still feared she might wake up and find it had all been a dream, but when he pushed the back door open with the toe of his boot and the familiar aroma of cooking and wet dogs filled her nostrils, Irene knew that all this was real.

Martha looked up from stirring a pan on the range and her face crumpled with concern when she saw Irene. 'Lawks, what happened to you?'

'I hurt my ankle,' Irene said breathlessly as Jim set her down on a chair by the fire. 'It's nothing to worry about, Martha.'

'We was getting worried. Miss Maude was about to go looking for you when your brother turned up. He said you was always disappearing when you was a nipper and not to worry.' Martha turned back to watching the contents of the pot. 'I says you'd come back when you was hungry, but Miss Maude was in a bit of a stew.'

'Well, she's here now,' Jim said, shrugging off his greatcoat to reveal a smart suit that would not have looked out of place on a city gentleman. 'And I'm sure a cup of tea would go down well, or perhaps something a bit stronger – for medicinal purposes, of course.' He glanced at Irene with a mischievous twinkle in his dark eyes so reminiscent of their father's that she felt her throat constrict.

'Miss Maude doesn't hold with strong drink,' Irene murmured, turning her head away so that Jim would not see how she struggled to control her emotions. She did not want to make a fool of herself in front of Martha, and Miss Maude had just walked into the kitchen with a look on her face that would have turned fresh milk to cheese in an instant.

'Oh! So you've decided to grace us with your presence then, Irene.' It was a statement rather than a question. 'I don't suppose you gave a thought to the possibility that Martha might be worried sick about you. I don't allow things like that to put me out of countenance, but you could have shown a little consideration for our – I mean, her – feelings.'

'Hold on a moment, Miss Greenwood,' Jim said, laying his hand on Irene's shoulder and giving it a comforting squeeze. 'Irene has hurt her ankle and I think she deserves the chance to explain her absence. I'm sure she had no intention of causing either of you any concern.'

Maude's stern features relaxed a little and she inclined her head. 'Maybe I was a little hasty.' She turned to Martha with an imperious wave of her hand. 'Tea, please, Martha, and fetch the brandy bottle. We'll take it in the parlour if Mr Angel would be kind enough to help Irene to the sofa. And bring some clean linen and a bowl of cold water so that I can make a compress for her ankle.'

'Do this, do that,' Martha grumbled. 'Anyone would think I was a slave.'

Maude shrugged her shoulders. 'I don't want you eavesdropping outside the door, so you'd better join us. Don't fret, you old harridan, we'll await your coming.' She whisked out of the room and her footsteps echoed off the polished oak floorboards and she made her way to the parlour.

Jim lifted Irene from the chair despite her protest that she could walk. 'I'd best carry you, ducks. You should keep your weight off that ankle until it's been seen to. Anyway, it seems we've had a royal command, so we'd best not keep the lady waiting.' He glanced over his shoulder at Martha, who was still mumbling beneath her breath as she made the tea. 'I'll be back to help you with the tray, Miss Martha.'

Irene stifled a giggle at the sight of Martha's open-mouthed look of astonishment, which quickly turned into a delighted smirk. 'I see you've a way with the ladies,' she whispered as Jim carried her out of the kitchen and along the hallway to the parlour. 'You've been away for so long and there's so much I want to ask you.'

'I've been round the world more times than I can count, and seen a great many things. I'm a different person from the wild boy that I was when I left home.'

'Not too different, I hope,' Irene said, laying her head on his shoulder. 'You're still my big brother and I can't tell you how much it means to me that you have come back to us.'

He laid her gently on the sofa. 'It's been too

long, Renie. But I'm here now and I mean to make amends for everything.'

'Not before time, as far as I can see,' Maude said, brushing him aside and bending over Irene to unlace her boot. 'Don't hover, young man. Go and fetch the cold water and linen so that I can put a cold compress on this ankle. There will be plenty of time later for explanations and apologies for the way you treated your family.'

'Don't be too hard on him, Miss Maude,' Irene said when Jim was out of earshot. 'I'm sure he had good reasons for doing what he did.'

'Men are all the same,' Maude retorted, pulling her mouth down at the corners. 'They follow their own inclinations and be damned to the rest of us. And I'm not apologising for the bad language.'

'Miss Maude,' Irene began tentatively, 'before the others return, I must tell you something.'

'This will hurt a bit,' Maude said as she eased the boot off. She stared at the rough bandage that Dora had inexpertly applied to the injured joint. 'Whoever did this was no doctor.'

'No, but she was kind and she meant well.' Irene bit her lip as Maude unwound the makeshift bandage.

'Can you move your foot?'

Irene wiggled her toes, wincing with pain. 'Yes, but it hurts.'

'And I'd say it was your just desserts for poking your nose in where it doesn't belong,' Maude said crossly. 'Don't put on that innocent face, miss. I can guess where you went this afternoon and I don't imagine you walked to Romford. Anyway, I saw you drive past with that boy. I've seen him in the distance at the market and I'd recognise the Greenwood nose anywhere.'

'You're right, but I make no apology for going to Navestock. I wanted to find out if Farmer Kent was related to the people I know in London, but I had no idea that his wife was your sister.'

'I have no sister. She is dead to me.'

'And yet you kept her room just as it was when she lived at home.'

'Sentimental nonsense,' Maude snorted. 'You have Martha to thank for keeping the room clean and aired. Dora went behind my back and married the man who should have been my husband. She bore him a son and I remain childless.'

'But you have a nephew. He is a fine boy, but not a happy one.'

'That isn't my problem.'

'Isn't it?' Irene angled her head. 'I think he

needs his kind aunt and his cousin Arthur, which is why I made certain that they met. If I have interfered, it was from the best of intentions. I would not deliberately upset you, especially when you have shown me nothing but kindness.'

'Humph!' Maude cleared her throat and turned away as the door opened and Martha bustled in with a heavily laden tray, closely followed by Jim.

'There now, clear the way,' Martha said brusquely. 'Let me see to that ankle, Miss Maude, and you can sit down and drink your tea with a tot of medicinal brandy.' She beckoned to Jim, who stood behind her with a bowl of water clutched in his hands. 'Make yourself useful and tear that bit of sheeting into strips. We'll have you fixed up in a trice, Miss Renie.'

Irene met Jim's amused gaze over the top of Martha's bent shoulders as she examined the injured limb. He placed the bowl within her reach and began, quite expertly, Irene noticed, to rip the sheet into bandages, which Martha dampened in the water before applying them to the swollen ankle.

Maude sank into one of the chairs by the fireside, adding a generous measure of brandy to her tea which she sipped with obvious enjoyment. 'Now then,' she said in a more mellow tone. 'Irene has told me about her visit to the Kents' farm and her meeting with my sister and her husband, so we don't need to go through that again. I think it's time we heard from you, James Angel. I'm sure we are all curious as to the reason for your sudden reappearance after so many years' absence.'

'I know I am,' Irene said eagerly. 'And how did you know where to find me, Jim? Do sit down and tell all.'

Jim handed the strips of cloth to Martha and he pulled up a chair. 'Well, it wasn't easy.' He sat down opposite Maude and helped himself to a tot of brandy, which he drank neat in one gulp. 'When my ship docked at Queenhithe I went straight to Wood Street expecting to find Ma behind the counter as usual, selling jars of pickles and bottles of sauce. I found it closed and shuttered and no one in the adjoining shops seemed to know where my family had gone, although they told me that the departure was fairly recent and that they had heard rumours that Pa was in Newgate. I can't say that surprised me entirely, so I went looking for old Yapp. As luck would have it I spoke to a boy called Danny, who knows you well, Renie. He told me as much as he knew and directed me to Emmie's house in Love Lane.'

'And how is Emmie? Has she had the baby?'

Jim shook his head. 'Not yet, although I

believe the birth is imminent. She was most insistent that I bring you back to London so that you can be there at her confinement.'

'But that's impossible. Josiah would not allow it. He sent me away because of lies told to him by that evil Ras and his stupid brother.'

'Nevertheless, I think our brother-in-law might stretch a point when he sees how much it means to Emmie. I only met him briefly, but I believe that he is sincere in his affection for her and would not want to see her upset so near to her time.'

'And Ma,' Irene said with a hitch in her voice. 'How is she? How did she take it when you turned up out of the blue?'

'Like the wonderful mother she always was.' Jim's eyes were suspiciously bright and he swallowed hard, taking a second or two to compose himself. 'She never uttered a word of reproach for the way I left. She said she understood why I ran away to sea, and that almost totally unmanned me, Renie. I had to turn my head away in case she saw the tears that came to my eyes. I would have felt less guilty if she'd given me a piece of her mind.'

'She is a better person than I,' Maude said in a low voice. 'I don't think I would have been so forgiving.'

'No, indeed you wouldn't.' Martha rose stiffly to her feet and placed the bowl and what remained of the cloth on a side table. She poured tea into two cups, adding a tot of brandy and several lumps of sugar in the one she passed to Irene. 'My aching bones are getting too old for this sort of thing,' she muttered as she sank down on the nearest chair.

Irene sipped the strong sweet tea and felt the brandy sliding down her throat to warm her stomach. The effect was instant and even the pain in her ankle felt easier. 'But how was Ma in herself, Jim? Did she seem happy to remain in Emmie's house?'

'She did, but it won't be for long. Before I left town I rented a furnished house in Five Foot Lane, close to the river. As soon as you are fit to travel we will return to London and take up residence. If Ma wants to join us when Emmie's lying-in period is over, then of course she will be more than welcome.'

Maude put her cup and saucer down with a clatter. 'Brave talk, my boy, but have you the means to support your mother and sister? How will you live? Or do you intend to return to sea?'

'Leave the fellow alone, Miss Maude.' Martha drained her cup and looked longingly at the brandy bottle. 'It's none of our business.'

'None of yours maybe,' Maude snapped. 'However, I feel somewhat responsible for

Irene. I wouldn't like to see her return to London only to be pitched back into poverty.'

Jim gave her a reassuring smile. 'There's no need to worry on that score, Miss Maude. I've saved my money over the years and never squandered it when I went ashore. I have ample means to live on for the time being, and I intend to look into starting a business that will enable me to swallow the anchor and lead a life ashore.'

'You do?' Irene could hardly contain her excitement. 'That's wonderful news, Jim. What sort of business had you in mind?'

He helped himself to more brandy, offering the bottle to Maude who shook her head with a prim smile and to Martha who nodded eagerly. Having added a generous amount to her tea, he resumed his seat. 'I don't intend to sell sauce and pickles, that's for sure.'

'And what exactly is your plan?' Maude demanded.

'I've travelled far and wide, visiting most of the countries in the world, and my observation has been that the best way to make money is to give people what they want.'

Maude folded her hands in her lap, eyeing him suspiciously. 'And what is that, may I ask?'

'They crave entertainment, pleasure and a little excitement to brighten up their dull and humdrum existence. The common man longs for an opportunity to fill his pockets with money; preferably without having to work too hard for the privilege.'

Irene pulled herself to a sitting position, ignoring the stab of pain that shot through her ankle. 'Jim, do I understand you right? Are you thinking of opening a gaming house?'

Maude uttered a shriek of dismay and Martha choked on a mouthful of brandy.

'Exactly so, my duck,' Jim said, apparently unmoved by their obvious disapproval. 'People will say that the gambling streak runs in the family, but I've never fallen prey to the addiction myself. I've visited many gaming houses abroad and I have seen how they are run. Ours will be a legitimate business, mind you, all open and above board with no attempt to fleece the punters. However, I think it's time that the Angels recouped some of the losses incurred by the old man over the years. What do you say, Renie?'

She stared at him aghast. 'I can't believe you said that, Jim. It's the worst idea I've ever heard. You must have lost your mind.'

Chapter Nineteen

They had the first class railway compartment to themselves. Irene relaxed against the comfortable upholstery with a sigh of contentment. Not only was she reunited with her brother, but they were on their way back to London. She could look forward to having a proper home again and she would see Ma and Emmie very soon. Then there was the daunting prospect of venturing into business with Jim. No matter how much she had argued and protested that opening a gaming house was a terrible mistake, he would not be shaken from his purpose.

'Penny for 'em,' Jim said, smiling. 'You look like the cat that ate the cream, or maybe it was a big fat mouse.'

'A couple of rats more like. Don't think I've forgotten about the Sykes brothers, Jim. I won't be happy until they're sent away for life, preferably to a penal colony in Australia.'

Jim's smile faded. 'Now, Renie, I thought we had that out last night. I don't intend to put my money into a legal gaming house and then risk losing everything by getting on the wrong side of Vic and Wally.'

'But don't you see that's how they've got away with it for so long? Everyone is afraid to cross them, and they are so crafty that they've managed always to elude the bobbies. If you insist on carrying out your plan at least there might be some good to come out of it.'

Jim's sandy brows knotted over the bridge of his nose. 'What do you mean by that? What's going on in that head of yours?'

'Just that the Sykes brothers have got to be stopped. If they thought you were a serious threat they might come out in the open.'

'I'm setting up a legal gaming club, Renie. I don't want any trouble.'

She leaned towards him, gazing earnestly into his eyes. 'Things got bad after you left London. They will get worse and worse unless the cops smash the gangs.'

'I suppose by that you mean the ambitious inspector you told me about, and not the City of London Police force in general.'

Irene averted her gaze to stare out of the window. 'Don't tease me. I'm dead serious about this, and if you won't help me then I'll go after the Sykes brothers on my own.'

'You'll do no such thing, Renie. If you try anything stupid I'll put you on the first train back to Havering.'

This drew a reluctant giggle from her and she squeezed his fingers. 'I can just see Miss Maude's face if I turned up again and said I had come for good. I think she has enough to do coping with the farm and Artie, especially as he is determined to marry the lovely Betty. And now she has young Arnold to consider as well.'

'That's her problem, my pet.' Jim relaxed back in his seat and took a gold half-hunter from his waistcoat pocket. 'We'll be arriving soon if the train is on time. We'll get a cab and go to the house first, and then, if you're a good girl, I'll take you to Love Lane to see Ma and Emmie.'

'I'm still not sure that Josiah will allow me in.'

'You're with your big brother now, Renie. From now on we'll be persons of consequence and I think you'll find that things will be very different.'

Irene was about to tell him that she was quite capable of looking after herself, but she thought better of it. It wouldn't hurt to let him think that she was going to be mild and biddable, for the time being anyway. Jim only remembered her as an eight-year-old child and he seemed to imagine that he could still boss her about, but he was wrong. He would soon discover his mistake, but for the moment she was content to let matters lie. She peered out of the rain-spattered window at the cloud of steam billowing in the wind. 'It's raining,' she said, changing the subject. 'Everything looks so dreary when it's dull and wet.'

'Don't worry, poppet,' Jim said cheerfully. 'You'll soon be too busy to notice the weather. Tomorrow morning, first thing, we'll make a start on touring the warehouses to choose furnishings for the gaming rooms.'

She stared at him in surprise. 'I didn't realise that you'd found a suitable establishment.'

'Why do you think I rented a large house if not to use the ground floor for business? It makes perfect sense.'

'So we'll be living above the shop again.'

Jim's shout of laughter was drowned by a blast on the train's whistle as the engine decreased speed. He rose to his feet and lifted their luggage from the rack. 'Almost there. This is the start of a big adventure for us, little sister.'

Irene let the window down and inhaled the familiar musty, smoky smell of the city, with the almost overpowering stench from the glue factory mingling with noxious fumes from the gasworks, and she knew that she was back where she belonged. The countryside was peaceful and green, but at heart she was a city girl and soon she would see those she loved most in the world. Then, when she had assured herself that Ma and Emmie were doing well, Irene decided that she would take the first opportunity to visit Alice. She had so much to tell her. She might even venture out after supper this evening, although there was a distinct possibility that this would involve seeing Edward again.

Having met Edward Kent senior and seen how he treated Arnold, Irene could understand how his elder son might have built a stone wall around his heart in order to protect himself from a bullying and selfish parent. She had seen the tender side of his nature in his dealings with Alice, and if he had not been an enforcer of the law, Irene decided that she might have warmed to him sooner. During the long days in the country, she had come to realise that she missed crossing swords with Edward Kent, and that there was a fine line between hate – and love. Of course, she did not actually love him, but she had to admit that she was seeing him in a much more kindly light. Now, more than ever, she needed to have him on her side. It would be the first time that an Angel had colluded with the cops, but theirs would be a relationship based on their mutual desire to see the Sykes gang behind bars, and there it would end.

The train slowed to a crawl as it drew alongside the platform.

'Home at last,' Jim said, leaning out to open the door.

Irene alighted from the carriage. With her ankle firmly strapped up she was able to walk with barely a limp, and she followed in Jim's wake as he strode along the platform, pausing to hand over their tickets at the barrier and then heading for the cab stand in the street outside the station. Jim assisted her into a waiting cab and she reclined against the well-worn leather squabs that smelled of stale tobacco and Macassar oil. He climbed in and sat on the seat beside her, and every now and again she had to glance at him, just to make sure that he was really there. She couldn't help thinking what a handsome fellow he was, and she noted with pride that his years of training as a ship's officer had given him an undeniable air of authority. He had grown into a fine man and she was certain that they would do very well together.

The city streets flashed past the windows as the cabby urged his horse through the chaotic traffic. Drays, broughams, hansom cabs and hackney carriages vied for space with horse-drawn omnibuses, costermongers' barrows and tranters' carts. After the quiet of rural Essex, the sounds of the city were deafening and Irene heaved a contented sigh. She had been grateful for the rustic respite, but now she was ready to begin again.

'We're here,' Jim said, breaking into her reverie. He tapped on the roof of the cab. 'It's the first house on the left, cabby.'

The rain had ceased and rays of pale sunshine filtered through the clouds as Irene caught sight of their new home at the junction of Old Fish Street Hill and Five Foot Lane. In a street lined with soot-blackened brick buildings four or five storeys high, the house that Jim had chosen stood out from the rest by reason of ornate, if slightly rusted, wrought-iron balconies outside the first and second floor windows. The front door might once have been a glossy black but the paintwork was peeling off in huge blisters, and the brass lion's-head door knocker was in need of a good polish. The windows were filmed with grime and the stone steps were splattered with bird droppings, but it was nothing that could not be fixed with a bit of elbow grease and a general application of soap and washing soda. Irene picked up her skirts and waited for Jim to unlock the door.

'Welcome to your new home, Renie.' He stood aside, allowing her to enter before him. 'What d'you think?'

'How could you afford to buy a place like this, Jim?'

'I couldn't. It's rented, but one day I'll buy it outright, you'll see.'

Irene looked around the large entrance hall, taking in all the architectural details. Many years ago, she thought, this must have been an elegant town house, but now it was sadly neglected. The air was thick with dust, as if the house had been empty for some time, and there was a strong smell of dry rot and mouse droppings. 'It will need a lot of work to clean a house this big,' she said doubtfully.

'A lick of fresh paint will soon have the place shipshape and Bristol fashion,' Jim said, setting their bags down at the foot of the stairs. 'Come on, Renie, I'll show you round.' He opened the door on his right and ushered her into a large empty room. A gilt-framed mirror hung above the carved wooden mantelpiece and despite its fly-spotted appearance it added a touch of tired gentility to what might once have been a charming reception room. Dust motes danced in the sunlight flooding in through two tall windows which overlooked the street. 'I thought this would do for the salon,' he said with an expansive wave of his hand, and his voice reverberated off the high ceiling in a mocking echo. 'This is where the ladies would gather to drink tea and gossip.'

'While the men gamble away their fortunes elsewhere,' Irene said drily. 'Much as I detest all forms of gambling, I don't see why women should be excluded from enjoying a flutter at the tables if that's what they really want.'

He stared at her, frowning. 'I don't know where you get your ideas from, Renie, but that wouldn't do at all. The gentlemen would be completely inhibited by the presence of women, and by women I don't mean their wives or sweethearts. The females who frequent these places are not ladies, if you get my meaning.'

'Oh, I do,' Irene replied smoothly. 'You mean that no decent woman would be seen dead in a gaming house and those who do attend are dollymops and harlots.'

Jim's face flushed beneath his tan. 'Don't talk like that. It does you no credit.'

'Don't be such a hypocrite,' Irene said, laughing. 'I was raised on the streets and some of those women, as you call them, are my best friends. One day I'll introduce you to Gentle Annie and Fiery Nan and you'll see that they are just human beings, earning their living the best way they can.'

'I can see that I've been away far too long,' he said, shaking his head. 'I'm beginning to think that Pa deserved that prison sentence. He should have kept you and Ma safe instead of allowing himself to fall in with undesirables.'

'Don't be too hard on him,' Irene said,

following Jim out of the room and across the hallway where he opened a door on the far side.

'This will be the gaming room.' He stepped inside. 'Come and take a look, Renie.'

She entered the room, looking round and taking in the elegant proportions. It would certainly fit the purpose. She eyed Jim curiously. 'You are prepared to make money out of other people gambling, and yet you look down on Pa for that very weakness which led him to fall into the clutches of the Sykes brothers. I don't think I understand you at all, Jim.'

'Don't put me in the same category as those ruthless criminals. This will be a respectable establishment, more of a gentlemen's club than a gaming hell.'

'I don't see the difference. Men will still gamble away their hard-earned money and get into debt because of it.'

'They will have a fair chance here, Renie. There will be no marking of cards or fixing the roulette wheel. The only difference between us and the expensive gentlemen's clubs up West will be that we cater for ordinary middle-class men, not wealthy toffs. If I see a fellow who is betting more than I think he can afford, I'll put a stop to his gambling and send him on his way.' He strolled over to the fireplace and rested his arm on the mantelshelf, staring down into the empty grate. 'And as to the women, Renie, I want you to vet those who come through the doors. There will be no cat fights or brawling in our establishment. They will be expected to grace the proceedings and entertain the men over food and wine, but there will be no . . .' he hesitated, glancing at her over his shoulder. 'There will be no hanky-panky, if you know what I mean.'

Irene doubled up with laughter. 'We are not running a knocking-shop, is that what you are trying to say, brother?'

'Ma should have washed your mouth out with soap a long time ago, Irene Angel. You are a respectable girl and I don't want to hear you using gutter language.'

'I can't believe how prim and proper you've become,' Irene said slowly. 'I thought you would be more broad-minded after so many years at sea and having seen so much of the world.'

'My dear little sister, I've seen things that would make your hair stand on end, and it's for that reason that I want to protect you from the worst side of human nature.'

'And yet you want me to help you run a gaming establishment. I don't understand.'

'I've told you that this will be the best of its kind and properly run. I've saved hard to get enough money together to enable me to come ashore, but I'm not qualified for anything other than a ship's officer, and I know nothing of trade. This is the only way I can think of to make enough money to give us a reasonable standard of living. You must see that.'

She met his intense gaze and saw that he was in earnest. She realised that, despite his apparent self-confidence, he was asking for her approval. She gave him a reassuring smile. 'I understand, and I'm sorry if I've appeared ungrateful. I know you want to do your best by us and I'll help you in any way I can.'

He crossed the floor in two strides to give her a brotherly hug. 'Thanks, Renie. I knew I could count on you. Now come and see the rest of the house. You can choose your own room and I'll introduce you to Mrs Garnet, the woman I've hired to keep house for us. She's busy downstairs with a cleaning woman, they're trying to put the kitchen to rights as we speak.'

'We have a housekeeper?'

He threw back his head and laughed. 'Of course we have a housekeeper, as well as a scullery maid and a tweeny. I wasn't planning for you and Ma to cook and clean for us. No, Renie, from now on we're going to live in style. We'll work hard, but we're going up in the world.' He took her by the hand. 'Come, we'll have to hurry if we are to pay a visit to Love Lane.'

Irene hesitated. 'Jim, will you do something for me?'

'Yes, of course. What is it?'

'Will you go and see Pa in Newgate and make your peace with him?'

'You needn't worry, poppet. It was always my intention to visit the old rogue.'

An hour later, Irene had chosen her bedroom on the second floor at the rear of the house, well away from the noise and bustle of the busy thoroughfare. The view from her window was not particularly prepossessing, as it overlooked the back yards and outhouses of the buildings in Five Foot Lane, but at least she might expect nights of undisturbed sleep. It was not a particularly large room and was simply furnished with a pine bedstead, a burr-walnut dressing table and an oak clothes press with a pine washstand. Nothing matched, but the eclectic mix of furnishings gave the room a certain raffish charm. The carpet was faded and worn and the curtains were slightly frayed, but that was a mere detail and a fault easily remedied, if Jim could be persuaded to include such items on their shopping list. Irene would have loved to unpack and settle into her new room, but Jim summoned her, insisting they go down to the basement kitchen where he introduced her to Mrs Garnet, the cook-housekeeper, Ida the fourteen-year-old scullery maid and fifteen-year-old Flossie, the tweeny. Then, having ordered dinner for six o'clock, Jim hurried Irene out of the house, giving her instructions to wait on the doorstep while he went to look for a cab.

As they approached Love Lane, Irene prayed silently that there would not be a scene. Jim might be confident of her reception but she was not. Her eviction from the house was still fresh in her mind and she could not imagine that Josiah would have had a change of heart. The cab set them down outside the Tippet mansion and Jessie answered the door, but her pale face was unusually grave.

'How is my sister?' Irene asked anxiously. 'There's nothing wrong, is there?'

'The doctor is with her now, miss.' Jessie held her hands out to receive Irene's outer garments, but she kept her eyes averted.

'Is she – I mean, is the baby coming?'

'I think so, miss. There's been a terrible lot of screaming going on all afternoon.' Jessie took Jim's coat and hat, backing away with a scared look on her pinched features. 'You don't need me to see you upstairs, I'm sure.' She turned and ran in the direction of the back stairs.

'Who is it, Jessie? Who was that at the door?'

Irene looked up to see her mother peering through the banisters. 'Ma, it's me, Irene, and Jim too.'

'Oh, Renie. Thank God you've come. I was never so pleased to see anyone in my whole life.'

Irene raced up the stairs, stumbling over her long skirts in her haste. 'Is Emmie all right?'

'She's having a hard time,' Clara cried, throwing her arms around Irene's neck. 'The midwife has been here since last night and we had to send for the doctor several hours ago. They won't let me into her bedchamber and Josiah is quite distraught.'

Jim was close behind Irene and he slipped his arm around his mother's shoulders. 'Now, Ma, calm down, there's a dear. I am certain that the doctor has everything under control.'

Clara allowed him to lead her into the drawing room. 'You're right, of course. It's just the waiting that is so unbearable.'

'I know, Ma, but getting yourself all of a dither won't help Emmie.' Jim helped her to the sofa. 'You rest there like a good girl.'

'I think a glass of sherry might be just the thing,' Irene said, moving swiftly to a side table laden with an assortment of cut-glass decanters. She filled a glass with the amber liquid and gave it to her mother. 'Sip this, Ma.

I'll go upstairs and see how things are going with Emmie.'

Jim eyed her doubtfully. 'Oughtn't you to stay and keep Ma company? I mean, this is women's business. I'm just in the way.'

'Nonsense,' Irene said, trying not to smile at his obvious discomfort. 'I'm sure that Ma would love to hear all about our new house and your plans to start up in business.' Without giving him a chance to argue, she hurried from the room. She was halfway up the second flight of stairs when she heard Emmie's howls of pain. It sounded more like an animal in distress than the cries of a human being and Irene broke into a run. She paused outside the bedchamber and tapped on the door.

Moments later it opened just a crack and a woman wearing a white goffered cap and a starched apron peered out. 'Who is it?'

'I'm Mrs Tippet's sister,' Irene said, craning her neck in an attempt to see over the midwife's broad shoulder. 'May I see her?'

'She's in no fit state to receive visitors. Please wait downstairs.' The woman was about to close the door but Irene stopped it with the toe of her boot.

'She would want me to be present. Please ask the doctor if I may come in.'

'He's got his hands full. Go away, miss.'

'Renie, is that you?' Emmie's plaintive cry came from within.

Ignoring the midwife's protests, Irene barged into the room. 'It's all right, Emmie. I'm here.'

'I'm sorry, Dr Telford,' the midwife said apologetically. 'I tried to stop her.'

'Hold my hand, Renie,' Emmie muttered through clenched teeth. 'Don't leave me.'

'It's all right, nurse,' Dr Telford said, mopping his brow with a damp and crumpled handkerchief. 'If this young person's presence calms the patient, then let her stay.' He gave Irene a cursory glance. 'You won't faint or do anything silly now, will you, young lady?'

Irene felt slightly sick at the sight of her sister's swollen and distended belly but she shook her head. 'No, doctor, I'm not squeamish.' It was a lie, of course, but it drew a twisted smile from Emmie's pale lips.

'You never could stand the sight of blood, Renie. I remember the time—' Emmie broke off with a deep-throated cry of pain and she gripped Irene's hand so hard that she felt her bones must break.

'I can see the baby's head,' Dr Telford said, beckoning to the midwife. 'Come here, woman, and assist me.'

'You're doing well, Emmie,' Irene said in

what she hoped was an encouraging voice. 'Be brave, ducks.'

'That's right, Mrs Tippet,' Dr Telford said calmly. 'Breathe easily for a moment and when I tell you, try to push hard.'

When the command came, Emmie closed her eyes as she made an obvious effort to do as the doctor ordered and her grip on Irene's hands tightened.

'Well done, love,' Irene murmured through clenched teeth.

'I can't do it,' Emmie sobbed, falling back against the pillows with tears pouring down her cheeks. 'I'm going to die. I know I am.'

'Nonsense,' Irene said sharply. 'Don't talk rot, Emmie. Do as the doctor says and it will soon be over. You'll have a fine baby and Josiah will be proud of you.'

'Once more, Mrs Tippet.' Dr Telford signalled to the midwife. 'Have the towel ready, nurse. We're almost there.'

'It's all right for you,' Emmie snapped. 'It doesn't bloody well hurt you like it does me.'

'Now, ma'am,' Dr Telford said sternly. 'One last push.'

'That's it, Emmie,' Irene cried with tears springing to her own eyes. 'I can see your baby coming. Oh my . . .'

* * *

Something wet was falling on her face and trickling down her neck. Irene opened her eyes and it came to her slowly that she was lying on the floor beside the bed. The midwife's grim countenance was hovering above her like something out of a bad dream, and she was systematically splashing water onto her face. Irene struggled to a sitting position. 'What happened?'

'You fainted, miss. Luckily you fell flat on your back and not over the mother.'

The sound of a baby's cry brought Irene rapidly to her senses and she raised herself to kneel by her sister's bedside. 'Emmie?'

'It's a girl, Renie. A lovely little girl.'

'Are you all right, dear?' Irene asked anxiously. 'I thought you was a goner back there.'

'I've never been better,' Emmie replied, smiling happily at the red-faced infant swaddled in clean sheeting and lying in the crook of her arm. 'But I am a bit tired. All I want to do now is to sleep. Will you go downstairs and put my Josiah out of his misery? Tell him he has a beautiful baby daughter and remind him that he promised me a carriage and pair of my very own.'

Feeling slightly dazed, Irene stared down at mother and child with a sense of awe. A few minutes ago her sister had been crying out in agony, but now all that appeared to have been forgotten. Despite the tumbled curls clinging damply to her forehead, Emmie looked serenely lovely and blissfully content as she gazed at the tiny scrap of humanity clasped to her breast. Irene backed away towards the door. Suddenly she felt like an intruder. The midwife was busy clearing away the soiled sheets and Dr Telford had his back to them as he packed his instruments away in a leather bag. Irene left the room and went slowly down the stairs, holding on to the banister rail for support. Her knees seemed to have turned to jelly and she did not know whether to laugh or to cry.

She burst into the drawing room but came to a halt when she realised that Ma and Jim were not alone. Josiah and his sons were standing in a group by the fireplace in deep conversation with Jim, while Ma perched on the edge of the sofa, pale-faced and anxious. She turned her head to give Irene a pleading look. 'Renie?'

Irene ran to her and clasped her mother's gnarled fingers in her hands. 'It's all over, Ma. Emmie has a beautiful baby girl and they are both doing well.'

Josiah uttered a strangled cry of relief and rushed for the door. 'I must go to her.' He hesitated, turning his head to give Irene a dazed look. 'You are welcome to stay to dinner, Irene. All is forgiven on this wonderful day.' He left the room without waiting for a response.

'Well, aren't you the lucky one?' Erasmus said, curling his lip. 'You've got off lightly, Miss Irene.'

Ephraim nodded in agreement. 'You are fortunate indeed. If it were not for the happy event I doubt if Father would have been so forgiving.'

Sparked into retaliation, Irene glared at him. 'I am not the wrongdoer as your brother well knows, Ephraim. And I doubt if either of you would be so complacent if my sister had produced a son instead of a daughter.'

'Renie, don't,' Clara cried.

'Leave my sister alone,' Jim said angrily. 'I know the full story and neither of you come out of it well.'

'You've only heard her version,' Erasmus said, smirking. 'She's a strumpet and a liar.'

Jim squared up to him. 'And you, sir, are a rake and a libertine. I would take great pleasure in flooring you, but I would not wish to upset my mother or sister by a display of fisticuffs.'

'You're a lout and a bully.' Erasmus backed away from him. 'But what can one expect from the son of a common felon?'

Jim fisted his hands but Irene caught hold

of his sleeve. 'No, don't, Jim. Can't you see that that is exactly what Ras wants?'

'He's not worth it anyway,' Jim said grimly.

Keeping well away from Jim, Ephraim cleared his throat. 'I think you had better take your leave now. I will make your excuses to Father.'

'Gladly,' Jim snarled. 'You are a pompous idiot, sir. And your brother is a despicable cad and a coward to boot.' He seized Irene by the arm. 'Come on, we're leaving. I promise you that it will be a cold day in hell before I return to this house.'

Clara uttered a low moan. 'Oh, no. Don't go like this. Say you're sorry, Jim. Like it or not we are all one family, and I don't want there to be another rift.'

Irene sank down on the sofa, wrapping her arms around her mother. 'Don't distress yourself. Come home with Jim and me. We've got a huge house with lovely big rooms and servants too. We'll look after you.'

'And who will take care of Emmie and the baby?' Clara said, gulping back tears. 'You have put me in a terrible position with your quarrelling. I am the one who is stuck in the middle, and I am not a well woman. Have pity on me, Jim. Apologise to Ephraim and Erasmus. Make your peace with them, for my sake.'

Irene shot a pleading look at him, but the stubborn set of his jaw was so reminiscent of their pa that at any other time she would have laughed. 'Please, Jim. We can't abandon Emmie and the child.'

Ephraim held out his hand. 'I am prepared to accept an apology if you are man enough to make it, Mr Angel.'

Jim eyed him with contempt but his expression softened as he turned his head to look at his mother. 'You could come home with us now, Ma. We could put all this behind us, and I will look after you.'

Clara shook her head. 'I know you would, son. But if I leave now I am abandoning Emmie and my granddaughter, and that I cannot do. Maybe later, when I am certain that my girl has recovered from the birth and the baby is thriving, but for now I must stay here and depend on the generosity of my son-in-law.'

Reluctantly, Jim shook Ephraim's hand. 'I apologise then, but only for Ma's sake.'

Erasmus struck a pose, angling his head and grinning. 'And what about me, old boy? You called me some harsh names.'

'You are beneath contempt, sir. One day we will settle this like grown men, but for now just think yourself lucky that circumstances prevent me from following my inclination to wipe that smug smile off your face.' Jim bent down to drop a kiss on his mother's forehead. 'We won't wait for Josiah, but we will return soon.'

Clara smiled through her tears. 'Thank you, Jim. I know what it must have cost you to do the right thing, and I'm proud of you, son.' She patted Irene on the cheek. 'Go with your brother, my dear. It's a great comfort to me to know that you will be living close by and that I will see you again very soon.'

'You will, Ma. We'll call again tomorrow and that's a promise.'

'I'll ring for Jessie,' Ephraim said as if determined to have the last word. 'She will see you out and I will make your excuses to Father.'

'Don't bother,' Irene said, rising to her feet with all the dignity she could muster. 'We may have to put up with you for Emmie's sake, but don't think that I've either forgotten or forgiven you for your treatment of me because I haven't and never will.'

They arrived home to find that Mrs Garnet was in a state of agitation over dinner, which was long overdue and quite spoiled. 'On your first night too,' she said, covering her face with her pinafore. 'What will you think of me? I am a fine cook, but I cannot perform miracles.'

'Please don't distress yourself,' Irene murmured. 'I am not very hungry.'

'Bread and cheese will be more than welcome,' Jim said firmly. 'And some fruit or cake with a bottle of wine will go down nicely.'

'Just this once won't hurt, I suppose,' Mrs Garnet said grudgingly. 'But they were fine lamb collops, all gone to waste. Anyway, I've lit the fire in the breakfast parlour, sir. I'll send your supper up as soon as it's ready.' She left them with a disapproving sniff, and stalked off in the direction of the baize door which led to the back stairs and the servants' domain in the basement.

'We'll sit in the parlour, then, and eat in front of the fire,' Jim said cheerfully. 'It will be like the old days in the flat above the shop.'

Irene took off her bonnet and shawl, tossing them onto a hall chair. 'Not quite, Jim. We had little enough to eat when Pa had been on a spree, and often sat before an empty grate for lack of coal and kindling.'

Jim led the way to a wainscoted room at the rear of the house where, as promised, a fire blazed up the chimney. They ate their meal sitting in front of it, toasting their toes and drinking wine. When Flossie had cleared the dishes, Jim smoked a cigar while Irene sipped coffee. 'We'll do very well here, I think, Renie,' he said, tapping ash from the Havana into the grate. 'I'm going out for a breath of air. You'll be all right on your own, won't you?'

Irene smiled. 'Hardly on my own, Jim. There are three servants at my beck and call. I think I will enjoy living like a lady.'

He rose to his feet. 'Good girl. I'll see you in the morning, and then we will make a start on setting up in business. Get a good night's sleep. You'll need all your wits about you tomorrow.' He strolled out of the parlour, leaving a trail of scented cigar smoke in his wake.

Irene put down her coffee cup and a quick glance at the marble clock on the mantelshelf told her that it was half past eight. Too early to think of going to bed, and yet too late to pay a call on Alice – or was it? She had become used to retiring early in Essex, but that was country living, and she was eager to see Alice again. She had so much to tell her that it could not wait until morning, and it was not far to Robin Hood Court. She could walk there in less than ten minutes.

She did not bother to inform Mrs Garnet that she was going out. Jim had given her a house key and she had been used to coming and going as she pleased from the shop in Wood Street. There was no difference now, she thought as she let herself out of the house, locking the door behind her and slipping the key into her reticule. She set off at a brisk pace, heading towards Cannon Street and continuing up Bread Street, crossing Cheapside and then turning into Milk Street.

There was still plenty of horse-drawn traffic clattering over the cobblestones, but fewer pedestrians were about at this time in the evening. Irene ignored the salacious offers from men lingering in pub doorways, and she hurried past them. She was out of breath by the time she reached the dark slit between tall buildings that led to Robin Hood Court, and for a moment her courage almost failed her. Vague scuffling sounds emanated from its gloomy depths that could have been caused by humans, or perhaps it was simply feral cats out hunting for food. She fixed her gaze on the glimmer of light at the end of the dark tunnel, and clutching her shawl a little tighter around her shoulders she entered the alleyway, treading softly. She was only halfway through when she heard the sound of footsteps behind her. She quickened her pace to a trot and then a run, but whoever was following was drawing closer by the second. She was already short of breath and her heart was hammering against her ribcage. She slipped on the mossy cobblestones and would have fallen but for a pair of strong arms that encircled her like a band of steel.

Chapter Twenty

Irene screamed and struggled in vain. 'Let me go.'

'Hold still. I won't hurt you.'

She would have known that voice anywhere. 'Inspector Kent, you frightened the life out of me.'

He released her instantly. 'What in the blazes are you doing out alone after dark?'

She felt a sudden urge to laugh, although the situation was far from funny. 'Is that all you have to say to me? Don't you want to know where I've been and what I've been doing these past weeks?'

'Come to the house. We can speak more easily indoors.'

'Am I being arrested?' Irene demanded as he took her by the arm and propelled her towards the moonlit court.

'You wouldn't find it so amusing if I had been one of the Sykes gang.' His tone was ice cold and Irene subsided into silence as they approached the house. She waited while he searched his pockets for his keys.

'I came to see Alice. I've been out of town for some time and I was anxious about her.'

'And yet you couldn't find time to write to her and let her know that you were safe and well?'

Irene was stung by his scathing tone even though there was some truth in his accusation. 'I had to leave town in a hurry. I wanted to write, but I didn't know what to say.'

'She was worried about you. I don't like to see my sister suffer. She has enough to bear without you adding to her misfortune.'

'I'm sorry if she was worried about me, but I'm not very good at putting my thoughts down on paper.'

'That's no excuse. A few words would have put her mind at rest.' He held the door open for her.

'Well I'm here now, so you needn't go on about it, and I don't need you to lecture me about walking out alone after dark. I'm perfectly able to look after myself.' She could not see his expression in the dimly lit hall, but she sensed his continued animosity and she was unaccountably angry and hurt by his cold reception. She followed him into the parlour, but in the soft glow of the firelight she saw that Alice was not in her usual place on the sofa and her throat constricted with fear. 'Where is Alice?'

'It's late,' Kent said, shrugging off his greatcoat. 'She will have been in bed for half an hour at least.'

'Is she unwell?' Irene asked anxiously.

He shook his head. 'She tires easily,' he said, striking a vesta and lighting the candles. 'Gladys has a key and she comes in every evening just before nine to put Alice to bed.'

Irene sank down on the sofa with a sigh of relief. 'All right, Inspector Kent. I admit that I behaved badly towards Alice and I am sorry for it, but I did not mean to neglect her. I had a lot on my mind.'

'Why did you return to London? Why didn't you stay in Essex where you were safe?'

She stared at him in surprise. 'If you knew where I'd gone, why didn't you tell Alice?'

'I knew where you were, but I didn't know the reason for your sudden departure from London. I did my best to reassure her that you had come to no harm, and being the good-natured girl that she is she made all kinds of excuses for your thoughtlessness.'

'I didn't come here to be lectured by you,' Irene retorted hotly. 'If you must know I was falsely accused of wrongdoing and my brother-in-law threw me out on the street. I had no choice but to leave London.'

He acknowledged this with a curt nod of his head. 'So why have you returned now?'

'Always the cop,' Irene said bitterly. 'Why don't you take me down to the station and lock me in a cell?'

'This isn't a game, Irene. If you have any intention of meddling with police business regarding the Sykes brothers, then I beg you to reconsider.'

'I'm not stupid, Inspector Kent. As it happens my situation has changed for the better. My brother returned from a long sea voyage and he came to Havering to fetch me. He has rented a large property in Five Foot Lane and we intend to set up in business there.'

He stood with his back to the fire, eyeing her intently. 'What sort of business?'

'I don't think that's any of your concern, Inspector.'

He frowned. 'Your brother was a seafarer and now he wants to live ashore, is that so?'

'Yes. He has come home for good.'

'Which leads me to wonder exactly what kind of business venture could be run from a private house.'

Irene was silent for a moment as she battled with conflicting emotions. She was hurt and angry but she also longed to confide in him, and to seek his approval for her plans. At a loss to deal with her feelings, she resorted to sarcasm. 'You're the detective. You work it out.'

'I would hazard a guess at a gaming house.

I think that you and your brother intend to try to beat the Sykes brothers at their own game.'

He was so close to the truth that it took her breath away. 'I think I've wasted enough of your time,' she said coolly. 'Perhaps you would be kind enough to tell Alice that I called and I'll come again tomorrow afternoon.' She made for the door but Kent was too quick for her and he barred her way.

'No. We are not leaving it like this. You have put yourself in danger by returning to London. The Sykes brothers have spies everywhere and no doubt they already know that you are in town.'

'Why would they be interested in me?'

'My men have been keeping them under surveillance for months. It was reported to me that a boy calling himself Jim Angel paid a call on the Sykes brothers in Blue Boar Court not long before you left London.'

She returned his steady gaze, although her heart was beating so fast that she was afraid he might hear it pounding against her ribs. 'So how does that involve me?' she demanded, assuming an air of innocence.

'Gladys told me that a seafarer called Jim Angel had been making enquiries about his family who used to run a shop in Wood Street. Someone, a neighbour I think, told him that Yapp might know where you had gone, and that led him to Danny. Given that Jim Angel turned out to be a man, it was not hard for me to guess the identity of the boy who thought he could take on a gang such as the Sykes.'

'You're wrong. It wasn't me. Now let me pass.'

He leaned against the door, folding his arms across his chest. 'Not until you have listened to what I have to say. You and your brother would be mad to attempt to play the Sykes brothers at their own game. In the past they have shown no mercy to those who invaded their territory, and you would be no exception. If Jim Angel applies for a gaming licence I will make certain that it is refused, and if you open up an illegal house I will see that you are closed down within a week.'

'What is it to you? Why won't you leave us alone?'

His brow darkened. 'I don't want to see you lying on a slab in the dead house, Irene. The law will take care of the Sykes gang and I promise you they will be brought to justice.'

'How can I have any faith in the law after what it has done to my pa? I don't trust the police, and I don't trust you. Now let me go.'

He moved away from the door. 'You must trust me, Irene. It's your only hope.'

'You are a copper first and foremost. You're no different to the rest of them.'

'And you are a wayward, stubborn creature,

but God help me I care what happens to you. I admire your spirit and your bravery and I don't want to see you crushed by your desire to seek revenge on Vic and Wally Sykes.' He took her by the hand and his expression softened. 'Trust me, Irene. Stop this folly and allow me to protect you.'

For a wild moment she was tempted to believe him. The touch of his hand was sending shivers down her spine and causing her pulses to race. She wanted to believe in him, but somehow she could not bring herself to abandon the prejudice that had been bred into her since childhood. He was a policeman and that put them on opposite sides of the law, and he was the son of a callous bully. Inspector Edward Kent had the same blood coursing through his veins as his father – a man who had brought misery to the women who loved him. It would be so easy to give in to his demands, but that would be a leap of faith she was not prepared to take. 'I don't believe a word you say,' she cried, taking refuge in anger. 'You are only interested in seeking promotion. You don't care if my pa spends the rest of his life in Newgate and you are afraid that I might succeed in bringing the Sykes brothers to justice when you have failed.'

'You are terribly wrong. Please consider what I have said.'

'Once a copper, always a copper.' Irene spat the words at him. 'Just leave me and my brother alone to get on with our lives.' She wrenched the door open and ran from the house. She heard it slam behind her but she did not look back. The chill of the night air made her gasp for breath and her legs felt as though they had turned to jelly. When she reached the alley she stopped to lean against the wall while she caught her breath. She had thought he might pursue her but he had not. 'So much for his concern about me walking home on my own,' she muttered. 'Well, I don't care what you say, Inspector bloody Kent, neither you nor the whole of the City of London Police force are going to stop me. I'm going to see the Sykes brothers punished if it's the last thing I do, and I'm not going to stop until I get Pa released from jail.' She braced her shoulders and headed for home.

Irene did not mention her visit to Robin Hood Court when she set off for the furniture warehouse next morning with Jim. He was in high spirits and she had no intention of passing on Kent's threat to block his application for a gaming licence, or his promise to close them down if they went ahead without a permit from the magistrate. Jim was full of plans for their new venture and he assured her that he had everything in hand. He hoped that they would be able to open for business in less than a week, provided that the painters could finish the two main rooms in time. 'That was where I went last evening,' he said, relaxing against the worn leather squabs of the hansom cab. 'I had the names of artisans recommended to me by an old seafaring friend who came ashore a couple of years ago and has started up a wine importing business with great success. You must meet him, Renie. He's a good fellow and is still unmarried.'

Irene giggled in spite of the nagging worries that beset her. 'Are you trying to marry me off, Jim?'

He grinned. 'Well, I don't see you as an old maid, my dear. And Gilbert is a steady chap with good prospects. You could do worse.'

'You can put that idea out of your head right now. My one aim in life is to get justice for Pa and to put an end to the Sykes gang.'

'Now, Renie, don't get carried away, poppet. You know I'll do anything I can to get Pa freed from jail, but we must avoid antagonising Vic and Wally at all costs. I haven't forgotten what they do to people who get in their way and it isn't pretty.'

'But Jim, I thought—'

'No, Renie, we're not going to do anything illegal. I didn't spend ten years at sea, saving every penny of my wages, to risk losing the lot when I finally came ashore. I grew up watching the old man fritter away any money that came into his hands and I saw Ma dragged down by hard work and poverty. That's all in the past and I'm going to make our fortune. From now on we're going to be respectable citizens.'

Irene absorbed this in silence. Jim and Emmie both seemed to share the same ambition, but hers was simpler. She wanted to see Pa free and her family reunited; she could think no further than that.

Jim tapped on the roof of the cab with his malacca cane. 'Stop at the warehouse on the corner, cabby.' His face was alight with anticipation as the vehicle slowed down and came to a halt. 'This is where it all begins.' He leapt out and held up his hand to assist her from the high vehicle. 'You can choose the colours, but I will pick the style of furnishing.'

Irene had not been looking forward to a morning spent selecting tables and chairs but once inside the huge building she began to take an interest. By mid-morning they had ordered tables, chairs and sofas for the gaming and reception rooms. They went on to a fabric warehouse and chose curtain material, which the obsequious salesman assured them could be made up and delivered in less than a week.

Jim had laid out a small fortune but he brushed aside Irene's fears that they had overspent, and he treated her to luncheon at a chophouse in Upper Thames Street.

'Now then, young Renie,' he said, wiping his lips on a starched white table napkin. 'There's another thing which I ought to mention before we go any further.'

Irene swallowed the last morsel of spotted dick and custard and licked the spoon. 'What is that?'

'Clothes, my dear girl.' Jim angled his head, casting a meaningful look at her faded gown that had once belonged to Emmie. 'You appear to be rather short in that department.'

'Are you saying that I look shabby?'

'No, of course not. Well, perhaps a little. What I mean to say is that you ought to find a dressmaker who could fix you up with something a bit smarter, if you know what I mean.'

'I do know exactly,' Irene said, smiling at his obvious embarrassment. 'I'm still wearing Emmie's cast-offs. I could do with a new skirt and blouse.'

Jim took a wallet from his breast pocket and peeled off a crisp new ten pound note. 'You need more than that, ducks. A whole wardrobe more like.'

'Put it away before someone sees. That's too much, Jim. I can't take it.'

'Don't be silly, of course you must. Dressing you like a lady is all part of the plan to establish ourselves as a respectable gaming house. I'm not going to encourage the riff-raff from the docks to frequent our establishment. I want the well-off punters who will behave themselves, not drunken dockers and sailors.'

Irene glanced nervously at the other diners but thankfully they all seemed too intent on eating and drinking to take any notice of them. She snatched the note and tucked it into her reticule. 'Well, if you're sure, but this would keep us in food and coal for couple of months or more.'

Jim leaned back in his seat, preening himself. 'Not in the way I intend to live, Renie. We're going to have the best of everything. I've done with living rough at sea and now I'm going to enjoy the comforts of life ashore. You'll see.' He beckoned to the waiter. 'I'll settle up here and then I'll walk you home.'

Irene shook her head. She fully intended to spend the afternoon with Alice, but she did not want to get into a long explanation as to how she had become involved with a copper and his family. There were some things that it was better to keep from Jim. 'If you don't mind, I'll go straight to the dressmaker that Emmie uses. I know where it is and it's not far from here. I can find my own way home.'

'Capital,' Jim said happily. 'Pay her extra to get at least one suitable gown finished before the week is out. I want to open the doors to the first punters as soon as possible.'

Irene rose to her feet, wrapping her shawl around her shoulders. 'The sooner I get there the better, then. I'll see you later.' She blew him a kiss, and squeezing past a corpulent gentleman, part of whose large bulk hung over the edge of his chair, she edged her way between the closely packed tables and out into the street. The atmosphere in the chophouse had been thick with steam and tobacco smoke. The smell of roast meat and hot fat clung to her hair and clothes as she hurried along the street, heading not for the dressmaker's rooms in Bread Street but for Robin Hood Court. She was desperate to see Alice and she was fairly certain that Kent would not be there at this time of day.

She found the door unlocked and she let herself into the house. 'Alice, it's me, Irene.'

A cry of delight from the parlour was all the encouragement that Irene needed. She entered the room and went straight to the sofa to give Alice a hug. 'My dear Alice, I am so pleased to see you and so ashamed that I did not write to you, but you know how it is. I am not much of a hand at letter writing.'

'I have missed you so much, and I don't care

about anything now that you are here. Edward told me that you had called last night. I was extremely cross with him for not waking me.'

Irene drew up a chair and sat down. 'Yes, I was silly not to have realised that it was so late, but I am here now, and I have so much to tell you.'

'Have you? How exciting.'

Irene had intended to recount the details of everything that had occurred during her stay in Essex, but now it did not seem to be such a good idea. Perhaps it was best if Alice remained in ignorance of the love triangle involving her father and the Greenwood sisters. Irene improvised wildly. 'Did Edward tell you that my brother has returned after a ten-year absence?'

'No, but Danny did. He couldn't wait to pass on that tasty morsel of gossip. I hope you don't mind.'

'Of course not. I had given up hope of ever seeing Jim again but he arrived in Essex, taking me completely by surprise, and now he has rented a house in Five Foot Lane where we are to start up in business.'

'No! How thrilling. What kind of venture is it to be?'

'A gaming house. But I'm afraid that Edward does not approve.'

'I don't suppose he would,' Alice said

seriously. 'He doesn't tell me anything about his work, and I have to rely on Gladys to keep me up to date about what is going on in the outside world. She says that there are gangs at work who terrorise innocent people. They make their money from illegal gaming establishments, and by threatening shop-keepers with violence if they don't pay huge amounts of money for protection from other street gangs.'

'That is true, but our establishment will be more like a club for respectable city gentlemen. Everything will be legal and above board.'

'I don't doubt it for a moment, and I'm sure it will be a great success. Now tell me about your sister. Has she had her baby?'

'I arrived back in London just in time for the birth. She has a beautiful baby girl and I intend to visit them on my way home from here.'

Alice sighed. 'How lucky you are, Irene. You can come and go as you please.' Her lips trembled, but she reached out to lay her hand on Irene's arm. 'I don't mean to sound envious; it's just that sometimes it is very hard to be shut up in one room day after day with no hope of getting out into the fresh air, or doing things that other people take so much for granted.'

Irene grasped her hand and held it to her

cheek. 'How thoughtless I am, Alice. Here am I, chattering on like one of the rooks in the tree outside our old shop, and you have to sit there listening to my prattle. I am quite ashamed of myself.'

'You mustn't feel like that. Now I feel bad for upsetting you, when you have spared the time to come and see me and bring me such exciting news.'

'I'm just angry to think that you should have to spend your days a prisoner in this room, which, if you'll forgive me for saying so, is dreary enough at the best of times. I know that Edward takes you out when the weather is good, but he really should provide you with some permanent means of transport.'

'It's not his fault. He has so much to do and so little spare time.'

Irene acknowledged this with a slight inclination of her head. 'Even so, we must think of a way to get you out of the house more often.' She rose to her feet, staring down at Alice with a thoughtful frown. 'I will think of something.'

'You are leaving already?'

'Yes, but I will return tomorrow.' She leaned over to kiss Alice's pale cheek and she patted her on the shoulder. 'Things will change for the better, I promise you.'

* * *

On her way to Love Lane Irene stopped off at the dressmaker's basement home and had her measurements taken for a whole new wardrobe. She left armed with a list of the material necessary to make up two skirts, three blouses, two afternoon gowns and two more to wear in the evening, and an assurance that at least one gown would be finished within the week. Tomorrow, Irene decided as she strolled along Wood Street, she would take a cab to the West End to do her shopping. She would need new boots and at least two pairs of shoes, and if she had enough money left from the ten pound note she would buy gloves and a shawl. It was an exciting prospect and she felt like a rich woman. She quickened her pace, striding along with new-found optimism and confidence.

On her arrival at the house in Love Lane, Irene went straight to Emmie's room where she found Ma sitting on a chair by the bed with the baby cradled in her arms, and Emmie propped up on pillows with a radiant smile on her face.

'What a pretty picture,' Irene said appreciatively. 'May I hold the baby, Emmie?'

'Of course, but be careful. You must support her head.'

'What are you going to call her?' Irene asked, taking the sleeping infant from Ma's arms as if she were a fragile piece of porcelain. 'She is so tiny.'

'She will grow fast enough,' Clara said, smiling proudly. 'She'll be running round the house before Emmie knows it.'

'Caroline,' Emmie said. 'She is to be christened Caroline Clara.'

The baby opened her eyes as if in answer to her name, and she stared up at Irene.

'She has such dark blue eyes. She looks at me as if she knows me.'

'They will darken to brown, just like Josiah's,' Emmie said, holding out her arms as the baby began to cry. 'Give her to me, please. It's time for her feed.'

Irene passed the wailing infant to Emmie with a feeling of relief. Babies were fine until they cried, and then they were best handed back to their doting mamas. 'I'll go then, and leave you in peace.'

'So soon?' Clara's smile faded into a frown. 'Won't you stay for a while, Renie? If you would help me downstairs to the drawing room I'll ring for some tea.'

'Of course, Ma.' Irene helped her mother from the chair, noting with a surge of concern that her mother's brittle bones felt increasingly like those of a fragile bird. She comforted herself with the knowledge that what Ma lacked in physical strength she more than made up for in spirit. 'I'll call again soon, Emmie,' she called over her shoulder as they left the room.

But Emily was apparently too absorbed in the pleasure of suckling her child to take much interest and she merely smiled and waved her hand. 'Yes. Thank you for coming.'

Slowly, with Ma in obvious pain, they made their way along the landing and down the stairs to the drawing room. As soon as her mother was comfortably ensconced in an armchair by the fire, Irene rang the bell to summon Jessie. 'How are you feeling, Ma?' she asked anxiously. 'Is the pain bad today?'

'Not more than usual, ducks. It could be a lot worse.'

'But there's something troubling you, I can tell.'

'Just the usual, Renie. I worry about your pa and the pain of not being able to visit him in prison is worse than all the rheumatics put together.'

Irene knelt at her feet. 'I haven't forgotten about him, not for a single moment, and I intend to do something about it now that I'm back in London.'

'That's all very fine, love, but what can a slip of a girl like you do? My Billy broke the law and now he's being punished.'

'He was foolish, Ma, and he got mixed up

with the wrong people, but he's not a criminal. You mustn't give up hope.'

'You won't do nothing silly, now will you, Renie? Promise me you won't.'

'Trust me, Ma. I won't make things worse, but I will get him pardoned if it's the last thing I do.'

'Don't talk like that, ducks. Many a true word is spoken in jest.' Clara glanced over Irene's shoulder as the door opened and Jessie sidled into the room. 'Tea and cake, please, Jessie.'

Jessie acknowledged Clara's request with a surly nod of her head and departed, closing the door behind her with a rebellious thud.

'That girl needs a lesson in good manners,' Irene said, rising to her feet. She brushed the creases from her skirt and a sudden thought occurred to her. 'Ma, have you any idea how much a brief would cost?'

'No, but I do know it would cost more money than we're ever likely to get our hands on.'

Irene remembered the huge sum of money that she was about to squander on new clothes. Why had she not thought of it before? She bent down to drop a kiss on her mother's grey hair. 'I won't stop for tea, Ma. I've got things to do.'

'Irene Angel, what are you up to?' Clara demanded.

But Irene was already on her way out through the door. She turned her head and grinned. 'You've just given me a wonderful idea. I'll tell you about it later.'

As luck would have it a hansom cab had just set down a fare a little further along the street and Irene hailed it with an imperious wave of her hand. 'The Tippet emporium, High Holborn, please, cabby.' She climbed into the cab and settled down to plan her course of action when she arrived at Josiah's shop. There was only one person of her acquaintance who might have had dealings with a lawyer whose fees would not be astronomical, and that was Erasmus. Much as she disliked him, Irene could hazard a guess that he had been up before the beak a few times in his short career and had obviously escaped with a mere caution or a small fine. His father would most certainly not approve of such goings-on, and she was not above using a bit of blackmail in order to get her own way.

The cabby set her down outside the impressive frontage of Josiah Tippet and Sons, Drapers, where the windows were filled with items designed to tempt female customers into the store. Ostrich feathers dyed in jewel colours were arranged in urns draped with silk scarves. Swathes of Indian muslin hung from invisible hooks like morning mist and bolts of satin, watered silk and cotton prints were draped in the semblance of a rainbow. It was enough to make a dressmaker's mouth water. As Irene approached the double glass doors a uniformed doorman ushered her into the establishment. Long counters with highly polished surfaces were manned by white-collared shop assistants with eager smiling faces. The walls were lined with shelves stacked with merchandise, and glass-topped stands were arranged strategically around the floor inviting closer inspection. Unable to resist the temptation, Irene peered into one of them and was amazed to see cases spilling over with buttons of every shape, size and description, from mother-of-pearl to millefiori. It was like looking into a wealthy woman's jewellery casket. She dragged her mind back to the business in hand as a young man wearing a black tailcoat approached her with an obsequious smile. 'May I assist you, madam?'

'Please inform Mr Erasmus that Miss Irene Angel is here and would like to speak with him on an urgent matter.'

'I'm afraid he's otherwise occupied, madam. I believe he is stocktaking.'

'I'm sure he can spare me a moment of his valuable time,' Irene replied smoothly. 'Please take me to him at once. There is no need to announce my arrival.'

'I – I don't know, madam. This is very irregular.'

'I am his aunt,' Irene said haughtily. 'He won't thank you for keeping me waiting.'

'Yes, madam. I'm sorry. Please step this way.'

Irene smiled to herself as she followed the flustered shop assistant. She had a score to settle with Ras and she was going to enjoy this.

Chapter Twenty-one

The assistant led her through a door at the back of the shop and along a narrow passage between racks tightly packed with boxes of all shapes and sizes. A lingering musty smell assailed her nostrils and the air was thick with dust and cotton fluff. She was ushered into a cramped office at the far end of the corridor.

Light filtered hazily through a small window which was partly obscured by shelves filled with sample books. Ras was seated behind a large desk which was submerged beneath a higgledy-piggledy assortment of ledgers and documents, some of which had fluttered to the floor and lay gathering dust on the ground. He did not appear to be doing anything more constructive than flicking pellets of paper at a daguerreotype of his father which hung on the opposite wall. He looked up with a guilty start and jumped to his feet as Irene entered the room. 'My dear Irene, this is an unexpected pleasure.'

'I'll come straight to the point, Erasmus,' Irene said coldly. 'You are a cad and a libertine and you have treated me very badly.'

He perched on the edge of the desk and his eyes hardened, although his lips were still stretched into a sickly smile. 'Come now, my dear. That's a bit harsh, isn't it? As I recall you led me on and then cried foul. That was not the action of a lady.'

'I don't pretend to be a lady, but I did nothing to encourage your drunken advances. You had me evicted from the house like a dishonest servant, and now I'm giving you the chance to make up for your appalling behaviour.'

'And if I choose not to do whatever it is that you want of me?'

'I have only to whisper a word in Vic or Wally's ear that you have shamed the daughter of one of their gang members and they will settle your hash once and for all. The Sykes brothers look after their own, Ras.' It was a bluff, of course, but she was counting on the fact that he would believe her. She eyed him contemptuously and was satisfied to see his cocky smile fade and his flushed cheeks pale to ashen.

'I say, old girl, there's no need for that sort of talk. You know it was all a ghastly mistake. I'll tell the old man so, if that's what you want.'

'Yes, that's a part of it,' Irene agreed. 'But there is something else. I need a lawyer who is not afraid to take on my father's case.'

'Why come to me? Lincoln's Inn is full of them. You could take your pick.'

Irene fixed him with a hard stare. 'You know as well as I that none of them would touch a case like this. My father was convicted of a crime that involved the Sykes gang and they are still at large. It would be a brave and very expensive lawyer who risked his reputation by taking Pa's side.'

'You've just admitted his guilt. Why waste money on a hopeless case?' Ras eyed her with a gleam of suspicion in his dark eyes. 'If it's cash you want you'd best look elsewhere. I'm afraid I can't help you.'

'All I'm asking for is the name of a mouth-piece who will convince a judge that there has been a miscarriage of justice.'

'You've got the wrong chap, Irene. I can't and won't help you.'

'I know what sort of life you've been leading,' Irene said softly. 'I'm certain you've only escaped jail yourself through having a bent lawyer. Now are you going to help me, or do I have to go to Josiah and tell him how you spend your leisure time?'

He stared at her with unconcealed dislike. 'I won't allow a silly young tart like you to blackmail me.'

'Then let's see how you like being thrown out on the streets and having to exist without your father's backing. If he knew that you creep out at night to visit gaming hells, opium dens and brothels he would cut you off without a penny.'

Ras slid off the desk, flexing his hand as if he would like to strike her. 'You bitch.'

'That's right, hit me,' Irene taunted. 'Let's see what Josiah thinks of a son who strikes a defenceless woman. Touch me and I'll scream so loud that all your staff and customers will hear me.'

'I was just testing you, Irene,' he said, dropping his hand to his side with a sickly smile. 'You've got spirit, I'll say that for you.'

'Give me the name of your bent lawyer and his address and we'll call it quits,' Irene said evenly, although she was inwardly quaking. She had thought him to be little more than a cowardly fool, but she had seen a flash of suppressed violence in his eyes and that scared her. She smothered a sigh of relief when he turned back to his desk and scribbled something on a scrap of paper.

'This is my chap. He has got me out of several scrapes in the past and he knows when to keep his mouth shut. Mention my name and he'll take care of matters for you.'

Irene took the paper and put it in her reticule.

'Are you satisfied now?' Ras demanded.

She was quick to hear a note of anxiety in

his voice, and she smiled. 'Almost, but not quite, Erasmus. I want fifteen yards of crimson silk taffeta and a similar amount of sprigged Indian muslin. You can add matching thread to that order and enough lace for trimming.'

He curled his lip. 'Are you sure that is all?'

She was beginning to enjoy herself. 'You might include a skirt length of dove-grey bombazine and several yards of white cotton-lawn, enough for two blouses, and a sufficient quantity of mother-of-pearl buttons.' She made to leave the room, pausing in thc doorway. 'And you can have the order sent to my dressmaker. She is the same woman who makes your step-mother's clothes so her address will no doubt be on your books. Goodbye, Ras. I hope we don't meet again.' She stepped into the corridor, closing the door with a triumphant smile. The look on Ras's face had been priceless, and the dull thud of a projectile hitting the door behind her proved that she had scored a victory over the abominable Erasmus Tippet.

Outside in the street she took a deep breath of the damp air and it was only then that she realised she was shaking uncontrollably.

'Shall I hail a cab for you, ma'am?' The doorman was at her side, peering anxiously into her face. 'Where do you wish him to take you?'

'Holborn Hill,' Irene said firmly.

* * *

The office of Lester Fox, Solicitor and Commissioner for Oaths, was situated on the top floor of a five-storey building on the corner of Leather Lane and Holborn Hill. The ground floor housed an outfitters specialising in garments and equipment requisite for foreign travel, and the upper floors were given over to offices. Irene was quite breathless by the time she had negotiated five flights of stairs to the attics where the servants would have been housed in days gone by. The corridor was dimly lit by a single gas light that fluttered feebly in its glass bowl, emitting just enough illumination for her to read the inscriptions on the closed doors.

'Come.' A voice from within responded to her nervous rap on the solicitor's door and she entered, blinking as her eyes grew accustomed to the bright light. A waft of cool April air fanned her hot cheeks and papers fluttered about in the draught from an open window. A stronger gust tugged the door from Irene's hand, causing it to slam. She saw to her surprise that the dormer windows were flung wide open and half a dozen or more pigeons were balancing on the narrow window ledge, pecking at handfuls of corn thrown by a chubby, bald-headed man who sat behind a kitchen table which served as his desk. He turned his head and stared at her over the top of steel-rimmed spectacles and his pale blue eyes twinkled a welcome. 'Hello, young lady. What can I do for you?'

Irene glanced at the piece of paper clutched in her hand, checking the address. There was no mistake, and she raised her eyes to meet his questioning gaze. He looked nothing like her idea of a lawyer, crooked or otherwise. His smile was quite cherubic and although he must have been well into middle age his skin was remarkably unlined, giving him the appearance of an elderly baby dressed in a man's suit of clothes. He tossed another handful of corn to the birds, chuckling at their antics as they attempted to edge each other off the high windowsill in their eagerness to snatch the grain. 'My little friends are hungry today. Do you like birds, young lady?'

Irene stifled a shriek of horror as a large black rat emerged from a hole in the skirting board and made off with a crust of bread.

'Don't worry, my dear. He won't hurt you. He is like the rest of us in his daily quest to feed his family.'

'There are more of them?' Irene gasped, eyeing the hole nervously.

'Like me, he has a wife and young ones waiting for him at home.'

'But he's a rat – vermin.'

'We are all God's creatures, my dear. Now

pull up a chair and tell me how I might help you.'

Irene glanced round and saw a bentwood chair almost hidden by a pile of books and papers.

'Just tip everything on the floor and sit down. It's quite exhausting walking up all those stairs.' He took off his spectacles and polished them on a green paisley handkerchief while he waited for her to make herself comfortable.

Irene coughed as a cloud of dust flew up from the tomes and documents as they hit the floor. She perched on the edge of the seat. 'You are the lawyer, Mr Lester Fox?'

'I am indeed. A wily fox rather than a sly one, I think. Now may I ask your name, and what is your business with me?'

'I am Irene Angel and you were recommended to me by my sister's stepson, Erasmus Tippet.'

'I may have had dealings with that person in the past. Do go on, Miss Angel.'

Irene cleared her throat and launched into her story. Lester leaned his elbows on the table, listening intently while the pigeons got on with the serious business of feeding until the last kernel of corn had been consumed. With a great flapping of wings they flew off just as Irene came to the end of her narrative. 'Well,

Mr Fox, do you think there is any chance of an appeal being accepted?

'Lester, please, and I shall call you Irene. We will be informal in the office.'

'Yes, but what do you think? Can we clear my father's name and get him released from prison?'

He rose from his seat and began to pace the floor with a pronounced limp. 'I'm afraid the chances are slim while the Sykes brothers are at liberty. Without their conviction and confession it would be almost impossible to convince a judge that your father was a mere pawn in their game.' He came to a halt in front of her and he bent down to tap his right leg below the knee. 'Wood,' he said by way of explanation. 'When I was a young man I was greedy for money and advancement. I was foolish enough to agree to defend old man Sykes even though I knew he was a black-hearted villain. It was a hopeless case but I was too arrogant to see that and he was sentenced to transportation for life. I was lucky to survive the beating I received from Vic and Wally and my reputation as a lawyer was lost to me as well as my leg. I had to survive as best I could by taking on cases that no other lawyer would touch. I have more reason than most for wishing to see the Sykes brothers safely behind bars.'

'I'm sorry,' Irene murmured.

'I have learned to live with my disability,' Lester said, smiling. 'Vengeance is mine, saith the Lord. However, I may be able to help Him along, so to speak, but you will have to do your bit, Irene.'

'I will do anything you say. I want the Sykes brothers caught and sent to jail for life.' Irene opened her reticule, and taking out the ten pound note she laid it on the table. 'There is a retainer.'

Lester's hand shot out and he held the crisp note up to the light. 'Thank you. I cannot afford to work for nothing, although in this case I would be happy to do so had I not a wife and ten children to support.' He tucked the note into his breast pocket. 'Now, Irene Angel – what a lovely name, by the way – what I am about to suggest is not entirely legal and there is a considerable degree of danger attached to it.'

'I don't care,' Irene said firmly. 'Just tell me what to do.'

'Well, as I see it, we need to lure the Sykes brothers into a trap from which they cannot escape, and we need some bait that they can't resist.'

'And might that be a rival gaming house run by me and my brother?'

'Precisely so. I want you to let the Sykes

brothers know that you are setting up in competition with them. Make certain that they are aware that you pose a real threat to their monopoly and allow the information to leak out gradually. They must not be allowed to suspect your motives.'

'I understand,' Irene said breathlessly.

'And I think it would be best if you do not tell your brother what you are doing, as I fear he might try to stop you.'

'Thank you, Lester. I am very much obliged to you.'

He shook his head. 'Don't be. You are the one who will be running the risks. Vic and Wally are dangerous men, and if they suspect that you are trying to entrap them they will show no mercy. You must be careful.'

'I know what they do to people who cross them,' Irene said, rising from her seat. 'I will take care.'

Lester's smile faded. 'If they become sufficiently worried, they might send their ruffians round to show you that they mean business. Are you prepared for that?'

'Yes,' Irene said with a determined lift of her chin. 'It is the only way.'

'I have my spies,' Lester continued seriously. 'And if I hear of an intended raid, I will inform the authorities. You must have no direct contact with the police, even though you said that you have a friend in Inspector Kent.'

'Not a friend exactly. I am acquainted with his sister.'

'Yes, you told me that you had befriended his crippled sister, but you must stop your visits forthwith, or you might be placing her in danger.'

'Yes,' Irene said slowly. 'I see that now.'

'Do you fully understand the risks you will be taking, Irene?'

'I do,' Irene said simply. 'Someone has to stand up to the Sykes brothers and it seems that someone has to be me.'

'You are a brave young lady.' Lester shook her hand vigorously. 'I promise you I will use every weapon at my disposal to protect you and help to free your father.' He turned away to open the door. 'Now go home, my dear, and do not visit my office again. I will send word when I have something to tell you. Is there someone whom you could trust to act as an intermediary between us?'

Irene thought hard. 'Yes, there is Danny Priest. He works for Yapp the pickle and sauce manufacturer, and he lives with his mother at number seven Robin Hood Court. I would trust Danny with my life.'

'You may have to, Irene,' Lester said grimly. 'Danny Priest it is. Do nothing until he gives you a message from me. In the meantime, I will visit your father in Newgate and when I have spoken with him I will lodge an appeal through the normal channels.'

That evening at dinner Jim was in high spirits having secured a gaming licence with surprising ease. He was full of plans for the opening night, which could now go ahead at the end of the week. Irene was surprised that Kent had not carried out his threat to block the application, but she merely smiled and allowed Jim to talk. It was, she thought, almost as if he were an impresario who was about to launch a production on the London stage. He was single-minded in his ambition and it was painfully obvious how much this new venture meant to him. She struggled with feelings of guilt. Jim would be appalled if he knew that her enthusiasm for the project was based on her desire to break the Sykes gang. Her brother might have travelled the world, but she realised that he was an innocent when it came to the ways of the criminal fraternity, and that after so many years at sea he seemed to have forgotten the harsh reality of life in the East End. Jim obviously thought that by honest hard work he could make a better life for his family, and that they would be welcomed into the respectable bosom of the rising middle class.

Irene listened with a sinking heart, and she realised that it was even more important to keep her plans a secret.

'I've rambled on long enough,' Jim said at long last. 'Tell me what you did this afternoon. Did you visit the dressmaker and arrange for some new gowns?'

'Yes, and I went to Love Lane to see Ma and Emmie. You must make time to go there, Jim. Emmie will be very upset if you don't show any interest in your newborn niece.'

'I was planning to go this evening, as it happens. I hope I don't run into Erasmus or I fear I might forget myself and give him the thrashing that he richly deserves, but I want to see Josiah. I want to thank him for putting in a good word with the magistrate who granted me the gaming licence. Despite his idiot sons, Josiah is a steady fellow and he has the sort of business contacts that I need if I am to bring the more respectable element in society to our establishment.'

Irene remained silent. She had not altered her opinion of her brother-in-law, but he seemed to have taken a liking to Jim, although she suspected that perhaps Josiah was more concerned with his own advancement than theirs. Jim might think that Josiah was helping them out of family loyalty, but Irene thought it more likely that he could see the advantage of introducing his business acquaintances to a gentlemen's club similar to those patronised by the toffs up West, but a great deal easier and cheaper to join. She smiled and nodded her head. She would not spoil Jim's moment of triumph for anything.

'I want the merchants and bankers to bring their wives to the salon where they can socialise,' Jim continued happily. 'There are enough disreputable gaming hells in London, and ours will be quite different. I might even ask that Kent fellow along to the opening night. That would define the fact that we will be working to the letter of the law. What do you think, Renie?'

Irene gave a start at the mention of Kent's name. 'Yes, whatever you want, Jim. I was going to call on his sister this afternoon, but I'm afraid it slipped my mind. I'll go first thing tomorrow morning. I could take an invitation with me if you wish.'

'Splendid. I have had some printed on gilt-edged cards, which look rather fine. Perhaps Miss Kent would like to come too. The more ladies we have in attendance the better it will look to the city worthies.'

Irene had taken Lester's advice to heart and she had no intention of putting Alice in danger by visiting her, nor was she going to invite

Inspector Kent to the opening night, but she needed an excuse to go out alone the next day. She wanted to see Danny in order to make sure that he understood why he was being asked to act as go-between. She knew that she could trust him implicitly, but she was not certain whether he would take kindly to receiving instructions from the lame lawyer. She decided to seek Danny out at work and put her case to him in person.

Yapp's Pickle Factory was situated in an old warehouse overlooking Stew Lane Stairs and the murky waters of the Thames. As luck would have it, Danny was outside loading up the wagon. He greeted her with a gap-toothed grin. 'Miss Irene. What are you doing here?'

'I haven't come to buy pickles, Danny. I need your help.'

His jaw dropped and his eyes widened in surprise. 'Me, miss? What can I do for you?'

Briefly and as quickly as she could, having seen Yapp's face peering out through one of the grime-encrusted warehouse windows, Irene explained the situation. 'Do you think you could do this for me, Danny? It might be dangerous and you would have to be very careful not to be seen.'

He puffed out his chest. 'I ain't afraid of nothing and I'd do anything for you, miss. And if it puts the Sykes brothers behind bars, then that's a bonus.'

'And also,' Irene continued hastily as Yapp emerged from the doorway shaking his fist at her, 'I want you to put it about that there is a new gaming club opening next Saturday in Five Foot Lane. All are welcome as long as they have the money to gamble but they must dress up in their Sunday best. My brother won't allow anyone in unless they look respectable. Do you get my meaning, Danny?'

'Ho, there! Get about your business, you lazy lout,' Yapp shouted. 'There's to be no spooning with girls on my time.'

'Wait for the lawyer to contact you,' Irene whispered. 'Don't let me down, Danny.'

He tipped his cap and grinned. 'You can rely on me, miss.'

Yapp was advancing on them with a malevolent look on his face and Irene beat a hasty retreat. She spent the rest of the morning visiting her father's old haunts and handed out invitations to his former gambling cronies, assuring them of a splendid evening's entertainment if they attended the opening of the new gaming house. She was careful to avoid Blue Boar Court, but she knew that her exploits would soon reach the ears of Vic and Wally and that was just what she wanted.

As she walked along Fish Street she saw the

familiar figures of Gentle Annie and Fiery Nan emerging from a public house. She went to meet them and was rewarded with tipsy hugs and the almost overpowering fumes of jigger gin and unwashed female bodies.

'Where've you been, ducks?' Gentle Annie demanded, squinting at her with bloodshot eyes. 'Ain't seen you about for ages.'

'And look at you, all dressed up like a toff,' Fiery Nan said with a throaty chuckle. 'You ain't in the trade now, are you?'

'No, I wouldn't have the talent for it like you girls,' Irene said, smiling. 'It's a long story which I'll tell you when I have more time, but you can do me a favour, if you are so inclined.'

'Name it, love,' Nan said, hooking her arm around Irene's shoulders. 'We'll do anything for a mate.'

Irene took some invitations from her reticule. 'Come to the opening night, all dressed up in your finery and behaving like ladies, and you can have as much gin as you can drink. Bring some friends, but only if they clean up nicely and know how to behave.'

'What are you at, Irene?' Annie demanded, cocking her head. 'Why do you want us to dress up like dollymops?'

'It's a secret,' Irene replied, tapping the side of her nose. 'Do it to please me, and I'll tell you everything later.' She waved the invitations at them but Nan pushed her hand away.

'It's no good giving us those. None of the girls can read. Just tell us where to go and we'll be there.'

By the end of the week the rooms were furnished, carpeted and hung with new curtains. Jim had sent invitations out to Josiah's business acquaintances and had left hand-written posters in pubs and chophouses all round the city. Deliveries of food and alcohol had been arriving daily, and Mrs Garnet had taken on extra help in order to make small cakes and pastries to serve with tea and coffee or a glass of negus for the ladies in the salon. The wine and spirits were supposed to be reserved for the gentlemen in the gaming room, but Irene had no intention of disappointing the working girls and she had stashed a plentiful supply of hard liquor in one of the cupboards in the salon.

Irene's new gown arrived from the dressmaker's just an hour before the doors were due to open on Saturday evening. Mrs Garnet had reluctantly agreed to allow Flossie to act as lady's maid for the occasion, and she made a creditable attempt at arranging Irene's hair in elaborate coiffure. When Flossie had completed her task, she stared at her reflection in the mirror and was quite taken aback to see the elegant young woman gazing back at her as if she could not believe her eyes.

'You look lovely, miss,' Flossie murmured with a misty-eyed smile. 'A proper lady.'

'It's a miracle,' Irene replied, tossing her head so that her new gold earrings, a present from Jim, glinted in the candlelight. She rose to her feet, doing a twirl in front of the mirror. The swish of starched petticoats and the rustle of crimson silk-taffeta sent a thrill running down her spine. 'It's such a fine gown, but do you think the neckline is too low, Flossie? I've never seen such a lot of my own bosom unless I was taking a bath.'

'It's what the ladies up West wear, miss. I seen pictures of them in magazines. They got no shame, them rich women. They ain't afeared to flash their titties in company, so I don't see why you should be.'

Irene hitched her bodice up a little higher. 'You're right, Flossie. If it's good enough for the wives of the gentry, it's good enough for me.' She picked up the fan she had purchased that morning from a pawnshop on the corner of Leather Lane and she looped it round her wrist. 'Wish me luck. Tonight is going to be very important.'

'Of course, miss.' Flossie hurried to open the door for her. 'I'm sure everything will go well.

The master has worked so hard to make it right.'

Irene went slowly down the stairs, praying silently that she had not ruined things for Jim. Despite her hatred for everything to do with gambling, she could not wish to see her brother's business venture fail, but she was not going to allow personal feelings to deflect her from her plan to outwit the Sykes gang. Much depended on their success tonight; they must do well enough to convince Vic and Wally that Jim's club was a threat to their autonomy. She doubted whether any of Josiah's stiff-necked acquaintances would deign to come, and she could only hope that Pa's old friends would not let her down. She was descending the last flight to the entrance hall when she heard the door open and the sound of high-pitched female voices and laughter. She hurried round the curve in the staircase, only to find that Jim had forestalled her. Looking resplendent in his evening attire, he prepared to receive their first guests. Irene would have rushed down to join him, but she recognised Fiery Nan's voice and she hesitated. Things could go badly wrong if the girls had not followed her instructions to dress and behave like ladies. She held her breath.

Annie was the first to come through the door and Irene was relieved to see that she had taken pains with her appearance. Gentle Annie might not look like a soberly attired merchant's wife, but at least she was clean and tidy and her gown was not overly garish. Moreover she was clinging to the arm of a gentleman wearing a top hat and evening cloak. Irene recognised him as Tim the Toff, one of the stalwarts of the gaming scene, and an old friend of her father's. Tim was the youngest son of a titled and extremely wealthy family, but he was notorious for frittering away his allowance on gambling and loose women, although Jim would be blissfully unaware of this fact. Irene stifled the urge to run down the stairs and give Tim a hug. He might be a roué but he knew how to behave and he would not give Jim any cause for alarm or suspicion.

She began to breathe a little easier as Fiery Nan entered with her hand linked in the arm of a slightly less fashionable but tidily dressed middle-aged man, closely followed by Ivy and several others, who had all done their best to look the part but would be unlikely to withstand close scrutiny. Irene ran downstairs to hurry the women into the salon before Jim had a chance to exchange more than a few words with them. So far so good, she thought, painting a bright smile on her face. 'Welcome, ladies. I hope you will have a thoroughly enjoyable evening.'

Ivy threw herself down on the nearest chair. 'Give us the free gin, Renie, and we'll guarantee to have a fine old time.'

'Of course, but go easy on the booze,' Irene warned. 'And mind your manners in front of the other guests. No swearing, belching or farting. Remember this is a high-class establishment.'

This last remark was greeted with gales of laughter and Irene felt more than a little apprehensive as she poured their drinks. She could only hope and pray that she had done the right thing, but even as she handed out the last glass her attention was diverted by the salon doors being flung open to admit a group of middle-aged matrons. They paused on the threshold, eyeing the noisy occupants of the room with expressions ranging from curiosity to downright disapproval. Irene sallied forth to greet them and she took pains to ensure that they were seated well away from Annie and her friends. She cajoled, flattered and teased the frosty ladies into reluctant smiles and she plied them with cakes and negus. Irene had surreptitiously added a generous shot of gin to the warm concoction of port and lemonade and very soon the genteel ladies were chattering as loudly as any of the dollymops and prostitutes.

As the evening progressed, the extra staff

Jim had taken on for the evening were hard pressed to keep up with the demand for refreshments. In the convivial atmosphere of the salon, largely due to generous libations of gin, punch and doctored negus, it was hard to differentiate between the wives of respectable businessmen and the women of the streets. The air was redolent with the scent of port, lemon, spices, juniper berries and a heady mix of cheap and not so cheap perfume. The chorus of female voices rose to an even higher pitch as the consumption of alcohol increased. The noise was deafening and the fug in the room was almost unbearable. Irene slipped out of the salon into the comparative cool of the entrance hall just as the doorbell rang announcing a late arrival. There was no sign of the hall boy and Irene went to answer the urgent summons. She opened the door with a welcoming smile but it froze on her lips. 'Inspector Kent!'

Slowly, staring at her with unconcealed admiration, he took off his top hat. 'Miss Angel.'

She felt the blood rush to her cheeks and her heartbeat quickened. She tried not to appear too pleased to see him. 'Is this a police raid, Inspector?'

'As you can see, I came alone.'

'Why are you here?'

He raised his eyebrows with a quizzical half-smile. 'Are you going to let me in, Miss Angel, or must I stand on the doorstep all night?'

Irene glanced nervously over his shoulder. She was certain that the Sykes brothers were having the place watched, and the last thing she wanted was for them to see her hob-nobbing with the cops. She took a quick look up and down the dimly lit street. There did not seem to be anyone lurking in the shadows. 'You'd better come in then,' she said, standing aside to allow him to enter.

'You and your brother are taking a huge risk,' Kent said, closing the door behind him. 'You do know that, don't you?'

'We are just trying to earn an honest living. Jim was granted a gaming licence. We aren't doing anything illegal.'

With an exasperated sigh, Kent dropped his hat and gloves onto the hall boy's chair and he seized her hands, gazing deeply into her eyes. 'Don't bandy words with me, Irene. I warned you before about the dangers of getting involved with the Sykes brothers. It seems you chose to ignore me, and I may not be able to protect you from them if you continue with this foolhardy enterprise.'

'You're hurting me, Inspector,' Irene said, wincing as his grip tightened to emphasise his words.

He released her immediately, but his gaze did not waver. His eyes blazed with suppressed anger, but she was quick to recognise anxiety as well as frustration in his tense expression.

'I'm sorry, but I need to make you see sense. You must not try to play the Sykes gang at their own game because if you do then you and your brother will certainly be the losers. I've seen the handbills and posters that you've plastered all round the city pubs and I know what you are doing. You want to antagonise them into overplaying their hand. I understand that you want justice for your father, but you are going the wrong way about it.'

She had a sudden urge to smooth away the lines of worry that creased his brow, but she withdrew her hands from his grasp and clenched them at her sides. 'You want to smash the gang too,' she said, hoping that she sounded calmer than she was feeling. 'Why would you care what happens to Jim and me?'

He opened his mouth as if to reply and then he lowered his gaze, shaking his head. 'I know what you think of me, and it is not flattering. You've made your feelings towards me quite plain, but I am begging you to stop this farce. You are endangering not only yourself but also my sister. If the Sykes brothers discover that you and she are friends she will be in mortal danger.'

'I wouldn't do anything to harm Alice,' Irene cried passionately.

His expression softened and he acknowledged her sincerity with a slow smile. 'I know that, Irene.'

She turned away from him, afraid that she might betray her feelings by a look or the tone of her voice. 'Please tell her that I can't come to the house for a while. Make some excuse but don't frighten her or allow her to think that I don't care. I wouldn't want her to think badly of me.'

Kent took her by the shoulders, turning her to face him. 'Alice will understand, but it's not just for her that I'm concerned; it is for your own good that I'm begging you to stop this foolishness. Leave the Sykes gang to the police.'

She almost melted at his touch, but she was determined not to make a fool of herself and she met his searching gaze with a defiant lift of her chin. 'And leave my pa to rot in jail for the next six years? No, that's asking too much.'

'I will do what I can for him when the time is right, but for now you must allow the law to follow its due course.'

'Well it hasn't done a very good job so far. The wrong man has gone to jail and the villains still terrorise the streets.' Irene chose her words carefully. She must be as clinically detached as he appeared to be. Now was not the time to cloud her judgement with emotion. 'I have nothing more to say, Inspector.'

He raised his hand as if about to plead with her and then lowered it, shaking his head. 'I can see that I'm wasting my time, but if you don't heed my words you could bring disaster on your family and mine.'

She moved swiftly to the street door and wrenched it open. 'Goodnight, Inspector. Thank you for the warning, but I suggest that you would do better to take Alice to the safety of your father's farm instead of keeping her caged up like a poor little canary in that dreary house.'

'What do you know about my family?'

Irene winced at the harsh note in his voice, but she knew that at last she had pierced his armour-like shell. 'I visited the farm when I was staying with Miss Greenwood at the Round House. I discovered that she is your stepmother's sister, and I learned of the family feud that has kept them apart for years.'

'Miss Greenwood is an embittered old spinster who disowned her sister when she married my father. She is nothing to Alice or me, and we mean less than that to her.'

'Maybe, but did you ever give her a chance to help you, or even consider the possibility that a lonely, childless woman might welcome a sweet girl like Alice into her home? Was it concern for your sister or your own pride that made you uproot her and bring her to live in London where she has to rely on the kindness of neighbours?'

'I think you've said quite enough.' Kent snatched up his hat and gloves. 'My family matters don't concern you.'

'Maybe not, but I care about Alice. Are you sure that you haven't put her needs a poor second to your ambition?'

He strode past her, ramming his hat on his head as he negotiated the shallow stone steps. Pausing when he reached the pavement, he turned to give her a searing look. 'Think about what I have said, Irene, and don't antagonise the Sykes brothers any further. Leave police matters to those who are paid to protect innocent citizens.'

'I can't do that.'

'Then I will have no alternative but to close your establishment down. It may take me a little time, but believe me I will do so unless you promise to stop playing this foolhardy and dangerous game.'

'It's no game, I assure you,' Irene retorted angrily. 'You have had plenty of time to sort the gangs out and you have failed. I just hope your men will be ready and waiting when Vic and Wally show their hand, as I've no doubt they will.'

'I'll have you watched day and night for your own safety, but my officers will have orders to arrest you on the spot if they catch you acting in a way which might provoke the Sykes brothers.'

'If you lock me up you might lose your last chance of breaking up the gang. Consider that, Inspector Kent.' She slammed the door in his face. She had had the last word, but it was a Pyrrhic victory.

Chapter Twenty-two

Irene was a great deal more upset by her confrontation with Kent than she had thought possible, and yet deep down she knew that beneath the cool air of officialdom his concern for her safety was genuine. In the dark hours of the night, she lay awake with his angry words repeating over and over again in her head. She was furious with herself for allowing this man to invade her thoughts and dreams, but she was even more determined to see the Sykes brothers brought to justice. No matter what Edward Kent said, she could not leave matters to the police. The plan which formulated slowly in her head was simple. She would wait until she heard that Pa's appeal was coming up before the court, and then she would pay a call on Vic and Wally. She would flaunt the success of their gaming house under their noses. She had seen the way they worked and she was certain they would not be able to resist the challenge. They would come round mob-handed and they would be caught.

In the days that followed, Irene discovered

that Kent was true to his word and each time she left the house she was aware that she was being watched. On one occasion she spotted Constable Burton lurking rather self-consciously in the doorway of the bakery just a little further down the street, but she pretended that she had not noticed him and continued on her way to Love Lane. With the house run by servants and Jim fully occupied with paperwork, she had little to do in the daytime and she often accompanied Emmie when she took Caroline out in her brand new perambulator. It made Irene smile inwardly to think that the polite nods and greetings they received were from people who not so long ago would have crossed the street rather than acknowledge two poor girls from the pickle shop.

At the end of a fortnight, when Irene was just beginning to think that Lester Fox had failed in his attempt to launch an appeal against her father's sentence, Danny arrived at the house in Five Foot Lane bursting with the news that Billy's case would be coming up before the magistrate in a week's time. Mr Fox had not committed anything to paper, but he had told Danny to warn Irene against doing anything rash. The Sykes brothers would have learned of the appeal and they would be leaning heavily on prospective witnesses in order to prevent them from giving evidence against them. Irene was not, under any circumstances, to do anything to antagonise Vic or Wally. Danny emphasised the last part of the message by tapping his right leg below the knee. 'Wood,' he said, winking. 'That's what Lester told me to tell you. Unless you want to end up similarly disabled, he advises you to keep quiet and leave everything to him.'

Irene nodded her head, but she had no intention of complying with Lester's instructions. She patted Danny on the shoulder. 'Don't worry, I won't do anything silly. But there is something you can do for me, if you will.'

'Anything, miss,' Danny said, beaming. 'You can trust me.'

'I want you to give Alice a message from me. Tell her that I have been planning an outing for her and I will call on Monday morning, but she is not to mention it to her brother as it will be a surprise.'

'A surprise,' Danny repeated, grinning. 'She'll like that.'

He won't, though, Irene thought grimly. If Edward knew of her plan to take Alice to the safe haven of the Round House he would be furious. But she had already put this important part of her strategy into action by writing a letter to Miss Maude, giving a very brief outline of the events which conspired to make life in London extremely dangerous for the crippled girl. Quite how she was going to get Alice to Havering Irene did not know, but get her there she would, and it had to be done before she faced the Sykes brothers and issued a challenge that would flush them out of their cover like two plump partridges. She gave Danny an encouraging smile. 'Good boy, Danny. Go now and give Alice my message, and please be careful. Don't go anywhere near Blue Boar Court or speak to anyone who might have dealings with the Sykes gang.'

'I ain't that daft,' Danny replied, flushing from the roots of his hair to the tidemark on his neck. 'I'm your man, Miss Irene. You can trust me.' He sauntered off whistling a popular tune.

Irene glanced up and down the street. There did not seem to be any spies lurking in doorways or behind lamp posts and she closed the door with a sigh of relief. She could hear Jim issuing instructions to the servants in the gaming room and sounds of furniture being shifted about as the charwomen cleaned the salon. She needed time to think and she made her way upstairs to her bedroom, where she slumped down on the edge of the bed, sinking into the soft feather mattress with a sigh. Until now she had been in denial of the shocking truth: her feelings towards Edward, for she could no longer think of him just as Kent or the inspector, had suffered a sea change. And yet, if she were being honest, she knew that this had not happened overnight. Right from the start he had had the power to arouse her emotions. Love and hate were supposed to be different sides of the same coin; perhaps in the beginning she had mistaken one for the other, but not now. During the long, sleepless nights when her spirit longed to merge with his, and her traitorous body yearned to feel his touch, she had come to realise that she loved him more than life itself. In dreams he came to her and his lips claimed hers in passionate kisses that made her tremble with desire. It was all the more painful to awaken and discover that she was alone in her bed and he was as far away from her as the moon that hung in the sky like a silver sixpence.

She lay back against the down-filled pillows and closed her eyes. She had never felt this way about any man. She had thought that love was for silly girls who had no mind of their own, and whose lives would be incomplete without a man to lean upon. She had never given Emmie credit for having genuine feelings for Josiah, and had accused her in the past of marrying him for money and position, but she knew now that she had misjudged and maligned her sister. Emmie truly did love the pompous middle-aged draper and she adored her baby daughter. No doubt in the fullness of time she would give many more pledges of her affection to her doting husband.

The image of Edward's angry face flashed before her mind's eye and Irene raised herself to a sitting position, staring at her reflection in the dressing-table mirror. If he had had feelings for her in the past, he must surely despise her now. The thought was as painful as a knife in the heart. He had tried to tell her in his own reserved way, but she had rejected him out of hand. She had thrown away her chance of happiness and now, she told herself sternly, she must live with the consequences. She must not allow her own feelings to get in the way of seeking justice for Pa and all the others who had suffered at the hands of the Sykes gang.

Success would be bittersweet, but her reward would be to see her parents reunited.

Theirs, despite everything, was a true love story. No matter how badly Billy behaved, Ma had been devoted and loyal, and as far as Irene knew, Pa had never looked twice at another woman. Gambling was his vice, but perhaps his time in prison might have cured him of his guilty obsession. Irene rose from the bed and went to the washstand where she poured cold water from the jug into the willow-pattern basin. She splashed her face with water and patted it dry with a towel before going downstairs to check that the rooms were ready for the evening's entertainment. She must carry on as normal. No one, least of all Jim, must suspect that anything was amiss.

On Monday morning the sun was high in a cloudless azure sky. A warm spring breeze ruffled the feathers on Irene's new bonnet as she walked briskly in the direction of Robin Hood Court. She had dressed in her best and she knew from the appreciative glances she received from passers-by that she was looking very fine indeed. Tucked away in her reticule was the reply she had been waiting for from Miss Maude, and as she had hoped the good lady was only too happy to give Alice shelter until such time as it was safe for her to return to London. Maude went on to say that she had been to visit her sister in Navestock and they had patched up their differences. Arthur was well and he and Betty were planning a June wedding. Young Arnold spent as much time as he could in the smithy and Arthur had taken him in hand so that he was a much happier and better-behaved boy. Martha, Miss Maude said, was her usual crabby self, but she sent her love to Irene and was looking forward to seeing her again. Irene smiled. So far so good;

now all that remained was to persuade Alice to make the journey into Essex.

A quick glance over her shoulder revealed Constable Burton, who stopped immediately and pretended to gaze into a shop window which just happened to be a milliner's establishment. Irene stifled a giggle. Poor Burton, he would never be considered for promotion at this rate. She dodged into a doorway and to her relief he hurried past without spotting her. She waited for a few moments before leaving, and then she crossed the street to take a back alley which led into Cheapside. Satisfied that she had shaken him off, she went on her way.

The front door of the Kents' house was unlocked and Irene let herself into the hall. 'Alice,' she called. 'Alice, it's me.' The parlour door was open and Irene entered the room, but she came to a sudden halt at the sight of Edward, seated on the sofa. There was no sign of Alice.

He rose to his feet. 'I've been expecting you.'

'How? I mean why? Where is Alice?'

'I took her to the country yesterday. She is safe with Miss Greenwood.'

'You took her to Havering after all that you said?'

'I admit that I was in the wrong. When I thought it over I realised that you were right and that by keeping her here I was exposing her to danger.'

Irene sank down on the nearest chair. His words had taken her breath away. 'I'm glad you did so, but I didn't think you were acquainted with Miss Maude.'

'My mother and Dora were friends and as a small boy I was often taken to the Round House. I remember it well and I knew what you said was true, and that Alice would be welcome to stay there with Miss Maude and Martha. I hired a carriage and we journeyed into Essex.'

'You might have told me,' Irene said indignantly. 'I've been worried sick about Alice and racking my brains trying to think how I would smuggle her out of London.'

A tender smile hovered around his lips. 'I know. Miss Maude showed me your letter. She said it was just like you to put others before yourself.'

Irene felt a blush rising to her cheeks and she jumped to her feet, taking an agitated turn around the room. 'I don't understand. How did you know what I planned, and why are you here now? You couldn't have known that I was coming today, unless . . .' Her voice tailed off as she thought of Danny.

'That's right. But don't blame the boy. I happened to overhear him giving Alice your message. It was then that I decided I must act, so you see I have only done what you intended to do.'

She stopped in her tracks. 'Am I hearing things, or have you just admitted that I was right about something?'

He smiled, taking her hands in his. 'I did as you wished, but now I need you to do something for me. I want you to promise that you will abandon whatever scheme you are hatching with regard to the Sykes gang.'

'I can't do that. I have gone too far to stop now.'

He drew her closer to him. 'No, you have not. You must allow the courts to settle the matter of your father's appeal. Leave Vic and Wally to me, Irene. I beg of you.'

His face was so close to hers that she could feel his warm breath on her cheek. For the first time in her life Irene was tempted to give in, but a small insistent voice in her head warned her that all would be lost if she allowed herself to be swayed from her purpose. 'I would do anything for you, Edward,' she murmured as she leaned towards him as if drawn by a magnetic force far stronger than her own will. She drew back just as their lips were about to meet. 'But not that.'

His hold on her tightened and his eyes hardened. 'I'm warning you, Irene – no, I'm begging you to stop this folly.'

ALSO AVAILABLE IN ARROW

A Mother's Promise

Dilly Court

She would keep her family together, whatever it took . . .

When Hetty Huggins made a promise to her dying mother that she would look after her younger sister and brothers, little did she know how difficult this would be. But despite the threat of being turned out on to the streets by the unscrupulous tallyman and the never-ending struggle just to exist, Hetty is determined her family will never starve or want for a roof over their heads.

Longing for something better out of life than the daily grind of making matchboxes for a pittance, she dreams of setting up her own business. With the help of friends she sells hot potatoes on the streets and things begin to look up for them all. But when the tallyman comes calling, they are faced once more with a future full of hardship and despair.

arrow books

ALSO AVAILABLE IN ARROW

The Constant Heart

Dilly Court

Would she risk it all for love?

Despite living by the side of the Thames, with its noise, disease and dirt, eighteen-year-old Rosina May has wanted for little in life.

Until her father's feud with a fellow bargeman threatens to destroy everything. To save them all, Rosina agrees to marry Harry, the son of a wealthy merchant. But a chance encounter with a handsome river pirate has turned her head and she longs to meet him again.

When her father dies a broken man, Harry goes back on his promise and turns Rosina out on to the streets. She is forced to work the river herself, ferrying rubbish out of London and living rough. In spite of her hardships, she cannot forget her pirate and when tragedy threatens to strike once more she is forced to make a choice. But is she really prepared to risk everything for love?

arrow books